Dear Reader,

This year has been a very successful one for *Scarlet*! Our particular brand of romance fiction has captivated readers in North America and the UK, and we are also reaching audiences as far afield as Russia and New Zealand.

So, what delights are there in store for you this month? Characters from Angela Drake's book *The Mistress* are featured in *The Love Child*. Naughty-but-nice Ace Delaney from *Game, Set and Match*, returns in Kathryn Bellamy's new novel, *Mixed Doubles*. (But don't worry if you didn't read the authors' earlier titles – both of these books stand alone.) We are also absolutely delighted to announce the return to writing of much-loved romance author Margaret Pargeter, with a brand new book, *Misconception*, written especially for *Scarlet* readers. And finally, we are proud to bring you another author new to *Scarlet*: Tammy McCallum has produced an intriguingly different novel in *Dared to Dream*.

I believe this time there is something to appeal to all reading tastes. But if there is a type of romance (say, time travel, ranch stories, women-in-jeopardy novels) we are not featuring regularly enough to please *you*, do let me know, won't you?

Till next month,

Sally Cooper

SALLY COOPER,
Editor-in-Chief – *Scarlet*

About the Author

Angela Drake is currently receiving excellent reviews for her *Scarlet* novels on both sides of the Atlantic. Readers and reviewers alike seem to enjoy Angela's unique writing style, so we are thrilled to be bringing you her latest romance novel.

Angela is a Chartered Psychologist who has worked in the education services, helping children with learning problems. She is the published author of several romances and mainstream novels and has also written for the young adult market. In her spare time, the author enjoys reading, going to the cinema and listening to music.

Angela is married with one grown-up daughter and lives in Harrogate with her husband and other assorted pets!

Other *Scarlet* titles available this month:

MIXED DOUBLES – Kathryn Bellamy
DARED TO DREAM – Tammy McCallum
MISCONCEPTION – Margaret Pargeter

ANGELA DRAKE

THE LOVE CHILD

SCARLET

Enquiries to:
Robinson Publishing Ltd
7 Kensington Church Court
London W8 4SP

First published in the UK by Scarlet, 1997

A copy of the British Library Cataloguing in
Publication data is available from the British Library

ISBN 1-85487-987-1

Printed and bound in the EC

10 9 8 7 6 5 4 3 2 1

PART ONE

CHAPTER 1

There were just two competitors in the jump-off, a state of affairs designed to promote crackling excitement in the spectators and maximum tension in the riders.

The two of them stood at either side of the entrance to the show ring, studiously avoiding each other's eyes as they waited for the result of the coin toss to determine which of them would go in first.

They could not have been more dissimilar, at least at a casual glance. The young woman, blonde and porcelain-skinned, waited with a calm, almost impassive expression on her face, whilst the man strode to and fro, biting hard on his lips, his black eyebrows wrenched together in a furious frown.

At that moment they had only one vital feature in common: a steely determination to win.

The steward came to announce the order of jumping. Miss Xavier was to go first, Mr Saventos second.

Emilio Saventos permitted himself a brief smile of triumph. It was always advantageous to go last. You knew then precisely what had to be achieved, you had the opportunity to respond to the gauntlet thrown down by the adversary.

If Alessandra Xavier was disappointed with this result, she gave no sign of it. Gathering up the reins of her dark bay horse, Satire, she inserted the tip of her left toe into the stirrup iron and sprang up to land lightly in the saddle, her right foot deftly slotting into the corresponding iron. The mounting of the horse was achieved in seconds in one supple fluid movement.

Alessandra's grace and athleticism were instinctive, as natural and unforced as breathing. This sinuous female strength, combined with her classical finely carved features and her tall slender figure, created an overall impression of distinctive elegance which invariably inspired people to turn and look at her for a second time.

The steward at the entrance to the ring looked towards her, calling out her number. Leaning over Satire's neck Alessandra gave him a brief caress before riding him quietly into the ring. A sighing ripple of appreciation went through the crowd and then they gave a huge burst of applause as she raised her hat and inclined her head courteously in the direction of the judges' box.

Alessandra had become a very popular rider at this prestigious southern counties show, delighting the crowd with her style, her daring and her courage. The amateurs among them adored her speed and willingness to take risks, whilst the professionals were deeply admiring of her ability to work at one with her horse, those long fine-boned hands of hers as flexible as elastic on the huge Satire's reins.

She scanned quickly over the course: fourteen fences, their striped poles gleaming in the late afternoon sunshine. It was a pretty big course ending with a formidable double that had caused a good deal of trouble to over half of the original competitors.

Jumping the course for the first time earlier in the day Satire had almost had a pole down on the final fence, just managing to get himself lined up in order to clear it by a whisker at the very last moment.

In the first jump-off he had learned his lesson and cleared the course with inches to spare. But this was his third time in the ring in the space of two hours. He was tired and hot, and understandably flagging in motivation, his early morning sparkle now a little tarnished.

'It's all right, boy. You're going to do fine,' Alessandra whispered to him, noting how his long velvety ears pricked and swivelled at the sound of her voice. 'You just believe it.'

Take it steady, she told herself, recalling the words of her first riding instructor who had taught her that good riding was a partnership between you and the horse – that even the strongest horse could be controlled with a calm will and steady intentions.

People had said that Satire was too big for her, too powerful and self-willed. But she had spent two years schooling him, using her old instructor's philosophy based on endless patience and quiet but relentless insistence. It had paid off and Satire's performance had earned him his reputation as one of the most promising horses on the county championship circuit. And now he was on the point of winning a competition that could lead to Alessandra's being considered a worthy contender in the big national competitions.

She looked down at his huge shoulders and quarters. The glow from his dark coat was almost blue-indigo, and beneath it ran a complex network of cord-like veins twitching and rippling with expectation. She ran her hand lightly over them, feeling a huge surge of fierce protective affinity with the animal. The love of my life she thought to herself with a wry smile.

She sat down deep in the saddle and put Satire into a steady canter. Let him find his own level, she told herself through gritted teeth. Steady, steady. He'll do just great. No need to think of the clock until the last minute.

She turned him towards the first fence and saw his ears swivel once again as his concentration reawakened. He soon found his stride and despite his tiredness jumped willingly and with precision, meeting each fence just right.

They were over the water jump, over the wall and clearing the triple. They were doing fine. But their time was too slow. Far too slow. Alessandra could hear the murmurs of tension in the crowd. She recalled her huge ambition to win. A desire that amounted to a need.

She felt Satire tense as she squeezed her lower legs on his flanks. 'Go on,' she mouthed fiercely, unable to prevent her body stiffening with the sudden anxiety to pepper things up. Really get him going.

'Go on,' she urged him. 'Go, go go! Faster. Much faster. You can do it!'

They were turning into the last line of fences and

now, with the sour taste of possible defeat rising in her throat, she threw caution to the winds and urged him on with every fibre of her being.

It was risky. Satire could be a demon if you gave him his head. And now that he was almost at a full gallop and snorting with excitement he inevitably lost some of his control. He leapt like a nursery rhyme cow jumping over the moon, his front hoofs giving the top pole such a sharp rattle she was sure it would fall. But somehow it managed to roll back into its cups and stay steady. Alessandra, however, was nearly thrown over Satire's head. Grappling for the reins, both stirrups now lost, she could do nothing but hang on for dear life and leave the last fence up to him.

Satire went racing to meet it and was nowhere near on the right stride as he approached. A less bold horse would have taken the line of least resistance and stopped or run out – taken the safer course. But not Satire. He stood right back on his hocks so that Alessandra felt as though she were perched on the side of a cliff. She felt herself soaring skywards as he jumped around six feet in the air, landing a good three feet past the finishing tape at the other side.

Struggling to regain her balance and right herself in the saddle, Alessandra heard the wild cheers and claps of the crowd. Her heart swelled. She leaned down and threw her arms around Satire's great neck.

'You're a star,' she told him. 'A miracle. The very best.'

Riding back into the collecting ring, she passed Emilio Saventos on his way out into the show ring. He did not look at her. His stony black eyes stared straight ahead, his mouth a rigid clenched line.

One of the young grooms from Alessandra's livery stables, who had come along as a general helper, came running up to congratulate her. 'Fantastic,' she breathed. 'He was brilliant!'

'Yes, wasn't he,' Alessandra agreed, taking deep breaths. 'How was our time?'

'85.6 seconds.'

Alessandra looked down at the girl in horrified disbelief. 'As much as that? Oh hell, Saventos only has to keep his cool and he's the winner.'

Peering through the opening to the ring, she saw Emilio Saventos's magnificent Lippizaner stallion Ottavio soaring effortlessly over the first line of fences. His time must be half hers at this point, she thought with a hollow sinking feeling.

Her heart trembling she forced herself to watch as the splendidly athletic Ottavio ate up the course. Having been slightly jerky and uneven earlier on – probably on account of his rider being a hard-hearted bastard, was Alessandra's feeling – the horse had now truly found his form. His speed was breathtaking, his judgement superb, and as he came up to the last fences she judged that Saventos need do no more than than sit back and let it all happen.

But that was not in Saventos's nature. Not only was he going to win – he was going to trounce his opponent well and truly. Show Alessandra Xavier who was boss. Screwing his dark features into an expression of dangerous menace, he demanded an extra spurt of speed from the horse. Turning Ottavio in far too fast and sharply towards the final line of fences he had him on the wrong stride at the final double. Sailing with huge courage over the first fence, Ottavio found himself right up against the final one with no leeway at all for putting in an extra stride. Incredibly, against all odds, he managed a huge and heroic spring, jungle cat style.

The crowd gave a low communal roar for the spirit and determination of the beautiful horse. And he almost made it, but at the last moment was unable to avoid brushing his fetlocks on the pole. It wobbled, hesitated for a moment and then dropped to the ground with a dull thud, clocking up four faults and costing him the round, the class and the competition.

Even Alessandra had to admit that it was monumentally bad luck. Nine out of ten times a pole would have stayed put given such a small nudge. But that was show-jumping for you – you got the good luck sometimes, the bad luck others. It all came out fair in the end.

Saventos came out of the show ring, his eyes sunk into his sockets, silent rage seeming to radiate around him. Bad judgement and bad luck had been on his side and he was a bad loser. Ignoring Alessandra he rode straight out of the collecting ring back to the line of horse boxes beyond.

Alessandra turned to watch his grim exit and her mind raced with troubled speculation. Her thoughts were interrupted by a call from the steward for her to go back into the ring to collect her award. She and Satire walked forward to fresh applause, coming to a halt in front of the judges' box. The competitor placed third, an amiable Yorkshire lad riding a beautiful chestnut, took his place beside her. But there was no sign of Saventos. Eventually, when everyone was tired of waiting for the missing runner-up, the wife of the company director whose firm were sponsoring the event came forward to present the prizes.

Alessandra leaned down and took the silver cup with a slow smile of delight. It was only just beginning to sink in that she was truly the winner of this prestigious competition. All kinds of opportunities could open up now. And maybe at long last her parents, most especially her father, would finally see the sense in her pursuing a serious career in competitive riding.

Alessandra had played her cards very carefully as regards this long cherished ambition. Her parents were both top flight musicians and not unnaturally had been hopeful that she too, would become skilled in the music field. They had never been unreasonable, however; the pressure had always been low-key and subtle. But it had been there. And she had had the intelligence to understand things from their point of view.

Her father was, after all, one of the most highly regarded orchestral conductors in the world. It was not suprising that he should cherish musical ambitions on his only child's behalf.

And that was why Alessandra had gone along obediently with his wishes. Realizing in her mid-teens that there would be little to gain from fighting him, she had continued her studies on the piano, had gained honours in her final examinations and then gone on to the Guildhall School of Music for a three-year course in the practice and theory of music, graduating earlier in the summer.

8

She had done what he wanted, and whilst she had kept up her riding, it had been relegated to second place as a mere hobby. Alessandra felt that she had served her term in the service of music. And at last she was free. But now it was crunch time. What to do next?

The thoughts passed through her mind in the flash of less than a few seconds as she sat square in Satire's saddle, quietly glowing with this newest, most precious triumph.

'Well done!' said the chairman's wife, all decked out in pale turquoise linen. She looked incongruously pristine and dainty beside the muscled steaming horse. As Satire flung up his head and stamped a foot impatiently she gave a little start of alarm and darted smartly back to the safety of the spectators' box.

Satire and Alessandra cantered a swift lap of honour around the ring and rode out to thunderous applause. Emilio Saventos was waiting for her.

'You are lucky today,' he said grimly. 'It will not always be like that.'

'Most likely not,' she agreed coolly.

'That horse,' Emilio continued, looking at Satire with scorn. 'He is careless. He bangs his feet on the poles.'

'They all do sometimes. Even yours.'

'Ottavio just gave a little touch. He knows how to tuck up his feet. I have taught him.' There was menace in this statement, and a look of dark sadism on the young man's face which made Alessandra alert to his potential for cruelty. She wondered what methods he had used to train his beautiful horse to pick up his feet.

9

'You should use your spurs,' Emilio continued enlightening her. 'And your whip.'

Alessandra glanced down at Ottavio's flanks. Just beneath the round of his belly, to the side of the cruelly tight girth, were marks of savage cuts. Although healing now and well concealed with thick ointment they were nevertheless unmistakable signs of a wicked abuse of spurs. Anger fizzed inside her but she revealed no trace of it. Her face was cool and impartial.

'No,' she told Emilio quietly. 'I can win without the aid of brutality.'

His nostrils flared like those of a furious equine. He was as hot and hasty and uncontrolled as she was calm and considered. And what came next was so unexpected, so incredible that Alessandra found it hard later to gain a clear recollection of exactly what had happened.

As she pressed her legs on Satire, urging him to walk on past the sulking Spaniard, Emilio suddenly raised his whip high in the air and brought it down with a vicious crack. Maybe he had intended it just to swish through the air waves. Maybe his aim had been to give his own horse a shock. Whatever was intended the eventual landing place of the whip was square on Satire's innocent quarters.

Already excited from the competition and the noise of the crowd, and being unused to violence, Satire gave a huge buck and set off at a furious gallop. Almost instantly he found himself faced with the five-barred gate which guarded the entrance to a grazing field. Helpless to do anything but try to steady him, Alessandra sent up a prayer as the gate rushed towards them.

Satire's instincts were always to jump rather than run out or stop dead and that was what he did – hurling himself into the air and not surprisingly getting everything wrong. His jump was skewed, lifting him over the gate almost sideways. Losing his balance his control over his limbs vanished, causing him to catch his foreleg in the upright strut of the gate.

Alessandra was thrown clear to land on the grass, winded but unharmed. Getting to her feet she saw Satire lying on his side on the ground, his legs thrashing wildly, his eyes rolling in distress.

Distraught, she flung herself towards him, hot tears springing from her eyes. A little crowd of onlookers had gathered behind the fence, watching wide-eyed as she knelt beside the terrified horse. Grasping his reins in one hand she tried to soothe him with the other.

A splendid horse brought down is a pitiful sight and Alessandra's heart felt bruised as the horse looked up at her, dumb and helpless fright in his huge eyes. A lifetime seemed to pass as he lay there. And then with a huge effort he miraculously began to struggle to his feet. He stood on the cool grass, trembling violently, holding up his right fore-leg.

'Oh, please God, don't let it be broken,' Alessandra whispered. Wildly she looked around her. 'Go get a vet,' she shouted to the curious crowd.

A small child detached himself from the gaping group and ran off to the stables office. Within seconds a young woman in a white coat appeared. Climbing swiftly over the gate she ran up to Satire and bent to inspect his leg.

She looked up at Alessandra. 'Are you OK?' she asked gently.

'Yes, yes. What about his leg?'

She ran her fingers very gently over the bones of his lower leg. 'I think he's probably done no more than pull a tendon. Let's see if he can move at all. Try to get him to take a step or two.'

Tentatively Alessandra hooked her fingers in Satire's bridle and urged him forward. He made an uncertain hobbling step and then stopped.

The vet now ran her hand over his foot, and he winced, showing the whites of his eyes. 'Where's your trailer?' she asked Alessandra. 'I'll give him a pain-killing shot and then let's try to get him in there and really see what's what.'

Her heart beating with anxiety Alessandra gently led the hobbling Satire back to the luxury trailer her parents had bought for her on her eighteenth birthday. He managed to fumble his way up the ridged ramp and seemed reassured to reach the familiarity of his box with its sweet-smelling straw and a fresh feed already mixed and put out for him.

The vet made a more detailed examination and was able to reassure Alessandra that she could find no evidence of broken bones. She recommended bandaging the horse's leg with a cold water poultice.

'Just keep him very calm and quiet for an hour or so and then I'll look at him again,' she decided. Looking at Alessandra's white face, she asked if there was anyone with her at the show.

'My mother's here.'

'Why don't you go and find her?' the vet

12

suggested. 'I'll get one of the grooms to keep an eye on your horse until you get back.'

'All right.' Alessandra went out of the trailer, scanning the crowds, wondering if she might see the slight figure of her mother, Tara Xavier. But like her father, her mother was also something of a celebrity. She would have got caught up with some admiring crowd who wanted to know of her latest plans.

And maybe that was no bad thing, thought Alessandra suddenly realizing that she had a score to settle with Emilio, and that it would be best done now whilst she was on her own.

Although her legs still quivered with shock, she presented a picture of outward calm as she made her way along the line of trailers where riders, grooms and family helpers were all busy loading up their horses into boxes and trailers in preparation for the journey home.

She knew the Saventos trailer well. It stood slightly apart from the others at the end of the long line, a huge vehicle, if anything even more splendid than her own: a mobile palace for horses.

She could hear the agitated drum of hoofs as she approached the trailer. Her heart began to drum in response. The door of the trailer was shut, but not locked. Pulling it open she peered into the gloom beyond. For a moment, after the brightness outside, she could see nothing except darkness, but what she could hear told her enough.

There was the sound of a whip thudding onto flesh, the high pitched squeals of a horse in terror. Oh, dear God! Not content with bringing fear and pain to one horse Saventos was set on ruining another.

'Stop it!' she yelled. Hurling herself forward she sprang onto the figure wielding the whip, catching his upraised arm and then knocking him to the ground.

There were muffled curses of protest. Saventos, startled and unnerved, looked up at his attacker. Outrage flared in his face. 'Get out,' he shouted. 'English bitch, how dare you come in here?'

'Leave that horse alone,' she said, grasping his upper arm with steel-like fingers.

'I do what I like!' His black eyes flashed with fury. 'And I do not do what a *woman* tells me. Never do I do that.'

He snatched his whip out of her reach as she attempted to take it from him. 'It is my animal. It must learn not to make mistakes. And I do what I please with it.' He scrambled to his feet and raised his whip once more. The horse cowered away from him in the farthest corner, his fleshy pink nostrils splayed wide.

Alessandra understood that it was pointless to reason with this man. Maniacal intent beamed from his ferocious eyes. Uncharacteristically allowing her own internal demons of rage to drive her, she dashed out into the open air and returning to her trailer grabbed the lunge line stored amongst Satire's tack.

As she flew back to the scene of sickening brutality she swiftly manipulated one end of the flat canvas rope into a loose loop.

She was not surprised to discover that Emilio had not been at all deterred by being caught red-handed

14

maltreating his horse and was busy finishing the grisly proceedings which she had interrupted.

The shrill bird-like squeals of the horse rattled Alessandra's nerves and hardened her already firm resolve. Half closing her eyes in order to assess Saventos's position and distance she took careful aim and tossed the lunge line into the air, cowboy-style. The loop billowed out into a circle and dropped smoothly over Saventos's head to land around his neck, at which point Alessandra gave the rope a savage jerk to pull it tight.

Saventos made a gagging noise, the whip falling from his hands as he staggered around blindly, grasping at his throat. As he struggled, Alessandra stepped up close to him, reeling in the rope and keeping it taut. She wound her end of the line around the brass tethering hook let into one of the trailer's internal wood struts. Saventos found himself roped on a short line like a bullock in a cattle market.

Alessandra stood back surveying him. 'I've got you now,' she said quietly.

Saventos's head twisted round. He stared at Alessandra, his eyes bulging with disbelief. And steadily growing fear.

Alessandra picked up the dropped whip and advanced on him. She placed the thonged leather tip against his cheek, touching his skin with the lightness of a breath of air. Emilio's features twitched.

'You're the helpless one now,' she told him meaningfully, 'and I can do what I like with you, you bastard.'

'Get out,' Emilio said through gritted teeth.

'Bend your knee,' she told him.

'What?'

'Do it!' She tapped his jaw very softly with the whip to remind him who was boss and then gave his calf a little nudge with the tip of her toe.

Reluctantly he obeyed her. Alessandra grasped his raised shining leather boot and tugged it off him. Tossing the whip to one side she lifted the boot to Emilio's livid face, laying the cool steel of the razor sharp spur attached to its heel against his cheek.

He gasped and tried to squirm away, but Alessandra blocked his way and each small movement merely tightened the noose around his neck.

'I could make some very pretty patterns on your face, just like you've done on your horse's flanks,' she said.

He cringed away from her. 'No,' he gasped. 'No.'

'You pathetic coward,' she told him. 'You're not worth wasting my time on.'

She meant what she said. Although truly she thought that if anything serious had happened to Satire she could have spent some time doing this man some real damage.

Then suddenly she was utterly sick of Saventos and his brutality. No way would she soil her own hands with such tawdry behaviour as his. She flung the boot from her in a gesture of violent contempt. It landed at the door of the trailer, just missing making contact with the figure of a man climbing up the entrance ramp.

He bent to pick it up. 'What is all this?' he asked. 'What is going on here?'

'Justice,' said Alessandra. She swivelled to face the newcomer, fixing him with her disarmingly level gaze, whilst behind her Saventos was letting out the muffled bellows of a frustrated bull.

The man glanced briefly at him and then looked back at her. He was a powerfully built man with thick black hair and a square strong face. An open candid face, the face of a man who would be scrupulously fair, although not necessarily kind.

His presence had created a subtle but definite shift in the psychological atmosphere.

'Who are you?' Alessandra asked with faint challenge.

He raised his chin slightly. 'I am Raphael Godeval Saventos,' he said. A silence followed this announcement.

As Alessandra connected with the man's gleaming and compelling black eyes she realized instantly that he must be a relative of Emilio's. Not old enough to be his father though. Possibly an older brother. At this point she really didn't care very much.

With slow deliberation Raphael Saventos turned his gaze into the corner of the trailer. Observing the lathered, bleeding horse, his face revealed little open feeling but when he glanced once more towards Emilio it revealed a good deal. Displeasure, contempt, disappointment.

He spoke to Emilio rapidly in Spanish and the younger man turned his face away, his features jerking and twitching.

'I would ask you to release my nephew please,' Raphael said to Alessandra. He spoke in the manner of a man used to commanding and being obeyed.

Alessandra, who had grown up in the shadow of a forceful father, and was now – albeit unconsciously – beginning to emulate him, was not in the slightest intimidated. Out of politeness, however, she unwound the line from the tether hook and let it drop slack on the ground.

'I could report him to the judges,' she told Raphael Saventos, glancing at Emilio and then towards the distressed horse. 'Or the British Horse Society.'

'I believe I could do likewise,' Raphael said, his eyes glinting like freshly hewn coal. 'Regarding your own behaviour.'

She gave a dry laugh. 'I doubt that you'd get much joy. Here in England we're rather keen on the welfare of animals. I'd be let off with a caution. I'd probably be the heroine of the moment.'

She knew she was pushing things a little. Technically she supposed she could be charged with trespass at the very least, But then if anyone were to present evidence of what had been done to Ottavio (and at this point she was mindful of the availability of her camera equipment in the trailer) she had little doubt that leniency would be very much on her side.

'You won't report me,' she told Raphael steadily. 'Because you won't want the disgrace of your nephew's rotten behaviour to come to light. It would be too shaming wouldn't it? You Spanish have great pride. And whilst you do disgusting things to unlucky bulls in public, you have the grace to give them a sporting chance don't you? Matadors at least have the decency to face the bull running free and risk losing their own skins.'

Saventos was taken aback. Intrigued, infuriated, impressed.

'You think I should keep silent to preserve the honour of Spain?' he asked. His eyes glimmered with what could have been a spark of humour.

'I think you should keep quiet to preserve the honour of your family,' she returned, glancing at Emilio. 'If they have any to preserve.'

Emilio's eyes flamed. 'We are a very old Spanish family. Very high up. How dare you speak so of our family?' He flung the words at her, his face livid with fury. Releasing a flood of what sounded to Alessandra like pure Spanish vitriol, he erupted from the trailer, pushing rudely past her and Raphael and striding off to the big black Mercedes which was parked alongside.

Alessandra stared at Raphael. She was beginning to feel the effects of the long day's riding, all the tension and excitement. She thought longingly of a long soak in a warm bath. And then she thought of Satire.

'I see that I must apologize for my nephew,' Saventos said gravely with a touch of weariness.

'More important than that – who's going to look after this poor horse?' Alessandra demanded, marshalling her energies and squaring up to him again. As far as she was concerned neither Raphael nor his nephew were going to get away with mere expressions of emotion – be it tantrums or resigned regret – when an animal was suffering.

The devils, she thought with renewed fury. Both of them.

'Ah, yes.' Saventos looked at the horse and sighed.

19

Alessandra supposed that he would have no idea at all of the practicalities of caring for an animal. The thought kindled a flash of contempt for him, although another part of her mind could not help being impressed by his quiet and dignified demeanour in the face of the despicable and gutless behaviour of his nephew.

She moved towards the horse who trembled and cringed away, making her heart bleed for him. Such a beautiful, noble animal. Worth ten of Emilio Saventos any day.

She crooned softly to him under her breath, the beginning of an aria from Mozart's *Don Giovanni*. She had had years of singing training, but had never particularly enjoyed or used her skill until she discovered that it was a marvellous soother for troubled horses. Dogs as well for that matter.

The horse allowed her to stroke his nose. His large blue-black eyes became calmer. 'He needs sponging down with cool water. And these cuts need to be treated with a soothing antiseptic ointment – the old wounds as well.'

She looked across to Raphael, her face hard. 'And then all he needs is love and reassurance, although I don't suppose that he'll have much chance of that.'

'I will take care of him,' Raphael said. 'Please – believe me when I say that. You see, I had no idea . . .' He stretched out his hands in a gesture of supplication, his palms turned upwards.

She said nothing.

'You are Alessandra Xavier, I think,' he observed.

'Yes.'

20

'I must congratulate you on your win today and your superb riding.'

'Thank you.' She had half expected that he was going to congratulate her on being the daughter of the world famous conductor Saul Xavier, which was what most people did when they found out who she was. Saventos's reference to her riding slightly mollified her.

He was just on the point of some further elaboration when the young groom who had been so impressed with Satire earlier on appeared at the bottom of the ramp. Her eyes fastened on Alessandra, full of anxiety. 'Oh! There you are. Can you come straight away. The vet needs to talk to you about Satire.'

Alessandra gave a little gasp. 'Is he worse?'

The girl pressed her lips together. 'I can't say. You have to talk to the vet.'

'Right.'

As she walked past Raphael he put out his arm. 'Please. If there is anything I can do to help. You must tell me. Anything at all.'

She looked up at him: a handsome commanding man. An arresting and powerful figure. She did not, however, look long or hard enough to register that his face was filled with warmth and sincerity. Because of her concern for Satire she felt a distaste bordering on revulsion for anyone connected with Emilio.

'I don't want your help,' she said tersely. 'In fact,' she added over her shoulder as she ran swiftly down the ramp, 'help from you or any of your family is the very last thing I need.'

CHAPTER 2

Two hundred miles away, in the heartlands of Britain's once glorious industrial north, a competition of a quite different kind from show-jumping was building up to its climax.

The Leeds Piano competition, held every three years, is one of the most prestigious in the world. Young hopefuls from all over the globe fight for the chance to shine on the platform of the Leeds Town Hall – a stately old civic building guarded by two massive stone lions.

Only the premier orchestras and conductors are considered worthy of providing accompaniment for the brilliant budding virtuosos and in this particular year, on this particular evening, it was the highly acclaimed Tudor Philharmonic who were the chosen players, working under the direction of their chief conductor Saul Xavier.

Xavier stood facing them now, his long sensitive hands drawing the music from them with a compelling unseen power that bordered on magic. He held his tall slim frame very erect, his backbone a ramrod. But his hands were as fluid and graceful as a ballet dancer. Whilst his right hand moved gently to indicate the rhythm, his left glided and hovered, giving the players their cue to each gradation of musical dynamics and expression.

Musical connoisseurs in the audience marvelled at Xavier's total command of each piece, and the curious mixture of strength and ease with which he enslaved and controlled the players. Those of them who were female also sighed at Xavier's fantastic sexual appeal.

'How old is he?' they asked each other, not being able to believe their calculations which ended up at the number sixty – if not a year older.

'My God,' muttered one notoriously cynical journalist to her companion, 'I'd never realized he was so beautiful.' She paused, thoughtful. 'They say his wife's over twenty years younger and hasn't ever looked at another man since they got together. I'd usually say "utter bullshit" to that. But with this man. Well . . .' She stared up at the great conductor, allowing herself to be hypnotized.

The time moved on. The audience listened enchanted to a sequence of moving performances of the music repertoire's great concertos, the works of Schumann, Brahms and Beethoven. And now to finish with there was some truly rousing Tchaikovsky. As Xavier conducted, the young pianist crouched over the keys, beads of sweat running down his face and dripping onto the glinting ivory.

Tara Xavier held her hands steady on the wheel, allowing her gently pulsing Jaguar, with its arsenal of late twentieth century technology, to more or less drive itself. She was keeping her speed at a constant eighty and the miles rolled away like satin beneath the car's big wheels. In less than an hour they would be approaching Leeds.

Alessandra sat beside her mother, her face stone-like, her feelings numbed. With a huge force of will she forbade her mind to re-live the events of the past few hours. Instead she began to dig deep into the onion ring layers of memory, taking herself back through the previous two years, desperately trying to recapture hours of shining happiness. It was a hopeless task.

Tara glanced at her. They had travelled in silence for over an hour now. She longed to break through the wall of misery behind which Alessandra had barricaded herself. She longed to comfort her. But how? She heard the inevitable clichés queueing up to be said: *It will pass darling, the hurting will lessen, time will heal bruised emotions*, etc. etc. Exactly the kind of words that the self-contained Alessandra would shy away from in impatience and contempt. Alessandra was fiercely independent. She liked to make her own way, fight her own battles. Pity was an emotion she had no time for.

Tara reflected that for Alessandra at twenty-one this was the first real set back, the first true taste of grief. And Tara's own distress on her daughter's behalf was keen and bitter, like the turn of a blade within a tender wound. But having just celebrated her fortieth birthday Tara had reached an age when she knew that life contained a stubbornly regenerative quality. That pain did indeed pass, and that the capacity for joy would slowly seep back into the black void.

'Are you all right?' Tara demanded suddenly, dismayed at the total inadequacy of the question.

Alessandra turned to her. She let her cool grey eyes with their dark sapphire streaks – her father's eyes – move slowly over the small delicate figure of her mother. She made a small dismissive gesture. 'All right?' she echoed.

'Yes, of course I am.'

'My two loved ones,' Saul murmured, detaching himself from the champagne-swilling throng in the magnificent first floor suite of Leeds's grandest hotel, and moving forward to greet his wife and daughter as they stood poised in the doorway.

'So,' he smiled, passing an arm around Tara's slender shoulders, 'you have both come back to me safe and sound.' He bent and kissed her gently on her lips. Then looking into Alessandra's grave and beautiful face, he asked: 'Do you have any triumphs to tell me about? Of the equine kind?' His face took on a hint of gentle irony. 'As if there were any other triumphs my lovely daughter cares about.'

'I got the Champion of Show cup,' Alessandra said. 'How about that?'

'That's very good news. Wonderful in fact!' He narrowed his eyes slightly, as he picked up the signals that belied Alessandra's brave-sounding tones.

'Yes, isn't it. I must admit I was a bit surprised. I hadn't expected to do so well.' Alessandra suddenly turned her face away from her father's gaze. 'Look I'm just going to clean up a bit before I brave the musical throng.' She spoke in a rushing breathless manner, afterwards making a swift and abrupt exit from the room.

Saul watched her. He looked back at Tara, his eyebrows raised.

'Satire had a heart attack,' she said. 'Fatal.'

'Oh dear God.'

'It was all over in seconds.' Tara grimaced, recalling the appallingly sudden incident with horrible clarity. Satire had been standing in his box, perfectly calm, although still holding up his wounded leg. Tara had been listening with alarm to the young groom's vivid account of his mad leap over a five-barred gate when, without any warning, Satire had simply shrunk down to the floor of the trailer to lie there like a stone. He had made just one attempt to raise his head, and then a blood-chilling sound had come from deep in his chest: a terrible, gurgling choking noise. His head had sunk back.

The vet had come straight away. She had opened one of his eyes, and Tara had seen instantly that there was already a blue film of lifelessness over it.

'Was Alessandra with him?' Saul asked.

'No. I only wish she had been. She'd gone off to talk to one of the other competitors. It took a few minutes to locate her.'

He sighed. 'The shock must have been terrible.'

'Yes.'

They were silent for a few moments, looking at each other, their gaze full of understanding as they recalled past trials survived and anticipated those to be faced and overcome in the future.

Tara saw eyes swerving in their direction. Aside from the winner of the piano competition, Saul was the star attraction at this party. His temporary absence from the fray had been noted.

'So, what are we going to do for her?' he wondered slowly, refusing to bow to the pressure of mere social demands.

Tara looked up at him. She gave a brief wistful smile. 'I doubt if she'd let us do much, even if we knew what would help. She'll need to work this out for herself. Like you have always needed to do Saul. After all she is your daughter.'

Alessandra splashed cold water over her cheeks and forehead. She freed her hair from the thick plait into which she coiled it when she was riding. It swung around her face and neck in thick heavy waves.

She leaned forward and peered at her face in the mirror, curious to note that she looked completely normal. Inside she felt insubstantial and fragile and pale, but the mirror seemed to show nothing of this. Her face was always pale anyway, but she had expected something more dramatic to be apparent.

Oh well, at least she wouldn't have much difficulty in putting on a good show at the party, maintaining a good façade. She knew that her parents would let her keep her feelings to herself and that no one else would have an inkling of what had happened. There would be no risk of anyone trespassing on her privacy, trampling on the grave of Satire.

The silent speaking of her horse's name brought tears surging up into her eyes. She allowed two or three to spill over, then breathed in deeply, wiped her face, smoothed the fabric of her long clinging cream

27

dress over her hips and thighs and re-joined the celebrations.

'You see, for many years I have studied the life of Tchaikovsky in great depth,' the winner of the piano competition explained earnestly to Alessandra, deftly capturing a mound of cold meats from the buffet table onto his fork and transferring them rapidly to his mouth. He was in his late twenties, with a mass of curly light brown hair and a strangely innocent and unworldly look about him. 'I've read over twenty biographies. And, do you know, all of them tell a slightly different story?'

'Fascinating,' she commented crisply, trying to work out how this man was able to devour a huge plate of food whilst simultaneously presenting a lengthy monologue on the only true way to approach the thorny problems connected with the interpretation of the great Russian composer's music.

'He was a man of great complexity,' the reflective winner proclaimed solemnly. 'A troubled man.'

'A man of sorrows and acquainted with grief,' Alessandra commented drily. She wondered if the virtuoso pianist would pick up that particular quotation from the Old Testament, which was heavily featured in Handel's *Messiah*.

He didn't.

'A man of sorrows,' he echoed. 'Yes. That is quite a perfect description. Most apt and beautifully put.' He looked at Alessandra with renewed interest. 'You see,' he said, refuelling his fork and launching once again into his monologue, 'you have to know where the music is *coming from* if you are to play it with true feeling. Are you connecting with what I'm trying to say?' He stared at her, his large eyes rounding into two huge shining circles.

Oh only too well, Alessandra thought wearily. Having been reared in an intense and rarified musical atmosphere she had been on the receiving end of this kind of conversation many times before. She assumed an expression of saintly impartiality and tolerance. She had the impression that this talented young man had suffered greatly for his art. And now unfortunately it was her turn.

His output of talk continued unabated, as did his input of food. Alessandra tried to be sympathetic. She knew from experience that performing music was very physical. You felt sick beforehand, sweated all the way through and were starving with hunger when it was all over. Pretty much like competition horse riding.

'You see,' the pianist continued, fuelled with success, good food and the ear of a beautiful young woman, 'you can't play the music with true sensitivity if you don't understand the composer's heart and mind.'

Alessandra felt exhausted. Just at this moment she couldn't give a toss about the heart and mind of Tchaikovsky or any of that procession of dead musical scribes who had been such a vivid presence in her childhood and adolesence. She stared fixedly at her supper companion, trying desperately to give at least some impression of interest. She felt as though her eyes might revolve into the back of her head like the iridescent oranges and apples in an alleyway gambling machine.

She wanted to go home and lie down in the darkness and cry until all the veins and arteries and pipes in her body had run dry.

But when her mother came to rescue her from the philosophizing musical man of the moment, she went off bravely to continue doing the rounds. By now she was so weary she could hardly stand. She found herself shifting from one foot to the other like a bored pony. It struck her as she listened to the merry chatter of the members of the Tudor Philharmonic that musicians, whatever instrument they played, were all rather good at blowing their own trumpets.

Around midnight her father glided up beside her, prised her away from the balding tenor who was bending her ear with tales of his past triumphs, and quietly steered her to the door.

'Home!' he murmured in her ear. 'We've done our bit.'

In the corridor outside the suite her mother was waiting. She carried a light cashmere cloak which she threw around Alessandra's shoulders. As they stepped out into the night air Alessandra pulled the fabric around her, glad of its protection. Suddenly her body was trembling. Feverishly hot one minute, icy cold the next.

With Xavier at the wheel the Jaguar had them back in Oxfordshire in one and a half hours flat.

Alessandra swung herself from the car, looking up at the big mock Tudor house in which she had lived since she was a baby. Tears gathered again in her eyes. She recalled leaving the house the previous morning full of hope and anticipation, setting off to the livery stables, loading Satire into the trailer . . .

In bed she lay dry-eyed in the darkness waiting for the hours to pass. She knew that in the great scheme of things horses were not as important as people. She knew too that her parents were doing their best to understand her feelings. But she doubted that they could ever truly understand. They were all wrapped up in each other and in music. How could they appreciate just what Satire had meant to her? He had been her companion and friend. She had cared for him like a mother cares for a child. She had truly loved him.

She acknowledged that she was lucky because her parents were rich and generous enough to buy her another horse. But every individual animal was as unique and irreplaceable as a human. There would never be another horse like Satire.

She wished she could cry; shake with great strangled sobs which would release some of the pain. But the tears that had threatened earlier on now stubbornly refused to come.

It was eleven when she woke the next morning, alerted to the gentle but insistent knocking on her door.

She struggled to sit up, her head still full of dream-like images: black moths and sinister flying bats – and dead black horses.

Her father came in. He placed a cup and saucer on the table beside her bed. She saw the steam rising from it in a thin spiral. Beyond the windows a September sun shone with metallic brilliance.

She braced herself as memory and pain came roaring back. Her misery stabbed her afresh as though it had been lying crouched in a corner of the room just waiting for her to return to consciousness.

Her father stood looking down at her. 'So?' he said quietly.

'I'm OK,' she responded with slight protest.

He laid a cool dry hand on her forehead. 'We were worried that you might have got a chill. A touch of flu perhaps.'

She shook her head. 'I'll be fine.' She glanced up at him. 'You can sit down on the bed for a moment Daddy,' she added drily. 'Or are you about to fly away on some important mission?'

His grey eyes beneath their cowled lids flickered.

She gave a sharp sly laugh, sizing up the situation instantly. 'So where are you off to today?' she wondered. 'Paris? Munich? New York?' Her father worked all the time. Seven days a week, fifty-two weeks a year if he felt so inclined.

'Vienna.'

'Ah.' She reached for the cup and took a sip. It was hot chocolate. Her father always made it perfectly; just the right blend of chocolate and milk with a little dash of coffee to spice it up. But then all the things he chose to spend time on, however little, he did perfectly.

'I'm going to discuss the possibility of a new video series,' he told her. 'The aim is to sign up international artists to make films demonstrating and explaining their own individual interpretations of the great masterpieces.'

'Trade secrets!'

'Mmm. That is the aim.'

'A novel idea. And expensive I'd guess?'

'Prohibitively. I shall probably have to finance some of it myself to get it off the ground.'

'Hmm. Well, you'd better not stay here too long talking then! These are obviously vital discussions. You don't want to miss your flight and arrive late.' Her eyes glinted as she looked at him.

Saul gave a brief smile. He enjoyed verbal fencing with his daughter. But this morning, as he had entered her room, he had wondered if he might penetrate the wall of irony she had built around herself, make a small dent in the defence ramparts of her outward bravery. But he could see that, like him, she preferred to be left to herself. Sympathy could be as much an invasion as a comforter.

'Alessandra,' he said, 'you know that when you feel able to think of choosing another horse we shall be here for you to do all we can to help in your choice. Whatever you want . . .'

The words made her flinch. She tried not to let him see. It was too soon to be talking this way. Far too soon.

'And if I might offer a little advice,' he went on, 'I shouldn't waste time about it.'

She dipped her head and reached again for her cup. 'Thank you,' she said.

'There's going to be a big gap in your life now, you realize that don't you?' he went on softly but relentlessly. 'And I'm not talking solely about the loss of Satire. You have to consider your whole future now that you've completed your education.'

Alessandra licked her lips. She knew exactly what he was driving at. There was this huge issue looming. The way ahead – whether to travel down a musical path, or to choose another route entirely. After her success at the competition the day before it had been her firm intention to tackle her parents head on about her future. She had intended to tell them in no uncertain terms, absolutely finally and definitely, that she would not be pursuing a career in music. And after that she had been going to tell them of her plans to find an independent sponsor to help her in her ambition to develop her skills and to gradually build up a small stable of top class show-jumpers.

But now . . . Now she simply felt drained and weary. And full of an aching terrifying apathy. 'I know,' she agreed. 'You're right.'

He looked at his watch. 'Obviously we can't make any firm decisions now. But when we're all together again in a few days we must talk seriously. Yes?'

She nodded. 'Where's Mummy?'

'On a flight to Amsterdam. She's conducting a youth orchestra there tonight. She'll be home tomorrow afternoon.'

'Oh, yes.' Another workaholic.

He stood up. 'Mrs Lockton will be here as usual. She's already preparing some lunch to tempt you.'

Alessandra nodded again. She could see that her father had said what he came to say. That now his thoughts were moving away from her, moving on into the future hours of the day which he would spend engaged in vital negotiations in another country.

He bent and dropped a light kiss on her forehead, awakening in her a sudden urge to cling to him. She resisted it. And as he closed the door softly behind him, it occurred to her that by far the greatest physical contact she had had with another creature in the past two years had been with Satire.

She finished her hot chocolate drink, climbed out of bed and stood by the window watching her father's most recent black Porsche vanish down the drive, laying a funnel of translucent white smoke on the gravel.

For a few seconds she allowed a sense of emptiness to envelop her. And then she told herself not to be pathetic, took a shower and got dressed.

Downstairs, in the huge state-of-the-art kitchen, Mrs Lockton, who lived in the nearby village and came in every day to cook and housekeep, was sitting at the table peeling carrots and onions. She had worked for the Xaviers since before Alessandra was born. She was a grandmother now and Alessandra fancied she knew a thing or two about life, despite the fact that she often joked that she had only been out of the UK once.

She looked up and smiled at Alessandra. 'I'm really sorry about Satire,' she said simply.

'Thanks,' said Alessandra sitting down at the table and sighing.

Mrs Lockton's knife flashed rhythmically in the sun as she worked. The movements were curiously calming.

Always here for you, Alessandra recalled her father saying, talking of himself and her mother. But that was sadly exactly what they most usually were not. It was, in fact, Mrs Lockton who had always been here, just as she was today. Although today, being Sunday, she would only stay long enough to prepare lunch and then she would go back to her own family.

Alessandra considered the afternoon which stretched ahead. A mellow autumn afternoon which she would normally have spent going out for a long leisurely hack on Satire through the country lanes.

Mrs Lockton glanced at her. Whilst deeply fond of her employers Saul and Tara, and hating to harbour feelings of disloyalty, she really did think that in the circumstances one of them should have stayed at home today to be with their daughter.

But then, Alessandra was just the kind of young woman who would have been unnerved by such a major departure from the normal run of things. She would probably have been annoyed at the prospect of being cared for. She would most likely have felt patronized. Mrs Lockton had noted from her own children that to patronize was one of the greatest sins a modern parent could commit.

'I was going to roast a duck for lunch,' she told Alessandra in practical tones. 'Serve it with cherry sauce and garden vegetables. Does that sound OK? Can you face it?'

Alessandra, miles away in her thoughts, returned to the here and now. 'Duck? Oh yes. Perfect. I shall be fine you know. I'm not the type to pine away and starve.'

Mrs Lockton smiled and continued with her peeling, and in due course a splendid duck lunch was placed before Alessandra who duly expressed warm appreciation.

But after Mrs Lockton had left Alessandra ate no more than a couple of mouthfuls of the succulent duck breast before laying down her knife and fork with a sigh. As she leaned her chin on her hands

Allegro, the family cat who had been observing from a distance, now considered it safe to jump on the table. Eyeing Alessandra and judging that she seemed unlikely to put up much opposition he stealthily approached her plate, eyed her once more and then settled down, hind paws well folded, and began to tuck in.

'Thief!' she said softly, observing him impassively. 'This is highly forbidden behaviour. If my father were here something very unceremonious would happen to you.'

Allegro took no notice. When the phone began to warble he carried on unperturbed as Alessandra got up abruptly from the table.

'Yes.' She spoke with a crisp faint challenge almost identical to that of her father.

There was a brief pause. 'Am I speaking to Miss Alessandra Xavier?' enquired the caller.

Alessandra narrowed her eyes, tilted her head and frowned slightly. That deep ripe almost languid voice. A voice she hardly knew – yet unmistakable. 'Mr Raphael Saventos?'

'Yes. I must apologize for calling out of the blue. I hope I am not disturbing you and your family if you are dining.'

Such formality, Alessandra thought. 'No,' she said.

'Miss Xavier I heard that your horse had died suddenly . . .'

'Yes,' she cut in, the tone of that single word managing to convey that Raphael had better be careful. That he risked trespassing on sacred ground.

'I am so very, very sorry.'

37

'Thank you.'

'Miss Xavier . . .'

'Alessandra.'

'Miss Xavier, I have to tell you that I feel some responsibility for what has happened.'

'Do you? I think you flatter yourself.'

'Please listen to what I have to say, although I can understand why you would feel angry with me.'

'With your nephew perhaps,' she said coldly.

'I come from an old traditional Spanish family Miss Xavier. What my nephew does reflects on me.'

'Well given your nephew that's very bad luck on you,' she snapped back, immediately angry with herself for sounding so coarse and ungracious.

'How he behaved to you after the competition was unforgivable. I was mortified to hear of it.'

'Were you? How interesting. So are you telling me that what your wretched nephew did to my horse, possibly as a mistake, was worse than his beating the living daylights out of his own poor horse – is that it?' Her anger was glowing and genuine now – and there was not one shred of regret. 'I don't remember your seeming in the slightest concerned about that nasty little piece of work Mr Saventos!'

There was a significant pause. 'Is there nothing I can do or say to make things better? I had no idea of what had happened before Satire died. I knew nothing of it until a half hour ago. And now I want to try to make amends . . .'

'What a nerve!' Alessandra exploded. 'How could you, how could *anyone* dare to suggest making amends for the loss of my horse? I *loved* my horse.' Her voice faltered. Suddenly the tears that she had longed to shed began to bank up behind her eyelids. They spilled over and ran down her face and chin, dropping onto the handset. Swallowing hard and keeping her voice in check through a supreme effort of will, she quickly excused herself to Raphael and dropped the handset back onto its contact point.

After she had finished weeping, she rinsed her face in cold water and stood looking out of the window, tracking the jerky movements of a small bird which hopped busily amongst the golden leafmeal dropped from a still nearly-green horsechestnut.

Allegro, sated and oozing contentment, jumped onto the sink and rubbed himself against her arm. Smiling absently she tickled the soft tufty fur behind his ears.

And then, turning slowly back into the room, she picked up the phone and dialled the call back facility to discover the number of the last caller.

CHAPTER 3

Raphael Godeval Saventos waited in the lobby of his London hotel, unruffled and composed. Despite the casual nature of his clothes: simple cotton trousers and shirt topped with a well cut linen jacket, he projected an image of noticeable style and elegance.

In front of him on the low glass-topped table was an English afternoon tea of dainty sandwiches, buttered currant bread and light sponge cake. Balanced on his knees was a heavyweight British Sunday newspaper which he was reading with interest.

He noted the number of articles related to women's issues. Feminist issues. He felt duty-bound to read them with care, to discover any differences between the thoughts of Spanish women on these matters compared with those of the British.

Raphael felt that he knew a good deal about Spanish women. As a child he had suffered at the hands and tongue of his mother, who had spent her life rebelling against his decidedly traditional father. 'Macho, macho!' she would taunt him when invited to take more interest in the family wine business and curb her ambitions for individual job opportunities in the great world beyond the Saventos vineyards.

His mother had been strong and difficult and strident. And once he reached adolescence he had begun to avoid her company as much as possible, leaving her and his elder sister to brood together in the family house, spending ever more of his father's money in order to turn it into a palace of luxury crammed with precious antiques and art work.

Raphael, out in the vineyards and the winery during every spare moment when he was not involved in his formal education, had quite naturally and automatically allied himself with the males of the family: his father and his eldest brother Joaquin. And then tragedy had struck without warning, leaving him with the responsibility of maintaining the huge profits necessary to re-invest in the growing business and at the same time satisfy the seemingly insatiable monetary demands of his mother and sister. And, of course, Emilio.

He laid down his newspaper and picked up a sandwich. He was well aware that from early on in his life he had learned to be guarded and wary – perhaps most especially as far as women were concerned. His lips flickered with a brief rueful smile as he reflected that this was hardly surprising given the personalities of his mother and sister.

The thought of women prompted him to look towards the revolving doors at the entrance to the lobby. It was perhaps a little early yet. But he had no intention of not being there, instantly visible, when Alessandra finally arrived.

When he thought of Emilio's crass and brutish

behaviour towards her the previous day he grew hot with anger. Displeasure with Emilio was no novelty, the resentful overgrown boy was a constant source of discord and dissatisfaction in the Saventos household. But for him to have behaved so shamingly, showing himself up in such a crude and sickening light in the eyes of the coolly beautiful and seemingly high-minded Alessandra stirred up real fury within Raphael.

He had reluctantly concluded, when she hung up on him earlier, that she wanted nothing more to do with him or his family. He had been in the process of pondering on a new route of contact – perhaps after allowing a decent interval to elapse – when she had unexpectedly called him back.

Her manner had been puzzling. He had the impression she was not entirely sure of her motives for getting in touch with him. She had sounded disoriented, and somehow needy. There had been something in her voice that had made him insist that she see him that day.

'Today? Oh – well, I'm not sure,' she had said cautiously.

'Please,' he had insisted. 'Please give me a chance to talk to you and explain.' He had come as near to pleading as a man of his self-possession and pride would ever get.

'All right then.'

'Three o'clock?'

'Make it four. I'll be there.' And she had hung up again. Just like that.

He stared once more at the doors, willing her to appear. He was by no means sure that she would keep the appointment, that he would ever see her again. And the uncertainty gave him a sense of keen anticipation.

He took another sandwich and consulted his newspaper once more. Then suddenly she was there in front of him.

'Mr Saventos,' she said with formal politeness, extending her hand.

He jumped to his feet. 'Miss Xavier! I am so charmed to see you. And please – not Mr Saventos. Raphael.'

She gave a faint smile. 'All right. In that case it's Alessandra please.'

He settled her down in a seat beside him, clicked his fingers and summoned a waiter to bring fresh hot tea.

He saw that she had been weeping. And at the same time as his heart contracted in sympathy, so a different kind of interest in her stirred and quickened, planting a seed of feeling that was destined not to be crushed.

'What have you done with your nephew?' she asked with brittle irony.

'Banished him back to Spain,' he said gravely. 'In deep disgrace.'

She looked at him. Her large grey eyes shone with feeling. 'Good. May I have a sandwich?'

'Please. Go ahead.' He felt absurdly gratified that she should accept the hospitality he had laid on.

She drank her tea and ate steadily through a dozen or so tiny sandwiches. She appeared to have no unease in his presence nor in the curious and unhappy circumstances of their meeting.

'I'm starving,' she said, moving on to the buttered currant bread. 'I haven't eaten properly since the night before the competition.'

He clicked his fingers again and ordered more food. He wondered how she would react to an invitation to dinner later on.

'What did you want to say to me – to make amends as you put it?' she asked suddenly with startling directness.

He was caught unawares. He looked at her delighted with her openness and her serene composure as she sat there calmly devouring the tea he had provided. He was so used to hot tempered women, women who showed emotion to excess.

She was wearing one of those loose fluid dresses that fashionable young women currently favoured. It was of a slatey blue that intensified the dark flecks in her grey eyes. The bodice was supported on tiny thin straps and beneath it she wore a brilliantly white short-sleeved T shirt that framed her face with light. Her long legs were covered by her dress, only the ankles showing – golden and exquisitely shaped like her long slender feet in strappy flat sandals.

He was forced to admit to himself that it was a very long time since he had been so moved by a woman. In fact he couldn't remember ever having felt so *drawn*.

'There is perhaps nothing adequate I can say,' he confessed to her. 'But I have to tell you that you are wrong when you think I have no feeling for the suffering of animals.'

She laid down her knife, having sliced her sponge cake into precise sections. She looked across at him.

'Have I surprised you?' he asked.

'Yes,' she agreed.

'How so?'

'I somehow anticipated you'd make a few high sounding pronouncements of regret about the behaviour of your nephew. I thought that afterwards you'd invite me to dinner somewhere very grand. And after that – then the account would be squared so to speak.'

He stared at her, horrified at this cool assessment of his behaviour and motives. Moreover he had to concede that they might have applied to him in other circumstances. But most certainly not in this state of affairs. With her.

'I never thought you'd talk about anything as mundane and practical as the welfare of dumb animals,' she added in elaboration, softening a little.

'Oh dear. I can see you must think very very badly of me.'

'No,' she said, far too lightly for his taste, as though her opinion of him was of little importance. And then she shrugged.

He leaned forward. 'If you thought so badly of me, why did you come today?' he asked with low urgency.

Her eyes fastened unflinchingly on his. 'I'm not sure,' she said slowly. 'Because . . .' She frowned. 'Oh, I truly can't say.' She gave a little shake. 'I was lonely,' she finished softly.

His heart made a surge. Astounding himself he leaned across and pressed his hand over hers.

Alessandra merely smiled and made a small dismissive huffing noise. He could only assume she was mocking herself for her lack of eloquence in explaining the reasons behind her actions.

He allowed her to polish off the remaining bread and cake and then he said to her: 'I want you to come with me on a short journey. I want to show you something.'

He stowed her very carefully in the black Mercedes she had seen the previous day, then drove through the London streets with a swift assurance that reminded her of her father. They went north, connecting with the M1 and up into Bedfordshire, close to where the fateful show-jumping competition had been held. Dangerously near the place where Satire had collapsed and died.

Alessandra held herself rigid.

'Please, have patience with me,' he said. 'Not long now.'

They turned into the long pot-holed driveway leading up to a livery stables Alessandra had not visited before. Raphael parked the car beside the stable block.

'Come,' he said to her, opening her door and handing her out as though she were fragile and precious.

Placing his arm lightly beneath her elbow he guided her down the line of boxes. Around a dozen gleaming equine heads leaned over their wooden half doors, eyes alert, ears forward. A little breeze started up from the southern end of the block playing a teasing game with the horses' long manes, then moving on to rattle the latches on the doors.

Raphael stopped at the end of the row where the box appeared empty. But when Alessandra looked inside she could see a big grey standing well back in the shadows, the whites of his eyes gleaming.

'Ottavio!' she whispered.

'I brought him here last night,' Raphael explained, leaning over the half door and inspecting the Lippizaner's condition. 'I was told this was a very good place. That he would have the very best care.'

'Do you mind if I go into the box to see him?' Alessandra asked.

'Please,' said Raphael, much relieved that the sudden confrontation with Emilio's horse had not unleashed fresh distress for her, 'that is just what I had hoped you would want to do.'

He lifted the latch on the door and swung it open for her to enter.

Ottavio shifted his feet in noisy agitation, shying away slightly as she slid softly through the doorway.

Raphael heard her humming to him. And then actually singing to him – very very softly as she had the day before.

He watched her move towards the horse with supreme calm and tact. He saw how this method of approach, combined with her complete lack of fear of Ottavio's continuously drumming hoofs and rolling eyes, had an immediately reassuring effect.

Ottavio gradually stopped his pounding and his eyes were steady as he looked at his visitor.

Alessandra stood close to him and put her hand on his neck beneath the mane. He felt different from Satire. His neck was a great solid wall of muscle and his closely clipped silver grey coat was all wire and spring where Satire's had been sleek as velvet.

He was covered in a dark blue rug and she could not see the state of the wounds that Emilio had inflicted on him. But he was certainly much less distressed than he had been twenty-four hours ago. He no longer flinched when she made the slightest movement and the expression in his eyes was one of deep intelligence and patience. She could tell that he was a horse who had known good treatment as well as bad.

She put her arm around his neck and for a brief moment laid her head against him, breathing in the unique warm earthy smell of horse. A tiny spark of happiness flamed up inside her.

Raphael looked on, his feelings and senses stirred. He waited still and silent watching these two exquisite creatures begin to form an alliance.

'You said he needed love,' he commented to Alessandra some minutes later when she was at last able to tear herself away from her dialogue with Ottavio.

'Yes,' she agreed.

'Yes, exactly.' He ushered Alessandra back into the car and asked her to wait whilst he checked on a few details with the stable staff.

When he returned to the car he found that she was drowsing, her head crammed uncomfortably against the window.

She jerked into wakefulness as he started the engine. 'Sorry. Being sad seems to make you exhausted,' she said in a matter of fact way.

He nodded. 'Then why not sleep? Let me recline the seat for you.'

'No. No thank you,' she said correctly. But when they had been going for a mile or two her head began to droop and roll. He brought the car to a gentle halt in a lay-by and pressed his finger on a button which tilted her seat slowly backwards.

She was already fast asleep, her hands folded lightly over her stomach, her lips slightly parted.

He got out a thin cigar and lit it, inhaling quietly and breathing the smoke out of the opened window.

He looked down at her. Her thick blonde hair had fallen away from her face, revealing her wonderful delicate skin. Used to the smooth dark gold of his mother's and sister's faces he was enchanted with Alessandra's paleness. He marvelled at the translucent quality of her skin, as though you could somehow trace all the different components of her face.

The bones of her face were long and curved. It was a face he guessed some would find a little too elongated, a little too classically severe on a woman. He, however, found himself captivated at its strength and individuality. It was not a face of popularly accepted, chocolate box beauty, but rather the face of a heroic female warrior of earlier centuries. For Raphael it was a face which failed by a whisker to conform to what was considered conventional feminine beauty – and because of that was all the more magnetic.

His eyes lingered on the shape of her body through the moulding fabric of her dress. She had surprisingly heavy breasts for a woman whose bones were so long and sculpted, whose waist was so narrow. And there was a voluptuous swell to her hips and thighs.

Alessandra Xavier was a disturbingly desirable woman. And very very female.

As though she sensed the potential danger of growing male desire, Alessandra suddenly woke up. She turned to look at him, sleepily bemused for a moment. 'Raphael! In England men who gaze at women when they're unconscious are called Peeping Toms. They're not at all approved of!'

He crushed his dead cigar into an ashtray and smiled. 'Then I am once again mortified,' he said. He had the impression that if she had been left alone with her bleak thoughts she would not have been able to achieve the lightness of mood to make a remark of such dryness and irony. He flattered himself that he had given her at least a few moments of respite from her sadness. He had brought her a tiny fleeting gift of joy on this black day. And for that he was absurdly grateful.

He thought again about inviting her for dinner and then weighing things in the balance decided not to push his luck. 'I have something to ask,' he told her solemnly.

'Mmm. Go ahead.'

'I would like you to exercise Ottavio for me.'

She sat up straight and shook her hair back over her shoulders. She frowned, not understanding.

'I think it best for him to have a week or so to settle down before embarking on the journey back to Spain,' Raphael explained. 'Either flying or sailing – these can be bad experiences for a horse.'

'Yes, that's true.'

'So he must stay in England for a while. But I would like him to be ridden regularly – by someone with skill and experience. Someone who has a true understanding of him. Will you do this thing for me Alessandra?'

'Yes,' she said more or less instantly. 'Yes – I will.'

'I shall pay you of course. This will be a business arrangement.'

She turned to him. 'Of course.'

50

There was a minute pricking pulse of electricity in the atmosphere. Raphael understood that his comment about a business arrangement carried an implied suggestion that there could be other motives underlying his request. He hoped he had not been so clumsy as to upset her.

'And will you escort him back to Spain for me?'

'What? Oh goodness.' She laughed. 'What on earth will you ask me next?'

There was another tingling silence. Alessandra wondered if Raphael thought she had been attempting to flirt. Which she hadn't. 'Is Ottavio your horse?' she asked curiously. 'I thought he belonged to Emilio.'

'He is one of two horses which I keep in the stables at my home. Emilio has had some success with showjumping and so I allow him to ride my horses.'

'You don't ride yoursef?'

'Only for pleasure. Walking about the countryside.'

'Hacking.'

'Ah yes, that is the word, hacking. Emilio, of course, thinks that he owns all things over which he has power. I am afraid he had a big shock when I sent him off last night and kept Ottavio here.'

'Sounds like you were reminding him who was boss,' Alessandra commented, unable to stop herself smiling with pleasure on the contemplation of Emilio's humiliation. She imagined him, red in the face and snorting whilst Raphael coolly banished him and issued his decree about Ottavio's future.

There was no reply to this opinion and she glanced at Saventos with renewed interest. He was concentrating on his driving, his eyes fixed on the road ahead, his face impassive.

51

'What is your occupation Raphael?' she asked abruptly.

'I'm a winemaker.'

'You have a vineyard?'

'Oh yes. We grow all our grapes on our own land.'

'I see.'

'Do you know much about wine?'

'No. Well, a little. My father has a well stocked cellar.'

He nodded. 'Wine is my life work,' he said simply.

'And the horses? Are they your life hobby?'

'I wouldn't say that. An interesting diversion perhaps. I have little time for hobbies.'

She had the impression Raphael was a man who would not find it easy to relax. He would need the stimulus of relentless serious work in order to feel fulfilled. Rather like her father, in fact.

The thought prompted her to take another swift glance at him. But Raphael Saventos was not at all like Saul Xavier in his overall personality. And where in his work her father was flamboyantly, almost demonically, driven she guessed that Raphael would be silent and dogged in his pursuit of quality and excellence.

'So when you bring back Ottavio to Spain for me,' Raphael said slowly, 'I shall show you my vineyards and my winery.' There was great solemnity and pride in his voice.

'I haven't agreed on that request yet.'

'No. But I think you will. Have you been to Spain before?'

'I've been to Madrid. The opera house.'

He smiled. 'Ah yes. Well, there is much more to Spain than that.'

Alessandra was becoming intrigued. She had never, not ever, met anyone who didn't very soon get around to asking about her world famous father: Maestro Xavier, the great conductor. An international household name. But not, evidently, in Spain. Or was Raphael simply sublimely indifferent to music? She had given him two perfect opportunities to ask what it was like to be the daughter of the splendid Xavier. And he had quietly side-stepped them.

They were back on the motorway now. Raphael asked: 'Did you come to London in a car?'

'On the train.'

'Ah.'

'You could drop me off at the station. I can get a taxi home.'

'No. I would prefer to take you home myself. I would like to know you are safe.'

He brought the car to a halt beside the front door of her house an hour later.

'Will you come in?' she asked.

'I think not.'

'You won't be interrupting anything. My parents are away.'

He turned to her, his eyes illuminated with a spark of displeasure. 'You will be all on your own in this great house? For all the night?'

He projected such pure soft outrage that she laughed. 'Yes. I'm grown up you know.'

'You have no servants? No dogs?'

'No. We're not feudal in England any more!'

She could see his chest expand as he took a deep breath. She saw that he was deeply disapproving. She thought of her parents, their carefulness and correctness. She thought of her father's reputation as a man of infinite talent and judgement, a man beyond criticism. And Raphael was silently accusing him of negligence in his role of parent and protector. The whole idea of it struck her as very entertaining.

Looking at Raphael's deceptively composed features she knew that the last thing she must do was make light of his obviously genuine concern for her safety.

He was Spanish. He would be one of those old-fashioned men who never questioned the idea that women needed protection. From a man. Presumably to shield them from the unwanted attentions of other men.

'Look Raphael, you mustn't worry on my behalf. I've stayed here lots of times on my own. We have good strong locks and the neighbours can easily be contacted if there are problems.'

'Well . . .'

'And,' she added, quiet and polite, 'It's none of your business.'

His lips tightened. 'No. I am sorry. Forgive me.'

'Done.'

They spent a few moments discussing the ins and outs of her new temporary job with Ottavio. She found herself more or less giving Raphael a promise that she would escort the horse back to Spain in a few weeks. That she would spend a weekend at the Saventos winery.

He insisted on escorting her into the house. He stood in the hallway and shouted up the stairway in magnificently savage Spanish.

She laughed. 'What's all this?'

'I am shouting to any burglars or intruders. Threatening them with a fate worse than death should any harm come to you.'

'Really. If they've any sense they'll clear out fast.'

'That was my intention! And now Alessandra I shall very regretfully leave you.' He inclined his head formally. And then he took her hand and held it lightly in his. 'I am going to be bold enough to ask you one more thing. I ask you to promise to love Ottavio a little for me. Please, will you do this for me? I know he cannot take the place of the horse you lost. But . . .'

Alessandra pressed her fingers on his to reassure him. 'Yes, of course I will,' she said softly, her throat suddenly thick with feeling.

He stared down into her eyes. And then he released her hand. He walked swiftly through the door, not turning back.

'Good-bye,' she called to him.

She waited until the car had disappeared, its low growling hum fading and blending into the sleepy twittering chorus of the birds.

Allegro came weaving and purring around her legs. She lifted him into her arms. 'Well now,' she said to him slowly, tickling his chin so that purrs vibrated in his throat, 'that was Mr Raphael Godeval Saventos.'

Allegro closed his eyes. His purrs accelerated and intensified.

'Yes,' she agreed. 'I was impressed too.'

She walked around the house checking all the rooms. All was well. After a warm bath she slipped into bed and fell abruptly and deeply asleep.

CHAPTER 4

A week later, upstairs in her bedroom, Tara was packing a suitcase in preparation for a four day stay in Edinburgh. A list of names of university students who were hoping to be considered for an audition with the Eastlands Orchestra lay on the top of the chest of drawers. She glanced at them from time to time as she detached silk camisoles and skimpy panties from the neat piles within the tissue-lined drawers.

Tara had been music director and chief conductor of the Eastlands for several years now. Auditioning for new players was an ongoing part of her work – and one she took very seriously. Making mistakes could promote difficulties all round. She recalled one particular disaster with an arrogant young clarinet player, whose musicianship was beyond reproach but whose social skills bore similarities to those of a hungry urban fox.

The phone began to peal. She looked at her watch. Eight-thirty. She paused, dangling a cream lace basque from her fingers and glancing across to the extension beside the bed.

Instead of moving to pick it up, she stood quite still waiting to hear Alessandra's soft footsteps down the hall, the sound of her low voice saying 'Hello,' in a husky almost conspiratorial manner Tara had never noticed her using before.

As though in response to her thoughts, she heard the door to the drawing room open and the faint slap of Alessandra's bare feet on the marble floor. 'Hello?'

A pause.

'Oh Raphael!'

Another pause.

Tara closed the bedroom door quietly and switched on the radio. As usual it was tuned to the most serious classical music station and some stern Stockhausen issued forth, putting a stop to any further anxious eavesdropping.

Tara continued her stroking and folding and gradually her suitcase filled up. Her mind, as usual, turned keenly to issues connected with her work and, also as usual, with worries about her daughter. And yet Alessandra had never provided any real reason for anxiety. She had never been a drinker, a pill popper or a man chaser. She had never been a raver in any way, shape or form. In fact Tara sometimes wished that Alessandra had caused more trouble, provided something tangible to feed a loving parent's natural inclination to be concerned.

It was perhaps Alessandra's solitariness that had been most disconcerting. There had always been a circle of friends around, especially those connected with the riding scene. But they had always been kept at something of a distance. There had never been one special friend, either male or female. Tara understood, of course, where Alessandra's inclination for solitariness had sprung from. It had come most surely from the genetic inheritance given to her by her father. Because Saul, aside from his relationship with his wife and daughter was perhaps the most self-contained person Tara had ever known.

It had recently begun to worry Tara that the self-possessed Alessandra might never find anyone who could be as precious to her as Saul had been and still was for her, Tara.

When Saul arrived home at half past midnight, Tara was still up, pattering around the kitchen, poking about in the refrigerator and jotting down explanatory notes for Mrs Lockton.

Saul came in as soft as a cat, threw his car keys on the table and swore softly.

Tara looked around. The sight of him in evening dress, the stark black and white framing his austere hawk-like features, still had the power to send a sharp rapier of raw desire through her. 'What?'

He shook his head in a gesture of silent resignation. 'Don't ask. I thought I'd gone out to conduct music. Instead – what a circus!'

He sat down, his face tense with frustration. He was a compulsive perfectionist whose tolerance of anything less than flawless was almost non-existent. Unlike Tara he was unable to accept that live music, in the very nature of its spontaneity, could not always reach his required standards.

Tara smiled. Stepping close to him she wrapped her arms around his tense shoulders. 'I thought you had Andras Vanyi as your soloist tonight. The current darling of the keyboard.' She nibbled fondly at her husband's ear lobe.

'He played as though he were fighting his way through Hungarian goulash. And when I took him to dinner afterwards he insisted on bringing three friends who munched their way through the entire menu, accompanied by practically all of the wine list.'

Tara chuckled, imagining the fastidious, aesthetic Saul captured at a restaurant table in the company of four guzzling and drunken musicians. She let her slender white hands slide down over his shoulder blades, creep inside the lapels of his jacket.

'The Danemans were at the next table,' Saul added. 'Which did little to improve matters.'

Tara's caressing hands slowed and stilled. 'We haven't seen them for ages. Years in fact.'

'And that's how I prefer it. Daneman's pretty harmless, but I think on balance I'd rather keep at a safe distance from my former wife.'

Tara said nothing. She and Saul rarely spoke of Georgiana Daneman who had been Saul's wife for twenty years before the vibrant young Tara had come along and detonated her marriage like a torpedo exploding a placidly sailing ship.

Tara recalled her past troubled guilt at hurting another person so badly and yet not being able to stop herself. She recalled too Saul's cold displeasure when she had taken it upon herself to strike up a strange and uneasy friendship with the rejected Georgiana. She had thought she was being open-minded and generous. She had fancied herself a trail blazer, defying the usual conventions of suspicion and jealousy inherent in the eternal triangle. But as Saul had warned, it had all ended badly. Quite shockingly in fact, bringing about a train of horrors Tara preferred not to dwell on.

'Did she speak to you?' she asked Saul lightly, resuming her stroking.

'No. There were a number of polite nods and smiles. I think they were both highly entertained to see me suffering in the company of four incoherent buffoons.'

Tara couldn't help laughing.

'Stop it,' he warned softly.

In the bedroom he prowled up and down, restless and frowning.

'Oh, come to bed!' coaxed Tara, looking up from her audition list.

He reached out and picked up the cream basque lying at the top of her neatly packed case. 'I haven't seen this beautiful thing before.'

She smiled. 'No.'

'You're taking this with you to Scotland, before I've had a chance to make my comments . . .'

Her eyelids flickered, her pulse accelerated.

'It's an empty thing without you inside it,' he said drily. He tossed it lightly across to her. 'Put it on,' he commanded softly.

'It has twenty hooks and eyes!'

'Very well then. I shall help you fasten them and then I shall unfasten them. Very slowly.' He turned away humming to himself.

Her nerves tingling, Tara slipped out of bed, shrugged off her wrap and stepped into the wired satin and lace. She hooked up the first few fastenings. 'There!'

He turned back. His eyes beneath their hooded lids appraised her with hungry appreciation.

Tara smoothed her hands over her hips. She guessed that she was in the full flush of her ripeness as a woman. In her early thirties she had gone through rather a skinny phase – not deliberately; her body had simply seemed to absorb all she put into it and never transform it into surplus flesh.

But recently she had filled out a little, her breasts regaining the fullness they had had in her teen years, her hips rounding, the flesh smooth and firm.

Saul bent to slide the tiny eyelet fastenings into their hooks. As he did so he brushed the skin at the base of her breasts with his fingertips and the skin of her neck with his lips. She shivered.

'There!' he said, completing his task and resting his hands on her slender waist.

Tara raised her arms to his shoulders and he bent to kiss her lips. 'Let me look at you,' he said, pushing her gently from him and standing back.

Tara found that her heart was thundering with excitement and desire. She sent up silent thanks to God and nature for being kind to her, for not making her slack and wrinkled before her time. She supposed that most women, with a husband so much older, would not have to worry on that score. But with a husband like Saul, lean and fit with a body as hard as a gun, gathering ever more magnetism as the years went on, she felt a growing need to guard all her female armoury.

'Turn around,' he said.

'You controlling devil,' she whispered, obeying him in a slow, half drugged manner. She felt his eyes

61

move from her waist to the swell of her buttocks, exposed beneath the fringe of lace. There was a tingling breathless pause and then she felt his hands on her, stroking the soft mounds, sliding his fingers into the crevice where she was already wet and glistening. Fully ready for him.

Ah! After twenty-two years, still his sensual power over her was absolute.

Later on he got up and went downstairs, poured whisky for them both.

He came back and handed her a glass. 'There.'

'Mmm,' she murmured, feeling herself coming slowly down from the magical place he had taken her.

'So. What have you to tell me?' he asked, slipping into bed beside her.

'I'm looking worried am I?' Was there anything he didn't pick up on?

'I sense traces of anxiety.'

'Damn you!' She smiled at him, her glance sharp and slanting.

'My guess is that they will be either maternal or musical.' He took a sip of his whisky. 'Most likely the former.'

She sighed. 'Yes.'

'So, then. He's still phoning her is he? The mysterious Spaniard?'

'Yes.'

'And that's making you worried. But why? I take it he's simply checking up on the welfare of his horse. Some people do have this strange attachment to four-legged creatures.'

'Our daughter for one. Don't mock it.'

62

'I wouldn't dare.'

'Huh!'

'So, don't keep me on tenterhooks my darling. Tell me what's behind this growing anxiety of yours. I do take it seriously you know.'

Do you? Tara wondered silently. Sometimes she felt she knew no more about Saul than she had all those years ago when he had unexpectedly invaded her life, singled her out and shone the full beam of his charisma on her. 'I can't quite put my finger on what's behind it. That's the problem. Oh, what the hell! It's most likely nothing.'

'Tara!' he said with grave reproach. 'Tell me.'

'She's being very quiet, very self-contained.' That sounded lame and pathetic. What else? Tara wondered. And how should she describe it?

'So? Isn't that how she always is?' Saul responded soothingly.

'Mmm. But this past week it's been much more marked. And you know she hasn't mentioned Satire once since he died. Not once.'

'Perhaps her grief is too private.'

'Yes, maybe.' Tara frowned into her drink. 'I just feel there's some new kind of secrecy about her.'

'Ah,' he said abstractedly, seemingly disinclined to elaborate.

No, she thought, it's more than that. I feel that Alessandra's on the brink of doing something unexpected. The kind of thing we've never had to worry about before. She took another sip of her whisky, then drained the glass and put it on the table.

Glancing up she saw a look of careful and remote deliberation on Saul's face. It struck her that he had already forgotten her feeble sounding concerns about Alessandra and had moved on to other issues. He was most likely wrestling with some point of interpretation regarding Mahler's *Resurrection Symphony* which he was conducting in Rome at the end of the week.

She wriggled herself down under the covers and decided to say nothing further.

Alessandra, lying in bed in her room at the other end of the house, had heard her father come in, heard her parents go into their bedroom and then drowsed through the next half hour or so before her sharp ears picked up her father's soft footsteps on the stairs.

The thought of her parents making love – whilst something she had been used to ever since she came into adolesence and the full knowledge of the issue of sex – reminded her that she was too old now to be living at home.

Whilst a student, she had rarely been at home, spending the vacations travelling on work assignments, or simply travelling as most of her fellow students did.

But having returned home again after graduation she had found a subtle but definite shift in the atmosphere of her childhood home. It had seemed to her that now that she had completed the childhood and youth tasks her parents had set for her, she was more of an equal with them. And with that feeling came a new self-awareness. But if she continued to stay at home, she would still remain their child: the odd one out at the apex of the family triangle.

She put her arms behind her head. It was time to move out. Move on.

'Are you going to exercise Ottavio again today?' Tara asked, trying to sound light and non-committal over a breakfast of fruit, toast and coffee. There were just the two of them. Saul had set off around six o'clock to drive to Manchester to rehearse the Hallé orchestra, which he was guest conducting that evening.

'Yes,' Alessandra replied in careful even tones. 'You know I shall. That's the arrangement I agreed to. I go every day to exercise him.'

'And how long will this go on?' Tara ventured.

'Another day or two.'

'Oh!'

'And then I'm taking him to Spain.'

Tara dropped her toast. It landed on her clean cream trousers, butter side down. 'Damn!'

'I'm sorry I didn't tell you before. I wasn't sure of the dates.'

'It's OK,' Tara smiled. 'We don't expect you to give us a chart of your comings and goings.'

Alessandra gave her a long steady stare. 'Daddy doesn't. But I'd hazard a guess you'd rather like me to.'

'No,' responded Tara promptly, returning the stare and thinking that Alessandra was getting more like Saul every day. But she could still handle him. Just.

'Really?' said Alessandra lightly, managing to manoeuvre her own toast into her mouth without dropping it.

'Yes. And I'd guess if I were completely disinterested in your comings and goings you'd be decidedly offended. And wouldn't I know about it?'

Alessandra smiled. 'Yes. You're right. That would be just something else for me to grumble about. I'm a real pain in the butt aren't I?'

They looked at each other and smiled in mutual amusement. The tension in the atmosphere eased.

'So when are you going to Spain?' Tara asked tentatively, picking off the buttery marmaladey mess from her trousers.

'The day after tomorrow.'

Tara jerked with fresh alarm. 'What! How?'

'By road and sea.'

'You're taking that great trailer by yourself to the ferry and then goodness knows where? With a horse in it?'

'France actually. And then across the border to Spain. Raphael lives in the north east of Spain. It's not all that far.'

Tara felt herself assaulted with brutal and unwelcome information. Driving through France. Negotiating the transfer to Spain. A man called Raphael!

'You can't drive one of those great horse trailers on your own through France. Think of the dangers! Those young students who've been murdered . . .'

'I shan't be driving on my own. There'll be a groom from the stables coming with me to Southampton and then Raphael will meet me at Le Havre.'

'Raphael,' echoed Tara with motherly caution.

'Yes. Raphael Saventos. Ottavio's owner. That's his name.'

'Oh.' Tara rubbed her cheek worriedly.

'Anything wrong?' Alessandra asked coolly, but

with faint provocation.

'No.' Tara looked with pleading at her daughter. 'It just sounds so *foreign*,' she said pathetically.

'Mummy! And that from a woman who flies round the world regularly several times a year, more international than a swallow.'

She's right, Tara wailed to herself silently. I'm an international, world jet-setter and yet the name Raphael Saventos strikes terror into my heart. When linked with my daughter that is. She glanced at Alessandra trying to hide any signs of the mother-hen-like anxieties going on inside her. She saw Alessandra in two days' time, leaving the house in order to set out on a long and difficult journey. Leaving on her own because both she and Saul would be elsewhere.

'I wonder what would Daddy say?' Alessandra mused, eyeing her mother with faint mockery. 'If he were here listening to this conversation.'

Tara considered.

'I'll tell you,' Alessandra offered cheerily. 'He'd give one of his long cryptic looks and then he'd say: "So! You're off to Spain." And after that he'd go back to thinking about important things like Sibelius symphonies and Benjamin Britten operas.'

Tara was forced to smile. Alessandra was right. Which was of course, she reflected without any rancour, why she, Tara Silk, was a good jobbing conductor whereas her husband Saul Xavier was a worldwide revered maestro.

67

CHAPTER 5

The ferry left Southampton harbour in the early evening. It would sail through the night and dock in Le Havre early the next morning.

Down in the diesel-smelling lorry deck Alessandra checked carefully on Ottavio's comfort and safety in his palatial trailer before making her way up the narrow iron stairways to the passenger sections of the boat.

She went to stand at the stern, watching the white ruffled channels stirred by the propellors which stretched out into the distance as though the boat were carving a moving signature on the water. Above her, outlined against a darkening sky, an escort of sea birds dipped and screeched, forever on the watch for food, their squeals intensifying at any hopeful sign.

She shook out her hair and let the wind race through it. The cool stinging sensation gave her a thrill of wild abandonment. She was going to Spain. On her own. To see Raphael Saventos's vineyards. And him!

During the night the ferry hit stormy weather and Alessandra woke to the boat's lurching dips and rolls.

Having always previously travelled by air when going abroad, she had never experienced anything like this. Her stomach began to feel tender and unsteady. She told it to behave itself but it took no notice. She was astonished. She couldn't remember being sick since she was a small child.

But within an hour she was hanging miserably over the toilet, her insides heaving painfully as her supper all came back.

She crawled once again into her bunk. The boat continued its pitching and tossing, and at frequent intervals she had to leap out yet again to retch over the toilet.

In the morning, white-faced, shaky and exhausted she went to feed Ottavio. He looked at her with wary reproachful eyes and completely ignored his breakfast.

'Oh dear, not you too. Poor boy,' she crooned to him stroking his nose and scratching behind his ears in an effort to cheer him up.

The ferry was late docking and there was a delay through customs. Alessandra looked down from the lofty driving position of the horse lorry and felt the familiar exhilaration of being in a foreign country, freed from her origins. But there was a quiet rumble of fear also. Whilst a very experienced traveller she had not travelled alone in a non-English-speaking country before, and had certainly not been faced with the problems of driving a huge vehicle on the right – or rather wrong – side of the road.

'Keep right, keep right,' she kept telling herself as she negotiated the snarl of the Le Havre Docks traffic.

Raphael had said he would meet her in the car park of a service area just beyond the exit from the docks area. She kept her eyes skinned, her hands tense on the lorry's big wheel. Behind her, in the back, she could hear Ottavio shifting restlessly on his straw. She felt a sudden weight of alarming responsibility.

Supposing Raphael had got held up. Supposing he had had an accident on the road. Supposing Ottavio needed veterinary attention. Supposing her own sickness had had nothing to do with the boat and she got sick again . . .

Oh for goodness' sake! she chided herself angrily. She took a deep breath and groaned a little as her bruised stomach protested at being so brutally disturbed.

With relief she spotted the service station Raphael had mentioned. She turned into the entrance and parked the lorry at one end of the vast park.

She got out, scanning the huge space and its massive juggernauts, then walked slowly towards the service area, making for the entrance to the café and other traveller facilities.

She was sure Raphael would be waiting, highly visible and deeply reassuring as she approached the automatically sliding doors. When she was unable to see him her heart began to beat more quickly.

She looked around the teeming foyer, trying not to allow feelings of panic to take a hold.

And then she noticed a small plump man standing beside a vividly flashing gambling machine. He was wearing a crumpled grey suit and he carried a placard which he held against his chest. It said on it: 'Miss Alessandra Xavier'.

She walked up to him. She pointed to the card. 'That's me,' she said.

He stared at her and then gave a brief smile. 'Señorita Xavier. You are she?'

'Yes. Who are you?'

'Señor Saventos is sending me to you,' he said. 'I am Ferdinand.'

'Oh, I see,' she said, which was far from the case. She felt desperately disappointed.

'There is trouble for Señor Saventos,' Ferdinand elaborated gravely. 'So he is not coming for driving you.'

Conjecture flashed through Alessandra's mind. She was aware of her face tensing into a frown.

'Is trouble with his mother and sister. If you live with women there is always trouble,' Ferdinand added grimly.

Alessandra could tell that he had not been hired for his discretion. She remembered Raphael's mentioning that in addition to Emilio, his mother and sister still lived in the family house, but he had given no indication of any problems. She had the sudden uncomfortable thought that this 'trouble' Ferdinand spoke of could be to do with her – and her imminent arrival.

'Please, coming now,' he said urgently, walking briskly towards the exit doors and gesturing her to follow him. 'We must be driving all day and all night to get to Spain.'

Alessandra found herself having to run to keep up with him. He had obviously spotted the Saventos horse lorry and was making a rapid bee-line for it.

He stood at the driver's door and held out his hand. He said something to her in Spanish.

'Oh yes,' she replied, suddenly understanding and handing over the ignition keys.

Ferdinand sprang up into the driving seat and activated the engine revving it up furiously. The wheels moved slightly. Good grief he's going to set off without me, thought Alessandra, sprinting around to the passenger side and hurling herself in, having the impression that her agitated travel companion was capable of anything.

She sat in frozen silence as Ferdinand propelled the lorry into the traffic with the force of a cork exploding from a bottle.

Once they got onto the teeming autoroute he sailed out into the fast lane and pressed his foot to the floor.

Alessandra was used to being driven at speed. Her father was a demon behind the wheel and her mother was no slouch. But they were both extremely vigilant and skilled drivers. She would have trusted her life to them in the most hazardous of situations. Watching Ferdinand now, crouched over the wheel like a not very intelligent bear being pursued by an army of cunning hunters, she would not have trusted him to post a letter.

'You should slow down,' she said to him. 'It's not a good idea to drive so fast with a horse in the back. You could upset him.' She knew as she spoke that she was whistling in the wind. Ferdinand did not understand English. And even if he had understood, she doubted that he would have taken any notice.

Miles sped by. Miraculously they were still on the road and alive. Alessandra found that there were periods when she became accustomed to the lorry's furious speed, almost indifferent to the dodgem car antics of the other drivers. And then suddenly full consciousness would kick in and she would feel a beat of pure terror.

After three hours of enduring Ferdinand's crazy driving she quietly suggested to him that they should stop at the next service point which was coming up soon. Ferdinand made no immediate response. She wondered if he had heard her, or had simply not understood what she was getting at and decided to ignore her.

'We must stop. You will be tired,' she insisted, wishing she knew some basic Spanish. Glancing at his furiously concentrating features and at his hands gripping the wheel like clamps she realized stronger measures were required. She threw herself against the back of her seat and groaned loudly, clutching her stomach.

Ferdinand turned.

'Sick!' she said. 'Very sick.' She clapped a hand over her mouth.

Now Ferdinand took notice. The expression of horror on his face suggested that he might soon be feeling the same. Within minutes they had left the madness of the autoroute and were stationary in another huge park. Ferdinand switched off the engine and Alessandra sighed with massive relief.

For Ferdinand's benefit she went through the charade of dashing to the toilets before rejoining him in the busy foyer.

He looked at her anxiously as though she might be about to blow up. She smiled at him. 'Better,' she said. He nodded energetically. He seemed all set on returning to the lorry and setting out again without delay but she insisted that they stop for a few minutes for rest and refreshment. She took him into the café and ordered coffee and croissants.

Sitting opposite the glowering and uncommunicative Ferdinand across the plastic-topped table she felt a sudden rush of irritation that Raphael had sent this totally inadequate driver and travel companion to escort her to Spain. It felt like some kind of insult. Surely not deliberate.

She realized that she had been hoping for great things from Saventos, that until now she had hardly dared admit to herself the full force of the let-down she had felt at not seeing him in Le Havre.

So what was I expecting? she asked herself with mocking irony. Some kind of virtuoso performance – a show of old-fashioned Spanish chivalry? Oh come on, Alessandra!

No, not chivalry an uninvited inner voice countered slyly, *simply someone to put you first!* She frowned, squirming away from such drippily sentimental thoughts.

She looked back at Ferdinand. Watching his hands she noticed that they shook uncontrollably as he raised the cup to his lips. Understanding flashed suddenly within her. She cursed herself for her silent criticism of the inept Ferdinand because he was a mere stand-in for Saventos, because he was short and ugly and spoke no English. Who was she to criticize? She might speak fluent French and German but she only knew around two words of Spanish. But more important than that, she recognized

74

Ferdinand's deep unease in having had to cross France at a minute's notice, meet a strange English woman and take charge of a huge horse lorry. It had all been too much for him. And driving on the French autoroutes was scaring him out of his wits.

Oh hell, she said silently to herself. She got up and went to the counter and bought a brandy. She went back to the table and placed it in front of him.

He looked at her anxiously. 'No!'

She reached for the ignition keys which lay beside his plate on the table. 'Yes,' she said. 'I shall drive.'

'No!' he said again. 'Señor Saventos . . .' His eyes were wide and desperate.

'Señor Saventos won't know anything about it.' She put her fingers over her lips. 'I shall not say one word.' She gestured to the brandy. 'Now drink it. You'll probably need it.'

Having checked on Ottavio who stood patient and resigned in his stall, she climbed up into the driver's seat and turned the ignition key. Ferdinand stared ahead as unresponsive as a stone as she negotiated the exit to the service point and rejoined the frantic flow of the autoroute. She kept in the slow lane for a while and then, gradually gaining confidence, moved into the next lane and maintained a steady cruising speed. Suddenly they were part of the rhythm of the road, beating in time with its throbbing pulse. She began to relax. She switched on the radio. Beside her Ferdinand sat back in his seat, his head gradually drooping onto his chest.

They reached the most eastern point of the French/Spanish border south of Carcassonne at around midnight. 'España!' exclaimed Ferdinand suddenly coming to life.

Alessandra was stiff and tired. They were in quiet open countryside now, the road almost deserted. She guided the lorry into a lay-by, turned off the engine and stretched.

'I driving now,' said Ferdinand firmly.

'You'll have to,' she returned. 'I'm whacked.'

He chuckled. He seemed like a different man now he was back in his native country.

'Is it far to Señor Saventos's house?' she asked.

'Far?'

She made an elastic movement with her hands. 'Far,' she said opening her hands wide, 'not far,' she explained closing them.

Ferdinand nodded. 'Is not far to Señor Saventos. Is quickly,' he added gaining confidence by the second.

Alessandra sighed with relief.

It was very dark now. The sky was a thick bluish black. Clearly there was no town nearby to send up a luminous orange glow and detract from its satiny perfection. The brilliance of the stars seemed exaggerated and exotic. Definitely foreign stars, Alessandra thought with a smile as she recalled her mother's worried repetition of Raphael Saventos's very foreign-sounding name.

From what she could see of the darkened countryside it was flattish and very expansive, the horizon stretching away far into the distance and merging imperceptibly with the sky. They went over a bridge and she saw a swift glitter of water below.

She had a sudden overwhelming sense of strangeness and isolation. She reflected that she had absolutely no idea where she was going, knew none of the

76

people to whose house and estate she had been invited. Had she been foolishly impulsive in agreeing to escort Raphael's horse to Spain and to meet Raphael on his own territory? All on her own.

Oh stop it! she told herself. You're just dog tired. Pull yourself together. This is a wonderful adventure.

After a while Ferdinand leaned forward over the wheel and began to accelerate. Alessandra, waking from a half doze realized that they were nearing the end of their journey. In the back of the lorry Ottavio set up a stamping with his feet.

'Stopping soon,' said Ferdinand.

They passed through ornate gates. Alessandra peered into the darkness. She fancied she could see the shapes of vines, crouched against the earth. Rows and rows of them. Infinite. A thrill of excitement fizzed inside her.

She could see larger buildings, but only dimly. It was very dark. She looked at her watch. Two in the morning. She supposed this would be the low point of the night for the Saventos family and all its workers. A winery would no doubt start up soon after first light.

Ferdinand weaved the lorry around a maze of tracks and then suddenly they ran out of road and he stopped. 'End,' he exclaimed triumphantly, jumping out.

Alessandra climbed down from the lorry, her limbs stiff from the long hours of sitting cramped and still. Recalling setting off from England early the day before she felt as though she had travelled half way around the world.

The smell of the air was soft and strangely musty, quite unlike the night air of Oxfordshire.

She saw a tall figure come around the corner of a large barn-like building close by. He began to walk quickly, then broke into a run.

She felt her hand seized and pressed very strongly in that of Raphael Saventos. 'Alessandra! I am so very sorry about the mix up, that I could not bring you here myself. Please, once again I have to ask you to forgive me. But from now I shall devote myself to you. Welcome to the Saventos vineyards. Welcome to Spain!'

It's all right! she said to herself silently, listening to this heroic speech and experiencing a shining stab of inward pleasure. It wasn't a mistake after all.

She looked up at him smiling through her fatigue. He looked dark and mysterious, yet at the same time deeply solid and reassuring.

Devote himself to her indeed! How dramatic. How Spanish. How splendid.

CHAPTER 6

Alessandra woke, her eyes prised open by a bar of sunlight inserting itself into the gap between the two halves of the big casement window which she had opened before she fell into the large carved bed, throwing herself back exhausted on the piles of white pillows.

Raphael had brought her to the room himself. He had led her through a complex maze of interior courtyards lit with dim lamps and filled with lemon trees in pots, their spicily fragrant leaves rustling in the night breeze. He had insisted on carrying all of her bags and had placed them reverently on a dark carved oak chest before withdrawing with a curiously formal, 'Good-night.'

She stretched, tossing back the covers and luxuriating in the warmth of the morning air, which curled itself round her limbs like something solid and tangible.

She looked around her. The walls of the room were painted white and hung with wooden-framed paintings of rolling green landscapes under brilliant blue skies. On the floor were earthy terracotta tiles, and a sprinkling of soft cream cotton rugs. The casement window reached to the floor and the hems of the long yellow and white striped curtains surrounding it brushed against the tiles with a soft sighing sound in the light breeze.

'Oh,' she murmured smiling at the room as if in greeting. 'Oh yes!'

She got out of bed. The tiles beneath her bare feet were very faintly tinged with warmth where the sun had touched them.

She opened the window wide and stepped outside onto the little balcony. It had a small balustrade painted in dark green and gold – the sort of balustrade much favoured in operas, behind which magnificently robed prima donnas would posture, tossing down flowers and songs to their forbidden lovers lurking in the garden below.

Alessandra, in her simple long white T shirt, scanned the scene beneath her which, although satisfyingly foreign and exotic, did not appear to contain any signs of human life at all, romantic or otherwise.

Immediately below her window was a terraced garden ribbed with narrow flights of steps whose borders were punctuated with earthenware pots from which a bright profusion of flowers and leaves cascaded. At the base of the steps was a stone terrace and garden chairs and a table set in the shade of an arc of eucalyptus trees.

To her left she could see a long low building with a tiled roof of pale apricot. It had a row of arched doors down one side and she guessed it must be the stable block. Behind it was an enclosed pasture. She could see

Ottavio at the far end placidly grazing, pulling in steady rhythm at the grass. She watched him, her heart giving warm little beats. She remembered how in the night when they had brought him out of the lorry he had thrown up his head and given a long piercing whinny of pleasure. And then, set free in the field, he had kicked out his hind legs in the air and dashed up and down like a crazy colt, bucking and snorting.

She turned now to look beyond the garden to the acres of flat terrain stretching out as far as the skyline. It was totally covered in endless rows of vines, their lines meticulously straight with thin strands of dark russety earth showing through in between. As she looked at the vines a kind of shimmer seemed to come off them through the bright haze of sunlight.

'Wow!' she murmured. She noticed a stillness in the atmosphere and the curious unfamiliar silence only found in the deep countryside. She listened carefully. There were just brittle fragments of bird song, and from somewhere in the depths of the house the sound of plates being stacked.

She closed her eyes and turned her face to the sun. For a moment she had a sense of pure and primitive happiness in simply being alive.

'Alessandra!'

She gave a little start and her eyes snapped open. Looking down she saw Raphael standing at the top of one of the rows of steps watching her with a thoughtful expression on his face. 'I am waiting for you,' he said smiling.

'Oh.'

'Yes. It is late. Come along. We shall have our breakfast out here.'

She was showered, dressed and out in the garden at his side in ten minutes flat. He jumped up from his chair as she approached and settled her down beside the table. It was covered in a long cream lace cloth and was laid with white and yellow crockery and silver cutlery which flashed in the sunshine.

There was crusty bread piled in a basket, fresh fruit and sweet cakes and unsalted almonds in a brass bowl. Plenty of hot strong coffee also.

'No marmalade?' queried Alessandra. 'I thought it was a Spanish delicacy.'

'Marmalade from Seville,' he smiled. 'Yes we do eat it sometimes, but not in the open air. The insects are even more fond of it than we are. You must go inside if you want marmalade.'

'I'll stay here,' she said, looking across the garden to the vineyard beyond. 'It's perfect.'

His black eyes rested full on her for a moment, not teasing, not mocking, simply looking at her as though she were a portrait or a sculpture.

Alessandra ate some cake and drank two cups of coffee. Raphael, opposite her, stretched out his long legs and linked his strong golden brown hands behind his head. He looked around him; at the sky and the endless lines of vines. And then once again at her. He seemed perfectly relaxed and tranquil, as though he had all the time in the world. Moreover he seemed quite content to sit with her in companionable silence, not needing to plug each wordless gap with chat.

'I didn't know if I'd see you this morning,' Alessandra said eventually. 'I thought you would be busy.'

'Doing what?'

'Working.' She was surprised he had needed to ask. Surely it was obvious. Her father was invariably up and working by six. Constantly driving himself. And her mother almost the same.

He smiled. 'There will be plenty of time for work later on.' The smile turned to a grin. 'You know, I will tell you something, you are a true English lady, Alessandra.'

She bridled. His words conjured up pictures of leisured middle-aged women in Knightsbridge taking tea. 'A lady! Certainly not!'

'No, no. I'm sorry, I'm not making myself clear. What I mean is that you are very English. Always thinking of work, of business. Of being purposeful.'

She looked at him in amazement. 'But aren't you?' Isn't that *normal*? she thought.

'I'm a Spaniard. Sometimes we work as though demons were driving us. And then sometimes we just – live.'

Alessandra looked around her. 'Surely a place like this can't survive on haphazard bursts of effort.' She looked hard at him. He seemed to her different out here on his own territory. Before, in England, he had been a visitor, and at a faint disadvantage because of the shocking behaviour of his nephew. But now, on his own territory, he was unobtrusively, but very definitely, assuming a certain superiority over her.

She frowned. 'You're making fun of me Raphael. Don't! I don't like it.'

He smiled broadly. 'Now that you're cross those dark specks in your eyes are flashing like chips of sapphire.'

83

'And I hate that sort of flattery,' she said, beginning to feel heated, but speaking with icy coolness.

'Yes. So do I normally,' he agreed gravely. 'I apologize. But I can't help noticing these things. I'm very observant you see. And very frank on such matters.'

She connected with his level gaze and felt her defensiveness begin to melt.

'What is the matter?' he asked after a while.

'Things aren't going quite how I expected,' she told him simply.

'Ah. How did you expect things to go?'

She considered. It was hard to put into words. 'I'd assumed we'd talk about how Ottavio has been getting on with the schooling I've been giving him . . .'

'We have spoken a good deal about that on the telephone.' He tilted his head questioningly, making her wish she hadn't been quite so frank in responding to his query. 'What else?'

This polite yet insistent quizzing was unnerving. 'Well . . . I thought that you'd show me around the winery. And that I'd meet your family who live here with you.' *And that you'd explain to me what Ferdinand meant when he said there had been 'trouble' for you. Family trouble.*

'I am sorry. I seem to have failed you once again.' His tone was regretful but at the same time ironic. 'You assumed we would be very busy straight away doing worthy and productive things. You didn't think we would simply sit here together sharing a few quiet moments on this beautiful morning?'

'No.'

'Do you mind?'

She looked at him, understanding that she had collided head on with a culture and way of thinking very different from her own. She smiled. 'No.'

'I think that you feel uneasy because we are not being energetic and industrious. That is your English way. But now you are in Spain Alessandra.' His eyes gleamed and there was a low soft power underlying his words.

'Yes. I'll learn,' she said briskly.

'And I must learn not to alarm you too greatly,' he said, rising from his chair. 'So come along with me. I will show you the winery without delay. We will be very busy and occupied together.' He stood up and held out his hand in an eloquent gesture of invitation for her to follow him. They made their way up the steps. When they reached the top, Raphael walked past the entrance to the house and led her around its row of shuttered windows to its north-facing wall.

As they rounded the far corner of the house, she saw a complex of buildings set well back on its eastern side. The cluster was dominated by a high vaulted edifice constructed of wood, with a roof of dark tiles. As they walked around to the west front of the building Alessandra was amazed to see a façade of tall white columns surmounted with a high carved arch. Several broad steps of veined cream marble led up the entrance.

She stopped at the base of the steps and looked up. 'It's like a Grecian temple.' she said, marvelling at the brilliant white of the columns stark against a fantastic cobalt blue sky.

'But not quite as old,' Raphael told her smiling. 'My great grandfather's original construction of the winery dates from the early 1900s and my father had the Grecian façade added in the 1960s. It is really very new.'

'Impressive nonetheless,' said Alessandra. 'Like your English, Raphael,' she added, suddenly acutely aware of his ability to manipulate her native language, whereas she knew virtually nothing of his.

He turned to glance down at her, obviously gratified. 'I have been learning and practising since I was a boy. In our business we must deal with the British and Americans. They are our most important customers. And, of course, now we export to Australia too and New Zealand. To speak English is essential.'

'Mmm, well even so, you're unreasonably good at it,' she said, resolving to learn Spanish.

'I am never unreasonable,' he commented drily. 'Now come with me and see the wonders of our winery.' He went ahead of her up the steps. One or two men coming out of the building nodded courteously to him and there were brief exchanges in rapid Spanish. 'We have two main sections for you to see,' he told her, 'where the wine is made and where it is stored. We shall look at the processing area first.'

She stood beside him at the entrance to a hushed enclosed space the size of an auditorium in which a great orchestra could play. Its roof, high above her, was steeply arched and vaulted. Hundreds of tiny windows were let into each bowed strut, filtering the sunlight through to lie in a multitude of bright lozenges on the supporting wood.

On each side of the wall were enormous gleaming

steel containers, linked to each other by a series of fat pipes.

The hush in the atmosphere seemed almost reverent: a thick solemn peacefulness orchestrated solely by the steady ripe hum of some unseen machinery.

Alessandra let out a long sigh. It was hard to think of words adequate to express her reaction to this palace of wine-making.

Raphael stood behind her, observing the silent awe on her strong sculpted features. 'This is where the grapes are crushed and fermented, where the actual creation and processing of the wine takes place.' He paused. He laid a hand gently on her shoulder. 'Alessandra,' he said. 'I don't know what you know about wine and how it's made. I would just like to say to you that I am very happy to tell you all I know about the growing of grapes and the production of wine. But only as much as you want to hear.'

Alessandra looked at him. She could see that he was not teasing now. His words intrigued her. Having been used over the years to a procession of music players and teachers telling her more than she ever wanted to know about certain aspects of the production of music, Raphael's last statement was something of a novelty.

'You see,' he elaborated, 'I have learned over the years that what fascinates and excites me about the making of wine does not necessarily do the same for others.'

She absorbed this with a faint smile. Looking up into Raphael's tanned face and his magnetic black eyes, being aware of the closeness of his solid and yet graceful body, she had a sudden electric twinge. It was like a faint, delicious little breath of warm air on a cool day, or a harmonious chord gently resolving a strident musical phrase. It was the planting of a seed; something achieved in a few brief seconds that had the potential to grow into something that could last for ever. The sensation was fleeting and yet so strong that she gave a small shiver.

'No comments at all?' Raphael enquired smiling, taking her through into an adjoining storage area where countless bottles of wine were laid in horizontal stacks within great hollows in the walls, each storage pyramid being surmounted by a great gothic archway. The notion of so much wine all in one place was somehow incredible. Breathtaking.

'It's amazing,' she said at last, looking all around her. 'A cathedral of wine. I almost expect there to be an altar to the Greek god Bacchus along the east wall.'

His eyes kindled. 'An altar to Bacchus the god of wine!' he exclaimed. 'What a clever idea – then at each harvest I could kneel there and pray for a vintage crop. Yes, I like that suggestion very well.'

They went back into the open air. After the hushed shade of the winery it was like stepping into the dazzle of spotlights, the sun was so powerful now, mercilessly beating down.

'You must be careful not to burn,' Raphael said. 'The September sun here is very strong. And your skin looks very delicate.' He regarded her face and neck and her bare arms with an expression of great care and attention so that she found herself swallowing hard, as though trying to absorb some painful lump of emotion.

'I shall have to get a hat,' she said lightly.

'I shall drive you into town later on and you shall get one,' he responded.

At her request they walked around to the stable block and went to look at Ottavio. The horse saw them approaching and came walking purposefully up the field. Putting his head over the gate he pushed his muzzle gently against Alessandra's breastbone. She slipped her arm around his neck. 'You beauty,' she whispered to him. She saw that the whip marks on his flanks were almost healed, that he was once again perfect.

She was aware of Raphael's gaze on her again. Normally she hated men to stare at her, feeling that they were sizing her up as a possible conquest, or simply as a lump of tasty female meat. She stared up at Raphael with a tinge of challenge in her eyes – and then had to admit to herself that unwavering attention from this particular man was not unpleasant in the least.

'This is a little like a love affair I think,' he remarked, and she felt her heart give a tiny extra beat of sparky panic. 'You and Ottavio.'

'He's a marvellous horse,' she agreed with enthusiasm. 'Such discipline and potential. And he's so determined, so brave.' She ran the backs of her fingers down Ottavio's long nose. 'And yet he's such a kind horse. Very gentle. Chivalrous, you could say,' she added with a wry smile.

'I am pleased to hear that you are getting on with him so well,' Raphael said.

Once again she was surprised to find herself irresistibly urged on to confide in Raphael. She, Alessandra Xavier, who had worked for years on the knack of concealing her inner feelings – and had now got it down to a very fine art! She said to him, 'When Satire died there were a few desperate hours when I was convinced I'd never make a relationship with another horse again. In fact I seriously thought of giving up riding altogether.'

'And what are you thinking now?'

'That I'd like the chance to work with Ottavio and draw out the very best from him,' she said with naked frankness.

'Then why not do it?'

Alessandra threw him a sharp glance. 'You know that's not possible Raphael.'

'Why not?'

'He's not my horse.' Her eyes were hard now. 'And you're not thinking of selling him are you?'

'No. You are right. I don't wish to sell him.'

'So, then! Why tantalize me with the prospect of things that can't come about?'

His magnificent eyes glowed. 'Oh Alessandra. I can see that I've made you angry again.'

'Yes. I hate that manipulative sort of talk.'

'No, no. You haven't understood me. I'm not trying to manipulate. I'm simply trying not to say things so directly and brutally that you will be alarmed. Or even shocked.'

She frowned, trying to understand the complexities implied in the words. 'What? What things?'

'Well, you see it has been in my mind to suggest that you stay on here as my guest for a few weeks – maybe longer – and continue to ride Ottavio, bring him on a little more as you call it. And also I was going to ask if you would like to do some work with my other horse Titus? And after that – well . . .'

She looked hard at Raphael, her eyes widening. 'Stay on – as your guest?'

'There now, you see,' he smiled. 'My words have frightened you out of your wits!'

'No. Not frightened me, just surprised me.'

'I was going to wait until much much later to say this to you Alessandra. I had planned to lead up to it gently. You see I had a very traditional Spanish upbringing. As boys and young men our fathers and uncles and grandfathers taught us that a woman must always be treated with great respect and with the utmost caution. A man must tread very carefully around a woman's sensitive feelings.'

Alessandra gave a little snort. 'Good grief! What century were you living in?'

He gave a low chuckle. 'You may well ask that! However, as regards my suggestion, I'm not going to dismay you further by demanding an instant reply to that question. Instead I shall ask you another question.'

'Oh goodness!' She put back her head and laughed, showing him her perfect white teeth. 'What next?'

He reached out and patted Ottavio. 'I want you to tell me what in your view is the most important ingredient for success in competition riding?'

'The calibre of the horse,' she replied without hesitation. 'And I'm not talking about pedigree or an exclusive and expensive thoroughbred ancestry,' she continued, her face vividly alive with the energy of her thoughts. 'The horse could be ugly or even clumsy. But if it has natural ability and the will to work with you and the spirit to keep going even when things get really rough – then it will succeed. Do you see what I'm trying to say?'

'Yes, oh yes I think I understand very well what you are trying to say.'

'And so what is the most important ingredient for success in making wine?' she asked with a slow smile, turning and leaning back against the bars of the gate, looking up at him, the sapphire streaks in her eyes glinting in the sun.

Raphael felt almost assaulted by the openness of her gaze. He thought he should turn his face away from her in case she should see the rapture steadily growing there and be alarmed. 'Calibre,' he reiterated softly. 'The excellence of the grapes. Without grapes of quality one cannot produce wines of quality.'

'So grapes and horses have something in common,' Alessandra said with slow irony. 'In order to make their mark in the world they must both have superb potential. But without the sensitivity of the winemaker or the rider to bring them on, they would never be able make it on their own. The rider has to school the horse, maybe for years, before it can have success, and I suppose,' she added considering, 'the winegrower has to gain a lot of experience before they can transform an excellent grape into a great wine.'

'Yes, that is exactly right,' said Raphael, looking down at her with great satisfaction.

'I'd like to learn about it,' she said. 'Winemaking.'

'Then you shall.'

'Does Emilio work in the winery?' she asked.

Raphael made a brief dismissive grunt in his throat. He turned away, looking over the vines. 'He works under sufferance.'

There was a breathless beat of silence and Alessandra had a sense of having touched an especially tender spot. Perhaps too painfully.

'Where are your family Raphael?' she asked with quiet directness. 'Aren't I going to meet them?'

'My mother and sister are in Barcelona,' he said shortly. 'They will be back tomorrow.'

'And Emilio?'

'He is having a short holiday.' His face was hard and closed and Alessandra was coming to understand that Raphael Saventos was a man who held a store of very private thoughts and feelings in the fortress of his mind.

'That sounds like a euphemism for telling me that he's been banished.' she commented.

'A euphemism,' repeated Raphael. 'That means an evasion, a pretty covering up of an ugly truth – yes?'

'Yes.'

'You're a very perceptive young woman,' he said.

'Did you send him away – because I was coming?' she went on with gentle persistence.

He closed his eyes. He took in a deep breath and let it out as a long despairing sigh. 'Ah, in the Saventos family we must always have such drama,' he said regretfully, conveying a good deal behind the words. 'We are so proud and so hot-headed, sometimes even violent.' He reached out and took Alessandra's hands in his, holding them with calm authority. 'You have such sureness, such strength Alessandra. I know that nothing my family can do will harm you.'

As Alessandra absorbed these puzzling and disturbing words, the powerfulness of hidden feelings vibrated through his hands into hers and for a moment she felt her view of the world fracture into pieces and then slowly reform itself in a new shape.

CHAPTER 7

The following evening, when Isabella Saventos and her daughter Catriona arrived back at the winery from their shopping jaunt in Barcelona they found that the young woman from England, whom Raphael had most astonishingly invited to visit, had not only arrived, but seemed quite settled in.

Far too comfortably settled as far as they were concerned.

As Isabella's silver BMW coupé slid smoothly up to the entrance of the house, she had glanced to her left and been astonished to see Ottavio being ridden round the field by a tall young female whose long fair hair fell in a thick gleaming plait from the rim of her velvet riding hat.

Isabella had never seen Ottavio ridden by anyone other than Emilio, and the sight of it gave her a sharp jolting shock. She knew from the terse brief details Raphael had volunteered that the young woman who had agreed to escort Ottavio back to Spain was a rider. Vaguely Isabella had thought of her as some kind of glorified groom who would naturally be able to climb up on a horse and exercise some control over

94

it. But to see this girl, a perfect stranger, mounted on Ottavio – a priceless Lippizaner – in Emilio's absence seemed like some kind of sacrilege. What could Raphael be thinking of to allow it?

She narrowed her eyes in conjecture, recalling Raphael's recent displeasure with Emilio because of some incident or other in England. She recalled too Emilio's fury earlier in the week at being banned from riding either of his two horses in the future – well, yes technically they were Raphael's horses she had admit, but Emilio had understandably always thought of them as his own. Raphael's cool delivery of this debarment had provoked a scene of unprecedented rage and hostility. Truly when Emilio had gone down into the vineyard with a lighted flare she had feared that the whole of the Saventos wine empire, built up over nearly a century, might go up in smoke. She had been forced to admire Raphael's skill in defusing a potential conflagration.

In private Isabella acknowledged that Raphael might have justification in prohibiting Emilio from riding Ottavio for a time, but surely that did not mean that the horse was to be used for the amusement of all and sundry.

She and Catriona exchanged looks, their eyebrows raised.

Whilst they had spent a good deal of their two day trip arguing and fretful – which was their habitual way of relating to each other – they now bonded together as a solid impenetrable unit in the face of the enemy. Two women defending their territory against the invasion of a strange female – prepared to be as hostile and devious as vixens.

And they were a formidable duo for anyone to reckon with, either male or female. Isabella at sixty-four was still able to command admiration, despite the undeniable leatheriness of her olive skin and the deep grooves running from her nostrils to the edges of her full, deep-red lipsticked mouth. Her hair, still abundant and black (the colour now dependent on artifice, not nature) was shoulder length. It was shiny and sleek, pulled back tight and smoothed with some glossy preparation so it looked as though it had been painted to her head. The fat knot at the nape of her neck was secured with a black silk scarf, its ends trailing down her back and rippling attractively as she moved.

But more daunting than her mature charisma was the ferocious determination of her personality. Ever since childhood she had sought not only to get her own way but to dominate. And because she had been a woman growing up in a very male-dominated and traditional country she had had to fight hard to achieve this.

Catriona was similarly self-willed, but lacking her mother's grace and style. She was, in looks, very much like her dead father – her features square and unremarkable. She had aroused a good deal of speculation in the family, and amongst the far-flung land-owning neighbours, by her choice to remain at home and not to marry. Was she in some way abnormal? they wondered. Did she have some special ambition of her own to pursue. In fact Catriona had never done very much at all in her life, beyond dabbling in the buying and selling of antique *objets d'art* and supporting her mother in playing the role of surrogate mother to Emilio. Her face had a permanently dissatisfied look as though she were criticizing the world and blaming it for its failure to provide her with the enjoyment and fulfilment she truly deserved.

Both of them, the arrogant mother and the disaffected elder sister, were heavily dependent on Raphael for the maintenance of their luxurious, leisured lifestyles. And like many dependents they clung on tight to their benefactor, whilst at the same time resenting him.

Raphael had had genuine reasons for sighing when Alessandra had questioned him about them.

Isabella stepped from the car, raising her head in a gesture of pride and arrogance, staring towards the house and resisting the temptation to take yet another glance at the long-limbed usurper riding Ottavio. She was wearing a dark red dress and a great deal of heavy gold jewellery, both of which looked particularly handsome against her dark olive skin. Like her son she was tall and solidly built – a woman of weight and presence. Her friends and acquaintances were in the habit of describing her as handsome rather than beautiful.

Catriona had the Saventos solidity, but none of Isabella's or Raphael's natural animal grace, either in her figure or her movements. She shambled from the car, her expensive green linen suit crumpled and hot-looking. She too wore a good deal of jewellery, which like her mother's was solid gold and had been painstakingly crafted in the early part of the nineteenth century. And yet strangers passing her in the street would probably have marked her down as a woman in cheap clothes and fake jewellery who was trying hard, but failing, to look exclusive.

She and Isabella passed through the inner courtyards leading to the main reception rooms of the house. Isabella flicked a scarlet-nailed finger at one or two of

97

the leaves on the lemon trees, checking that they were not drying out – or dusty, notching up points of complaints with which to browbeat the servants.

Progressing into the airy expansive drawing room she stood quite still, her eyes roaming over the fat ceremonial sofas upholstered in brocade, over the expansive pale oriental rug, over the ornate eighteenth century mirrors gleaming at each other from opposite walls. She noticed that a single slab of sunlight had sneaked beneath the not completely drawn blinds, lying there in defiance. It would probably have been like that for an hour or so now, given every opportunity to bleach her fabulous rug. A serious bone to pick with the servants was duly noted.

Isabella raised her chin, her nostrils flaring slightly as she reviewed her room, passing on from the negligence of the servants and focusing on something quite different. She stiffened as though daring the scent of an intruder to mar the perfection of her magnificent salon.

She crossed to the piano, a treasured nine foot Bechstein which had belonged to her grandfather. She saw at once that the music on the stand had been rearranged. She had left her fat book of Beethoven's Sonatas open at the *Pathétique*, the Adagio movement. She remembered doing that quite clearly. And now it was Schubert's music that had been brought to the front, the *Impromptu in A flat*.

Isabella touched the keys lightly. 'She has been playing my piano,' she murmured to herself, with mingled feelings of outrage and righteous satisfaction.

Catriona, in the doorway, leaned against the dark wooden frame looking dishevelled and exhausted. 'I'm going to take a bath.'

'Yes, good,' said her mother abstractedly. 'I shall do the same when I've checked on the dinner preparations.'

Catriona sighed. 'I'd been hoping for a quick supper. An early night.' She had actually been thinking of watching TV in her room with a bottle of vodka and iced tonic to hand.

Isabella straightened her spine. 'Oh no. We shall take dinner around the family dining table. We shall have the old silver out and the Limoges china.'

'Good grief!' muttered Catriona.

'Raphael can select one of the premier wines from 1981. That was a very good year for us. Where is Raphael by the way? Have you seen him?'

'He went into the field. He's talking to the girl.'

'Ah!' Isabella chewed at her lip. Her face took on a musing look.

Catriona privately thought that her mother was wasting her Machiavellian energies dreaming up ways to intimidate some horsey girl from England. The girl was probably going back to that dreary damp country without delay in order to jump about in a wet field over evil-looking fences and fall in the mud. All right, so she had been riding Ottavio. So what? He was just a horse.

'Why don't you wear your yellow dress this evening?' Isabella suggested. 'The one with the full sleeves. I've always thought that suited you very well.'

'Mother,' said Catriona, turning away and preparing to go to the refuge of her bedroom without delay, 'I'm nearly forty and I shall wear what I like.'

Isabella was not put out. In fact she suddenly felt cheered. Catriona might not be interested in putting on a grand show and intimidating this interloper. But for her, having arrived at a stage of life when things could seem all too predictable, the prospect of donning her full regalia and having an unexpected challenge to deal with had a decided touch of adventure about it.

She went majestically through to the kitchen to speak with María, who had once been her nursemaid and had stayed with her through her marriage, sticking to her like the seal on an imperial letter and eventually turning herself into the best housekeeper in the north of Spain. María, whilst as stubborn as a mule, could be relied on to produce a splendid dinner, even at the very shortest of notice.

'We dine at eight,' Raphael told Alessandra, holding Ottavio's reins as she sprang from his back. He put on a mockingly grave face which made her laugh. 'The ladies of the house of Saventos have returned.'

'I saw them,' Alessandra told him. It had mischievously crossed her mind as she watched Isabella Saventos standing looking imperiously up at her house that someone should have thought to run up a standard over the central balustrade.

Raphael saw that Alessandra had no anxieties whatsoever about meeting the women in his family. But then why should she? She had no idea of their potential for drama and excess and feuding. Neither did she have any inkling of his own anxieties about this meeting. She had no idea that for him Alessandra was already weaving herself into the complex tapestry of the Saventos dynasty.

Alessandra took off her riding hat and rubbed her

100

hand over her forehead which was slippery with warmth and moisture. 'I'm not used to riding in this heat,' she commented with a rueful grin.

There was a red line across her forehead where the rim of the hat had pressed against her skin and Raphael had to hold himself back from laying his lips against it. 'You will get used to it,' he said, without thinking what the words might imply until he had said them.

'Will I?' She glanced up sharply and he had a sudden notion that she might have taken a glimpse into his feelings after all. She was a remarkably shrewd young woman.

She bent to slacken Ottavio's girth. Raphael had noticed that the horse's comfort was very important to her. She never jerked the reins tight, never tugged at Ottavio's mouth or dug into his flanks with the heels of her boots. Unlike Emilio, of course, who did all of those things and would never have bothered to consider that a horse might be happier walking back to his stable with a slackened girth so that he could breathe more easily.

He looked at the back of her lowered head as she worked on buckles and straps. She had plaited her hair so that the first knot started very high up, almost on the top of her head. The tail of the plait reached half way down her back and had a silky fat bulk about it which was both satisfying and heartbreakingly seductive.

Straightening up Alessandra met his steady gaze and felt the power of his attraction to her like an electric force. She was not unfamiliar with the experience of men falling in love with her – a Bavarian flautist in Salzburg the year before had been so besotted he had threatened to melt down his silver flute into a molten ball if she would not take his ardour seriously. But she had never experienced any reciprocal feelings of infatuation. In fact the breathless loss of self-control suffered by her various admirers had seemed both incomprehensible and slightly pathetic.

But now, here in Spain, in the correctly formal yet overwhelming presence of Raphael Saventos, she was beginning to understand what the big fuss about falling in love might be all about.

'I've never ridden a horse of the calibre of Ottavio,' she told Raphael, aiming for a calm even tone as they walked together to the stable block. 'I would say he's in the world class league.'

'Then I shall take your word for it.'

'Oh no. It's just my opinion. I'm not a world expert.'

Raphael judged that her opinion of Ottavio was good enough for him. 'What about Titus?' he asked.

Alessandra laughed. 'He needs a lot of schooling. He's got a huge jump in him but he's a bit crazy.'

Raphael nodded. 'I suspected so when I bought him. I thought it was time for Emilio to have a challenge, you see.'

Alessandra glanced up at him. He had that unreadable, secret look on his face that she had seen once or twice before. And the very faintest of smiles – just a little chilling. 'Tell me more!' she said.

'Emilio had everything easy,' said Raphael. 'Beautiful toys when he was small. An expensive motor-bike at sixteen, a succession of new cars. It is one of my mother's main hobbies to indulge him, you see. He is a very spoiled and thus a very dissatisfied young man. That, of course, is not his fault. However when I bought Titus I was hoping that it would give him the chance to enjoy the satisfaction of being faced with a hurdle and being able to deal with it. Is that the correct expression?'

'Clear it.'

'Ah yes.'

'And did he clear it?'

'I think he fell on his face,' said Raphael.

'Literally and metaphorically?'

'Quite so.' He looked into her eyes and there was a sharp connection of shared feeling between them.

'Titus reminds me of Satire when I first got him,' said Alessandra. 'Everyone said he was a crazy horse, and that I was crazy to take him on. My father said he was like a five litre engine with no brakes – which was a pretty neat summing up. And Titus is a bit the same.'

'Your father was not worried for your safety?' Raphael asked swiftly.

Alessandra gave a little snort. 'Good heavens no! My parents have never kept me on a tight rein. I've always been allowed to make my own mistakes and learn from them. And in any case,' she added, looking with amusement into Raphael's sternly concerned face, 'Satire was a handful but he wasn't dangerous. And neither is Titus.'

'Ah,' he said softly.

'What Titus needs is some experience in steady hacking around country roads,' she informed Raphael in a business-like manner. 'Teach him how to stop and start. And how to survive a life that doesn't include constant breathtaking excitement.'

'Yes, I see.'

'It's just my opinion,' she said.

She walked Ottavio into his box and began taking off

his tack. As she removed the saddle a faint haze of steam rose from the horse's moistly warm back. She began to wipe him down with a sponge soaked in tepid water. Raphael leaned over the half door, watching her.

She straightened up. 'Does it bother you?' she asked. 'That my parents gave me such freedom?'

'I'm afraid I don't know very much about English ways. As I have told you, here in Spain some of the older families like ours are still very – traditional.'

'Does that mean controlling? It doesn't seem to have been happening with Emilio.' The sapphire streaks in her eyes glittered.

'Oh my dear Alessandra,' he said, shaking his head slowly. 'How you like to put me in my place.'

'I don't think I should flatter myself on that score.' She smiled to herself, dipping the sponge into the bucket once more.

'Not controlling,' said Raphael thoughtfully. 'I don't like that word very much. Perhaps protective. Yes?'

She paused, the sponge resting for a moment on Ottavio's rounded haunch as her mind suddenly began skating back through her childhood and adolescence. She had always been deeply appreciative of her parents' reluctance to control and manipulate her. The only real constraint they had placed on her had sprung from their overwhelming desire to initiate her into the world of music. But aside from that there had been great freedom, not only psychologically but physically. After all her father had rarely been at home. Protective, she mused, protective . . .

Alessandra went downstairs and into the drawing room promptly at five minutes before eight and was surprised to find it empty. The blinds had been raised as the sun had now disappeared, departing with slow drama in a blaze of blood-red and gold.

The room had a silent expectant air about it, making Alessandra feel faintly uneasy and exposed. The house beyond seemed silent too, like a deserted ship, although if she listened hard she could hear faint sounds of pans rattling in the kitchen which was reassuring.

She went to stand by the piano and idly fingered the keys. Then she sat down and began to play. Haydn this time – and from memory. The edginess fell away as she felt herself drawn into the piece. With a pedigree and upbringing like hers there was no way Alessandra would ever escape the irresistible lure of music.

Some time later Isabella came in, followed by Catriona who she had dragged from her room in her desire to present a united front to the visitor. Catriona had grudgingly put on an electric blue silk dress which she had bought in an exclusive fashion shop in Madrid the year previously and which was now a shade too tight. She was uncomfortable in her cream high heels and her cheeks were warm and flushed from the rapid consumption of two large vodkas as she dressed.

Isabella, magnificent in glowing emerald green, had piled her hair in a coronet on her head so as to accentuate her long neck. Both of them clinked with jewellery, having discarded none of the gold they had been wearing earlier and merely added more.

Isabella stopped dead just inside the doorway, having heard the sound of the piano and seen the figure sat behind it.

Alessandra looked up. She rose gracefully to her feet smiling with welcome and anticipation, simply attired in the fluid cream dress she had worn at the party following the piano competition. She had undone and washed her hair then plaited it again, thinking that a flying mane might appear somewhat wild in the rigid formality of the Saventos drawing room. She wore no jewellery apart from two tiny silver dolphins in her ears. Her parents had brought them back from their recent Athens trip and she had loved them on sight. 'Señora Saventos,' she said warmly, moving across the room and extending her hand.

Both Isabella and Catriona were taken aback at this composure in the younger woman. They were used to visitors outside their circle being awed and intimidated on meeting them. They were both in their different ways daunting, besides which there was a certain unspoken reverence due to the whole notion of the Saventos reputation and wealth when newcomers entered its precinct.

Isabella found herself in the awkward position of not knowing quite how to behave in the face of all this calm assurance and easy elegance.

Alessandra was, in fact, in a similar position, and not quite as confident as she appeared. She wished most fervently that she could speak Spanish.

At that moment Raphael walked through the door. 'I am so sorry,' he said, positioning himself to stand close to Alessandra. 'There was a telephone call from one of our supermarket customers. I was not able to cut them short.'

Neither his mother nor his sister smiled. They simply stared at him, their dark eyes wide and reproving.

106

Alessandra glanced up at him and he looked down. His eyes were full of concern as though he had left her to the mercy of a hostile army. She felt his nearness, the heat from his strong solid body, and was suddenly overwhelmed, a warm wave of some unknown emotion washing up inside her, flooding her vital organs. She turned her face quickly away from him. *This man*! an inner voice whispered. *Only him. For ever.*

The atmosphere was thick with emotion and conjecture.

Raphael spoke a few brief phrases in Spanish at which Isabella raised her head and looked glinty and dangerous for a moment like a latter-day dowager queen.

'I was explaining to my mother and sister that you are a successful British rider,' Raphael said to Alessandra, 'that you have been working with Ottavio at my request.'

She nodded, sensitive to the expression of displeasure on the other two women's faces.

Raphael said something further in Spanish and Alessandra heard the words Saul Xavier.

Isabella's eyes flickered. She spoke back rapidly to Raphael and again the words Saul Xavier were included. Catriona came suddenly on the alert, the expression of disdainful boredom left her face.

'You are Maestro Xavier's daughter,' Isabella said to Alessandra with great ceremony. She shook her head at Raphael, chiding him. 'And my son is not telling me . . .' she groped for the further English words to express what she felt about this revelation, and the fact that it had been witheld from her until now.

Gazing gravely at Alessandra for a brief instant, Raphael then turned back to his mother and said, 'It is quite true that I have not talked before about Alessandra's father, and I know she also has been wondering why that should be.' He looked down at her seeking her confirmation.

'Yes.' Alessandra's eyes, held by his, were enormous.

'This is not because I do not think it is important that she should have such a famous and renowned father. It is simply that Alessandra is – herself.'

As these significant words were being absorbed, María came in with a heavily ornate silver tray on which there was a champagne bottle and four tall cut glass goblets. Raphael took the tray from her and set about opening the wine.

Isabella made a little sound in her throat and then gestured graciously to Alessandra, inviting her to sit on one of the sofas.

'I am afraid,' she announced regretfully, 'that my speaking of English is not good.'

'It's a lot better than my Spanish,' Alessandra said. 'I feel ashamed to be here in your country and not speak your language.'

Isabella made a graceful movement with her hands, a pretty show of forgiveness for this shortcoming.

'But I'm going to learn,' Alessandra added with quiet determination.

Raphael, handing her a glass of wine which was bubbling very friskily, smiled down into her eyes, his approval clearly evident.

'I wish you luck. It's a pig of a language,' said Catriona.

'It is a *beautiful* language,' protested Isabella frowning.

'This is our new sparkling wine,' Raphael told Alessandra, holding out his glass to gain the light from the window in order to inspect its contents carefully. 'Do you like it?'

'Oh yes.' Just at that moment Alessandra thought she would have enjoyed fermented cabbage leaves had Raphael selected and poured them for her.

'I guess your father will only drink French champagne. The real thing,' observed Catriona. Her English accent was faintly tinged with American which gave it a certain charm, going some way to redeem Catriona's general lack of grace. 'He would not think so highly of cheap Spanish imitations,' she added with an undisguised touch of malice, flashing a glance at her brother.

Alessandra thought of the bottles of vintage champagne stacked in racks in the cool room beyond the kitchen at the Oxfordshire house. 'Yes,' she said evenly, 'he does drink French champagne, but now I shall be able to introduce him to something fresh and different.'

They went through into the stately, oak furnished dining room and the evening proceeded as it had begun, moving along in a series of jerky interchanges and unspoken scrutinies and conjectures. Presided over by Isabella the whole occasion was very gracious and polite, but at the end of it Alessandra felt exhausted.

Isabella insisted on escorting her to her room in order to make sure that she was entirely comfortable. Having inspected the room and noted that it was suitably airy, that the flowers were fresh and that the bed had been turned down properly she bade Alessandra a dignified good-night.

She turned at the doorway, the huge gold charms on her bracelet clashing together. 'We must talk of your father's work before you return to England,' she said. She spoke very slowly and carefully as though she had been rehearsing the words all evening.

'Yes,' said Alessandra. 'Certainly.'

Isabella took a little breath. 'You must be staying with us as long as you want to,' she said.

'Thank you,' said Alessandra, equally carefully. She felt as though she had suddenly stepped onto floorboards which were delicate and cracking.

'But I think you will be wanting to go home soon,' Isabella added, slipping through the door. 'Your parents will be wanting you to be with them, I know.'

Alessandra sank down on the bed. 'Phew!' She kicked off her shoes and pattered to the window.

Outside at the bottom of the terrace steps she saw Raphael walking up and down. Even from this distance she could smell the faint fragrance of his cigar.

As if he felt her eyes on him he looked up towards the window. He raised his arm in a slow gesture of acknowledgement, as intimate as an embrace.

CHAPTER 8

Tara held the phone to her ear long after Alessandra had replaced the receiver at her end – miles away in Spain. She stood in silent reflection for a time and then went out of the house and walked down the garden, listening to the sigh of wind in the branches of the willow trees which screened the formal part of the garden from the swimming pool area beyond.

She recalled seeing the garden for the first time more than twenty years before. She had been only eighteen, brought to the house by an ardent Saul who had willingly abandoned his wife in order to be with his young mistress.

Wandering down the lawn and idly picking out the odd blade of grass that had seeded itself amongst the roses, Tara remembered the girl she had been then; young and brimming with hope, totally caught up with the magnetic Saul Xavier, body, heart and soul. She had been headstrong too, daring and impulsive – and two months pregnant.

What a nest of hornets she had stirred up, she thought allowing a wry smile to curve her lips. She wondered if she had known what lay ahead, what intrigues and struggles and sadnesses were in store, if she would have acted any differently. And knew instantly that she would not. She would have done exactly the same as she did then.

She had been powerless to resist the fervent intensity of romantic and erotic love. And even now, at more than twice the age she had been then, the thread joining her to Saul was still pulled tight.

She stood for a while looking up at the branches of the great monkey-puzzle tree that stood in the center of the lawn, commanding and yet comically eccentric. She thought about her career – her professional development as a musician. Her early promise as a virtuoso violinist had been cruelly ended through damage to the vertebrae in her spine in a car accident and she had eventually taken up conducting instead. She judged she was a good conductor. She was sensitive, authoritative and patient. Orchestras liked her and worked well with her. She was popular with audiences and the radio networks. But she sometimes wondered if she had been little more than competent, if she had ever formed a truly innovative and creative idea on the interpretation of the world's great masterpieces.

Saul was a great innovator, of course. He always seemed to find something new to say about a piece he was conducting. But then he was a man. A husband not a wife, a father not a mother.

It seemed to Tara that however hard you tried as a woman, you never seemed to manage to generate enough creativity to pour into your work *and* into people. And maybe the simple answer was that there could never be enough for both. It just wasn't possible. Men had got that worked out – maybe not at a conscious level, just through instinct. Men didn't even try to divide their store of energies. They kept the bulk of it for the wholeness of their self-fulfillment.

And this was why, she concluded, reaching out to touch one of the tree's prickly branches, Saul at this moment was busy in a planning meeting with his musical agent Roland Grant in London, and she was drifting in a desultory way around the garden and worrying about her daughter in Spain.

In the last few days the phone conversations with Alessandra had become increasingly brief and brittle.

They had been fine at first. Alessandra had been warm and chatty, offering information freely. She was staying on at the Saventos estate for a few days, having a marvellous time helping out with the schooling of Raphael Saventos's horses. They were fantastic horses, Ottavio a real winner, the other horse a real challenge. Alessandra had worked out a short term schedule for bringing them on and Raphael had given her a free hand to put it into practice. It was a wonderful opportunity.

Tara had heard the excitement and enthusiasm in her daughter's voice and been tremendously happy that Alessandra seemed to have found a temporary respite from her wretchedness over Satire's death.

But then the calls had become less frequent, and when they came she had sensed a growing reluctance on Alessandra's part to say very much. A guarded and defensive tone had crept into her voice as though she were saying to her mother: 'Keep off, let me get on with my life on my own'.

And now it was almost two weeks since Alessandra had left for Spain.

Tara looked around as she heard a soft roaring beyond the gates. Saul's black Porsche came up the drive, flashing past her and drawing up in front of the house in a spray of flying gravel. She went across the lawn to meet him, watching him uncurl his long figure from the car. She speeded up suddenly into a run, desperate to be close to him.

'Darling!' He took her in his arms and kissed her forehead under her hair.

Tara seized him before he drew away, pulling his head down so that she could meet his lips.

He grunted with satisfaction.

'I thought you were going to be late,' she said.

'I decided to be early for once.' He took her hand and led her back over the grass, swinging her arm as though they were newly fledged lovers taking a secret stroll. 'Roland was in one of his leisurely moods, so I decided to use a maestro's trick and up the tempo a little. He found himself having to speed up to prestissimo. We got to the concluding chords rather more quickly than he expected.'

Tara chuckled. 'All right Saul, you don't have to remind me that all of us poor sidekicks are under the control of your iron thumb.' She made a small grimace. 'Anyway I'm glad you did gee him up,' she added. 'I needed you.'

'Yes?'

'Even more than usual.'

'Ah.' He looked into her eyes. 'The subject must be Alessandra,' he said.

'Yes. I'm getting worried.'

'Did you think I hadn't noticed?'

'No. But sometimes you choose to ignore me when I start behaving like a mother hen.'

'Mmm. So, tell me, what is the latest development in the Spanish saga?'

'The latest development is that she's no intention of telling us much.'

'And is that new?'

'No, but then usually she's not miles away in Spain at the same time as not telling us about what's going on. If you see what I mean!'

He gave one of his grave inscrutable smiles. 'She's in Spain with a respectable old Spanish family. She's well and apparently happy. Need we be worried?'

Tara sighed. 'Oh Saul!'

'Very well. I shall take your concerns seriously. So then, let's look at this situation dispassionately, discuss it rationally.'

Silently Tara gave a dry laugh. Could he really be dispassionate? About his daughter?

'Let me guess at the roots of your worry,' he said. 'First of all, she's still very young.'

'Yes.'

'But of an age to make her own decisions – yes?'

'True, but for heaven's sake Saul, she's got very little experience of the grittiness of real life. And what does she know about this man she's gone to stay with? What do *we* know about him?'

'His intentions might not be honourable – is that it?' Saul glanced mockingly down at her. The deep sapphire flecks in his cool grey eyes glinted. 'Come along now Tara. Alessandra is capable of handling any unwanted advances.'

'Yes, but supposing they're not unwanted.'

There was a pause. She judged that at last she had got through to him, rattled his composure. Saul was after all a flesh and blood man – both a lover and a father.

He startled her by saying, 'So you're saying we should be worried about Alessandra's setting out on the road to sexual experience?'

Tara gaped at him. 'The road to sexual experience! Saul, we're talking about a milestone in the life of our daughter. How can you be so cool about it, so clinical?'

'Not clinical – logical, balanced.' His carved features were immobile and austere.

Tara gave a snort of frustration.

'No, don't dismiss what I say. Think Tara! Think back! There was a time when you used to worry that there was no special boy-friend for Alessandra, that she seemed to give all her affection to the horse. Isn't that so? Can you deny it?'

'No.'

There was a time,' he continued with soft menacing challenge, 'when you used to be worried that she was gay.'

'No!'

'Oh yes. Be honest. You never said so. You never used the word. But it was at the back of your mind. I could almost see it written there.'

'Yes,' she agreed in a whisper. Tara was suddenly reminded of herself at Alessandra's age, a young mother with a baby, and a stolen lover whom she

116

worshipped like a god. Looking up at Saul now, those memories re-awakened, she felt a stab of white-hot primitive desire for him.

'Saul, don't make things hard for me,' she said quietly. 'I know I'm a hyprocrite. I know I'm implying that my daughter shouldn't be free to choose her relationships or give in to spontaneous sex urges – in other words to do exactly what I did when I was three years younger than her . . .'

'Quite,' he said drily.

'But Alessandra hasn't got started on her life yet. She still doesn't know what she wants to *do* with it!'

'Did you?'

'Yes. I wanted to be a virtuoso violinist. I still wanted that even when you came along like a great hurricane and swept me off into your seething musical world. And I did achieve it. You *know* all that.'

'Yes,' he said, 'you did.' He spoke with genuine feeling.

'Alessandra has no career, no ambitions, apparently no plans. That worries me.'

'No ambitions! I had the impression she wanted to be a world class show-jumper. Or have I been badly mistaken?'

'Oh yes that!' Tara frowned, nibbling on her lip. 'But do you know Saul, I'm not sure how serious she ever was about that.'

'No? I seem to recall some earlier parental discussions when we went over all the ins and outs of that particular desire of Alessandra's. It was a kind of girding of the loins, polishing up our defensive armoury for when she finally faced us with it.' He smiled down at her, his eyebrows raised. 'Isn't that so?'

'Yes. I haven't forgotten,' she said a little sharply. 'I know that was what we were expecting. But you see, if she had been passionately wanting to be a competition rider, I don't think she'd have gone through all those years of music training.'

'You don't?'

'I certainly wouldn't!'

'No my darling, you wouldn't. But then Alessandra is not you.'

Tara put a hand up to her forehead. 'Saul,' she exclaimed in exasperation, 'I think if you go on being so calm and cool I shall turn violent.'

He put his arm around her shoulder and pulled her to him. 'You're still the little tigress I fell in love with,' he told her silkily. 'Now, come along, tell me in plain and simple language, what has Alessandra been saying to you to bring all this on? Mmm? Did she phone just before I came?'

'Yes.'

'And?'

Tara let out a large sigh. 'Oh, I don't know. I can't quite put my finger on it.'

'When is she coming back?' Saul asked, cutting straight to the heart of the matter.

'She didn't say. I suppose that's just it.'

'So why didn't you simply ask her?' Saul enquired reasonably.

'It just didn't seem the right thing to do. I had a feeling that if I'd started badgering she'd have become angry with me.' Tara looked defiantly up at her impassive husband. Sometimes his impartial, god-like view of things drove her wild. And sometimes it had the effect of making her desire him with an urgency of raw passion that could still amaze her. Was this persistently glowing sexual urgency based on a yearning to try to pierce through his shell of omnipotence, she wondered with sudden insight. 'Why didn't *you* ask last time you spoke to her?'

'I haven't spoken to her in the last week.'

'No,' said Tara. 'You've hardly been here.'

There was a tiny missed beat. 'Is that a reproach?'

'No.'

'I think it was.

'Saul, I understand your life and the way you've arranged it, and it's OK by me. I'm not a clinging little wife who needs to winge about her husband "never being there". And anyway, I've hardly been blameless myself in respect of always "being around".' Looking back now on her hectic professional life in the past ten years Tara had a horrible feeling that she might have somehow failed her daughter. She also had a strong sense that it was worse to have done that as a mother than a father. She gave a wry smile. How her own mother Rachel would laugh if she heard her say that. Whenever Rachel had offered exactly the same opinion Tara had firmly slapped her down.

She supposed that at some deep level in her anxiety there was a fear of her daughter's becoming caught up in some wild and turbulent love affair; of Alessandra's somehow losing herself to someone else. There was a troubling resonance about Alessandra's being in Spain with Raphael and her – Tara's – own heady headlong tumble into love all those years ago with Saul. The sins of the mothers, she thought with wistful irony. But it was not sin that bothered her, it was something else. Something she couldn't quite grasp and identify.

Saul pressed her arm. 'So what are we to do,' he asked with a faint smile, 'about our errant daughter?'

'Nothing,' said Tara regretfully. 'After all what *can* we do?' Except worry she added to herself silently.

For a breathless moment she thought he might be going to counter her negative resignation and offer some positive suggestion, some brilliant way of resolving things. She still had fantasies about Saul's being able to arrange all things as he wished. Even other people's lives.

He bent his head to hers. 'I have to agree with you. We can probably,' he said softly, 'do very little, I'm afraid.'

They turned and walked slowly back to the house.

She had a sense of their having discussed her concerns about Alessandra like an item on an agenda. And the subject being now closed.

Tara rested her head against him, thinking of her marriage and of the enormity of her love for both Saul and Alessandra. Loves of a very different kind, each with their own joy and richness and sadness. She resolved to phone Alessandra early the next day and try to make amends for the difficulties she felt she had placed between the two of them through her poorly disguised quizzing and worrying.

'So,' said Saul, sliding his hand around the curve of her breast. 'Will you allow me to take you out to a lovely dinner my darling? I've already booked a table. And after that, when we come back and have the house all to ourselves, we can enjoy a long slow meal of another sort. Mmm?'

CHAPTER 9

Raphael and Alessandra rode out into the lush green grasslands that stretched for miles beyond the borders of the vineyard.

They had fallen into the habit of taking the horses out in the early morning for a gentle hack. Raphael, under the guidance of Alessandra, was giving Titus some basic tuition in starting and stopping as she had previously recommended.

'He's coming along very nicely,' she commented, watching Titus's head move rhythmically up and down, Raphael's strong slender fingers lightly controlling the reins.

'And I?' Raphael asked solemnly. 'Am I too coming along very nicely?'

'Oh, I shall make a good rider of you yet,' Alessandra said, looking straight ahead and smiling to herself. 'Emilio will have to look out when he gets back.'

'I think Emilio will have to look out for a good deal when he gets back,' Raphael commented. His tone was ironic, but his face expressionless.

Alessandra looked around her, taking in the soft luminous glow of the morning. The sun was well up, but not yet powerful, and the horses could move about freely without becoming uncomfortable. They had kept up a good brisk canter for the last mile, and now they were enjoying a quiet walk with the horses on a loose rein.

Raphael had suggested that they take a longer ride than usual this morning so that he could show her the canal system which passed close to the vineyard.

'When my great grandfather first came here in the 1900s he found a dry and arid land,' he explained to Alessandra as they moved forward. 'I think scrub is the word you would use for it. People said that he was a fool to think about establishing a winery here. They said that the land would never produce any good grapes. But he was not a man who could easily be put off. He liked this place. He could feel its possibilities in his bones.'

'It sounds to me,' intervened Alessandra, 'as though your great grandfather was pretty stubborn and determined – rather like you in fact. So – he decided not to take any notice of what all the faint-hearted pessimists said.'

'Stubborn and determined! Are these compliments?' enquired Raphael.

'Oh yes.'

Raphael gave a low chuckle. 'Thank you for that Alessandra. Well you are right. My great grandfather stayed on here. He found out that although the climate was very dry the land here could produce very aromatic fruits. Very fragrant, very *pungent*.' He turned to her. 'I like that word don't you?'

'Yes.' She smiled at his delight in pulling especially descriptive words out of the extensive hat of his English vocabulary.

'He also found that the variation in temperature between day and night in the prime growing time of the year was such as to be very beneficial to the plants.'

'In what way?'

'It was very steady, not going up and down too suddenly.'

'Is constancy of temperature especially important in wine-making?' Alessandra asked.

'It is crucial. Plants don't like swings between the hot and the cold. And the pressed grapes in the vats don't like these fluctuations either. That is why when my great grandfather built the winery he had the roof especially designed with all those little windows put into it. The reason for this was to maintain a more or less constant temperature in there you see. Of course nowadays we can do that through modern heating methods.'

'Your great grandfather sounds to have been quite an innovator.'

'Oh yes. He must have been a rather special person altogether.'

They surmounted a little ridge and there below them was a glittering ribbon of moving water. Alessandra could hear it rushing and bubbling busily within its concrete banks. 'It's more like a river than a canal,' she commented in surprise. 'It seems to have a life of its own.'

'The network here was very carefully planned to bring the maximum amount of water into the region,' Raphael told her. 'This was happening at the same time as my great grandfather was doing his planning. As he was constructing the winery so the water was being brought to the land making it richly fertile – just as he needed, and just as it is today.'

'What a wonderful story,' Alessandra said simply. 'I have always thought so.'

She gazed at the shifting glinting water, fascinated. She looked back to the vineyard, to the white columns at the entrance to the winery, just visible in the distance, gleaming in the sun. 'So here at the Saventos winery you literally turn the water into wine.'

'Yes,' he said. He gave her a long look, as though he would stamp her features forever in his mind. 'Yes,' he repeated at last. 'What a beautiful way to describe it.'

They walked on. Alessandra turned her face up to the sun and breathed in the fragrant air. The last few days had been magical – not quite believable. In Alessandra's mind they were like a glowing yet unfocused tapestry formed from the weather, the drama of the changing light in the sky, the wine, the scents in the air, the grace of the horses. And at the centre of the image was Raphael – his voice and his eyes and his presence burrowing deep into her senses and her mind.

Alessandra felt herself drawn ever closer to him, wanting to discover everything about him, to know what he knew, to feel what he felt.

In the midst of her blossoming admiration for him, she had an acute and growing intuition of his loneliness. He gave an impression of huge strength and sensitivity. And yet there was a deep stoicism in his personality, and an underlying sense of sadness. He seemed to her compellingly entwined and at the same time trapped within the web of his family, bearing a heavy burden of responsibility for supporting two spoiled and idle women – and the absent brutish Emilio. She did not think that things were at all easy for Raphael in his role of director of the wine business and head of the family.

An icy courtesy had prevailed between her and the Saventos women in recent days, since she had stayed on beyond what would have been considered a normal period for a casual visitor.

Isabella had been undeniably gracious. She had even gone so far as to permit Alessandra a glimpse into the world of her artistic ambition, into the huge art studio which had been especially built for her at the back of the house where the light was perfect.

Once inside her sanctum, Isabella had come fully to life. 'I am being an artist,' she had announced theatrically to Alessandra. 'For many many years now, I am being an artist.'

But it appeared that Isabella had been constantly frustrated in her artistic ambitions. She had informed Alessandra with eye-glinting ferocity that composition and painting were the great enthusiasms of her life but she had been most cruelly prevented from allowing them to flower as they should. Haltingly, in her idiosyncratic English, she had managed to get across the bitter message that had she not been born a woman and saddled with the responsibilities of caring for a family she would have devoted herself wholeheartedly to art. And, most likely have become a success. She would have had canvases hanging in the prestigious contemporary galleries in Madrid.

Isabella had whipped a white sheet from her easel and shown Alessandra the huge canvas on which she was currently working. It was a turbulent whirlpool of colour, the oils put on with a knife, so thick that they seemed almost edible. Alessandra had already seen other examples of Isabella's work around the house. All of them were abstracts, explosions of darting lines and wildly wayward geometrics. Alessandra had gazed at them with curiosity, presuming that they represented some kind of reflection of Isabella's personality.

She had been reminded of her father's often asked question regarding a piece of music and the way to truly understand it. 'What is this *about*?' he would demand.

Asking herself that same question about Isabella's paintings Alessandra had been able to come up with no more apt word than anger. And possibly also confusion. She had not felt disturbed about this, or in any way intimidated by the older woman. But she had certainly felt curious about her. And because she was beginning to sense the full power of Isabella's self will and her brittleness, she had found herself even more strongly in sympathy with Raphael than before.

Isabella had also invited her to play the piano once again. She had sat upright on the sofa, her hands regally folded, listening with great attentiveness. Afterwards she had made no comment on Alessandra's interpretation or technique, but had enquired if she considered the Saventos piano to be a good instrument.

Alessandra had said yes – which was true. She had wondered with silent amusement what the reaction would have been if she had said no.

But Isabella's attempts at friendly cordiality had a forced and desperate edge to them. Alessandra knew that the older woman could hardly wait to hear that the unexpected guest from England was leaving.

Catriona, in contrast to her mother, had not been much in evidence, spending long periods in her room or driving off into the nearby town. Alessandra wondered if this was her usual pattern of life, or if she was lurking and brooding, distancing herself at the furthest point of the uneasy female triangle that had formed in the house. What Catriona and her mother said to each other in private Alessandra found it hard to guess.

During the hours of the afternoons when, even though it was now late September, it was much too hot to school the horses, Isabella and Catrionia retired for a long siesta whilst Raphael attended to the winery, and Alessandra had got into the habit of sitting in the shade on the terrace and learning Spanish words from the huge dictionary he had found for her in the family library.

She had begun compiling a list of the words she found she most frequently needed to use. During family mealtimes she attended carefully to all that was said. Raphael patiently translated each item of Spanish conversations into English for her benefit. And very gradually words and phrases were beginning to mean something. She was not yet able to frame more than the simplest responses, but she was beginning to understand quite a lot.

Ferdinand too had been a great ally in this respect. He had turned up on a number of occasions to help Alessandra with the heavier work of caring for the horses and cleaning the stables. Working together they had formed an easy going and amicable friendship. When she had asked him if he would help her to learn his language he had been highly flattered and only too ready to oblige.

These reflections were suddenly interrupted as she saw a small village coming into view. It nestled into the palm-like bowl of a dip in the land below, bathed in sunlight and looking like a settlement from centuries long past.

Alessandra could make out the network of alleyways between the houses, the walls all whitewashed, the wash peeling from the relentless onslaught of the sun and the storm rains. The small white houses with their apricot and terracotta tiled roofs were a pleasing jumble of heights and sizes. Tall branches of orange trees thrust their leafy tops over some of the houses and flower-filled pots stood on the numerous balconies which projected into the alleys. Some of the pots had been wired to the outer rails of the balconies and their trails of bright geraniums gleamed white and scarlet and pink.

As they rode nearer she could see the rows of scuffed and delightfully shabby back doors of the houses. People went in and out, carrying shopping baskets and pushing bicycles. She heard the sound of a guitar from somewhere deep in one of the houses, a long melancholy tune from the *bel canto*.

Raphael made a small gesture and they brought the horses to a halt and let them stand, the reins dropping slack.

'Yours is a very beautiful country,' she said eventually to Raphael in careful Spanish.

He nodded. She felt his eyes move from their consideration of the village and rest on her, his gaze quite open and unembarrassed, slow and leisured, taking her in.

I don't want to go home, she thought suddenly in a kind of excited panic. I want to stay here in this magical place. I want *this* to be my home.

'Tell me about your father Raphael,' she said quietly, returning to the English language once again. 'You've never spoken about him. Not once.'

'He was killed,' Raphael said simply.

128

'I'm sorry,' she said. 'Sorry that I asked,' she added, fearing she had caused him unnecessary pain.

'No. It is right for you to ask. You need to know these things,' he said. 'It happened one day in the summer, just before the harvest. My father and my brother Joaquin were on a tractor driving down in the bottom part of the vineyards. The tractor over-turned. We have never found out the reason. But they were both crushed.'

She said nothing, simply allowed her silent sympathy to reach out to him.

'I was the one to find them,' he continued calmly. 'I did not see the bodies, because the tractor was lying on top of them.'

He turned to look directly at Alessandra. There was a deep and nakedly simple expression of grief on his face. She saw the way in which it intensified the lines carved onto his skin.

She reached out her hand to him and he took it in his. He said, 'I sometimes think of the two of them. How they would be talking as they drove, discussing the readiness of the grapes for picking. Wondering if these grapes would be part of a harvest and a vintage they would remember in years to come. But they never saw the years to come. The did not even see that autumn or that harvest.' He paused, drawing in a long breath. 'You know Alessandra – ever since that time I have had a great respect for both life and death.'

'How old were you then?' she asked.

'Sixteen. My brother was twenty-two, my father forty-five. They were young strong men.'

'And you took over the running of the winery?'

'Of course.' He gave a short dry laugh. 'Who else

was there? I left school. I did not go to university. I worked and worked to kill my grief. And now I have worked in the vineyard for half of my life.'

Alessandra tightened her fingers around his. He smiled, his lips curving in an expression of great sorrow and great sweetness for a man of such self-containment and strength.

'Alessandra,' he said abruptly, 'when you first arrived in Spain I asked you if you would stay here for a little time as my guest . . .'

'Yes. I remember.' She felt her heart begin to beat heavily.

'I had truly wanted to propose something else to you. But I did not like to rush you. You were alarmed anyway with my other proposal,' he added smiling at the recollection.

'Please Raphael, say what it is you want to say,' she told him, looking down once more at the village.

'Very well. Will you consider staying here on a permanent basis in order to ride and train the horses so that they will be ready for competition work?'

'You mean – you want to employ me as a rider for your stables?' She frowned, puzzled, trying to pull herself out of the sombre mood his previous story had elicited.

'No. That is not what I have been thinking.'

'What then?' she asked, her heart giving sudden frantic leaps.

'I want you to ride the horses under my sponsorship.'

She was amazed. 'You want to be a sponsor for me? Sponsoring's a very serious commitment – very expensive.'

'Yes.' He smiled. 'I know.'

'A British rider being sponsored by a Spaniard?' she queried.

He looked displeased. 'You would not be sponsored by *me*. You would be sponsored by the winery. That would be quite in order. There would be no clash of nationalities.'

'I'm sorry Raphael. I didn't mean to cast any aspersions on Spain. I was just pointing out a logistic difficulty.' She tugged at his hand, forcing him to turn and meet her eyes.

'Yes. I understand.'

'I think Spain is wonderful,' she said impulsively, longing for the hurt and defensiveness to leave his face. 'I think it is magnificent to be Spanish.'

His hand almost crushed hers in its ferocity of feeling. 'So what have you to say to my question?' he asked.

'I don't know. I need to think about it.' She had felt tremendous elation and anticipation before he framed his request. And now, strangely and perversely, even though he had offered to fulfil an ambition she had longed for for years, she felt disappointment. She had had a sense, quite unrealistically and fantastically, that he might have been about to ask her something else. And the thought had brought her breath to a painful halt in her chest.

'Yes, of course you do. Please forgive me for putting you under pressure,' he said, retreating once more into polite formality. 'We will talk of it later.'

They turned the horses back in the direction of the winery and walked on in silence under an intensifying sun.

CHAPTER 10

When the telephone rang Tara sprinted across to it as though it was on the point of making a sudden bid for escape. She picked up the receiver, listening anxiously, trying desperately to swallow the piece of toast she had placed in her mouth just before the phone came alive.

She could hear similar sounds of listening at the other end, and then a voice saying rather impatiently, 'Mummy?'

'Yes. Oh darling, it's so good to hear from you.' Immediately Tara cursed herself. She could hear her little speech through Alessandra's ears, altogether too gushing and grateful and worriedly mumsy.

'It's only a couple of days since we last spoke,' Alessandra said.

'Yes, yes I know.' Calm down, Tara told herself. 'How are things then?' she asked, wincing now to hear the garishly false brightness threaded into her words.

'Fine.'

'Oh. That's good. How's the horse coming on?'

'Ottavio?' Alessandra gave a little snort. 'He's not exactly at the stage of "coming along". He's a well

132

established top flight horse. He was when I first started riding him.'

'Yes.'

'You knew that Mummy.'

'Yes.' Tara agreed faintly, resisting an urge to say something apologetic. She recalled a distant time when she and her own mother used to have similarly jerky and tortured conversations, except then it had been Tara who had played the exasperated and commanding role Alessandra had now taken on.

'How's Daddy?'

'Oh, he's well.'

'Busy is he? Dashing around the world twice before breakfast?'

Tara forced herself to produce a merry-sounding laugh. She reflected that Saul, having recently told her of his resolve to spend a few precious days at home, had gone off at a minute's notice the afternoon before, following a phone call from Roland Grant to ask if he would take over from another maestro who had unexpectedly walked out of rehearsals and vanished into thin air. In truth Tara was not quite sure *where* Saul was. 'Something like that,' she agreed.

There was a pause. 'And you Mummy. Are you busy?'

'Oh, the usual.'

'Which is?'

'Rehearsing the Eastlands Orchestra for the annual series of autumn concerts. Oh, and I've agreed to lead a conducting seminar that's coming up at a music convention in Cambridge next week. I'll have to brush up a bit for that!'

'No you won't. You're a really good conductor Mummy. Always very well brushed up.'

'Thank you!' Tara felt a rush of warmth. 'To be quite honest, I'm making a real effort not to get my diary too full this season,' she continued, swept along on a burst of impulsive need to confide. 'I think I'm getting a bit old and tired. Perhaps it's burn out!'

'Nonsense.'

'No, truly. I do quite seriously think it's time I stopped buzzing around like a frenetically busy bee. So when you come home we could do a few nice things together,' she ventured, trying to hit a balance between hesitancy and over confidence. 'We might have a day in the West End, or maybe drive up to the Yorkshire Dales.'

Alessandra made no instant reply. Tara thought she heard a sigh.

'Have you any plans for coming home in the next week or so?' Tara enquired feeling as though she had embarked on a high wire.

'No.'

'I'm sorry?' The simple starkness of that one word, although it had been stated with perfect calmness sounded horribly serious and brutal.

'No, I haven't any plans for coming home. I'm staying on here.'

Tara gripped the receiver so tightly her nails dug deep red scores into her palm. 'Staying on,' she echoed stupidly. 'For how long?'

'Indefinitely.'

'*What*?'

'Raphael has offered to sponsor me.'

Tara blinked with incomprehension and then astonishment. 'As a rider?'

'Yes, of course. What else?' Alessandra sighed heavily and then she chuckled. 'Come on Mummy, stop behaving like a mother hen.'

'I'm expressing a natural parental anxiety,' Tara responded sharply.

'What about? Surely not my career. Listen – you and Daddy have been worried for months about what I was going to do with my life after I graduated. Well, I'm going to do what I've always wanted. I'm going for the high jump. Of the horsey type. And it will all be fine. I shall have the money I need and all the facilities to really make a go of it in show-jumping, all quite independent of you and Daddy.'

'Yes but . . .'

'But what? Look, don't spoil things for me Mummy. I'm absolutely over the moon about it. This is exactly the kind of opportunity I've always dreamed about.'

There was a silence.

'And I promise I'll come home in a month or two and let you see that I'm perfectly sound in mind and body.'

'Yes.'

'What is it that's bugging you?' Alessandra demanded fiercely.

Tara sighed. 'It's all so sudden. And we don't know anything about . . . your sponsor.'

'Oh that's it. I see. Are you going to make a few more politically incorrect remarks about foreigners?'

'Oh, the arrogance of youth,' Tara exploded, adding bitterly, 'And I should know about it. I was just as bad myself.'

'Yes,' Alessandra agreed brutally. 'So I've gathered. Except on top of everything else you ran off with Daddy when you were three years younger than me.'

'Yes.' Tara sighed. This was the first time Alessandra had faced her with the knowledge that she, as a newly fledged adult had given some thought to her mother's youthful impetuosity and formed some judgement on it.

'Mummy,' continued Alessandra dangerously, 'I think we should all have the freedom to make our own decisions, as long as no one else gets mangled up in the process. And all I'm doing is starting out on a new career. Raphael is going to be my sponsor. I'm not eloping with him.'

'Oh God,' Tara whispered.

'All those sighs are a bit rich coming from you Mummy. You're not going to accuse me of sleeping with him are you? That would be a touch hypocritical. Anyway you've no need to worry, there's nothing in the agreement between me and Raphael that says I have to go to bed with him.'

Tara found herself shying away from her daughter's words as though they were glowing pokers. *Go to bed with him. Running off, others getting mangled up . . .*

'And in any case,' said Alessandra, screwing the knife deep into the wound she had opened, 'Raphael isn't married. So even if I did sleep with him – so what! I wouldn't be pinching him from anyone else. Besides which I'm a big girl now.'

'Yes,' said Tara wearily. 'You're right.'

'Oh Mummy,' said Alessandra, 'look, I'm sorry for saying all those things. It's just that I don't see how you can come over all concerned and righteous when you . . .'

'Yes, I understand. It's all right,' Tara cut in quickly, hardly able to bear the guilty contrition in her daughter's voice.

She felt suddenly sick and dizzy. 'Let's not say any more. We'll talk again soon and make a new start.' Swiftly she put the phone down. Her stomach under her clenched hands was bruised and tender. Rushing to the lavatory she just made it in time, straining and then vomiting into the basin. Deep in her gut a raw mean pain grated. Her periods had become irregular recently and when they came they were heavy and painful. Any kind of emotional upset could trigger things off like dam gates opening.

Panting and groaning softly she went back to the kitchen and switched on the kettle. 'Oh, Saul!' she exclaimed, thumping her fist on the marble-topped unit, 'why are you never here when I need you?'

Alessandra slotted the phone back into its housing on the wall. When telephoning home she always used the receiver in the stable block. In the house there was the ever prowling presence of Isabella, making her uneasy and unable to speak freely.

She walked outside and stared across the lush land which stretched endlessly to a vivid blue horizon. Where the two met there was a faint border of deep indigo gently shimmering in the late morning heat. Despite the warmth in the atmosphere Alessandra felt a faint malicious draught of cold air prickle over her skin. The way she had spoken to her mother jarred in her ears, the echoes taunting her. She grasped the rope of her hair, plaited in preparation for riding, and held onto its plump comforting end. And then without warning, she found herself starting to cry. The violence of the sensation shocked her. She could hear the huge sobs wrenching their way out of her, surging up in broken gasps. She dashed back frantically into the stables and let herself into Ottavio's stall.

Following his morning's schooling Ottavio was contentedly munching at a hay net she had hung up for him. Tearing a fresh wadge, he turned towards her, his huge eyes faintly curious but quite untroubled. His confidence in her was total. Putting her arms up around his neck she pressed her head against him and let the tears spill freely.

Her lack of control terrified her. She, Alessandra, who was always so cool, so strong. And now tears were gushing out of her in a great flood. She had never had a feeling in her life to compare with this. And yet everything should be just wonderful for her, exactly as she had told her mother it was. Or rather how she had *shouted* to her mother that it was.

Why had she needed to shout? What had driven her to be so hard and cold and cruel? To her mother whom she really loved, who was her friend?

She clutched onto Ottavio with a desperate unknown yearning. She conjured up an image of herself winning on him at Olympia, the great Christmas show. She saw herself bending to take the challenge cup from some duchess or princess. The sobs merely accelerated, so that he turned his head towards her and pushed his nose against her chest.

'Oh pull yourself together Alessandra,' she muttered eventually, scrabbling about for a handkerchief, not finding one and having to rub her nose and eyes on her hand.

She stretched her spine and took deep long breaths, one after the other. Ottavio regarded her with gently impartial eyes. 'Promise you'll never breathe a word of this to anyone,' she told him softly, patting his rump and running her hand over the wiry cascade of his tail as she let herself out of his stall and walked back to the house.

Isabella was in the inner courtyard, watering the lemon trees in their pots in a way that seemed to Alessandra more to demonstrate a point than anything else. Immediately she heard Alessandra's footsteps, the older woman turned and looked around, a brief flashing savagery in her face. With a sickening jolt Alessandra understood that her phone call to England had been listened to. And whilst Isabella's English was only fragmentary, it was competent enough to understand the essentials.

Isabella would surely be aware now of the proposition that Raphael had recently put to Alessandra. She would also know that it had been accepted.

Alessandra wished she knew if Raphael had revealed anything of his intentions to his mother, or if the news had been broken to Isabella solely through the stealth of her own eavesdropping. She was coming to learn that openness was not one of the strategies favoured in the Saventos family. Their emotions seemed only able to survive in a tensely fragile atmosphere of half truths and secrecy.

'Good morning, Señora Saventos,' Alessandra said very politely in Spanish.

139

Isabella inclined her head in coldly formal acknowledgement. Her gold bracelets tinkled faintly as she withdrew her hand from its attentions to the lemon tree. She was wearing white this morning. Her olive skin glowed beneath the heavy linen fabric and her immaculately smoothed black hair, caught in a bright crimson silk scarf, gleamed in the sunlight. Alessandra fancied she could almost see the little rapier points of hostility dancing around its shiny halo.

'I've been out in the field riding,' she said, continuing in Spanish, pleased to be able to recall all the necessary words without difficulty.

Isabella dipped her head once more. Alessandra could tell that the older woman had no idea what to say to her, how to deal with her. Except that her face said very clearly that she resented Alessandra fiercely both for being in her house and for always looking so at ease there. Alessandra was fairly confident that Isabella had not registered any signs of her earlier distress, even though she was sure her face must still show screamingly obvious evidence of her weeping. She guessed that it was Isabella's habit to be far more concerned with looking into her own feelings rather than examining or sensing those of others.

'Raphael has gone into the town for a business meeting,' Isabella said, speaking in very rapid Spanish so that Alessandra had to jerk herself into full attention to catch the words. 'He will not be back until this afternoon.' She peered at Alessandra, as though these words were some sort of challenge. A gauntlet thrown down. *You didn't know that did you? He doesn't tell you everything!*

When Alessandra merely smiled politely in response, she added with severity, 'I shall be taking lunch in my studio. I have a lot of work to do. I have asked Maria to serve your lunch out on the terrace.'

Alessandra knew this was both a rejection and a deliberate insult. The family never dined out of doors during the hottest hours of the day when the sun could burn and the insects were out in force.

'Thank you,' she said, rapidly calling up the newly acquired words from her memory and adding swiftly, 'That will be nice. I like dining on the terrace.'

Isabella's eyes glimmered, as she turned to make a gracious and meaningful exit. She had not failed to register a neat point scored by the enemy.

Unaware that she made a very pretty scene, sitting under the shade of the eucalyptus in her pale green top, cream cotton trousers and big straw hat, Alessandra sipped wine and turned the pages of the British Horse Society's *Manual of Horsemanship*. From time to time she raised her head from the book in order to make pencilled notes on the jotting pad open on the table.

The sound of an approaching car's engine seeped gradually into her awareness, making her heart give a small spring. She looked up, expecting to see the big black Mercedes coming up the drive. Longing to see it, in fact, she realized with a painful jolt.

She took off her dark glasses, frowning as she registered a much smaller black car, sleek and crouched and aggressive. She swallowed, feeling her throat go dry. She recognized the car, she recognized the long-boned head of the driver. What, she asked herself in astonishment and growing concern, could her father possibly have in mind by turning up out of the blue here at the Saventos winery?

141

In a gesture of self-protection, as though to offer herself some small screen of concealment, she put on her dark glasses once again. There was a jagged tug from the past as she watched the tall, spare, figure move towards her, the gait loose, easy and panther-like. Her father: the idol of her childhood, the hero of her youth. Her friends used to say that he was so fantastically attractive he was 'to die for' even though he was quite old.

Slowly she stood up to greet him, smoothing her clothes, tentatively fingering the rope of her hair, still in its shiny thick plait. He moved close. His lips were curved in a dry quizzical smile, his arms stretched out to her.

For a trembling moment as he came close and she looked at him, his features became mobile and liquid, and suddenly Raphael was there before her eyes instead . . .

'Alessandra!' Her father's voice was dry and faintly mocking. He bent and his lips lightly touched each of her cheeks in turn.

Blinking and frowning slightly she returned to the here and now, to the carved, hawk-like features of her father, quite unlike the strong solidity of Raphael's dark head and his wonderful firmly substantial body . . .

She realized then, confronted so unexpectedly with her father, how potently Raphael's image had imposed itself into the whole fabric of her thoughts.

'Daddy!' she exclaimed. And then, as though she were an established inhabitant, she said, 'Welcome to Spain.'

CHAPTER 11

'So,' said Saul, sitting down and looking slowly around him. 'You seem to have found yourself a rather beautiful corner of Spain.'

'Yes.' Alessandra, behind the protection of her dark glasses took the opportunity to scrutinize her father at leisure. Confronted by him so suddenly, so unexpectedly, she was overcome with a feeling of closeness to him. There was also a sharp sense of how much like him she was. It had never struck her quite so forcibly before. But now that she looked at him and recalled her own image in the mirror as she interwove her plait that morning, she could see how the lines of her own face were developing according to his example.

'What are you thinking?' he asked, reaching out and grasping the half empty unlabelled wine bottle and studying the colour of the wine within.

'That I'm proud to be your daughter,' she said simply.

He looked up from his examination of the wine. 'Thank you.'

'And what are *you* thinking Daddy? And what are you doing here?'

He smiled, noting the undercurrent of challenge in her tone. He held up his hands in a delicate gesture of truce. 'I've been in Barcelona, doing a rescue conducting job.'

'Really? What happened to the other guy? Did you tie him in a knot and thread him through the strings of the concert hall's nine foot grand? Is he still there, screaming to be set free?'

'He's probably screaming somewhere or other,' Saul agreed with a twisted smile. 'The poor man had a nervous breakdown apparently.'

Alessandra shook her head. 'Dear, dear. Toppling off the podium into madness. Occupational hazard. You'll have to watch out Daddy!'

'Mmm. *Great wits are to madness near allied and thin walls do their bounds divide,*' quoted Saul. 'That's from John Dryden, I think. Although I'm not sure I've got it accurately word for word. I remember my uncle used to quote it to me when I was a boy.'

As they smiled at each other, enjoying a little mutual teasing, an amicable skirmish with words for weapons, María came purposefully down the steps, like a guard dog who has sensed the presence of a stranger within the walls of its domain.

She came to stand by the table. She looked at Alessandra. She looked at Saul.

'This is my father, María,' Alessandra explained in Spanish.

'Ah!' María nodded to him with great politeness. 'Will your father be wanting something to eat?' she asked Alessandra, who turned instantly to Saul to make a swift translation.

He shook his head in a smiling negative, murmuring that he would be quite happy to enjoy the wine.

Alessandra spoke again to María who said she would bring another glass.

'Well, well,' remarked Saul watching María's stately progress back to the house. 'I see you have acquired the skills of a translator. I'm impressed.'

'I'm only up to household bits and pieces so far. And a few horsey phrases.'

'Nevertheless . . .'

There was a short pause. 'Have you been speaking to Mummy recently?' Alessandra asked him.

'Since when?'

'Since this morning?'

'No.'

Alessandra chewed on her lip.

'I'm getting a strong whiff of scepticism,' said Saul drily. 'But it's the truth. I did try to contact her this morning. But first of all the line was busy and after that the answering machine was switched on.'

'OK. I believe you.'

'Why do you ask?'

Alessandra saw María returning and waited until she had delivered Saul a tall green glass with swirls of bubbles trapped in its stem before saying, 'We had a rather inharmonious conversation earlier on. I said some things, she said some things . . .' She took the bottle from her father's hand and poured from it into the glass before him.

'Ah well,' he observed with a smile, 'the two of you were always able to produce a few sparks.'

She sighed. 'Yes, but now I wish I hadn't been so ready to scrape a match over her sandpaper.'

Saul gave a low chuckle. He raised his glass. 'I drink to your and Mummy's health my dear.'

'And yours,' Alessandra responded, taking a drink of her wine.

'So – what did you say to make your mother prickly?' he enquired.

'Oh! So it's all my fault is it?'

'I should have thought,' he said mildly, 'knowing and loving the two of you very well as I do, that there was tension and prickles on both sides.'

Alessandra smiled. 'That's a very charming and subtle way of attempting to provoke me into a full confession of my supposed sins Daddy. So don't think I didn't notice.'

Saul took a second sip from his glass. 'This is a most excellent and complex wine,' he said.

'It's from the harvest of five years ago. The weather in the early months of that year was especially good for that particular grape variety.'

'Which is?'

'Oh, I think you should guess!'

He took another sip, chewed a little, considered for a while. 'Tempranillo, I should think. A very traditional Spanish grape. On its own I think, not blended with any other variety.'

She made a little grimacing grin. 'Yes, of course you're right Daddy. As usual.'

'And is Mr Raphael Saventos who owns this apparently excellent winery a very traditional Spanish man?' Saul wondered.

'I think he probably is,' Alessandra responded with a cool admirably similar to that of her parent. 'Although, of course, I don't know so many other

146

Spanish men to compare him with.' She took off her dark glasses and faced Saul square on, eye to eye, and, she hoped, adult to adult.

'So what are your supposed sins?' he asked in a manner that implied nothing more than idle curiosity.

Alessandra felt prickles of sweat break out under her armpits. Slowly and carefully, without any distractions of emotion, either nervily defensive or aggressively assertive, she told Saul about Raphael's offer of sponsorship for her riding ambitions.

As she had expected, he took it all perfectly calmly. He said very little, although no doubt he thought much. His responses were mainly limited to the odd murmuring of, 'Ah' and 'I see'. But these were merely acknowledgements of her explanations rather than any judgemental comment. Alessandra knew that her father would already have formed a firm opinion on what she had told him. She also knew him to be a man of huge restraint, one who had no difficulty in saving up what he had to say for later.

'Interesting,' he concluded at last when she had finished her short exposition. He drained his glass, stood up and said, 'Well, perhaps now you should take me to see the horses of the Saventos stables.'

'You really want to?'

'Most certainly.'

'It's not compulsory Daddy,' she teased. 'I know you're not a true horse enthusiast.'

'Perhaps not. But I am an enthusiast of anything – be it on fours legs or not – which forms an integral part of the whole future of my daughter.'

As they stood together in the stables, Saul with his

head bowed slightly as he listened with meticulous attention to Alessandra's enthusiastic description of Ottavio's abilities and Titus's potential, the figure of Isabella suddenly appeared in the doorway. In the context of the warm dung-fragrant stables, with their wood planked walls and their carpeting of straw and grit, she projected a darkly dramatic image of glamour and artifice.

'Oh!' exclaimed Alessandra startled. She had never known Isabella to visit the stable block before. And looking at the older woman's pale lemon silk gown and delicate designer suede court shoes she didn't think it was a particularly good idea now. 'Señora Saventos!'

Isabella was staring at Saul. Her magnificent black eyes flashed with accusation as she looked from him to Alessandra. 'María is telling me that we have a – high up visitor,' she said in slow halting English. 'You should have come to tell me straight away,' she mouthed to Alessandra in a hissing Spanish aside.

Saul raised an eyebrow. Just a fraction. Alessandra noticed instantly, but suspected Isabella had not.

'Please be introducing me,' Isabella instructed Alessandra, seeming oblivious to the displeasure she might be causing the famous father by treating his daughter with the authoritative impatience she usually reserved for the servants.

Alessandra did as she was asked, her face calm and politely neutral.

Things now being on a satisfactorily formal footing, Isabella shifted into charming hostess mode. 'I am sorry but my son is being away in Lérida,' she told Saul, gesturing to him to follow her back to the house where she found her attempts to pin him down as a passive guest on one of the fat sofas in the drawing room scotched by his restless propensity for pacing and observing.

He made an immediate detection of Isabella's artistic endeavours, pausing to scrutinize one of her colourfully hectic canvases which hung on the wall opposite the windows, boldly signed with the intials I.S. 'This is your work Señora Saventos?' he enquired, swinging round to face her.

'Yes.' Isabella's breathless anxiety made her seem suddenly vulnerable.

'I must congratulate you,' Saul said. 'Painting is a very difficult and complex skill. I have never mananged to achieve anything in that field myself.'

Isabella licked her glossy crimson lips. She glanced up at Alessandra and there was a faint pleading in her proud eyes. *Please tell me what your father says about my work* she was asking.

Alessandra managed a translation, although she realized that converting her father's elegantly formal sentences into Spanish was going to stretch her to the full.

After an hour or so of stiffly polite conversation, conducted in conjunction with the consumption of María's offering of tiny cups of black coffee and sweet cakes, she found herself becoming exhausted. And longing and longing for Raphael to return.

At six, having accepted Isabella's pressing offer to stay for dinner, and then overnight, Saul departed to the guest bathroom suite to take a shower.

'Your father is a very great man and a supreme

149

artist,' Isabella observed to Alessandra before sweeping away to her own bathroom and further changes of attire. She made it sound as though she were the first person to form this opinion.

'Yes, he's a very special and talented person,' Alessandra agreed.

'And I gather that your mother too does a little orchestral work?'

'Yes.'

'But she is not, of course, of your father's stature?' Isabella raised her well plucked eyebrows.

Alessandra was suspicious, wondering what Isabella was getting at. 'My mother isn't as famous as my father,' she agreed. 'But she's a first rate musician.'

'Yes. I understand. But then,' continued Isabella with a creamy smile, 'there are many good musicians, but only a few great maestros.' Apparently well satisfied with this summing up, Isabella left the room with the smugness of one who knows how to drive home the winning dart with style.

Alessandra stood quite still, clenching her hands together tightly in order to stop herself pursuing Isabella and giving her a slap.

It seemed like a long long time until dinner. Alessandra went back onto the terrace. She sat down with her book for a while, and then, her concentration all gone, got up to stand looking down the long driveway, willing Raphael's car to appear.

But it was after seven when he returned and he went straight up to his room to change. She did not see him until the family had all gathered in the drawing room to take pre-dinner sherry and wine.

And then she could not talk to him freely because Isabella and Catriona were on their most horribly stiff and prescribed behaviour, with Isabella ensuring that Saul was manoeuvred into the position of centre stage as the fêted guest of honour. A role with which he was quite at ease and by no means averse to.

With Isabella taking firm command the conversation proceeded in uneasy jerks, swerving between English and Spanish spoken and understood with wildly fluctuating sophistication.

At dinner Alessandra found herself constantly glancing at Raphael, who was placed diagonally opposite her on the far side of the table. She wondered if Isabella had deliberately arranged the seating so that he was at as great a distance from her as possible. If she had, she could not have been more successful at making her, Alessandra, feel quite desperately bereft.

Dinner, however, was less excruciating than it might have been as Raphael, now taking the lead as host, appeared determined to keep the conversation as impersonal and genial as possible. In his beautiful, elegant and almost one hundred percent gramatically faultless English he engaged Saul in a brief discussion about international affairs, afterwards going on to say a little about the current politics of Spain. He then asked courteously about Saul's future musical plans.

Saul smiled. 'If you were to ask Alessandra that question she would say – "Daddy's plans! They usually don't vary from jet setting around the world from one concert hall to another bullying hapless orchestras to play the music of hapless dead composers." And, of course, she's quite right!'

Alessandra found herself watching Raphael anxiously, wondering how he would respond to this deadpan self-mockery. She saw that he looked amused. Then for a brief moment he turned to her and his eyes connected with hers. She sensed an expansion in her chest and a curious sighing sensation in the pit of her stomach.

Saul picked up his wine glass, swirling the wine and gazing at it with appreciative assessment. He turned to Isabella. 'This is most excellent wine Señora Saventos.' he said to her.

'Thank you,' Isabella smiled, much gratified. 'Raphael!' she commanded, reverting to Spanish, 'tell Señor Xavier something about our wines.'

Catriona let out a small suffering breath as though to say, 'Not again!'

'We live in a land of heroes and history,' Raphael told Saul in whimsical tones, 'and here at the Saventos winery we like to produce our wines with a blend of traditional techniques and modern innovation.' Having said this, he made a rapid translation for the benefit of his mother who made a regal gesture of agreement.

'We are very old family,' Isabella told Saul, who nodded with appropriate sensitivity.

'So,' he said, looking around and taking in all the Saventos family members, 'in your wine making, you have a commitment to both traditional techniques and novelty?'

Raphael nodded confirmation whilst Catriona looked as though she could hardly bear to endure another second spent in the discussion of wine.

'We like to stay in the very top of the techniques,' Isabella burst in on a triumphant rush, having spent the last minute or so painstakingly stitching the words together.

'*In the forefront,*' murmured Catriona, glancing at her parent with a look of supreme irritation and disdain.

For a moment Isabella gave an impression of such confusion and defencelessness that Alessandra felt true sympathy for her. She watched Isabella turn in appeal to Raphael who gave her a gently reassuring smile. It was a gesture of such kindness and sweetness that Alessandra felt herself grow warm and weak with love.

Saul took a leisurely swallow of his wine. 'Señora Saventos,' he told her graciously, 'whatever techniques you employ here at the Saventos winery must be truly excellent. The wine speaks for itself.'

In obedience to Isabella's decree, Alessandra and Saul were sent into the garden after dinner to admire the full moon and enjoy a few moments in private.

'The good señora will no doubt be hoping that I shall be making every effort to persuade you to come home,' Saul remarked, as they looked over the acres of vines, their leaves mysterious and spectral under a silvery light.

'Oh yes,' Alessandra agreed, turning from the view to look covertly back to the house, straining her eyes to catch a glimpse of Raphael.

'And will you?'

She looked up at him, her throat tender and full. 'No Daddy. I won't.'

He smiled. 'So then – there we are! The decision is made,' he said lightly. And before she could form a

153

reply he had dropped a swift kiss on her forehead and disappeared back into the house.

He would be in bed and asleep in around five minutes flat thought Alessandra, sleep being in the main at his beck and call, just like everyone and everything else.

She walked slowly up and down the terrace, recalling the night when she had seen Raphael pacing to and fro with his cigar. She went backwards and forwards, waiting, hoping. But he did not come to join her.

Lights began to go out in the house. Soon María would be wanting to lock the doors. Feeling bereft and at the same time trapped within the rigid conventions and proprieties of the Saventos household, she made her way up to her room resigning herself to having to wait until morning before seeing Raphael again.

Only seven hours to live through, she told herself sternly, alarmed to feel tears swelling once again behind her eyelids.

As she turned the brass knob leading to her room she felt the little silky hairs rising erect on the back of her neck. A shadow moved in one of the alcoves flanking the big casement window at the end of the corridor.

A figure moved forward. She felt an arm around her waist, a dry firm hand pressed over her mouth.

'*Amor*,' she heard whispered in her ear. 'I thought you were never coming.'

CHAPTER 12

Raphael pushed her ahead of him into the room. Closing the door behind him he turned her to face him. There was no need for him to draw her into his arms, for she was already folded against him, sighing with bliss. Besides the joy that began to filter into the whole of her being, she felt an overwhelming sense of relief, as though at last she had found the solution to some wonderful mystery which she had been seeking all of her life.

She let her body rest against him, whispering his name over and over, aware that her limbs were weakened and trembling.

'Say it again,' she whispered to him, her lips pressed against the fabric of his shirt, her eyes beginning to overflow with pent up emotion.

'*Amor!*' His breath was warm against her hair. '*Amor!*'

'Oh Raphael!' she breathed. 'Do you really love me? Do you?'

'Oh my dearest, most wonderful beautiful Alessandra. I have been mad for you. Almost crazy. Right from the start. Surely you must have known.'

'Yes I think I did know. But it was in that part of me where knowing is half dreaming and half wishing. Where you think it can't be really true, because it's too good to be true!'

'It is true,' he told her. 'I love you my most precious Alessandra.'

She sighed, pressing her face closer into his chest.

He reached down and placed his fingers under her chin, tilting up her face, so that he could look at her. 'Come now then *amor*. Let me have a kiss.'

His lips united with hers and she found herself swimming down to some soft warm heaven where all troubles floated away and rapture was the name of the boat she sailed in.

She thrust herself fiercely against him, wanting to blend herself into him. 'I feel a little crazy too,' she told him, 'crazy with happiness. I didn't understand just what was wrong before – until now.'

'Wrong?' He pushed her very gently away from him. His dark eyes beamed down at her in the moonlit room.

'Ever since we spoke that morning when we were sitting on the horses, looking down at the village.'

'Yes.'

'I felt I should have been so happy and pleased when you asked me if you could be my sponsor. But somehow I felt let down. All the rest of that day I felt hollow – and so very lonely.'

'I understood that only too well,' he said tenderly. 'My heart bled for you my love. But you must realize that I was in the same position. I felt such despair, because I could not make myself speak my real feelings. I asked you one question, my most precious *amor* but all the time I was wanting to ask you something quite different.'

She gave a low cry. 'Oh Raphael, what was it you were going to ask me?' *Were you going to ask if you could be my lover?* she thought wishing and wishing.

He paused, seeming unable to speak.

She reached up and kissed him again, this time very lightly her lips merely making a tingling brush over his. 'Perhaps you wanted to ask if you could be my lover,' she dared to say, understanding in a flood of joy that she could say whatever she liked to him, because the trust between them was so strong.

'No,' he said, and his voice was almost harsh.

She gave a small gasp and drew back.

He pulled her to him again. 'No! I was going to ask you to be my wife.'

She looked at him, her eyes enormous. As the incredible words sank into her consciousness, so happiness washed slowly and heavily through her. She felt a huge release from all the tensions of the past days since she had come to know this marvellous man. And after that she felt a sensation of miraculous blossoming, as though she were a curled bud, dropped into gently nurturing water, her petals unfolding, reaching up and swelling out to form a great, lush beautiful bloom. 'If you had asked me that question on that morning,' she told him, her voice as thick and mellow as honey, 'I would have said yes without a moment's hesitation.' She undid a button of his shirt and slipped her hand inside, so that he released a small groan. 'And I *do* say yes now.'

He was very still, holding her near him. He said,

'Do you really want to take me on my love? Me and my troubled family – and Spain?'

'Yes,' she said, bending her head and kissing the smooth warm skin of his chest. 'Yes, yes, yes.' She noted that he had asked if she *wanted* to take on all these things, not if she simply felt able to. Love swirled through her in a fresh swooping wave. She felt his hands stroking her plait, luxuriating in its silky plumpness. His fingers teased the skin of her neck and she drew in a sharp breath, suddenly understanding the meaning of animal desire. She said to him, suddenly mischievous, 'I don't expect you to believe this, but I've never really kissed a man before. In fact where men are concerned I'm a complete novice.'

He gave a grunt of approval and deep satisfaction. 'I had guessed. You have a purity about you that is rare in modern young women.'

'I shall need careful handling,' she murmured, a little dart of fear springing up, then dying like the fading sparks of a sky rocket. She could never have anything to fear from Raphael.

'You shall have it,' he said, sliding his hands softly down her back and over her hips. Tiny points of electricity sparked her skin beneath her clothes where he touched. 'But I don't want you to be my mistress. I want you to have all the respect, and all the honour, that is due to you for your most pure and beautiful code of living. When we make love, my sweetest *amor*, when your virginity is taken, it will be in the solemnity of the marriage bed.'

'Oh Raphael,' she breathed. 'That sounds like sheer poetry – and it simply makes me long for you more.' She stared up at him. 'Now I've met you,' she told him with faint irony, 'I'm not sure if I can stay as pure as you'd like to think of me.' She felt herself throbbing and opening up for him, the blood thundering hot in her veins.

'We need not wait,' he said, stroking her face. 'We can arrange a simple civic ceremony in just a few weeks, days possibly.'

Excitement surged up. To be married to Raphael without any waiting. To lie in his bed and have him make love to her.

'I think I should speak to your father in the morning before he leaves,' Raphael insisted quietly, as though she needed some further persuasion.

Alessandra gave a dry laugh. 'Oh I can just hear the two of you. Chewing the fat over me in my absence. And both of you behaving so correctly and formally. You'll be so traditional and polite. Will you be demanding that I'm handed over to you with a hefty dowry in tow?'

'Ah, you are making a mockery of me!' He tightened his finger around the top of her arms.

'No, never.' She tilted her face up to him. 'But I do like to see the droll side of things.'

'I can see,' he said, 'that you are going to need some very stern handling.' He pulled her to him and this time his kisses were heated and full of demands.

As they clung together, their lips meeting ferociously, their hands roaming over each other, Alessandra began to understand how love-making might be as energy releasing and, perhaps, even as violent as physical combat. How it could be a kind of ecstatic, seething struggle – not for supremacy but in pursuit of the ultimate fusion and rapture that can be created between two people.

After a considerable time, watched by an impartial moon from the open casement, Raphael lifted her into his arms and laid her gently on the bed. He stood up, looking down at her. And then he bent to give her one last sweet good-night kiss, before slipping softly through the door.

'I take it,' Saul said to Alessandra, carefully skinning a white peach, 'that you understand fully what you're doing in accepting Raphael's offer of sponsorship.'

Alessandra, dreamily crumbling a roll onto her plate and unable to eat a single mouthful of breakfast, murmured that she did.

'I expect that you and Raphael have discussed the legal implications of this plan,' he continued, popping a section of peach into his mouth. 'And I should advise you to consult our own lawyers in London, and not leave everything to the legal advisors here.'

'Mmm,' said Alessandra.

Saul took a sip of black coffee. His steely eyes viewed his daughter with speculation. 'I have to say that, whilst I have a great admiration for Saventos and his winery, I really do think I should warn you against rushing into any sort of business arrangement with him without very careful thought and preparation.'

'Yes,' she agreed.

'Alessandra!' he said sharply. 'Listen to me. You're a girl on your own in a strange country. You've known this man no more than a few weeks. Caution my dear! Caution!'

Her eyes slanted towards him. 'So what are the dangers involved? What's on your mind Daddy?'

'The usual. Fear of your being short-changed, cheated, manipulated, exploited.' He held up a hand to silence her impending protest. 'Listen to me darling. I'm not suggesting that Saventos would do any of these things. But to put oneself in the hands of a very rich, very powerful man, can be potentially hazardous.'

'I wonder what Mummy would say to that,' Alessandra enquired thoughtfully, shooting her father a level look. 'Isn't that rather what she did? With you?'

Saul pressed his lips together. 'It was for love,' he said simply. 'It was not a business arrangement.' His voice was perfectly calm, but she saw the glint of warning in his eyes. 'For love,' he repeated half to himself.

'Daddy,' she said, relishing the thought of the ace up her sleeve, pausing just a fraction of a second to savour the moment before she played it. 'I should have told you this sooner – but it's love for me too. Raphael has asked me to marry him.'

Saul's hand was still for a moment as he raised another slice of peach to his mouth. He placed it between his lips, chewed briefly and then swallowed. He picked up his coffee cup. 'And you said yes?'

'Yes.'

He took a sip, carefully replaced his cup on the saucer. 'To make a longstanding emotional commitment to another person is, of course, the most important, most serious decision any person has to make in a lifetime,' he observed without drama. 'You do, of course, appreciate that?'

'You rushed headlong into a commitment with Mummy from what I've heard,' Alessandra countered, daring to bring out into the open things she had long pondered on. 'Dropped everything to be with her.'

Saul gave a wry smile, seemingly unperturbed. 'I was forty,' he said with soft emphasis.

'Yes. And she was eighteen. Just as "impetuous" as me apparently. And three years younger.'

'Yes.'

'And it wasn't marriage.'

'No.'

'So you can't really object can you Daddy?'

'Oh no,' he agreed. 'I haven't an argumental leg to stand on. Besides which you're of age, free to do what you wish.'

She paused, waiting.

He said, 'I can only speak for myself. You must talk this over with Mummy as well.'

'What are your reservations then?' Alessandra demanded.

'Most likely simply a parent's shock when they realize that the little child they once knew has grown up,' he said evenly. He knew that voicing the other things that concerned him: Alessandra's readiness to tie herself to a foreign culture, maybe a new religion, but most of all to this clearly tortured Spanish family, would be of no avail. She would do what she wanted. And indeed that was right. Who was he to say what might or might not work out for her? Even though she was his daughter and he knew her better than nearly any other human being in the world. He had learned through the years that one could not even say with any certainty what was good for oneself.

162

'If this is what you really want, I give you my full blessing,' he said eventually.

'Oh Daddy,' she responded in a great warm rush of feeling, 'you can't possibly imagine how much I adore him, I'm so desperately in love.'

'Ah,' he cautioned, 'I can indeed imagine. I was – I am – just as in love with your mother.'

'He calls me *amor*,' she whispered, her face rapt.

He considered, then gave a sigh. 'That does seem to relegate "darling" to the doldrums,' he commented drily.

'Raphael would like to – speak to you before you go,' she said.

Saul nodded. A small smile of irony curved his lips. 'Am I ready for this? The role of the heavy, serious father. Must I demand to know his prospects – given that I already know his intentions?'

Alessandra grinned. 'How would I know? This is strictly men's talk isn't it?'

Saul was highly impressed with the winery. He told Raphael that in England such a place would already have been elevated to the status of a national monument. 'We're struggling you see with our productive industries. The old stalwarts like mining and car building are either dead or dying. But this . . .' He waved an arm, taking in the architecture, the machinery, the raw produce from the grapes fermenting in the great steel vats, 'this is production and export on an impressive scale.'

'Thank you,' said Raphael simply. 'We are always seeking for ways to develop and expand. Until recently we only used the traditional Spanish grapes, but now I am adding other grape varieties to our production.'

'Another example of your philosophy of fusing the old and the new,' said Saul.

'Yes,' said Raphael smiling. 'But I must not bore you with talking endlessly about wine. I must speak to you about Alessandra.'

'Yes. She is very special,' Saul said softly, looking away from Raphael and gazing up at the winery's astoundingly complex roof structure.

'She has told you that I've asked her to marry me?' His voice though courteous was full of pride and determination.

'Yes – she has.'

'And do I have your – sanction?'

Saul felt himself suddenly to be in an absurd situation, being asked to make some kind of judgement on this clearly exceptional and deeply worthy man. He felt that he was being placed fair and square in the role of heavy father. It was a role he had never aimed for, nor was it one he wanted to take on. And yet Alessandra's happiness was so very precious to him.

'My wife and I have thought a good deal about Alessandra's future through the years,' he said eventually. 'We simply want her to be fulfilled and to experience her allotted portion of life's joy.'

'You think I cannot give her that?'

'I'm not saying that Raphael.'

'No, but you are giving me a feeling that you are uncertain about it.'

Saul slowly shook his head.

'You are an Englishman,' said Raphael, his dark eyes glowing. 'I think perhaps I am just a foreigner to you. The English do not like foreigners. They do not really trust them . . .'

'Sadly I have to agree with you,' Saul admitted. 'As a general rule. But I hope I'm not guilty of prejudice as far as you yourself are concerned and in fact, I don't believe that I am.'

'I may be a foreigner,' said Raphael with great dignity, 'but I am also a human being. Have you warned Alessandra against me?'

Saul was becoming more impressed by the minute. He realized that this man loved Alessandra with a passion maybe equalling his own raging fervency for Tara when he had first come to know her. 'I've made one or two remarks about the difficulties of two cultures coming together. All the attendant problems.'

'Ah yes.' Again the dark eyes glowed. 'But you see, despite our different nationalities, our human instincts are so perfectly matched. Alessandra is everything in a person that I find it natural to love. And I know that for her I am the same.'

Saul looked hard at him, and was not surprised to find that he did not flinch.

'And yes,' Raphael continued, driving his hands into his trouser pockets, 'I know that there are difficulties to overcome. I have told her quite openly that my family is not easy. That here in rural Spain we have a liking for battles and drama.'

Saul bowed his head for a moment, recalling the two women in the dining room the night before, considering the worm of envy and hostility that could eat with disastrous consequence into the apple of Raphael's and Alessandra's undoubted love for each other.

'I want to marry Alessandra as soon as possible,' Raphael said quietly. 'We could have a civil service within the next few weeks. And afterwards there could be a blessing in churches both here in Spain and in England.'

Saul's heart took a huge plunge. Suddenly he was faced with the thought of losing Alessandra. His child had grown into a woman, and the love that had grown with her was now to be transferred to another man. All quite natural, of course, what a father would expect and wish for. And all, at this stage, quite inevitable. Bridges had been crossed.

For a fleeting moment he recalled the terrifying moments of an early morning in a Cornish village years ago. Unthinkable deeds had been perpetrated there, driven by the devils of rage and revenge. In his ears he heard the heart-wrenching sounds of the little Alessandra screaming in misery and bewilderment. He recalled his desperate search for her, how when he had at last found her she had held out her round baby arms to him. 'Daddy, daddy . . .' He recalled his heart swelling with such love it caused him physical pain.

Slowly he reached out, took Raphael's hand and shook it warmly. 'As long as you take the very greatest care of my daughter,' he said, with just a hint of silky warning, 'then you do indeed have my sanction, and my most sincere blessing.'

Their eyes met briefly, sparked with a complex of powerful emotions.

Saul walked out of the dimness of the winery into the clanging brilliance of the sunlight. Although it was

166

not yet eleven, and he had enjoyed a perfect night's sleep, his limbs felt heavy and exhausted.

He knew that these feelings would pass. He would drive away from the winery and, as he neared the next orchestral rehearsal, opened the score of a Brahms symphony or a Beethoven piano concerto, so he would be put to rights again. More or less.

But how the hell was he going to convince Tara?

Alessandra watched the lean figure descend the steps from the winery. She got up and went to meet him, her love for him huge. It had always been a force in her life, but at this moment her pulsing love for Raphael was spilling over onto every creature on earth, creating new sensations, intensifying those already established.

Saul took her arm in his. 'You can breathe easily again. We didn't come to blows. He's not lying on the winery floor with his blood leaking out like wine from a shattered bottle.'

'Ooh!' Alessandra winced.

'I hadn't realized it was all to happen so soon,' he commented non-committally.

'We need to be together,' she said.

'Yes.' He paused. 'When will you speak to Mummy?'

'Later. As soon as you've gone.'

'Very well.'

She pressed his arm. 'Daddy, it'll be all right. Truly. You mustn't worry about me. I'm so very very happy.'

'Mmm.'

'Don't be like that Daddy. I know you see me as some kind of exile, buried here in the Spanish countryside. But you see I'm beginning to love Spain – because it's the country of the man I love.'

Saul smiled. On no account would he let her see how this kind of speech from a beloved only daughter could carve gasping sighing wounds.

She was insistent. 'Say you like him too. Please. Say that you're pleased.'

He laughed. 'You always knew how to get your own way. I've been wrapped around your little finger all these years.'

'Nonsense. Now say it!'

'I wish you all the happiness you could wish darling. And, truly, I think Raphael is a most worthy consort – even for you.' He wrapped an arm around her shoulders, pressing hard, instructing his muscles to communicate nothing but joy on her behalf, on no account to give anything away of his gnawing reservations.

As he prepared to leave, having shaken hands regally with all the family, Alessandra followed him to the car and leaned in to give him a final kiss. 'Off you go – jetting around the world again,' she teased.

'Good-bye my darling.' He ignited the engine. 'Oh, and one last thing,' he said, swivelling his eyes towards the house, 'If you ever feel the need to watch your back, then I should look out for the sister rather than the mother.'

CHAPTER 13

Strolling back from the stables later that day Alessandra heard a long electrifying shriek come from the house. Then another, and another. A powerful but distorted song of rage and fury, as though some diva soprano had finally gone mad on stage.

Alessandra understood immediately what was going on. Raphael was telling Isabella of their marriage plans. And Isabella was clearly not pleased.

She felt a twinge of alarm. She had been warned that there would be drama and hysterics, but this seemed frighteningly serious – over the edge.

Sitting on the terrace in the late afternoon sun, Alessandra waited for Raphael to emerge from his mother's onslaught. She tried to imagine him. Would he be standing, head bowed and proud and silent, simply allowing the screams to rain down on him – waiting until the tempest gradually blew itself out? Or would he be quietly remonstrating in that stern manner he could adopt when he was displeased? Whatever his tactics, she was confident that Raphael would know better than anyone how to deal with his histrionic parent.

Even so a grub of unease crawled into her guts, wriggling itself insidiously.

At last all went quiet. Raphael emerged from the house, his face dark. He came to sit beside her. He said nothing for a while, just let out a long shuddering sigh.

Alessandra leaned over and wove her fingers through his. She waited.

'I am afraid she is angry,' he said.

Alessandra raised her eyebrows. 'I had rather gathered that.' She tightened her fingers around his. 'Oh Raphael, I'm so sorry.'

'It will pass,' he said. 'She is so very *Spanish* you see. She knows all too well how to quarrel.'

What has she against me? Alessandra found herself asking silently, a tiny spark of anger lighting and then dying. 'Maybe being Spanish and knowing how to rant and rage and get all your feelings out in the open is better than the way we English do things,' she said, tilting her chin up and aiming to sound steady and reasonable.

'And how do you English do it?' he asked tenderly.

'We try very hard not *do* anything if we can help it. That's the whole point you see. We've got a real hang up about expressing our feelings. We hide them behind a wall of politeness. I suppose basically we're afraid of our feelings, ashamed to admit having them at all.' She glanced at him. 'That's rather stupid isn't it? I suppose it makes us feel safe to be so cool and calm. But then sometimes, when the cork pops out of the bottle, things can be even more dangerous . . .' Her lips curved in a slow smile of irony.

170

'Oh my darling Alessandra, what a lovely speech,' he said in a low rush of passion. 'And how I love you. More and more with every hour that goes by.' He gave another sigh. He didn't seem able to stop sighing. 'But I'm afraid that even though my mother is able to face up to her feelings and scream out loud, it does not mean that all will instantly be well.'

'Isn't there always sunshine after a storm?' Alessandra said, stretching out her legs in front of her, and refusing to be drawn into his dark mood of quiet despair. 'It's a kind of global concept, from when time began. Think of that lovely passage in Beethoven's *Pastoral Symphony*. You can almost feel the sun coming out, the clouds blowing over, the thunder rolling gently away.'

Another sigh.

'What was the problem for your mother?' she asked gently. 'When you told her about you and me?'

'I think she simply can't face up to the fact that her son has finally decided to be married. You see she has had me for thirty-two years as her son. She has always seen herself as being the first woman in my life. And now she must step down from her pedestal.'

Alessandra snorted. 'Oh, come on Raphael! I can't take that on. It sounds like something out of a seventeenth century history book!'

For a moment his eyes flashed. 'I told you before,' he said, his voice sharp, 'in these pockets of rural Spain, the emotions of centuries long gone by are still present, stalking the terraces and the mountains.'

'Nothing but ghosts!' said Alessandra flatly.

'But ghosts which still walk.'

171

'Oh dear!' She just couldn't take this seriously.

'You mustn't make light of it, Alessandra,' he warned. 'I am afraid there are difficult times ahead for us.' He paused. 'Perhaps you are feeling that you would like to change your mind.'

She turned on him, suddenly angry herself. 'Never! And you don't really mean that do you? Raphael! How could you dare to suggest that I might run out on you just because things aren't flowing nice and smoothly? How dare you even think that, after what we told each other last night, what it felt like when we touched. Surely when we held each other you must have known that I was yours for ever.'

'Oh my beautiful *amor*. I think if you were to leave me I would die very slowly of a damaged heart. But I would hate to imprison you in a cage of . . .'

'Yes?'

'Oh,' he covered his eyes with his hand, 'I don't know how to tell you what I feel. But look at us now! Don't you see what's happening. Because of my mother, already we are in a kind of conflict you and me.'

'No!'

'Yes. A little so anyway. My darling Alessandra I simply could not bear to put you through anything at all that was unpleasant to you, unless you truly wanted me so much that you were certain you could bear it.'

She stared at him. 'Well, I do want you that much,' she said flatly, her voice fierce with the power of her feelings.

She got up and placed herself on his lap. Then,

unheeding of any of the watching eyes from either the house or the winery, she bent her head and pressed her lips on his with some force. She felt his answering response as though a bolt of high voltage electicity had passed through him.

Moments passed and then suddenly Ferdinand came running up, shouting and gesturing excitedly. Alessandra levered herself from Raphael's knee with great dignity, having the thought that now she was about to become the mistress of the Saventos estate perhaps she might need to gather together the armoury of her English reserve – at least in public!

She beamed a faintly steely glance at Ferdinand whom she had come to like and respect greatly; just a little warning to let him know she expected the same from him.

'Señorita Xavier,' he responded with gravity, acknowledging her with a courteous bow of his head. He then turned to Raphael and started to gabble in agitated Spanish at break-neck speed.

Alessandra caught only a few words. She gathered there were problems connected with the winery. Murmuring to Raphael that she would 'leave him to it' she went off to the stables to check on the horses.

As she was giving Titus's mane an extra brush, whilst at the same time working out a fresh schooling programme for him in her head, wondering if he was ready for her to put him round a five-foot-six course yet, Ferdinand burst into the stables. He seemed to be in an even greater flurry of agitated anticipation than before. And still gabbling away at an alarming rate.

'If we're going to speak in Spanish you'll have to slow down,' Alessandra told him, illuminating her words with appropriate gestures.

'No. No. You are understanding in Spanish fast, fast,' protested Ferdinand.

'Not everything,' she smiled, putting her brushes back in the box and letting herself out of Titus's stall. 'So, slow, slow please.'

Controlling himself with obvious difficulty, Ferdinand managed to convey to her that a buyer from a big chain of UK supermarkets had turned up to talk to Raphael about a potentially huge order for wine.

'Turned up!' echoed Alessandra. 'Don't these people make appointments?'

'Yes, yes,' said Ferdinand gleefully. 'She should have come next week. She's made a mistake. But Señor Saventos was very charming and of course he didn't send her away, even though he is very busy with other things.' Here, he broke off and looked at Alessandra meaningfully. 'Well of course a businessman like Señor Saventos wouldn't be so stupid as to tell her to go. She might not come back!'

'Quite,' agreed Alessandra. She was beginning to feel as excited as Ferdinand.

'Yes. And she's a very attractive lady.' Ferdinand made gestures indicative of sexy feminine curves in the air and rolled his eyes.

'Really.'

'We could get a big, big order. Everyone could be rich! Señor Saventos gives good bonuses you know. So if he sells a lot, we get a lot.' Ferdinand paused, frowning a little. 'Oh, but I'm talking too much. Women don't like to hear all about business matters.'

'This one does,' Alessandra assured him. 'Go on.'

'You see Señorita Xavier, Señor Saventos is an old country man of Spain but he is modern too. He knows about the unions and he understands the workers too. He would never try to pay people less than the minimum wage. He is a good boss, because he respects us.'

'Yes. I can see that,' said Alessandra, her heart throbbing with warmth and pride as she thought of Raphael becoming ever more alert to the depth of his sensitivity and feeling for social justice.

'Not like Señor Emilio,' added Ferdinand, his eyes closing to slits, his features twisting into a grimace of dislike. 'If he got his way he would treat us all like dirt. I tell you señorita, it would make him very happy to grind us all under the wheels of his fancy cars just like the French aristocrats used to crush the peasants under the wheels of their carriages before the revolution.'

'Really,' said Alessandra, affecting polite interest, whilst at the same time carefully filing away that interesting viewpoint in her mind. She had almost forgotten about Emilio. Now she was warned with a little jolt that there was yet another hurdle in store to be cleared.

'In fact, Señor Saventos is a very splendid man altogether,' Ferdinand announced brightly.

'Yes, he is.' Alessandra smiled. She realized that Ferdinand was intrigued with the scene of passion he had witnessed earlier and was fishing for more information. But she had no intention of passing any on. Not until she and Raphael had had the chance to discuss together in what way the announcement to the staff should be handled.

She felt a keen anticipation of all that she and Raphael would share together, pooling their ideas not only on the intimacy of love, but on the day to day running of their lives, and this great wine business which Raphael had kept insisting would soon become hers as well as his. She saw them together through the years, sharing everything, holding nothing back from each other.

'And now,' said Ferdinand, 'I must go and tell Señora Saventos about our visitor.' He gave Alessandra a slow wickedly conspiratorial wink. 'I shall get in big trouble if I don't keep the Señora informed.'

Alessandra, watching him go, had the impression she herself might be in big trouble with Isabella for being the one Ferdinand had decided to inform first. She recalled Raphael's words about his mother having to step down from her pedestal. And suddenly neither the words nor the idea seemed as fanciful and anachronistic as she had first thought.

She left the stables and went back to her favourite spot on the terrace. She sat for a while, thinking things through, looking out over the vines and then watching the sky where, for the first time since she had been in Spain, there were clouds banking up from the east. As she watched they swelled with breathtaking speed, joining together to form a lowering grey lid which fastened itself down over the house and the surrounding land. She felt the first warm fat drop of rain on her cheek. And then, without warning, there was a torrent; huge heavy drops falling around her like exploding eggs, bouncing up from the terrace. Low stormy rumbles sounded in the distance.

Seeking the shelter of the house, she found herself in immediate confrontation with Isabella, who had clearly been waiting for her, and was looking extremely beady.

'Come with me,' Isabella snapped, walking on purposefully ahead in the direction of her studio.

In other circumstances, with other people, Alessandra would have laughingly protested to find herself ordered about in such a high-handed manner. With Isabella, on this thunderous afternoon, she decided the best form of response was a quiet acceptance of the older woman's agitation and anxiety. She followed Isabella to her studio, keeping outwardly calm and in no way permitting herself to fall into the trap of trotting along dog-like in order to keep up with her commander's frantic footsteps.

Walking into the studio some seconds after Isabella had arrived there, Alessandra paused, looking into her future mother-in-law's eyes with a steady level gaze.

Isabella's silent fury swirled around the room. Beyond the windows the outer storm was lashing itself into a commensurate state of rage. Rain whipped around the winery, vaulting off the roof and streaming down the walls in glistening ropes.

'We shall speak in my language,' Isabella announced tersely in Spanish. 'I will speak slowly, so that you can understand me.'

'Very well. I'll do my best,' said Alessandra softly – in English. 'I'll speak slowly too.'

'You are meddling in things you don't understand,' Isabella began.

Alessandra was outraged. 'I beg your pardon?'

'You come here from England. You know nothing of my son, you know nothing of Spain and now, after just a few weeks, you have trapped him into asking you to be his wife.'

'Señora Saventos,' Alessandra said, with all the soft menace of her father's silkiest and most dangerous tones, 'if you were not the mother of my future husband and therefore deserving of my consideration and a little respect, I should walk out of this room and refuse to speak to you.' She was not sure if Isabella understood all of this, and maybe that was no bad thing. She said quietly in Spanish, 'Raphael asked me to marry him. I did not trap him.'

'You have no understanding of our family,' Isabella said. 'We have suffered terrible tragedies. Things you could not begin to imagine . . .'

'Yes I can imagine. And I've heard about the tragic death of your husband and your son. And I'm very very sorry,' said Alessandra, interrupting. 'But those aren't reasons for me not to marry Raphael.' She made a halting translation into Spanish.

'Ach!' Isabella exclaimed. 'You know nothing, *nothing*!'

'Then tell me what it is I should know!'

Isabella stared at her, astounded at her calmness and her boldness to challenge. 'You should know,' she said, her eyes flaring, 'that a marriage between you and Raphael is out of the question.'

'Why?' She reached out and held onto the arms of a chair, finding that her limbs were trembling.

'Because here in Spain, we are very proud and very strict. We don't know about English ways. We don't want to know. And, tell me this; how could you ever be a good wife to my son, when you know nothing of our Spanish ways?'

'I shall be a good wife to your son, because I love him,' Alessandra said very slowly and clearly. 'And I agree with you that Spain is old fashioned in some ways and different from how we are in England, but once I'm married to Raphael it will become partly my country too. And our children will be half Spanish and half English.'

Isabella drew in a deep theatrical breath and closed her eyes briefly. Outside the windows the storm was reaching its climax, the thunder shaking the house, the sky a livid deep blue sparking with blinding silver flashes. 'You are young,' she said eventually, 'you think that you have all the answers to making a perfect life. But you are mistaken.'

Alessandra let a pause fall. 'Why don't you like me?' she demanded evenly. 'What is it about me that makes me unsuitable as a wife for your son?'

Isabella flushed dark red.

'Is it because I'm not Spanish? Is that it? Is that *all*?' In the firm set of her face, Alessandra made it clear that she was going to have no truck whatsoever with objections on the grounds of prejudice and an unreasonable hatred of all things foreign.

Isabella turned away from her, then swung back. 'And have you thought about Emilio? How will he react to this ridiculous whim of Raphael's?'

'Whim? Raphael and I love each other,' Alessandra burst out, mystified and cruelly hurt.

'After a few short weeks! How can you know?'

'I can't say. But we just can,' said Alessandra. 'And we *do* know. It wouldn't make any difference if years and years went by. We'd still feel exactly the same.'

'You come here and steal Emilio's horses . . .'

'No! I won't have that. I worked with the horses at Raphael's request. You should apologize Señora!' Alessandra unclenched her fingers from the back of the chair and straightened her spine. Anger thudded through her.

'Very well,' Isabella agreed, relenting a little. 'I made a mistake to use the word steal. But for Emilio, to have you come here and take over his horses was like a torture. Raphael should never have done that to him.'

'Emilio deserved it. He ill treated his horses. He forfeited the right to work them. And in any case, they're Raphael's horses aren't they?' Alessandra found herself in full spate, like the rain coursing down the windows. She recognized that she was less in control of herself than she would have wished, but her feelings of honour and fair play had been roused. There was no way she would allow herself to be abused and denigrated, not even by a formidable Spanish dowager who was the mother of the man she adored.

'When Emilio found out that you had been riding his horse and that you were coming here, he was so beside himself and so jealous, do you know what he did? He went down into the vineyard and set fire to some of the new vines. That was how crazy and full of anger he felt.'

Alessandra was horrified. 'Then he should learn some self-discipline,' she said stiffly.

Isabella shook her head. 'You have no idea about Emilio or his feelings. That is what I meant before. You – you *English* Alessandra, have no understanding at all of the powerful feelings in this family. We are part of a great tradition, shared by all the old families in Spain.' She raised her head, a proud queen of her dynasty and her domain. 'Our heritage is enormous, like the vast fields surrounding our winery. Our lives are like great ancient tapestries. They are woven from all of our struggles, all of our tragedies. They are in our hearts and souls and in our blood. You could never ever feel all of that.'

'Maybe not. But I belong to a tapestry of my own,' said Alessandra with stubborn determination and pride. Good grief, would this endless exhortation on the magnificence of Spain, on its intransigent declaration never to let any foreigner share its great passions and fires and darknesses, never stop? It seemed to go on and on, repeating its insistent theme like one of her father's treasured vinyl discs that had developed a hairline crack.

Yet, even though the theme had been constantly rammed down her throat, it was not one which repelled her. Alessandra had a sharp flash of sudden insight into her growing desire to be admitted to the mysterious fortress of Spain's secrets, even though that jealously guarded palace might be fraught with all kinds of danger.

She looked beyond the silently raging Isabella to the world outside the window, the glorious countryside of unspoiled Spain. The rain had stopped and everything glistened. Already a pale sun was probing translucent silver and gold fingers through the clouds. The blue of the sky was re-establishing itself, the birds had started to sing, and the world was at peace again.

'Señora Saventos,' she said calmly and very slowly, switching once again into her own language. 'Your son, Raphael Godeval Saventos has asked me to be his wife. I have agreed and my father has given us his blessing.' She paused. 'Do you understand?'

Isabella raised her head, and Alessandra knew that her meaning had been followed quite clearly. 'So don't think that I'm prepared to be spoken to like a servant who's displeased you,' she added. 'And don't think either that I shall be packing my bags and running away back to England.'

Isabella's face was shaken by a wave of overwhelming emotion. As Alessandra turned to leave, she called out: 'Wait! You think you know everything don't you? You think you have an answer to everything I say! You foolish girl.'

Alessandra turned back. 'What now?' she demanded harshly.

'You will never have Raphael's undivided love,' Isabella said with slow meaningfulness. 'Never.'

Alessandra pondered the words. Her limbs felt weak again. A coldness stole through her. She saw a gleam of triumph in Isabella's eyes, the exultation of a woman who holds a trump card higher than an ace.

'Can you guess why?' Isabella asked, her bracelets jingling softly as her hands twitched in agitation.

Alessandra breathed deeply. 'I don't like guessing games,' she said with disdain.

'There is another woman in his life,' Isabella said, allowing the words to roll around her mouth as though she were savouring a flavorous fleshy peach stone before finally spitting it out.

182

Alessandra stared. Her world rocked. 'I don't believe it.'

Isabella gave a dry laugh. 'Ask him. I am surprised he hasn't told you.'

'I don't believe you,' Alessandra repeated.

Isabella merely raised her very beautifully arched brows. 'Simply ask him. Or Catriona. Or Emilio.'

Alessandra found herself taking in tiny rapid breaths, almost panting. She forced her mind to work. 'He may have had love affairs,' she protested. 'That's only natural for a man of his age.'

'Yes,' Isabella agreed in syrupy tones. 'Only natural.'

'I didn't expect that he would have been living here like a monk,' Alessandra continued shortly.

'Certainly not,' said Isabella.

'So where is she, this woman?'

Isabella shrugged, smiling. 'She lives in Granada.'

'That's miles away from here.'

'Yes. And what difference does that make? One can love someone who is at the other end of the world.'

Alessandra felt that she had tumbled over a cliff edge into the waters of a roaring torrent. One couldn't think whilst being bombarded with sensation as she now was. The only thing to do was find some calmer clearer waters in which to breathe more freely.

Once again she made her way to the door. She turned. 'You're confusing the past and the present,' she told the contemptuously gloating Isabella. 'The woman you're talking about is in the past. But *I*,' she announced with strong clear determination, 'am in the present.'

CHAPTER 14

Raphael sat on Alessandra's bed and gently pulled back the sheet from her face and shoulders. She had wrapped herself in the bleached white fabric like a mummy in a tomb. Now, as she felt herself disturbed, she began to emerge from sleep. Her eyes felt heavy and drugged and it seemed that in waking she was having to swim up from the very depths of her unconscious mind.

He touched her neck and her shoulders with tender fingers and then bent down to her and kissed her forehead.

Alessandra blinked, trying to regain a grasp on reality after having fallen into such a deep sleep.

'You have had a long siesta my darling,' said Raphael, watching her with concerned eyes, guessing that her uncharacteristic retreat to bed in the late afternoon must have been prompted by some traumatic event.

Alessandra stared at him, allowing his beloved face to stamp out the image of her dream: Isabella in her studio, stabbing with her brushes, making her bracelets clash furiously together as she frantically slashed great swathes of blood-red anger onto her canvases.

'You're not ill *amor*?' he said with a touch of alarm, seeing such raw distress on her face.

She shook her head. 'I was suddenly just so very tired. It's probably the heat, I've still to get used to it.' His strong solid presence brought a calm joy stealing into her. 'Have you finished your business meeting?' she asked.

'Yes.'

Alessandra raised herself on one elbow. 'So tell me! What happened?'

'We have the prospect of a very big order, extending over an initial period of two years, with an option for further business after that.'

'That's wonderful news!' She had the same sense of sparkling excitement that came with a win at a big show-jumping event. 'Did she try to screw you down to a cut-throat price?' she asked curiously.

'Yes – she tried. I resisted. We came to a compromise.' He smiled. 'How do you know about such things *amor*? This "screwing down"? Tell me that mmm?'

'I read the newspapers. I like to know what goes on in the world outside horses and music. And I want to learn all about your wine business.'

'Yes.' He stroked her cheek. 'And it gives me great pleasure that you do. And I shall do all I can to teach you.'

She stretched her arms and flexed the muscles of her shoulders, fully awake now, the dream banished. 'Raphael,' she said slowly, 'I may be a virgin, but I'm no innocent. There are quite a lot of "worldly" things that I know about.' She took a long breath and let it out slowly.

Her look and the twist of her smile held a faint challenge that he was instantly aware of. 'I am sorry darling, I don't quite follow what you're trying to tell me.'

She stared at him, wondering how to broach the delicate issue that burned in her mind.

'You are angry with me,' he said softly, and his brow creased.

She shook her head, then looked swiftly away from him.

'Alessandra,' he insisted, giving her arm a little shake. 'What is it you want to tell me? Something is very wrong.'

There was a pause.

'Is it my mother?' he demanded. 'Has she been upsetting you?'

'You could say that. Yes.'

He closed his eyes. 'I knew this would happen. She will have said cruel things to you, no doubt.'

'Yes.'

'Alessandra, my darling – I am so sorry. But when she gets to know you better . . .'

'Raphael, it's not so much what your mother said about me that's worrying, it's what she said about *you*.' Alessandra wriggled herself into a sitting position. The sheet slipped down over the roundness of her full breasts, leaving them exposed. She looked down at herself and then at Raphael. As their glance locked and held, a bolt of desire reminiscent of the violence of the rain and thunderstorm earlier darted between them. Reining in her passion, naked and proud, she faced him head on with her challenge.

His eyes glittered like jet. 'What did she tell you?' he asked, and his face was hard and austere.

'That there is another woman you love.' The words fell into the silence like flinty stones.

His head jerked around. 'No!'

She stared at him. She could sense his silent fury.

'No!' He was shouting now. 'How could she fill your head with lies like this?'

Alessandra put her hand on his arm. 'I didn't believe what she told me either. There was just one horrible little moment when I wondered . . .' She felt a spark of guilty shame, asking herself if she was telling him the truth. She wanted all of her words to him to be truthful, she wanted there to be no secrets between them. But she was not entirely sure that she was innocent of concealment. Dark, undefined suspicions still lurked insidiously at the back of her thoughts. And yet, with all her heart she longed to trust him.

He took a heavy breath. 'I shall speak to her. She won't be allowed to get away with this.'

'Look . . .' Alessandra began.

'No!' he decreed, silencing her. 'No more. We will say no more about it. I will not have you upset with having to discuss cruel lies that have sprung from jealousy and bitterness.'

'I believe in you Raphael,' Alessandra said quietly. 'Whatever lies anyone tells. And there is nothing to be ashamed of – for either of us – in having had lovers in the past.'

'But *you* haven't!' he cut in swiftly.

'No. But if I had I wouldn't be guilty about it. And neither must you be.'

He jumped up and began to pace about the room.

He looked grim and dark and unreachable. She could hear him muttering to himself in Spanish. He came and sat down once again on the bed. 'I am sorry for seeming to be so hard and so angry,' he said. 'There have been one or two loves in my life. But that was a long time ago. In the past.'

Alessandra smiled to herself, breathed a sigh of relief. *In the past*. Just as she had said to Isabella. She took his hand and placed it between the cleft of her breasts. 'You know that I'm yours,' she whispered, her eyes wide with love. 'You know that all of my body is waiting for you, just you.'

She took his hand and guided it to the other cleft between her legs, covered with the sheet. 'All the most secret parts of me. They are just for you.'

He gave a low groan. 'Oh my *amor*.' His head bent and his lips brushed over each of her breasts in turn, in a soft sighing caress. His fingers pressed into the valley of the sheets, exerting pressure on the tender sensitive flesh at the root of her legs but having no contact with it.

'Having you now makes me ashamed to think of other loves in the past. That is why I seem so angry and full of guilt. You are so beautiful to me Alessandra, so pure and wonderful and strong. You are all I could ever want. Thinking of my past life with any other woman makes me sickened with my own weakness.'

'But that's crazy!' She shook her head in disbelief. 'You're being too harsh in judging yourself. Having a lover isn't a weakness. It's nothing to feel ashamed about. Oh Raphael! Is this yet another thing about being Spanish that I don't understand?'

Suddenly he burst out laughing. 'Most probably. We are a very strange breed of people!' He made a sharp dismissive gesture with his hand. 'Now, I don't want to talk any more about the past. Look, there is something I have brought for you.' He reached into his pocket and took out a small tooled leather box. It was old and battered looking, the gilding around its edges scuffed away in places.

'It's a ring,' whispered Alessandra.

'Yes. It was my great grandmother's ring. My father left it to me in his will.' He opened the box and tilted it so that she could see its contents. Standing nobly against a cream satin lining was a ruby, as fat as a bird's egg, set in heavy gold and surrounded by twenty glittering diamonds.

'It's perfect,' Alessandra said, moving her head slowly in wonder. 'Simply perfect.'

Raphael smiled. 'Rubies are not to everyone's taste. If you hadn't liked it I would have had to think about what else I could give you. But I can see that you do like it my *amor*.' He took the ring from its box and slid it onto her wedding finger.

Alessandra started at it. The stones glinted up at her, like a host of living fires. 'Why didn't your father leave it to your mother?' she asked, having the disturbing thought that Isabella was going to be fuelled with fresh fury when she saw Alessandra wearing a priceless family ring.

'My father liked to preserve some things from his family to pass on as he wished. And my mother does not regard a ruby as a precious enough gem to wear on her fingers. Haven't you noticed that she wears nothing but diamonds?'

Alessandra gave a low chuckle. 'No. But now that you mention it . . .'

'Shh,' he said, tilting her face up so he could kiss her. She flung her arms around him, holding him very tightly, pushing herself against him, longing and longing for him as he kissed her into a state of helplessness.

Eventually they drew apart from each other with huge reluctance, smiling and promising each other the most wonderful gifts of passion once they were married and could give in fully to their desire.

Raphael sighed. 'Now my *amor*, get up and wash your beautiful face, put on your most beautiful dress and come down for your first dinner in *my* house as *my* fiancée.' He reached down to her again, giving her one last lingering kiss.

Almost immediately after he had left her there was a soft knock on the door. María slipped quietly into the room. She was holding a portable telephone in one hand and a glass of chilled white wine in the other. She said in clear slow Spanish, 'Your mother from England has been calling you. She said I mustn't wake you if you were sleeping, but that she would like to speak to you as soon as you were awake.'

Carefully she placed the wine on the table beside Alessandra's bed. 'Here is something to refresh you as you dress,' she said, her lined sunburned face full of knowledge and kindness.

'Oh María, you're so good!' Alessandra exclaimed.

'And see, I've brought you a telephone you can use here in your room, so you can have a nice talk in private.' María's black eyes, sunk within the folds of glossy leather skin, sent out silent messages about her employer which she would never dream of voicing.

'Almost too good to be true,' Alessandra added, her eyes twinkling as María discreetly vanished.

She took a sip of wine and dialled her home in England. Tara answered after only one peal. 'Oh Alessandra. Thank goodness!'

'What's the matter Mummy?'

'Oh nothing much. Just that I've heard from Daddy that you're about to get married.'

'Yes. So?'

'So, isn't it all a bit sudden?'

'Is this leading up to a parent-style lecture?' Alessandra enquired, her voice cool.

'No.'

'That's what it sounds like.' Alessandra wished she could make herself come across more warmly, less brittle. But somehow, she couldn't.

'I'm sorry,' said Tara, her voice low and genuine. 'I suppose I felt a bit hurt because I seemed to be the only one not in the picture.'

'I did try to contact you earlier,' Alessandra broke in, instantly defensive. 'There was no reply, and the answering machine wasn't on.'

'No. I forgot to set it. I was out for a while.'

'Somewhere interesting?'

'I was in Cambridge, for a planning meeting on the conducting seminar.'

'Music matters?'

'Yes.'

'That's OK Mummy. First things first,' quipped Alessandra sardonically without thinking too much about it. When she did think she was horrified to think she might have implied some longstanding grudge against her mother for the time she had invested in music over the years.

'Look I'm sorry I was out when you were trying to contact me,' said Tara.

'It's all right. I got used to it you know, years ago!' Oh hell, thought Alessandra, another blunder. Why did she keep saying these things? Was it because deep down she really did feel a grudge?

There was a horrible pause, mother and daughter both longing to find some bonding point in the emotional chain stretched across the miles, and not being able to discover the right linkage to grasp.

'Daddy said that you and Raphael are thinking of getting married fairly soon,' Tara ventured hesitantly. 'Do you know when that will be?'

'Not yet.'

'Daddy's going on tour in Russia for a few weeks,' she offered, again tentative.

Alessandra understood the message behind those words instantly. 'It's all right Mummy,' she said, doing her very best to sound loving and understanding. 'We're not planning on a big occasion. We shan't be expecting you and Daddy to turn up at the drop of a hat. There'll probably be just me and Raphael and one or two witnesses.'

'Yes,' said Tara. And then, faintly, 'Oh dear.'

'What's the matter?'

'I feel as though I'm letting you down somehow.'

'Well you're not. And I'm perfectly fine. Very very happy in fact.'

'Good.'

'What did Daddy say after he'd visited here?' Alessandra asked curiously, listening out keenly through the pause which followed, a silence she found highly suspicious.

'He thought Raphael was a very . . . impressive man.'

'He is. So there you are! No need to sound so doubtful Mummy. Did Daddy say anything else?'

'Naturally. What would you expect when your only child suddenly takes it into her head to marry a virtual stranger?'

'Oh for goodness' sake!'

'Listen darling, please don't be angry about this. But quite honestly I don't think Daddy was totally happy about your situation . . .'

'It's my life not his,' Alessandra snapped. 'He's always done exactly what he wanted. And you've done almost as well yourself.'

'Yes,' murmured Tara.

Her tone of faint martyrdom inflamed Alessandra and she was on the point of making some searingly sarcastic retort when she suddenly hauled herself back from the brink. 'Oh poor Mummy!' she exclaimed.

Tara gave a small chuckle. 'Not at all. And don't you dare start pitying me! I'm very proud of my record of behaving badly.'

'I think you're probably behaving much better than I am just at this minute,' said Alessandra honestly.

'Look darling, will you promise me to give this whole thing a long second thought?' said Tara impulsively, spurred on by Alessandra's sympathetic warmth, and inadvertently shattering the newly built sense of trust.

Alessandra lifted the phone from her ear and stared at it.

'No!' she shouted, 'No!'

CHAPTER 15

Catriona was positioned by the drinks tray when Alessandra arrived in the drawing room for the Saventos family's pre-dinner ritual gathering. Ignoring the variety of fine wines on offer, Catriona had poured herself a large vodka and tonic and was sipping it whilst gazing out of the windows, her face arranged in a bored and indifferent expression. She was wearing a dress of plum coloured silk and had a huge tasselled scarf in pinks and burgundies slung over her shoulders. Gold chains hung with old coins dangled in heavy ropes from her wrists and around her throat. 'Hi!' she said casually to Alessandra over her shoulder.

'Hello.' Alessandra poured herself a glass of wine.

Catriona turned. 'Nice dress,' she said.

Alessandra, in a plain lemon tunic – and very conscious of the huge ruby ring on her finger – smiled in acknowledgement.

'I hear congratulations are in order,' Catriona offered in her excellent English with its Spanish rhythm and Americanized vowels

'Thank you.' It struck Alessandra that whilst

saying very little, Catriona nevertheless managed to convey the impression that Alessandra's engagement to Raphael was either too boring or too unlikely for his sister to contemplate seriously.

'Mother's still getting dressed,' Catriona volunteered in laconic tones. 'So you can breathe freely for a while – and I can have another drink.' To emphasize the point she returned to the drinks tray and sloshed more vodka into her glass. 'Anyway you will be safe from dear Mother's evil tongue this evening. Raphael has invited the supermarket buyer to stay on for dinner.' She grimaced and made a small contemptuous sound in her throat. 'So we'll all have to be on our best behaviour.'

Raphael came in at that moment, followed by a young woman with short shiny brown hair, dressed very neatly in a navy suit. He introduced her as Penny Barker, who came from Birmingham and was one of a small team of senior wine buyers for one of the UK's biggest chain of supermarkets.

Penny, in her early thirties, was lively, sharp-eyed and – as Ferdinand had earlier indicated – amply curvaceous. She shook hands all round with enthusiasm. On meeting Alessandra, she exclaimed, 'Oh I have to say I'm so relieved to meet someone English.' She looked around at Raphael and pulled an apologetic face. 'Sorry Señor Saventos. I'm sure that was highly politically incorrect. But I'm off-duty now.'

Raphael laughed. 'It is quite all right. I can imagine that we Spanish are not all that easy to put up with!'

'You're easier than some people I have to deal with,' said Penny with cheery frankness. 'I often spend days tasting and trying to buy wines and the vineyard owners give you absolute hell. It's as if you're their enemy – even with the prospect of a tasty slice of potential business dangling in front of them.'

Raphael placed a glass of oaked chardonnay into her hands. 'I think this was the wine you were most impressed with earlier. Well now you can drink it instead of spitting it out.'

'Oh what bliss. Cheers everyone!' said Penny, raising her glass.

'Just one minute!' said Raphael, crossing to Alessandra and laying his arm briefly on her shoulders. 'I'd like to say that we shall be drinking a very special toast. Alessandra and I are going to be married,' he announced quietly.

'Wow, how super!' cried Penny. 'Well, congratulations. And even more cheers.'

'Cheers,' echoed Catriona, her eyes lazy with some clouded, undefined emotion.

'This is a very special day for me,' Raphael said softly, giving Alessandra's profile a long, intense stare. He put up his hand briefly and touched her cheek, making her skin tingle with tiny sparks of excitement.

The atmosphere in the room was suddenly electric with the strength of their feeling for one another. Alessandra was sure that the other two women present must feel it as a force in the atmosphere. Never having been in love before, she found herself in a state of dizzy exhilaration. She had never realized that you could adore someone with the depth and fervency with which she adored Raphael. She had never guessed that you could love another person with all of your being, and feel this wonderful, glorious sense of closeness.

I'm all aglow with energy and joy, she thought, feeling that her body was flooded with light, as though all the doors and windows of her heart had been flung wide open to greet the sun.

As she looked at Raphael, his dark eyes burning into her, she felt that she could withstand any of the difficulties which inevitably seemed to lie ahead. She felt as though she were bursting with love – for him, for everyone. In fact she was sure that she had been handed a limitless supply of the stuff: love by the sackful that she could dig her hands into like confetti at a wedding, tossing it into the air so that it would fall on everyone around.

'It most certainly is a special day,' Catriona agreed with a blasé smile. 'My mother and I had begun to think Raphael would remain single for ever.'

A tiny pause fell. For a moment even the exuberant Penny was quiet, sensing something faintly sinister hidden beneath the words. Something not entirely in keeping with the mood of a celebration.

'Come on everyone, drink up,' said Catriona. 'I don't like to be the only one filling up my glass yet again.'

At dinner the conversation moved along in a quirky mixture of English, Alessandra's budding Spanish, and Isabella's comically clumsy attempts to demonstrate to Penny that she had a good grasp of both languages.

Isabella was even more dressed-up than usual. Her bold, very Spanish dress was a mass of swathes and folds and pleats, emphasizing her handsome stately figure – most especially her impressive dowager's breasts. It was a dress of bright red, the colour of an English pillar box, and it clashed violently with Catriona's plum. She wore so many heavy clanking bracelets that it was surprising she could lift her arms in order to cut up her food.

Her conversational overtures were almost exclusively directed at Penny. Occasionally she would turn to her son or her daughter in order to seek help with an English word that eluded her. But having made a brief nod in Alessandra's direction after making her dramatic entrance into the company, she gave no further sign of registering her presence.

Why? thought Alessandra baffled. *Why?*

Reflecting on this as she sectioned up a slice of goat's cheese and cut herself a clump of fat grapes with the heavily ornate silver grape scissors bearing the Saventos family crest, Alessandra gave a small start as she heard Isabella announcing to Penny that her grandson Emilio would be returning home the next day after a business trip in Italy. The grandmotherly tones were ripe with pride and indulgence and Penny nodded with appropriate smiling politeness.

Alessandra, quietly vigilant, was not slow to note the glance that passed between Catriona and Raphael. Business trip indeed!

Isabella went on to explain in halting wooden English that her grandson was considering taking up motor racing, and that she was very proud that he had asked her to sponsor him in this ambition.

Alessandra saw Raphael's face freeze into sudden stillness. He got up abruptly from the table and busied himself opening further bottles of wine which stood waiting on the heavy oak sideboard. Alessandra could feel the silent tension seething within him. She wanted to get up and wrap her arms protectively around his beautiful muscular body.

'These young men and their sport!' Catriona commented in a slow drawl. She took a cigarette from a slim gold case, drawing on it deeply and daring her mother with a long look to say anything to stop her. 'What is your sport?' she asked Penny, squinting at her through the haze of smoke which had risen up.

'Oh, the usual,' said Penny brightly. 'A bit of tennis. Films, theatre, the odd concert. I used to be a great night-clubber but I've got past it.'

'Classical concerts?' Catriona asked.

'Yes, sometimes.'

'Alessandra's father is the conductor Saul Xavier,' Catriona told her, glancing at Alessandra with a little smile, then turning back to Penny to see if the information had sparked off any interest.

'Really,' exclaimed Penny. 'How fascinating!' She laughed, 'I hardly ever meet anyone famous.'

'I'm afraid you aren't now,' said Alessandra drily. 'I'm simply the daughter.'

'Oh well, these things rub off,' said Penny. She stared at Alessandra thoughtfully, frowning a little. 'Isn't your mother a conductor too?'

'Yes. And she's rather good at it,' Alessandra said firmly. 'She used to be a brilliant violinist as well, when she was younger.'

Penny looked deeply impressed. 'I already knew about that. I read an article about the two of them recently in one of the Sunday supplements.'

Catriona, cigarette dangling between long pink nails, leaned slowly back in her chair allowing Penny to hold the floor.

'They seem to have had a frightfully romantic life,' said Penny to Alessandra. 'Running off together when your mother was only a girl.'

'No, they didn't run off together,' said Alessandra crisply. 'My mother moved in with my father. He was married at the time you see, and his wife wouldn't give him a divorce. And I was already on the way!'

'Oh!' Penny's smile was becoming uneasy. 'Well, I did have the feeling it was all terribly romantic,' she concluded lamely.

'I suppose it was,' Alessandra said. She looked at Catriona, and then she looked at Isabella, wondering how much the older woman had understood of this rapid interchange of information in a foreign language.

Catriona turned to her mother and drawled away in Spanish for a few moments. Her mother ran a tongue around her lips and began to fiddle agitatedly with her diamond rings.

Alessandra felt Raphael come up behind her, a significant and reassuring presence. He reached over to refill her glass. '*Amor*,' he breathed in her ear, 'be careful.'

Alessandra turned to look at him. *It's all right* she told him with her eyes. As she gazed up at him another great flooding wave of love washed through her. The sensation led her to conjure up a sudden image of her parents twenty-odd years ago. She began not only to understand, but also to feel, how they must have been totally swept away by their feelings for each other.

The reflections triggered a sharp revitalization of her love for both of them, together with a huge surge of pride. It must have been so hard for them, she said to herself, as she contemplated the protracted and stubborn resistance of her father's awful first wife Georgiana to give in graciously and agree to a divorce.

'I seem to remember the article said your mother had been stopped from playing the violin through some tragic accident,' said Penny, making a brave attempt to plug the uncomfortable gap of silence that had opened up.

'My parents had a car accident,' Alessandra explained in calm clear tones. 'My mother suffered some damage to the vertebrae in her neck, the ones that carry that part of the spinal cord which controls the nerves linking to the middle fingers.'

'How dreadful!' said Penny.

'You'd never know. The damage isn't obvious at all in everyday life. And she can still play her violin, but not to concert standard.' Alessandra felt sudden tears swell up into her eyes when she recalled the way in which her mother's apparently glittering career had been so brutally cut short. How brave she had been. Never complaining about what she must surely have felt as a terrible loss. Must still feel.

Her parents never talked about that sad accident. There seemed to be a shadow around it, a halo of some secret darkness too painful to contemplate.

When the cheese and dessert were finished the company returned to the drawing room. Catriona poured further drinks and lit another cigarette. Alessandra glanced at her from time to time, having the impression that, in contrast to her usual apparent boredom and her longing to escape to the privacy of her own room, Catriona was rather enjoying herself this evening.

The conversation lurched along through the safe topics of the Spanish countryside and the best shops to patronize in Barcelona.

At ten-thirty a taxi arrived to take Penny back to her hotel in Lérida. Raphael went to escort her to the outer door and to wish her farewell.

Without his presence Alessandra found the room suddenly stifling even though the evening air, filtering in through the windows, was sweet and fresh with the aftermath of the earlier rain.

Catriona continued drinking and smoking, seeming quite content to sit in silence. Isabella, however sat bolt upright on the sofa, her eyes flashing, her breathing deep and heavy. Again Alessandra was reminded of a diva opera singer; a proud and stormy artiste waiting in the wings before making her big entrance.

Coming back into the room Raphael made some quiet and non-committal comments on the success of the evening. His eyes linked with Alessandra's, tender and desirous.

Isabella's head jerked up. She rapped out a short speech to Raphael in rapid Spanish.

The response on his face was one of such fury, Alessandra feared for a moment that he might commit violence on his parent.

Isabella threw her head back and flung out an arm, pointing her finger at Alessandra. Again she released a volley of machine-gun fire Spanish.

Alessandra caught one or two words. '*Hija natural.*' She wrinkled her brows, trying to make connections.

'Enough!' shouted Raphael.

'Oh spare us Mother,' murmured Catriona in her best drawl, glancing at Isabella with weary contempt.

'*Bastarda!*' proclaimed Isabella triumphantly.

'What does "*hija natural*" mean?' Alessandra asked Raphael with deadly calm.

'It doesn't matter,' he said in distress. 'You must take no notice.'

'Tell me. I shall only look it up in the dictionary.'

'It means love-child,' Catriona cut in sweetly, rolling the words around her tongue.

Alessandra stood up and crossed to the sofa, standing looking down at Isabella. 'So, you think you have made a great point do you?'

Isabella flinched, tossing her head like a startled thoroughbred horse.

'Yes, I was a *love-child*,' Alessandra said, her voice trembling with passion and yet full of confident authority. 'And I'm proud of it. I'm proud of my parents' love for each other. And yes, I was a "*bastarda*" when I was born. But not any more. My parents are married. My pedigree is faultless Señora Saventos. Just as noble as any of the Saventos family. I have nothing to be ashamed of either in my past or in my family. Quite the reverse in fact.'

Isabella looked up at her, eyes hard and full of disdain. 'Hah!'

'Have you understood what I said?' Alessandra demanded.

Isabella gave a stiff nod. She said nothing.

Raphael stepped up to his mother and spoke to her in firm stern Spanish.

Isabella waited until he stopped speaking. She took a long inward breath. 'My son tells me I must apologize,' she said to Alessandra with icy coldness.

There was a moment of waiting. And then Isabella got up from the sofa and, without saying another word, walked slowly from the room, her face conveying supreme disdain. It was clear to all of the observers that her whole bearing was in no way suggestive of one who has conceded defeat – in fact quite the reverse.

CHAPTER 16

The storms which had hit northern Spain the previous afternoon moved swiftly north west, and in the early hours of the next morning they were making their rumbling way over the south of England.

Tara, lying in bed drowsing, listened to the sudden stirring of the trees in a hurricane-like wind and the relentless slap of the rain on the windows. As thunder cracked across the sky the foundations of the house trembled, and the metallic lightning, striking through a chink in the curtains, illuminated the room with momentarily blinding brilliance.

Saul had set off for the airport some time ago. He had slid out of bed as softly as a cat, sensitive to her need to sleep, because he knew that she was on edge and unhappy about their daughter. But Tara had hardly slept all night. She had noted his every sigh and movement, and as he moved away from her so she reached out and pulled him back, desperate to have him close before he left on his extended Russian tour. He had made love to her with exquisite and lingering tenderness and then he had left the bed, dressed swiftly and slipped away.

After the whine of the Porsche's engine had faded into the clamour of the storm, she had at last managed to lose herself in the comforting embrace of a light sleep.

Now suddenly her drowsy peace was disturbed. She found herself gripped with a raw grating pain which seemed to echo the turbulence outside. As she came fully awake the bewildering sensation of intense, generalized hurting focused itself between her pelvic bones. Her uterus felt as though a clamp of iron had been fastened around it.

She sat up in bed, doubled up, bracing herself against the spasms, her arms winding themselves protectively around her belly. Whimpering softly she rocked herself to and fro. The sheets beneath her felt suddenly warm and wet. Looking down she saw the dark stain of blood seeping from beneath her thighs.

She blinked. Surely it was not that time of the month. She found it hard to remember. She supposed the lovemaking with Saul could have disturbed the delicate mechanisms of her internal organs. Her breath shivered in her throat. 'Oh dear God!' she gasped. The pain was now a dark droning turbulence, and when she stood up in an attempt to make for the bathroom her legs nearly collapsed beneath her. The waves of pain beat within her like a storm tide against the rocks.

With a huge effort of will she got herself to the bathroom. And in time, very gradually, the red throb of pain began to dwindle and fade. She started to breathe more freely.

She ran a bath and lowered herself into the fragrant hot water. Slowly and most blissfully, the pain was relinquishing its hold on her, retreating to a far horizon. And outside the window she could see a vivid white sun pushing through the storm clouds as the violence in the sky moved away.

'Aah,' she breathed shaken and weakened. Despite the warmth of the water she found herself shivering. And then suddenly she cried out, her voice ringing through the empty house, in a bleak forlorn lament, 'Oh Alessandra! Oh Saul!'

In Spain, Alessandra lay in bed, watching the sun rise. The clouds were soft spun and luminous, outlined first in deepest blue, then pink, then gold, their shapes stretching and contracting like mysterious cellular organisms under a microscope.

Raphael had laid her in bed the evening before. Following her angry but dignified upbraiding of Isabella in the drawing room, once she was alone with her adored fiancé, Alessandra had sunk into a reflective silence, licking around her mental wounds like an animal bewildered at having been set upon for no known reason other than existing.

'Does your mother truly hate me?' she had asked him, her eyes never leaving his face as he kissed her and then tenderly began to undress her. She stroked his wonderful thick hair, and the smooth skin at the base of his neck. And yet at the same time she was re-living the pain of the closing moments of the evening, hearing yet again Isabella's angry words, full of loathing.

'No. But I'm afraid she's jealous of you my darling. You're young and you're very beautiful, and she is old and she feels her female attractions are all vanishing. I suppose we should both try to be forgiving,' he finished, his mouth closing around one of her rosy nipples and sucking at it gently.

Alessandra closed her eyes and gave a low sigh of pleasure. 'Love-child,' she murmured, echoing Isabella's accusation, but speaking with wistful tenderness, not contempt. 'What a curious, old fashioned expression. And yet it has a kind of beauty to it, don't you think?'

'Yes.' Raphael took up her nightdress and raised her arms so that he could slip it over her naked body.

'I really meant it when I told her I was proud to be just that,' Alessandra said, sinking into his arms, her body warmly aroused and throbbing.

Raphael held her close. 'You were splendid to-night my dearest most precious *amor*.' He ran his hands gently down the length of her body over the thin cotton fabric.

'Do you mind?' she asked abruptly. 'Do you mind that I was born out of wedlock?'

He laughed. 'My darling it is *you* that I love. Simply you, the wonderful woman that I'm holding in my arms now. For me, nothing else matters.'

'I thought perhaps,' she persisted, 'that for a very traditional Spaniard an irregularity of birth might be quite a drawback. Even in England you know, there's still a lot of emphasis on that kind of thing in the upper classes. Some families would kick up a major fuss if their son wanted to marry a *love-child*.'

'I can only tell you that this son doesn't care a damn,' he said, lifting her off her feet and dropping her onto the bed. 'Now will you please stop talking and allow me to give you a proper kiss.'

After some delicious moments when their lips fused and their tongues moved sensuously together, he eventually withdrew from her with a deep sigh.

She caught his hand as he raised himself from the bed. 'The son may not give a damn,' she said softly, 'but what about his mother? It really did seem important to her.'

'His mother will just have to learn not to meddle in her son's affairs,' Raphael had responded shortly. And he had spoken in that firm hard way she knew meant that the subject was to be closed.

Alessandra waited until the antique clock on the landing had struck six and then she got up, dressed quickly in her jodhpurs and a light sweater and went down to the stables.

Ottavio and Titus both came to the edge of their stalls to welcome her, hanging their heads over the wooden doors and watching her with grave and loving eyes. She gave them some sugar crystals she had saved from the night before, because these were their particular treat.

She watched them munching in comical unison, the rubbery movement of their lips and the crunching of their teeth rhythmic and soothing.

'No jumping this morning,' she told them. 'We'll go for a nice gentle walk.' She guessed that Raphael wouldn't be able to join them that morning. He would have urgent paper work connected with Penny Barker's visit, and she had seen him running up the steps to his office in the winery as she let herself out of the house. She respected his work, understanding that he was not able to spend more than a few hours a day with her. She supposed the example of her parents had taught her that two people can love each other passionately despite their need to have lives of their own as well.

She slipped the bit into Ottavio's mouth, hooked the bridle deftly over his ears and fastened the throat lash. The luxurious leather saddle made pleasing creaky noises as she levered it onto his back and leaned beneath his belly to catch the end of the girth.

Next she put a snaffle bridle on Titus, coupled the rings with a thin chain linkage and fastened on a strong lead rope. Swinging herself up onto Ottavio she gathered up the slack of the lead rope and, encouraging Titus forward to follow him, walked both horses out into the stable yard and down the long drive.

They walked on keeping an even and steady pace. It was unfair when riding one horse and leading another to expect frequent changes of pace. Her aim this morning was simply to give them some exercise and keep them supple. They went out beyond the vineyards, Titus walking with his nose just level with her knee, and circled round the vast fields, where the grass was blooming and shiny from the recent rain. After a time, when she could see that there were no distractions of agricultural vehicles she allowed the horses to have a trot, and after that a brief canter.

Pleased with their responsiveness and obedience, she walked them gently back home under a ripening sun.

As they turned into the drive leading to the house

she heard the low roar of a car's engine. The noise was coming from the *autovía* leading to the minor road which eventually linked with the driveway. Within seconds a bright red sports car came hurtling up behind them, curving a swerving arc in a screech of tyres to avoid hitting them, then pulling up with a great scraping of loose stones some yards ahead.

Ottavio, a balanced and experienced horse, laid his ears flat, shied dramatically, then was instantly under control once more. Titus, however, violently unnerved and upset, began to plunge and buck, exerting random violent pulls on the lead rein.

'Hell!' exclaimed Alessandra furiously, leaping down from Ottavio and running to calm the terrified Titus. Having managed to settle him, patting and stroking his sweating neck, she saw a familiar figure jump out of the car and come running back towards them, his wild black hair falling over his eyes, his face dark with rage.

'Emilio,' she said to herself through gritted teeth. 'I might have known.'

Emilio was gesticulating and shouting as he came nearer and Titus's response to the approach of his former rider was to give another buck and a huge shake of his head, whilst Ottavio, though still and placid, began to show a good deal of the whites of his eyes.

'You fool! Don't you know that cars slow down for horses?' Alessandra yelled at him in English.

'Stupid stupid girl,' he yelled even louder in Spanish. 'Thinking you can manage two horses at once. My horses,' he added in a ferocious growl.

Alessandra pulled herself together. Losing her temper was not something she did often, and she hated to be out of control. It dawned on her that the last time it had happened as badly as this was when she had threatened Emilio with a thrashing after he had beaten Ottavio. The feelings now were very similar. She thrust her arms by her sides and kept her whip pointing firmly to the ground. 'I was managing them fine until you came along. And they're Raphael's horses,' she said tersely.

'Hah!' exploded Emilio, sounding uncannily like his grandmother. 'You come here and take over my horses. You get your claws into Raphael. You think you can get him to marry you just like that.' He snapped his fingers, curling his lips up in disgust. 'You think you can take everything!'

Alessandra stared at him, slowly understanding that Isabella and Catriona must have been feeding him with information about her every action whilst he was away in Italy. She supposed it was not surprising, that she might easily have guessed what had been going on if she had bothered to think about it. Yet even so, she was jarred and dismayed. 'Think what you like,' she told Emilio in cool tones.

'He'll never marry you,' said Emilio spitefully. 'You wait and see. You think you have your feet nicely under our table, but you just wait and see!'

Alessandra saw red. 'Oh get the hell out of it you silly little boy,' she exploded. 'Go away and play with your shiny new toy.'

Clicking to the horses to walk forward, she pushed past him and went on up the drive, steering a wide berth around the ostentatious red car – whilst at the same time noting with a swift assessing gaze that it was a brand new, top of the range Ferrari.

Smouldering quietly she untacked the horses, sponged them down with cool water, gave them each a feed and went back to the house to shower and change. Standing under the jet of warm water she decided that she would break her usual habit of not disturbing Raphael at work and go and seek him out for a few moments. Her feelings were raw and touchy. She badly needed the reassurance of his presence. She had no intention of telling him about her clash with Emilio, perhaps not to talk much at all. She simply needed a few moments to be with him, close to him, breathing the air he breathed, inhaling the calm strength of his love for her.

As she pulled on light cotton trousers and reached for her shirt, there was a knock on the door. This was not a light questioning knock like María's, more of a dictate. 'Alessandra. Please open the door,' a voice commanded in shrill tones.

Isabella. Oh hell!

Alessandra wrenched on her shirt and, still doing up the buttons, opened the door. 'Good morning Señora Saventos,' she said with formal politeness.

'I have something to show you,' said Isabella shortly. She walked into the room with all the authority of the mistress of the house. Crossing to the oak chest against the wall, she laid a large envelope on its polished top.

Alessandra looked at it. Her mouth dried.

'Look inside,' said Isabella. 'Go on!'

Alessandra was alarmed to find her fingers trembling as she raised the flap and pulled out the paper within. It was a sheet torn from a glossy magazine, a glamorous black and white photograph showing a striking couple at some obviously exclusive function.

For a few seconds the image seemed to dip and swim before Alessandra's gaze. She blinked rapidly, forcing her eyes to focus properly, commanding her brain to take in the hateful information before her. She saw Raphael in evening dress with a woman standing beside him. The woman was blonde and exquisitely groomed, with a very appealing face and a charming figure. Her hand was laid possessively on Raphael's arm, and she was looking up at him as though he were the most wonderful man in the world.

'This is the woman I told you about,' Isabella said, although Alessandra already knew. 'She is from one of the most aristocratic families in Spain.'

Alessandra felt her stomach lurch and swoop. She could think of nothing to say.

'She is Raphael's mistress,' said Isabella, emphasizing the word. 'His *amor* for many years.'

Alessandra dropped the photograph as though it had been set alight. 'No,' she murmured.

'Yes,' said Isabella.

Alessandra sank down on the bed, her legs suddenly weak and disobedient.

'You said it was all in the past,' Isabella continued, her black eyes glinting and merciless, her bracelets clanking like armour. 'Look, look here!' She indicated the date at the top of the page. The printing was tiny and Alessandra had to peer at it closely to make it out. The date was a recent one, no more than two months ago. In fact it seemed that the photograph must have been taken little more than a week or so before she had first met Raphael.

'You see,' said Isabella with huge satisfaction. 'This is all in the present. Not the past.'

'No,' said Alessandra dully, the horror seeping in. Desolation flooded through her in a cold cruel wave. 'No, no, no.' Her voice faded into nothing.

CHAPTER 17

'*Amor*!' Raphael rose from his desk, instantly appreciating the depth of Alessandra's distress.

Ferdinand, busy repairing a window frame damaged in the storm, swiftly put down his tools and quietly melted from the room.

'Raphael,' Alessandra said, her heart beating in lumpy painful leaps, 'you haven't been telling me the truth.'

She spoke perfectly calmly, even though this was one of the most difficult sentences she had ever uttered. She knew that she would never have been able to say this to him unless she had simply plunged in. She felt like a terrified child perched at the edge of a diving board above a cold, bottomless pool with all the escape routes cut off.

There was a short pause when both of them were very still, standing facing each other head on, their gazes locked.

'I mean it,' said Alessandra. 'It's serious.'

'Tell me!'

She opened her mouth and then closed it again.

'Tell me,' he insisted. 'Anything. I must know.'

She swallowed hard. 'You told me about women in your past, your former 'loves'. That's what you called them.'

'Yes. Well then?'

'Loves, you said. In the plural. More than one. Somehow that doesn't sound so important.'

'So important as what?'

'As one particular woman. One very special woman.'

His gaze swooped down for a moment. 'Go on.'

She gave a great heaving sigh. 'Raphael, do I really need to say any more? Do I have to spell it all out, word for word? I don't know if I can.'

'What has someone been saying to you?' he demanded angrily. 'My mother was it, or maybe my sister?'

She stared at him, realizing that there were depths to him she hadn't even begun to guess at. 'Let me describe someone to you,' she said. 'A charming blonde woman in a designer dress at some classy function just a couple of months ago. She seems to be very loving and devoted, staring at you as though you were some divine being. Are you going to tell me you've never heard of her?'

He drew in a long sighing breath and raised his head in that gesture of pride and noble resignation that was so uniquely his own. 'You are talking about Luisa Victoria de Mena. She is the heiress to the estate of a prominent and very wealthy Spanish family. She is also the wife of a senior politician in the government.'

'And she's also the mistress of Raphael Godeval Saventos?' suggested Alessandra, her heart cold.

'No.'

'You deny it? I can't believe you could do that Raphael. Do you think I'm a complete fool?'

'She was my mistress. A long time ago.'

'I saw the date on the photograph, it was taken literally just a few weeks ago,' Alessandra insisted, her voice filled with despair.

'Yes. That's quite true.'

'Well then . . .'

'I was invited to a dinner in Madrid at the end of the summer. It was a government sponsored dinner held in honour of a number of private company owners who were presented with awards. Luisa happened to be there with her husband. After dinner she came to talk to me and congratulate me on my award. We were photographed together. That is all.' His face was bleak as he completed this terse speech and then gave a long shuddering sigh.

'No,' she said shaking her head. 'I won't be fobbed off with that. I didn't come here to interrupt your work just to be told yet another part of yet another story.' Her eyes blazed at him, alight with anger. 'Because that's what you've been feeding me with so far isn't it Raphael? You haven't lied to me, you simply haven't told all of the truth. And maybe that's as bad as lying!'

'No. Don't say those things!'

'And don't you dare look at me with such an angry face,' she shouted at him furiously. 'I've done nothing wrong.'

'I'm not angry with you,' he said relenting instantly. 'I'm angry with myself. Can't you see that? I was an adulterer, low and shabby!'

'When was this affair with Luisa de Mena?' she asked, her face hard. 'I need to know – and I need to know the truth.'

'It started seven years ago. It ended one year ago.'

'Six years. You were with her for six years?' Alessandra's mind leapt about wildly, not knowing if this was a good or bad thing to be hearing.

'We couldn't meet very often. She lives mainly in the south and also in Madrid. And she is married. We had to be very careful, and very patient.'

'Did you love her?' Alessandra asked.

'Yes, I did for a time.'

'Tell me some more,' she demanded softly. 'You must tell me Raphael, I need to know.'

'Very well. She's ten years older than me. She picked me out at a wine convention in Madrid. She took me to dinner and then she took me to her flat in Madrid and seduced me very prettily. I was charmed and, of course, flattered – and only too ready to be seduced.'

'Why didn't she get a divorce?'

'Oh, she never wanted to marry me. She just liked to have a young lover.'

'The calculating bitch!'

He gave a slow wistful smile. 'Yes, I'm afraid so. I didn't realize at the time, but now, of course, it's all quite clear.'

'Did she dump you then?' Alessandra asked brutally.

'No. Why should she? It could have gone on for years as far as she was concerned. I suited both her and her life-style. Why should she want to "dump" me?'

'You ditched her then?'

'Yes.' Suddenly he smiled. 'This dumping and ditching. These are words I don't know very well.'

'They're good ones aren't they? Evocative?'

He gave her a sharp glance. 'Is that what you're going to do to me now?' he asked, his voice low and dangerous. 'Dump me? Hmm – is that it?'

Tears welled up without warning in her eyes and spilled over. He took a step towards her and she flung herself into his arms. 'You bastard,' she wept.

'I'm a bastard for having been someone's lover and then dismissing her?'

'No. You're a bastard for not trusting me enough to tell me. Why couldn't you trust me?' She beat her hands against his chest, weeping, chiding – and suddenly in danger of collapsing into hysterical laughter.

'Because I've become so used to keeping secrets,' he said wearily. 'Because my mother and my sister are impossible. Telling the truth to them is like tying oneself to the stake and dropping a lighted match.' He was silent for a time. 'Do you understand?' he asked.

She looked up at him. 'I don't know,' she said slowly, her habitual confidence and sturdy optimism all fled. She felt vulnerable and exposed. She felt as though she were standing at the edge of a precipice, and that with the slightest wrong move she could topple over. She closed her eyes, feeling herself falling and falling, grasping only at darkness and emptiness.

'Alessandra . . .' He tried to stop her moving from his arms and then abruptly he let her go.

She stepped backwards, putting a distance between them. She could not look at him again. What she had seen in those last few moments had desperately unnerved her. His face had been full of fervour, full of ardour – all the emotions she had seen in his face before and adored. But there had been something else there too. Something she now recognized and which made her heart thud like a stone. For even now he was still holding back from her, and his eyes were dark with secrets.

She had shut herself in the stables. For over two hours she had stood beside Ottavio, talking through her thoughts, simply allowing them to pour out.

'Maybe I'm wasting my breath,' she said to him, her wet cheek against his warm sleek one. 'You're a Spaniard too aren't you? Maybe you're a lot like Raphael. You won't be able to get on my wavelength. Not ever. Maybe we're just not meant to be with each other.'

Ottavio pushed sympathetically against her, promoting a fresh wave of tears.

'So maybe I should just pack up and go home,' she told him. 'That would be the sensible thing to do wouldn't it? The kind of thing sensible people do in serious sensible books?' She stopped and blew her nose.

'I don't know if I want to be sensible,' she continued. 'In fact I don't think being sensible or not sensible is anything to do with it. Do you? It's all about love isn't it?'

Ottavio blinked impassively. She stroked her fingers down his cheek bone. 'I'd never dream of

221

saying a soppy thing like that to anyone else Ottavio,' she said sniffing, 'so don't you dare snitch on me.'

She frowned, having a vague recollection that as she prepared to leave Raphael's office she had told him that she didn't know if she could go ahead with the marriage. 'Did I really say that?' she asked. 'And if I did, did I mean it?'

Another tearful wave lapped up. 'If I went home and was sensible,' she informed Ottavio, 'a lot of people would be pretty happy and relieved wouldn't they? My mother most likely. My father too – although you never know with him. Isabella certainly and Catriona and the unspeakable Emilio.' She put her arms up around Ottavio. 'Oh I couldn't leave you to the mercy of that little jerk. I'd have to steal you away. And Titus too.'

Confused and in utter despair she sank down onto the straw and began to sob uncontrollably.

It was some time later before Raphael got to her. He had known immediately where she would have fled to. But there had been a minor crisis to deal with in the processing room and by the time he reached the stables she was well and truly barricaded in. It took him and Ferdinand a good half hour to prise the lock from the heavy stable door.

He lifted her from the straw and carried her outside into the sweet fresh air. Settling himself onto a wooden seat outside the tack room he pulled her onto his knee, pinned her arms behind her back and kissed her very thoroughly.

'Tell me you won't leave,' he commanded.

'No,' she protested, squirming away from him off his lap, pulling her plait round her shoulder and holding onto it; something comforting and familiar amongst all the confusion. 'Not until you tell me everything I should know. Everything!'

He bowed his head, letting his arms fall slack between his legs.

'The real reason your family hate me so much,' she insisted passionately. 'The reason your mother seems very happy for you to be an adulterer with an older mistress but doesn't want you to have me for a wife.'

He flinched and she was both sorry and gratified to see the hurt on his face.

'She would prefer me not to marry,' he said flatly. 'It would please her if I never married.'

Alessandra was astounded and baffled, but she was sure now that he was holding nothing back, that at last she would hear the truth. 'You mean she doesn't want you ever to get married? Not to anyone? Are you saying it isn't just me that she objects to?'

'Ah, now you're beginning to understand,' he said with a wry faint smile. 'I suppose I was a fool not to tell you everything right from the start.'

'You're not a fool Raphael,' she told him tenderly. 'That's not the reason you've been keeping secrets from me. These are family secrets aren't they? Secrets you hate, that you can't bear to share?'

'Yes.'

She took one of his hands in hers. The contact with his skin made her tingle with electric feeling. 'You can trust me,' she said softly. 'Anything. There's no need to hold back. You can tell me anything.'

There was a short pause. 'When my great grandfather came here, he put all his energies and all of his savings into creating the winery. He worked day and night to pay back his loans and debts. And gradually the winery began to thrive and he was making a profit. He became a rich man. He had a son who became even richer, and a time came when that son, my grandfather, wanted to make a binding will.' He broke off.

Alessandra squeezed his hand in sympathy.

'He and my grandmother had had four children. Two of them died when they were only babies. The remaining two – a boy and a girl – who were clearly very precious to them because of the loss of the others, had grown into adulthood. The girl was very beautiful and also very headstrong. Against her parents' wishes she married an Italian count. He was very charming apparently, but he turned out to be a gambler. He was always coming to my grandfather for money. More and more money to pay for his obsession. Eventually my grandfather realized that this man could drain him dry. Around this time his health began to fail and when he made his will he was anxious that his son, my father, must be protected from the count's demands in the event of his early death. He had a will drawn up stating that the winery and all of the proceeds from it should go to his son, who would have complete control over how much he chose to give to the remaining dependants.'

'So in essence, your grandmother and your aunt were cut out of your grandfather's will.'

'Yes. It seems very cruel doesn't it? But of course in those days it wasn't so unusual for men to have total control of family money.'

'What happened?'

'My grandfather died soon after, and my father duly inherited the winery and all of my grandfather's fortune – which was quite considerable by that time. We are a very rich family, as you've probably guessed.' He turned and smiled at her, raising his eyebrows.

'Mmm. I suppose I was aware, but only in a vague kind of way. I've been lucky,' she added reflectively. 'Money's never been a real issue for me, because there's never been any shortage.'

'I'm afraid money is a very real issue in this family,' he said bitterly, 'even though there's plenty!' He fell silent, his face lined with a dark meditative and very Spanish melancholy.

She rattled his arm. 'Don't stop there Raphael. Go on.'

'Very well. After my grandfather's death my father made a very generous provision for my grandmother. And he also helped my aunt, in so far as he saw fit. However when he died – very young and very suddenly as I told you – it turned out that the provisions of the family will had never been altered since my grandfather's original instructions were drawn up. When I found out what they were I was shocked. I was only very young then, and I fancied myself as a progressive; forward looking and liberal. This will seemed to me like something from a dark, feudal past.'

She took in a sharp breath. 'Go on.'

'My grandfather had had the will drawn up in such a way that the provisions were to be binding on the next generation – and the next, and so on. He had devised a will which was to stand as a blueprint for all future Saventos wills as long as the winery was in the ownership of one of the male members of the Saventos family.'

'That does sound a touch feudal! So what were, or rather are, these provisions?'

'They are complex as you can imagine, but basically they are aimed at ensuring that the eldest surviving son of each generation will take control of the winery. The incentive for those eldest sons is that they inherit full control of the vineyards, the land, the winery and all its profits, together with the total family fortune, provided that they marry and produce a legitimate male heir.' He paused, allowing Alessandra time to absorb this last piece of information.

'So does that mean,' she asked slowly, 'that at the present time you, as the only surviving son, but not yet married, don't have all those benefits?'

'That is right.'

'But if you marry and have a son of your own then you'll automatically get them?'

'Yes. It's grotesque isn't it?'

'Probably. But I'm still not sure I understand it all fully,' she said frowning.

'Let me help by telling you a bit more. At present my mother – despite the fact that she has little interest in the actual running of the business – has the power to vote for or veto important business decisions. For example I am very keen at present to expand, but she is more cautious. If I were to put proposals for expansion to the directors then she could use her vote against me at a board meeting. But should I marry and have a son, then the number of my shares will increase so dramatically that her vote will count for much less. She would no longer have the . . .'

'Clout?' Alessandra suggested.

'That's it. She would no longer have the clout to enable her to put a brake on my decisions.'

Alessandra made a little hissing sound through her teeth, gradually coming to understand the dark implications of the Saventos will.

'But you would never make her poor would you?'

'No, of course not. I should be more than generous. She is an impossible woman as I've told you. But she is my mother and I love her. And in any case she has considerable wealth in her own right, as her parents were rich. It isn't so much the money my mother is worried about. It's the loss of power, both for herself and for Catriona and Emilio.'

She stared at him. 'What do you mean?'

'Think of it. If I were to die now, then Emilio – provided he married and produced a son – would inherit everything. Moreover Catriona would stand to gain a far greater share of the family fortune than she would if I marry and have an heir – whether I had an early death or not.'

'Don't talk about dying – I can't bear it.' She moved close to him and kissed his lips fiercely. 'So when you and I get married, poor Catriona will have to find herself a job or a rich husband?'

He smiled. 'Maybe not a job. Somehow I can't see that, can you? But a rich husband, well yes, I think so!'

Very rich, thought Alessandra with dry irony, reflecting on Catriona's likely need for fresh jewellery, protracted idleness and a plentiful supply of vodka.

'But Isabella loves you,' Alessandra protested. 'She wouldn't want you dead!'

'No, of course not. Although it has often occurred to me that if I did die she'd be able to manipulate Emilio in a way she can't do with me. He's like a greedy, selfish little boy, you see. But he's also a little boy who's very frightened, very vulnerable.'

'What! Emilio? Never!'

'Oh yes. He often makes me very angry and I can't bring myself to love him. But I sometimes need to remind myself that his life-story began in terrible sadness. He was born just after my brother, his father died, and then his mother died whilst giving birth to him. My mother had to give up her weeping for all of the dead in order to look after him. She took him on as her own child. And Catriona has been a mother to him as well.' He paused and sighed. 'I'm afraid that being born out of calamity and having too many mothers has ruined him.'

Alessandra said nothing. She felt there was nothing she could say that would not sound trite or false. She remembered Isabella's passionate words about the drama and tragedy of the Saventos family.

'I think,' said Raphael, 'that my mother would feel she was still in control if Emilio were to take over the business. He puffs and blows and rages, but it's all hot air, and when he's with her he's like a lamb you know.'

He stood up, his movements sharp and abrupt. 'But enough of this. There's no question of my mother wanting to despatch me to the next life. What she wants is simply a continuation of what has been happening in the last few years. For her it

228

was ideal. I was settled with a mistress I could never hope to marry, leaving my mother as the queen of the household with the freedom to play devil's advocate with the business whenever it entertained her to do so, and to indulge Emilio to her heart's content.'

'Oh yes. Now I understand,' Alessandra said with a long sigh. *And then I came along – and threatened to disturb her whole world.*

'I hate it, this terrible will,' Raphael burst out in despair. 'It's wicked and archaic.'

'Can you do anything to change it?'

'I have had lawyers working on it for years. Maybe one day they'll come up with something. In the meantime – we just have to live with it.' He stroked her hand softly. 'You must understand, this will affect you too my darling.'

'You know that I don't care about the material things,' she said to him quietly. 'I want to share in your thoughts and your love and your heart. That's what matters, not the money.'

'But you're interested in the winery,' he reminded her sharply.

'Yes. Yes, I am.'

'You see Alessandra, I want you to become more involved in the winery. I want us to share in the challenge of taking the business forward into the next millennium.'

She felt an inner spark of anticipation. 'But what will Isabella think of that?'

'She will be furious. For a while.'

'So all her hostility and her raging about Alessandra the bastard "love-child" were simply smoke screens. Or should I say red herrings?'

Raphael gave a low chuckle. 'That's it. Red her-rings,' he echoed, enjoying this odd expression. 'She would have hated *any* woman who presumed to claim me. Without exception.'

After a long pause, whilst the joy surged up slowly inside her, she said to him, 'Raphael, you realize that we've both been talking as though our marriage is going ahead.'

His hand tightened on hers. 'And it is, isn't it? Please *amor* I know you had reason to be angry with me. I know that I've kept things from you and it was very wrong of me to do that.' He stared at her, anguish on his strong features. 'I thought I was protecting you. I thought if you knew all there was to know about my family that you'd go away and never come back.'

'*Tonto!*' she murmured, giving his lower lip a tiny nibble with her teeth.

'Yes, yes. I told you I was a fool.' His eyes glowed with feeling and urgency. 'Now! You must tell me immediately or I shall go mad. Will you still take me on? Will you marry me?'

The power of his plea hit her with a physical force. She had no chance of resisting him, even if she had wanted to. Despite all the new and dangerous knowl-edge he had given her, despite her full understanding of the enormity of what she was embarking on in allying herself with Raphael's family, the earlier doubts about Raphael himself were all swept away.

'Take you on,' she echoed, cradling his face in her hands, 'you and your mother, your sister and your nephew. And Spain. I must be crazy not to run home this minute. How soon can we arrange it?'

INTERMEZZO

He took her to the south because she told him she wanted to see the Sierra Nevada and the old Moorish cities of Seville and Granada which she had read about in history books. But also it was because she wanted to be with him whilst he gave himself the opportunity to breathe in the atmosphere of the place where his former love lived, so that he could lay old ghosts and start again.

Their marriage had been a quick but dignified civic ceremony, and afterwards they had gone straight to the airport in Barcelona and by the afternoon of the same day they were in Seville.

Raphael took her to the ancient Alcázar palace, and led her through its ornamental patios and sumptuously decorated chambers with their glowing tiled walls.

'You like it?' he asked.

Alessandra found herself swept up in a wave of sensation: being here with Raphael, just the two of them, alone in this astonishing monument to centuries of old Spain. 'It's amazing! I've never seen anything like this. I think it frightens me just a little.'

He laughed. 'I'm not surprised. This palace is full of stories, seething with them.'

231

'Some very bloody I should imagine,' she said, looking at the row of five skulls painted over the door lintel in the bedroom which King Pedro the Cruel had made for his adored second queen María more than five hundred years before.

'Oh yes indeed. King Pedro once murdered a guest from Granada, for the sake of one of his jewels, a great uncut ruby which was said to be priceless.'

'Not very hospitable of him.'

Raphael chuckled. 'Apparently Pedro was absolutely mad about his María. He rejected a Bourbon princess for her sake and he wanted to give her everything.' He looked down at Alessandra, his deep gaze telling her that his own feelings were just as intense. His eyes lit with a sudden mischievous gleam. 'There's a story that he made the gallants at the court pay homage to her by requiring them to stand in a queue to drink her bathwater.'

'Ugh!'

'One of them said he couldn't do this. He said that if he were to savour the sauce then he might desire the partridge also.'

'Aha, good thinking!' She leaned against him, feeling him warm and solid and heavy. She was loving every moment of being with him, seeing him freed from work and from his family, laughing and ironic and carefree. Her *husband*.

They went to sit in the gardens. A brilliant autumn sun shone down from a bright azure sky. It was warmer than in the north. The gardens were dusty with heat, the fronds of the palms and orange trees dulled and brittle.

And then it was time to move on. They picked up a

hire-car in the city centre and drove west into the mountains. In time the *autovías* narrowed to breathtaking metalled country roads hugging the sides of cliffs below which dark gorges yawned with dizzying steepness. Alessandra fell silent as Raphael concentrated on the challenge of manoeuvring the car along the perched looping roads.

It was dark well before they reached the village of Pampaneira. The night air smelled of aromatic plants and tobacco and rough country brandy.

The staff in the little hotel smiled in welcome and offered them supper even though it was nearly midnight.

Raphael raised his eyebrows, seeking her preference.

'Nothing,' she murmured. 'Just you.'

'Come then,' he said, taking her hand and leading her to the low white room with its huge carved bed and white frilled sheets.

He laid her on the bed and undressed her with slow tenderness, kissing each newly exposed stretch of her soft white skin. When she was naked, lying looking up at him, he turned her over and undid her hair, spreading it out across her back and stroking it with long heavy sweeps of his hand.

She felt herself drugged, helpless to do anything except lie in his arms, letting him pleasure her.

She woke in the night and heard it raining outside, a soft plump pattering that was like a lullaby. Beside her Raphael slept, his breathing soft and rhythmic.

She was overwhelmed with an unspeakable sensation of happiness. She recalled the moment he had brought her to a heady peak of shuddering, mind-swooping pleasure. It had been glorious, quite wonderful. But it was not only the moment itself that had been so precious, but the feeling that what she was experiencing was just a beginning for her. She knew that with Raphael she was going to sense things and feel things and see things that she had never even considered existed before.

The curtains whispered in the dark, and the rain filled the country air with scents dependent on the earth and the sky, rather than those created by human beings.

She touched Raphael's face with gentle fingers, tracing the lines of his strong bones and his warm firm lips. He made a deep sound of contentment, but did not move or wake.

Pulling the sheet back, she began to kiss his neck and then his shoulders and his chest. Moving down she rubbed her breasts gently against his stomach as her lips sought the insides of his thighs and the heavy warm maleness of him between.

She smiled as she felt him coming back to life.

'*Amor*,' he breathed, groaning with the pleasure she was giving him.

'You made such beautiful love to me,' she told him. 'And now it's my turn to do my share.'

He laughed, pulling her head up to his with firm hands. She began to tell him how much he meant to her. She began to apologize for not being more experienced in making love. But she would learn . . .

'You English,' he chided, 'how you like to talk and reason and explain instead of feeling and sensing things with your instincts.'

She began to protest. But he very soon silenced her.

PART TWO

LATE SUMMER THE FOLLOWING YEAR

CHAPTER 18

Georgiana Daneman, the beautiful ex-wife of Saul Xavier, emerged gracefully from the door of a Harley Street clinic and stood for a moment surveying London's elegant street of exclusive and expensive therapies.

Georgiana, now in her mid-fifties, was still, thanks to the formidably skilled and costly attentions of a succession of plastic surgeons, virtually as beautiful as she had been twenty years before. This did not prevent her from continuing to patronize the face and body doctors. In fact, when she looked in the mirror and found herself growing ever more youthful and lovely, she felt it necessary to be even more on her guard against the unseen finger of time, which she knew would become busy decorating her all over with wrinkles and sags if she didn't keep up a firm guard.

Today she had been talking over the benefits of a little lifting and tucking with one of her favourite scalpel wizards. Between them they had decided on some attention to her neck and chin, mindful of the spectacular success of some similar work on her eyelids and lips two years previously.

The prospect of a few days being pampered in the caring atmosphere of a luxury clinic was decidedly cheering. Georgiana had long ago decided that she didn't mind the initial bruising and discomfort caused by cosmetic surgery. Recovering from them gave her the chance to relax fully, stay in bed all morning reading and reflecting – or simply stay there doing nothing if she wished. And then after lunch there would be the pleasure of receiving visits from her friends who could be counted on to be delightfully sympathetic and admiring of her courage in submitting herself to yet more pain.

And Daneman, of course, was always prompted to become even more attentive than he was normally.

She smiled to herself. A new project, something fresh to look forward to was always pleasing. When you lived a life of unrelenting luxury and entertainment it was sometimes hard to discover a new peak of pleasure to scale.

She smoothed the skirt of her light mint green suit with perfectly manicured, fuchsia-tipped fingers and then put a hand up to her shoulder length blonde hair, checking that it also was behaving as it should.

Satisfied that all was well, she progressed down the small flight of steps and walked towards her silver Mercedes coupé. Settling herself against the car's thick buttercream leather she buckled her seat belt and inserted the key in the ignition.

Something drew her to look up. The neat figure of a petite dark-haired woman was running lightly down the steps of the clinic just beyond the one she herself had recently left. Georgiana's hand stilled. She watched the woman turn and walk briskly past the Mercedes. A red linen dress, cut to flare from a halter-neck swung jauntily as she moved.

Georgiana's heart gave a little spring of sharp recognition. She looked in her rear view mirror and saw the woman pause by a sleek Jaguar saloon in racing green, before vanishing into it through the driver's door.

Tara Silk – Saul's mistress!

Georgiana stared. Her heart jerked and speeded up. She had not seen Tara for ages, and to come across her so unexpectedly was something of a shock.

'Tara,' Georgiana whispered to herself, examining the feel of that once hateful name on her tongue and her lips. 'Saul's mistress.'

Well, of course, Tara was now his wife, and had been for several years, but Georgiana still thought of the younger woman as Saul's inamorata, the illicit lover who had seduced him with her throbbing youth and earthy sexiness and stolen him from his blameless wife.

She watched the Jaguar pull smoothly from the kerb and drive away. As the car passed close Georgiana took a quick covert glance. Tara was looking very charming, her thick hair cut into a shaped bob, the ends curled out like the petals of an upturned daffodil. Even in the flash of a second it was possible to see that her skin glowed, and that the flesh of her neck was alabaster smooth.

Georgiana swallowed down the saliva that had poured into her mouth. She waited until the Jaguar disappeared, waited a few minutes longer to be on the safe side, and then got out of her car and walked quickly to the entrance of the clinic which Tara had just left. The polished brass plate on the stonework beside the door bore the name of two consultants, both of them experts in the field of gynaecology.

Returning to the plush haven of her Mercedes Georgiana sat in silent contemplation for a few moments, her mind energetic with speculation. Her heart was still beating unusually fast and gradually she felt herself filling with a sensation curiously akin to excitement.

Tara guided the Jaguar through the crowded streets, her feelings a mingle of intense anticipation topped with a small cloud of dread.

She had been suspicious for around four weeks now but had relegated her speculations to a far place in her mind, occupying herself with the summer conducting seminars at the Royal College in Manchester, with preparations for the forthcoming season with the Eastlands Orchestra. And with a yearning desire to close the gap that seemed to have opened up between her and Saul ever since the news of their daughter's sudden marriage.

That she and Saul had not heard about Alessandra's wedding until after it had taken place had deeply upset Tara, who felt as though she had been alienated and rejected by her only child. But Saul had not been prepared to share in her distress. He had expressed the view that Alessandra was fortunate to be settled with a man she loved, a man who was wealthy and worthy and had been able to offer her the dignity of marriage at the start of their relationship – something he had deeply regretted not having been able to do for Tara when they first came together. As parents they should be grateful that things had turned out so well for their child.

Tara had looked into his stern, hawk-like features and been warned not to make any further protests.

Instead she had eagerly looked forward to spending a few days at the Saventos winery, visiting Alessandra and her new husband in the late spring. But the flying visit had done little to soothe Tara's jagged emotions. Somehow she had not managed to strike the right note with Alessandra. Their relationship had been rather as she remembered it during Alessandra's teenage years, with Alessandra slightly withdrawn and brittle, and Tara either exasperated and touchy, or desperately holding herself back from coming over as sentimentally maternal. It seemed to Tara that now Alessandra had Raphael, whom she clearly adored, she no longer needed anyone else. Not even her parents, and perhaps most especially not her worriedly doubtful mother.

'Raphael is a man of culture and sensitivity as well as a damn hard worker,' Saul had informed her sharply, when he had found her pacing around the grand Saventos guest suite wearing a frown of most decidedly maternal concern. 'He's one in a million.'

'Yes, I know. But that ferocious mother,' countered Tara, 'and the sister . . .'

'Alessandra's not married to them.' Saul had said, his grey eyes steely and cold.

Tara turned now onto the motorway, sighing and trying not to remind herself yet again how often Saul seemed to be away these days: foreign tours with his

241

Tudor Philharmonic orchestra, TV appearances in the States, master classes on conducting in China and Japan.

However it pleased her to remember that he was due to arrive home this afternoon and would be around for the next few days without any heavy engagements to occupy him. She would have him to herself and it would be bliss.

This evening they were to dine with their agent Roland Grant and then go on to the Barbican for a concert conducted by Michael Olshak, one of Roland's newest young stars. Tara recalled meeting the young flame-haired American conductor years before at the Music Centre in Tanglewood, Massachusetts, when he had been no more than a raw recruit. She could see him now, gawky and sensitive, hesitantly wielding his baton in front of the student orchestra.

And now he was one of Roland's rising stars. And once Roland shone his spotlight on you it was incredibly hard to sink back into the shadows again.

Joining the flow of the motorway she put her foot down, sailing into the outside lane and pressing ahead. Her mind went back to Saul, considering the various ways in which she could break her news to him. She wondered what his reaction would be. It was hard to guess – she herself was not entirely sure of the feelings surrounding this unexpected discovery. The only thing she did appreciate was the sheer strength of her feelings, even if they were a muddle: one minute surging and soaring, the next plunging into doubt and a dark thread of fear.

The gynaecologist had been brisk and practical

and communicative.

'Forgive my gardener's hands,' she had said with a wry smile, palpating Tara's naked abdomen with probing fingers before slipping on her gloves and beginning an internal examination.

Tara tried to relax. Her innards had felt tender and vulnerable.

'Remind me – how long is it since your last pregnancy?' the doctor asked, screwing up her features in concentration as she moved her fingers in slow gentle assessment.

'Twenty years ago.' Could it really be as long as that?

'And the pregnancy was terminated as a result of a trauma in a car accident?'

'Yes.' A trauma! The word seemed not to do justice to the experience. The crash and the events surrounding it had produced horrors her mind shied away from like a terrified horse.

'And you were told that you wouldn't be able to have any more children?'

'Yes.'

'Mmm.' The doctor went on probing, smiling faintly. 'We tend not to be so categoric and pessimistic these days.'

'They had to give me a dilation and curretage to get rid of . . . everything. I had the impression that the lining of my uterus had been badly damaged.'

'Mmm. But scarred tissue – providing it's not diseased – has a habit of repairing itself over time. Especially in young healthy women who have a good diet and a fulfilling life.'

'Is that right?'

'Yes.'

'So could I really be pregnant?'

'I can't say definitely yet. We'll have the results of the urine test soon enough.' The doctor glanced down again at the notes. 'Have your periods been regular?'

'All over the place. But then they've never been like clockwork.'

The doctor pressed her tongue through her teeth as she made a final pumping movement with her fingers and then withdrew them.

Tara sat up. She felt curiously light-headed.

The doctor peeled off her gloves and posted them into a white bin. She crossed to her giant-size desk and consulted Tara's notes. Having stared at them for a while she said, 'It's possible that in recent months you've started a pregnancy – or maybe more than one – and suffered an early spontaneous abortion. Does that seem likely?'

Tara suddenly understood what had been happening to her in the autumn whilst all the anxiety about Alessandra had been taking root and sprouting shoots that grew like Jack's beanstalk. 'Good grief! Yes! And I was so dumb I never put two and two together.'

'Not dumb. You were given the message loud and clear that you'd never have another baby. In your mind you'd completely ruled out the prospect.'

'That's absolutely spot on, exactly how I saw things.'

There was a soft knock on the door and a young woman came in. She handed the doctor a small slip of paper and then left as unobtrusively as she had come.

The doctor looked at the paper. Then she looked at Tara. 'The test is positive,' she said. 'It confirms that you are indeed pregnant.'

As Tara stared at the doctor in amazement she suddenly felt altogether different: empowered and splendid and utterly female because she was still able to create another human being in the secret darkness of her body.

She swung her legs off the couch, wriggled her dress down over her knees, replaced her shoes and went to sit in front of the doctor's desk. 'You talked about my having a recent miscarriage. What does that mean about the chances for this pregnancy?'

'It means,' said the doctor, closing the file of notes with a satisfied slap, 'that you should be careful and vigilant.'

'No horse-riding, athletics or alcohol.'

The doctor gave a confirmatory smile. 'And, of course, it would be wise to cut down on your work schedule which I gather has been somewhat hectic.'

'Aah. Yes. Of course.' Roland will not be pleased Tara thought wryly.

'And if there is any sign of bleeding or any undue pain you must call me immediately.'

'Yes.' Tara looked up at the doctor with a sudden new thought. 'Sex?' she enquired.

'Can your husband manage to be very gentle?'

Tara felt a tiny spark of thrilling desire, thinking of Saul. 'He's a man of great self-restraint.'

'Well then, that's all right isn't it?

Nearing the Oxford exit from the motorway Tara began to slow her speed in anticipation of crossing to the inside lane.

The crazy, incredible speed of the motorway suddenly hit her as though she had never been on such a road before. She recalled the day of the accident – the 'trauma' that had killed her baby and her budding career as a soloist. She remembered the dizzy speed of Saul's Porsche and his grim demonic expression as he gripped the wheel with fingers of iron.

She gave a little gasp of fear as the Jaguar made a tiny swerve in response to her trembling thoughts and responding fingers.

'Concentrate!' she commanded herself. She was pregnant. She must defend her defenceless baby. There was no longer just herself to think about.

Her hands damp and shaking she guided the car off the motorway with huge care, then relaxed as she joined the comparative calmness of the A40 main road.

Her car phone chirped. She flicked a switch and spoke into it. 'Yes.'

'Tara!'

'Saul!'

'Listen darling, I'm still in Munich. I can't get away.'

She felt a sudden emptiness.

'Darling – I'm sorry.'

She caught the note of slight irritation in his voice.

'Can't be helped,' she said drily. 'But don't complain if I find myself dying of loneliness and running away with a toy boy!'

What the hell had made her say that she wondered? Talking to her adored husband as though she were some flighty flirtatious middle-aged woman hankering for her youth and a bit of young muscle. Talking as though she could seriously be attracted to another man. Talking in exactly the opposite manner of a level-headed, loving wife who's just learned that she's having her husband's baby.

'You'd only regret it,' he said silkily, 'especially when I caught up with you.'

'Given the opportunities you're giving yourself for catching up with me these days Saul, I'd probably get away with it, no problem at all!'

'I'll be back tomorrow afternoon at the latest,' he said crisply, letting her know that he wasn't going to be drawn into further banter. 'Give my apologies to Roland for this evening will you?'

'Yes.' Suddenly she wanted to cry, she needed him so badly. Needed him right now.

The phone squeaked and crackled, cut off and then re-established the connection.

'I'll have to go,' he said. 'Enjoy the concert darling.'

'Yes.'

'With or without a toy boy.'

She stared bleakly at the phone as the connection went dead.

'You'll never guess who I saw today,' Georgiana told her husband, her blue eyes wide with animation.

They were sitting in a cosy expensive West End restaurant and Dr Daneman had been heavily engaged in studying the details of the menu as she spoke. He looked up, then smiled in the indulgent protective way he had become accustomed to using with Georgiana. 'No, I shan't. So please tell me!'

'Tara. Tara Silk.'

Daneman felt a glinty sharpening of his attention.

'It must be years since I saw Tara,' Georgiana said reflectively.

'Yes indeed. And how was she?' He ran a fingertip along the edge of the laminated menu card. 'Did you speak to her?' he added cautiously.

'Oh no! We didn't actually meet. I just saw her.' Georgiana tilted her head and allowed her curtain of precision-cut blonde hair to swing from her face in a most charming way. 'She didn't see me.'

Daneman made a swift decision on his menu choice and laid the card down. He felt his attention now fully claimed by Georgiana's piece of information. As an experienced psychotherapist he was never able to free himself from the need to look for hidden meanings behind seemingly innocuous words.

And in Georgiana's case he had some dark and complex prior experience which warned him of the need to be especially vigilant. Especially when the subject of Saul Xavier's second wife came up.

'And where did this "sighting" take place?' he asked, taking care to keep his voice light and detached, his smile gentle and uncomplicated.

'In Harley Street.'

'Ah.'

'I told you I was going to see my surgeon this morning,' she chided.

'You did indeed my dear. What is it to be this time?'

'Just one or two little nips and tucks to keep me very beautiful for you,' Georgiana said coquettishly, lightly tapping the underside of her chin.

'Mmm.' He smiled once again, as though he were an indulgent father humouring his vain daughter.

'I was leaving my appointment, just about to drive away. And then I saw her.' The thoughtful assessing expression in Georgiana's china-blue eyes intensified. 'I think it must have been fate,' she concluded, and her smile revealed a mixture of satisfaction and delicious prescience.

Daneman's nerve gave a little crackle. Beneath Georgiana's blandness there was the capacity for strong and seething emotions. For violence even. He was well aware of that, because before she had become his wife she had been his patient. He had taken her through countless hours of therapy, probing into her past, into her inner thoughts and fears. He knew Georgiana perhaps better than anyone else – as a professional therapist, as a friend and lover and lastly a husband.

As a wife Georgiana had always been astonishingly placid. Some might even describe her personality as bland. But Daneman knew differently. And his knowledge was not simply based on psychological theory, it was derived from a simple witnessing of her past deeds. Outrageous deeds, fuelled by crazed jealousy.

We all of us have sinister capacities, he reflected. Every one of us is a walking explosive. But the majority of us seldom need to release the safety valve that keeps guard on the boiling cauldron of our emotions.

Daneman knew that the marriage between Georgiana and Xavier had been creaking for some time when Tara burst onto the scene. Tara, by precipitating the final break between the great conductor and his wife, had exerted the final tiny thrust of pressure to spring the valve open.

'She was coming away from an appointment with her gynaecologist,' Georgiana elaborated, leaning over the table and lowering her voice. Her eyes glittered, leaving Daneman in no doubt that she was in a state of great excitement, speculations churning away inside her.

He watched her play with the food on her plate and considered the implications of Tara's being in the frame once more. Georgiana's own personal frame.

'I wonder why she needs to see a gynaecologist,' Georgiana mused.

'Any number of reasons,' Daneman said.

'I don't think she's ill.' Georgiana speared a tiny prawn on her fork. 'In fact she looked very well.'

'Most people who consult a doctor are reasonably healthy. They simply need a little tinkering with. Sometimes medical, sometimes no more than an offer of kindness and attention.'

Georgiana smiled at him, as indulgent as he had been previously. 'You were kind to me,' she said. 'When I was going through all that hell, you were the only one who really cared and listened.' She touched his hand, and then turned her face away, her gaze becoming clouded and distant. 'Hell,' she murmured again, speaking just to herself.

Normally calm and unemotional, Daneman felt himself stabbed by a prick of anxiety. He wondered if the time would soon come when he would need to confront Georgiana with the secrets he had long been keeping to himself.

CHAPTER 19

Alessandra watched from the bedroom window as Raphael emerged from the main door of the house and turned in the direction of the winery. He paused briefly, looking back, looking up to find her watching him as she always did.

He raised his arm and she raised her hand to her lips and held it out as an offering.

The ten months of their marriage had been an idyll, despite the continuing difficulties and hostility from his family. Perhaps, she thought, turning away from the window, it was the very fact of the family's rancour and opposition that had brought her and Raphael so preciously close. She sometimes had the feeling they were carrying on a delightfully secret love affair, gulping down their passion in eager snatches between Raphael's business life, her life with the horses and the ever present life with the family.

The novelty of being his lover was still as fresh as their first night together, their lovemaking just as heady and intoxicating, at a super high-octane level.

She loved the look in his eyes when he reached for

her, letting her know how much she meant to him. She loved his being there for her when the occasional tide of homesickness unexpectedly swept in.

When they were alone together they had got into the habit of talking to each other in Spanish. And now that she was steadily getting better and better at understanding and speaking she found that Spanish was a wonderful language, perfect for the private and intimate expression of their love.

But aside from the heat and exhilaration of sexual passion, she loved the simple everyday living with him, sharing in all the highs and lows of ordinary daily life, talking over business problems with him, providing a buffer and a sympathetic ear when his mother decided to act out one of her angry scenes.

'Terrible woman,' she murmured to herself with a smile, as she gathered up fresh towels from the big oak linen chest and slid a small white box from the far corner of wardrobe.

Releasing a small sigh, she went into the bathroom, turned on the taps, and then went back to close the door firmly and turn the key in the lock.

Only then, with the door secured and the rush of the water drowning out any sound, did she feel safe in carrying out the ritual that had recently become a part of her life.

She reached into the shiny white box with its pink and blue writing and brought out all the paraphernalia she would need for the test, lining it up on the shelf. There were two plastic phials and a little plastic dropper. The accompanying leaflet, which she had carefully translated and written out in English, told her that the dropper would turn blue if the result of the test were positive. She would see a circle form, a purplish or bluish circle which would hang suspended in the liquid of one of the phials.

She sat on the bath side, waiting, trying to be calm. The first time she had carried out the test, the requisite five minutes needed for the chemicals to react had seemed like a grim eternity.

Subsequent occasions had been hardly less stressful. Each time she started out with huge surging hopes and at the end of the five minutes was plunged into awful misery. The blue circle had never appeared.

But today she had the patience to wait until her period was a full six days late. Hope shimmered inside her, making her innards queasy and unsteady.

Out of superstition she tried hard to resist rehearsing the wonderful words in her head – the particular words she would choose to give Raphael the news that he was going to be a father.

She swallowed hard, her body swaying slightly, yearning towards the phials on the shelf. Her bare toes gripped the tiled floor. She pulled her plait around her shoulders, stroking it. And then she laid it down over her breast and folded her hands over her stomach. A casual observer would probably have concluded she was praying.

She looked at her watch. Five minutes couldn't have gone, surely. She looked at the phials. There was no colour in them, just white light gleaming through from the tiles behind. She screwed up her eyes, but saw only red furred globules beneath her lids.

'Please,' she whispered, '*please!*'

After ten minutes had gone by, she walked slowly to the shelf, poured the contents from the phials into the lavatory basin, packed all the equipment back into its box which she wrapped in a white plastic carrier and thrust it to the bottom of her travel bag. This in turn she would later place at the back of the wardrobe.

Filled with a calm stoic misery, she stepped into the bath. As she lay in the water she felt the beginnings of the familiar tiny grinding sensation which always announced the start of her period.

Ottavio was jumping like an angel. Having schooled him regularly all through the spring and early summer, getting up religiously at dawn to ride him before the heat became overpowering, Alessandra had brought him to the peak of his potential. His stride was now almost half as long again as when she had first ridden him. His natural precision in tucking up his forelegs whilst in flight over the fences was also honed to perfection and he had learned how to put on extra speed and cut corners without any loss of accuracy.

On this pink and gold summer morning, having jumped twice around the huge six foot practice course she had built for him, both Alessandra and Ottavio were now breathless and sweating.

Ottavio had done brilliantly, surpassed anything she had known him do before. She was certain that he would pick up several prizes in the show she planned to take him to in Barcelona at the weekend.

Having taken off his hot, steaming tack, she set to work sponging him down, using tepid water to soak her sponge so as not to give him the shock of a dead cold douse as he was cooling off.

She heard the roar of a car's engine in the driveway. In her mind she pictured Emilio sitting behind the wheel of his Ferrari, frantically revving the engine as though to proclaim his ferocious virility to anyone who might be listening.

Emilio spent most of his time driving the car at mad speeds around the country roads or tinkering with the packed contents beneath its huge bonnet. In fact the car was his constant companion, like a partner in a highly charged love affair.

Although Emilio rarely talked of anything but his future career as a world class racing driver, Alessandra saw no evidence of this ambition becoming a reality. He had had the odd few tutoring sessions with a retired Italian grand-prix driver, had attended some of the most glamorous international racing events, and he followed the sport closely in the newspapers and on TV. But so far he had not entered any organized events nor, as far as she could tell, done very much at all to begin building a career and a reputation for himself.

Alessandra began to wonder if the idea of being a motor racing driver was all a fantasy: a dream which Emilio had no firm wish to translate into reality. After all dreams were safer and more controllable than reality. She began to suspect that, having been overprotected by his grandmother and his aunt, the outwardly storming and bluffing young man had no real confidence for testing himself out in the real world. There were times when she felt almost sorry for Emilio.

She began to mix the feed for the horses, trying hard not to feel sorry for herself following the disappointment with the pregnancy test that morning.

In the early weeks of the marriage she had idly speculated on the possibility of becoming pregnant. The idea had been a hazy thought at the back of her mind, squirrelled away like a child's saved treat to bring out and gloat over from time to time. Maybe not now, she would think. But soon.

When four months had gone by she had begun to be slightly puzzled. She had always regarded herself as vigorously fit and healthy. Her body had always responded as she had wanted it to. If she wanted to improve her time on swimming sixty lengths, then she could do so. If she wanted to improve her dexterity on the piano then she had only to practise and it would happen. The same with the riding of course. But now, suddenly, her body was stubbornly refusing to respond to her wishes.

And with each month that went by her bewilderment grew, gradually blossoming into a full blown longing of intense desperation. Each time her period came she was filled with despair.

She had mentioned her concern to Raphael in a low-key way a few weeks before. He had simply smiled at her, cupped her face between his big sensitive hands and told her she must not worry.

And because he was so tender and loving and utterly wonderful she simply started to worry more. Having a child seemed to her like a gift she would bring him in return for all he had given to her. That she couldn't do so made her feel hopeless and inadequate. Sometimes she even felt tragic, imagining herself like a latter-day Spanish Infanta or a French Dauphine who had sailed off with high hopes to a foreign land in order to marry the Crown Prince and produce a son to cement the concord between their two countries. But she was a princess who turned out to be barren.

Barren, she muttered to herself, tipping the feed into Ottavio's stone shelf dish and listening to Titus shifting in his stall in anticipation of its being his turn next. Such a cold and cruel word.

'*Amor!*'

Hearing Raphael's voice, she turned. She felt a deep happiness just to see him again. But beneath it was this knawing undercurrent of sadness. She put her arms up around his neck and kissed him.

'Aah,' he said. 'I adore you. More and more, every day.'

'Even when I smell of sweat and tack-oil and horse?'

'Yes, even then I think I can bring myself to find a little love.' He stroked her forehead where the rim of her helmet had left a long red groove. 'And how did Ottavio do for you today?'

'He was brilliant.'

'No fences down?'

'Not one. Faultless.'

'Then I think we shall have a big win to look forward to at the weekend. The start of a splendid career – yes?'

'Mmm.' She laid her head against him, loving his firmness and solidity.

'That doesn't have the sound of your usual enthusiasm,' he commented.

'Oh.' She looked up. 'Doesn't it? Sorry.'

'Are you nervous my sweetheart? It's been a long time since you were in a big event.'

'Yes, that's probably it.' She paused, realizing that he was fully on the alert to the lowness of her mood. She raised her head with a little jerk and smiled. 'I'll get over it. Chewing my finger nails to the bone before a big event has never been my style.'

'No. Your nails are simply beautiful,' he said, taking her hand and kissing each finger tip.

'Stop being so disgustingly romantic,' she chided.

They walked from the stables out into the open air and looked across the rows of vines whose greenery was now lush and thick, the clusters of grapes hidden among them firm and fat. 'This has been a magnificent year for the grapes,' he observed with satisfaction. 'No frosts in the early spring, no rough winds to blow off the little buds of the vine flowers and just enough rain in the summer to ripen the fruit at a steady rate. If the weather continues to be so kind we shall be very very busy at harvest time.'

'I'll help,' she said eagerly. 'Anything. Any old job at all, no matter what.' She was gradually learning more and more about professional grand scale winemaking. She had read a good deal, watched Raphael and his team at work, and now she had seen nearly a complete year's cycle in the life of the vine.

'Thank you *amor*. There will be plenty for you to do, don't worry.' He pressed her hand, resting in his. 'Now, tell me,' he commanded quietly.

'What?'

'What is troubling you.'

'Nothing.'

'It can't be my mother or my sister. They're safe in Barcelona at the sales.'

'Terrorizing the assistants in the fashion stores!'

'Most surely. Now!' He turned her face to him, staring down into her eyes. With that powerful human instinct he had he was cutting like a sword right through to the heart of her hopes and her disappointments.

She felt the tears leap up behind her eyelids, felt her throat tender and swollen. 'I so much want a baby,' she blurted out.

He was silent for a few moments. 'And you will have one. All in good time.'

'No. Things aren't going right. There must be something wrong with me.'

'There is nothing wrong with you. These things sometimes take time.'

'We'll soon have been married for a whole year.'

'That is only a short time.' He was wearing his remote and intractable look, more daunting than any amount of shouting or stamping about.

She had a feeling that she shouldn't pursue this line of conversation. But now that he had opened up the wound that had been troubling her she needed time to lick around and explore it.

'I want to have your baby, Raphael,' she said with passion, her eyes shining with feeling. 'I want it so much it's like a terrible hurting inside me.'

She heard him sigh. She was suddenly unsure of how he was reacting to this driving passion of hers. Whether any man, even one as sentient and sympathetic as Raphael, could have any understanding of it.

'I want to give you a son,' she said, stiff and obdurate.

'No,' he said, for once raising his voice. 'I won't have this old fashioned kind of talk.'

'It's not old fashioned,' she protested, 'just something as old as time. A wife who adores her husband wants to have his child. Surely you too want a child, Raphael.'

'I would very much wish for us to have a child. Either a son or a daughter,' he said in a somewhat formal manner. 'And we will, all in good time.'

Alessandra thought of the Saventos inheritance and how having a son would satisfy the demands of the terrible family will.

'Don't think about the will,' he said sharply, accurately reading her mind. 'I won't have our lives controlled by that. We shall live our lives as we decide, not by the decree of some dusty old document.'

'Raphael, I couldn't agree with you more. But you have to admit it would be very convenient if we managed to do what we wanted and fulfil the demands of the will as well. It would be like beating it at its own game.' She stared at him, angry and pleading, but his face was very still, revealing nothing except his clear displeasure in the continuance of this conversation.

'I simply want to have your child,' she insisted, her eyes wild and flaring because of her desperation. 'Never mind about the wretched will – or the fact that your mother gloats at me daily when she looks at my stomach and sees that it's still as flat as a board.' She held her breath, hoping that the last remarks would have diffused the thunderous atmosphere developing between them.

'Aren't you happy just to be with me?' he asked, his eyes as hard and glinting as coal. 'Surely you're not turning into one of those women who can think of nothing but producing children, being a cow in calf.'

Alessandra gave a short, involuntary gasp. There was nothing she could think of in response to questions like that. She wished she had kept her mouth shut. She had never dreamed the conversation would go like this. Before, when she had been in any distress, Raphael's response had always been one of calm sensitivity and sympathy. She cursed her impulsiveness in letting the self-pity she had hugged secretly to herself for so long gush out, at the same time wondering what the sin was in talking to your husband about your future children.

'I have to go back to the winery now,' he said in pleasant neutral tones. 'I shall see you at dinner *amor*.' He leaned forward and gave her forehead a light kiss.

Alessandra considered running after him, and decided very firmly against it. Slowly, and keeping a discreet distance from him, she made her way back to the house.

As she stripped off her sweatshirt and jodhpurs and changed into white cotton trousers and an apricot T shirt, a huge wave of nostalgia for her home and her parents surged up. It was rare that she suffered from homesickness, but the sensation of yearning now carved out a raw hollow in her stomach.

She dialled the number of the Oxford house, but as usual was only able to speak to the answerphone.

Usually when this happened, she would leave a joky message, 'Hello there, you ever absent parents. Where are you? When you get a spare split second give a thought to your poor daughter.' And then she would put the phone down, half glad not to have had to engage in a conversation, feeling satisfied that her duty in contacting them had been done for another week.

Today, when she heard the recording of her father's precise answering message, she felt her throat swell with feeling and quickly dropped the receiver back on the handset.

Unable to settle to anything, and mindful of Isabella's absence, she felt herself drawn to the curtained drawing room, to the gleaming, shockingly underused grand piano. Sitting down at the keyboard she scanned over the shining keys and then raised her hands. Gradually the effort and concentration of making music began to smooth out her jagged feelings.

As she played she came to understand that whilst having a baby was of huge importance to her, avoiding any hint of estrangement from Raphael was even more vital. And so when he came in later to join her for a pre-dinner glass of wine she greeted him smiling and light-hearted.

He looked at her with his long steady look, and then he took the glass from her hands and took her in his arms.

CHAPTER 20

Tara sat in the Barbican hall with Roland Grant on one side and an empty seat on the other. She felt the absence of Saul keenly, and laid her bag and her coat on the vacant space in an effort to stop it looking so reproachfully unoccupied.

Roland, the mild mannered, silver-haired founder and director of an international musical management firm, was at his most gallant, unperturbed and charming.

'Did you know Tara,' he said confidentially, assuming his usual pretence of being everyone's ideal (albeit highly cultured) grandfather, 'that the best-selling author Miles King is negotiating with a mega New York publisher to sign up for a biography on Saul?'

Tara turned to him with a chuckle. 'Does Saul know?'

'Oh yes,' said Roland, swivelling his glance towards her, his deceptively gentle blue eyes as sharp as a knife-edge.

'Really.' Her smile felt uncomfortably tight across her face like an expanded waist band after a huge dinner.

Roland's eyes said 'Didn't you know?' But his voice said, 'I believe he's not entirely opposed. No doubt he'll be discussing it with you.'

'No doubt,' said Tara. 'When I eventually get to pin him down for long enough,' she added to herself sotto-voce, glad to see that conversations would have to be suspended as the orchestra were now all assembled and the leader taking his bow to the audience's applause.

There was a short expectant pause and then the orchestra gave a collective smile as their corkscrew-curled, red-haired conductor made his entrance, crossing through their ranks to the podium.

Michael Olshak was a rising star who, in the past few months, had suddenly captured the public imagination. This was mainly due to his undeniable gift of musical interpretation but also in part a reflection of Roland's gift of employing image makers who knew their stuff.

Although Roland was on the wrong side of seventy, he was still a trail blazer. Understanding that the inevitable way forward in music promotion lay in building up the images of those who made the music, he had set up a team of consultants who were top flyers in the publicity field.

Olshak, in his Armani evening suit, with his black silk shirt open at the neck and his wild flame hair cascading over his collar was a perfect icon of 1990s chic. He projected an individuality and sharpness of style that would surely last well into the new millennium.

'He catches the eye doesn't he?' Roland whispered to her in the falling hush. 'Now let's hope he can do the same for the ear.'

The concert opened with the overture to Rossini's *Barber of Seville*. The orchestra were in exuberant form, playing with a verve and excitement that produced a collective spine tingle. And yet, under Olshak's direction there was no loss of precision. It was a fresh and impressive rendering, ending in a climax of sparkling triumph and drawing a roar of acclaim from the exhilarated audience.

After prolonged applause Olshak left the stage in order to bring on the soloist who was to perform the next work. The enthusiastic applause subsided into a hum of excited murmuring amongst the listeners.

Roland leaned towards Tara. 'Not bad! In fact,' he remarked drily, 'Olshak's going to be seriously good, when he gets a bit more experience under his belt.'

A silence fell over the auditorium as Olshak returned to the platform with Lucy Cook, the violinist who was to play the Sibelius concerto. She was very young, having only that year won a national prize for the best under-eighteen musician of the year. She wore a fussy schoolgirl-style dress in shot pink and purple silk. It had puffed sleeves and a ballooning skirt and looked as though it might have been hastily run up by her mother the night before.

'Oh dear,' murmured Roland.

'Is she one of yours?' Tara asked.

'Not fully signed up, but we're after her. She plays like an angel even though she looks like a dog. Fortunately dog-like looks can always be put right which is more than can be done with dog-like playing.'

But when the girl started playing it occurred to Tara that it wouldn't have mattered if she looked like a gargoyle. The sound that came from her instrument had a brilliant and beautiful simplicity that made her catch her breath. This was a dark concerto, full of unresolved tensions and the girl seemed to have captured all of the feeling in her fingers and transferred it to the strings. There was intensity and passion in her playing as well as beauty.

Tara felt a huge pang, recalling the brief heady days of her own career as a violinist. She remembered the joy and sweet exhilaration of playing, the way in which the world of the here and now temporarily vanished as one sank down into the world and mind of the music and its composer.

But her hopes of a virtuoso player's career had all been snuffed out after the accident. She smiled wistfully to herself, the regret now no more than an occasional hazy melancholy. The damage she had suffered in the crash could have been a tragedy for her, and perhaps it would have been in other circumstances. But at the same time as she had lost her ability to play, so she had learned of the safe return of the one-year-old Alessandra who had been missing, kidnapped and taken far away.

When faced with the loss of a child, the loss of a skill, however precious, pales into insignificance.

As the music penetrated her emotions, Tara's thoughts moved lovingly through memories of the baby Alessandra and then onto the young woman into which she had grown. She felt a sudden intense yearning for her, a longing to hold her child in her arms again.

At the end of the piece the audience erupted into a thunder of appreciation. Some people were actually on their feet; there was stamping, cheering and whistling.

Roland turned to her. Then he reached into his pocket and took out a monogrammed silk handkerchief which he put in her hands. 'Here,' he said gently, supposing that Tara was mourning for her lost virtuosity. 'I think our ugly little duckling fiddler must be very good indeed to have you shedding tears.'

'She's marvellous. And I'm getting old and sentimental,' said Tara ruefully, drying her eyes. She recalled that pregnancy had always made her volatile.

She glanced at Roland, accurately guessing at his mistake regarding the source of her temporary sniffles. He'll think I'm full of nostalgia and on a roller coaster down to the menopause she thought. A mischievous smile lit her face. Oh, Roland, you just wait, she whispered to herself, her eyes sparkling – but no longer with tears.

They went to a dark bistro in Soho. Roland settled his talented, money-spinning flock at a tucked away table in a candle-lit corner and went off to order champagne. Tara had Michael Olshak on one side and the scrubbed schoolgirlish Lucy Cook on the other.

Tara had the impression Lucy would much rather have been tucked up in bed than sitting in a fumy steamy basement the size of a shoe box. The girl looked as though she were ready to fall asleep over the table.

Tara talked to her for a while about her playing, drawing Lucy out on the subject of the passions and pitfalls of playing the violin.

As the girl began both to liven up and relax, Tara became increasingly aware of Michael's thoughtful

267

blue eyes watching them. And that in the main, his focus was on her, Tara.

'Now,' said Roland, re-joining them, 'I think congratulations and celebrations are in order. Michael, I drink to the ever upwardly escalating spiral of your career, and Lucy I drink to your artistry and the launch of many glorious years of playing.' He raised his glass and looked at Tara. 'And you, my dear, I simply drink to you – with all my heart.'

'Roland! You're getting smoother and ever more polished and shiny with the years that go by,' Tara admonished him affectionately.

'Yes,' Roland agreed. 'Rather like a much dripped on fossil don't you think?'

After the general laughter, Roland began to outline his plans for the two younger members of the party. There would be tours to arrange and recording contracts to negotiate. There would be decisions to make on building up Lucy's repertoire, the concertos she would need to learn and have ready to perform in the next year.

Tara sat back, enjoying the opportunity to listen to Roland giving his own virtuoso performance now that the music was over for the evening. He was such a clever performer, in fact she would go so far as to say cunning. He soon had the shy Lucy eating out of his hand, not only agreeing to all his suggestions on the concertos she would most love to learn and the most prominent cities and concert halls it was essential she should perform at, but venturing to make suggestions of her own.

I wonder if she'll change her acquiescent tune when he suggests a trip to the hairdresser to do away with that pony tail and the straggly fringe, thought Tara entertained. He'll probably drive her there in person and afterwards they'll go on to Harvey Nichols for a complete new wardrobe. She sat back, sipping her mineral water, observing and listening, a wry smile on her face.

From time to time she and Michael connected with a swift glance and there was a frisson of shared amusement between them.

Eventually, when Lucy appeared in real danger of falling asleep over her empty dessert plate, Roland settled the bill and offered to take her home. 'I think you two are old enough to look after yourselves,' he whispered slyly, winking as he bore the drooping Lucy away.

Michael leaned back in his chair, stretched up his long arms and linked his hands behind his head. 'Freedom at last! Roland's a great guy but he never relents on the pressure does he? It's go, go, go the whole time.'

'When they lay him in his coffin they'll have to fasten the lid down hard,' she agreed, 'or he'll be out again manufacturing coruscating careers and hatching up deals!'

Michael replaced his delicate sensitive hands on the table and looked down at them. 'He wants to package me you know. Like a box of luxury chocolates.'

Tara laughed. 'Go on.'

'Worse, he wants to package me with Brahms.'

'What?'

'He wants me to record the most popular symphonies – as determined by computer read-outs – the violin concerto and the two piano concerti on a boxed set of discs. It's to be called the Olshak-Brahms collection. Can you believe it?'

'Yes. Are you going to do it?'

'Am I hell!'

'What have you got against Brahms?'

'Nothing. I've been totally in love with him and his music for years. Which is why I balk at recording his work packaged under a chocolate box cover where my name is bigger than his and my picture's all over the box and poor old Brahms nowhere to be seen.'

'Oh dear.'

'Grim isn't it? Grant's trying to sell me as a product and using the music just as a vehicle. Of course the big agents are all at it, creating and promoting "personalities". They have to keep up with the times or go under.'

'What will you do?'

'I'm leaving the multi-national recording group Grant placed me with and signing up with a small independent Danish company who are more interested in music and composers than with the mammoth egos of "big-star" conductors and their glossy images.'

An image of Saul flashed through Tara's mind. She wondered if Saul had also been in Olshak's mind whilst he was speaking.

'It sounds like a good idea,' she said evenly. 'What's the snag? No, don't tell me – money. They're going to pay you peanuts.'

'Not peanuts. Simply a fair wage for what I do.'

'Will you and Roland part company?'

Olshak looked thoughtful, and faintly sad. 'I don't know. I'm truly fond of Roland, but . . .' He shrugged.

'You were always an idealist,' said Tara. 'Do you

remember talking to me at Tanglewood all those years ago? We discussed the problems for a conductor of starting off Mozart symphonies.'

'Oh yes, I remember,' he said, his eyes staring hard into her face as though he wanted to look at her with great care so he would never forget.

'You were a true romantic when it came to talking about music.'

'I was a true romantic full stop,' he agreed. His face lit with an impish smile. 'Of course you know that I fell in love with you that day?'

'Oh, I guessed something of the sort.'

'You're laughing at me. But it was true, I did.'

Tara sensed the genuineness of the young man's warmth and the note of sincerity and uncomplicated friendship behind his faintly jesting words. She felt enormously grateful. She realized how starved she had been for affection and appreciation in the past months, with Saul so often absent and Alessandra finally gone.

'Let's get some fresh air,' he said suddenly. 'I'm beginning to feel stifled.'

They walked down Old Compton Street together, drawn towards the bright lights of Cambridge Circus. The pale ink-washed sky above them glowed with a citrus beam gathered up from a billion city lights. Olshak pulled her arm through his. It was a gesture of friendship and protectiveness and she did nothing to resist it.

'Did you have a happy childhood Michael?' she asked him suddenly.

He thought for a moment or two. 'Yeah. I guess I did. Nice parents, keen for me to do well, but not too pushy. A nice house, baseball classes in addition to the music ones. Oh – and a pair of twin kid sisters who were a pain in the neck. But, yeah – a good childhood. Why?'

'Saul had a desperately sad and lonely childhood. He was an orphan brought up by a dutiful but cold and remote uncle.' She paused. 'So you see, maybe there's a reason why he needs constant acclaim, constant reassurance that he's pretty damn good at what he's doing.'

Michael said nothing for a while and Tara knew that he was giving careful thought to what she had told him.

'And,' she added, with calm insistence, 'it goes without saying that Saul is one of the most brilliant musical interpreters of his generation.'

'I'm sorry,' Michael said softly at last.

'So no more side swipes at Saul – mmm?'

'No. Look Tara, I wasn't suggesting . . .'

'I'm sure whatever you were suggesting wasn't done deliberately. At least not in the sense of wanting to be hurtful. But it did hurt me a bit, because Saul's been the love of my life. And I still love him very much.'

Thinking with longing of the absent Saul prompted her to move closer to Olshak, to seek the comfort of a man's body pressed against hers. 'And when he's alone with me,' she concluded with faint admonishment, 'I live with the real man, not the image.'

'Oh Tara!' He put his arm around her waist. 'Tara, you make me feel as if I should be grovelling at your feet in shame!'

'Dear Michael, you're still a hopeless romantic.'

'Yeah.' He grinned down at her. 'Listen, let's take

the tube down to Trafalgar Square and do something crazy, sit on the stone lions or whatever!'

Tara found it was not too easy to climb onto the Trafalgar Square lions when you were wearing high heeled shoes and thinking of protecting your unborn child. So she perched on the side of the fountain instead and stared up at the soaring column topped with Lord Nelson's statue.

Olshak sat beside her. Easily, without any awkward hint of seduction, he wrapped his arm around her once again.

'Have you got a girl?' she asked. 'Or a wife maybe?'

'No wife. But I'm dating someone. She's nice. A cellist with the Boston Phil.'

'And where is she tonight?'

'Somewhere in the middle east. They're on tour.'

'So we're both poor abandoned souls.'

'I guess so.'

'Oh Michael,' she sighed, leaning her head against his shoulder.

'I've been thinking of you quite a bit these last few months,' he said. 'Ever since I saw you in Manchester back in the early summer.'

'Really! I didn't see you.'

'I skulked in the back row of one or two of your seminars. I was wearing a big Trilby hat to hide the curls, so you wouldn't spot me.'

'You silly boy! I wouldn't have minded!'

'Wouldn't you? Being stalked by a red-haired goof who fell in love with a married woman around ten years ago and still has a bleeding heart.'

'Stop it!' she laughed.

'It's OK. I'm not dangerous, but I still get a thrill

when I see your picture in the papers, or on a disc sleeve.'

She sighed.

'What's the matter?' he asked, sounding worried. Still holding her, he arched the top part of his body away a little so that he could get a proper look at her. 'You're sad aren't you?'

'A bit. And a bit mixed up. You can still be that, you know Michael, even when you get to be ancient and gone forty.'

'OK,' he said crisply. 'Are you going to tell me? Is it because of your career? Did hearing Lucy tonight stir up old memories? Tara, it was such a tragedy that your career got messed up in that accident.'

'My career as a virtuoso violinist had a full stop put on it,' she countered. 'But I still make music through my conducting. And that's what truly matters isn't it? Making wonderful music? I remember you saying just that in Tanglewood.'

'Yeah. And I haven't changed my mind.' He reached up and caressed her hair with delicate light strokes. 'It'll be OK,' he said. 'It'll all be OK – whatever *it* is.'

'Yes, I suppose so.' She drew in a long breath. 'It's mainly to do with my daughter. She went off to Spain last year, fell in love with a wealthy Spanish wine grower and married him within weeks. And since then I've only seen her once.'

'Is she happy?'

'Yes, I think so. He's a lovely man.'

'But?'

'Oh, I don't know. I suppose I had such hopes for her; that she'd do something hugely exciting and daring with her life.' She laughed. 'That sounds a little over dramatic doesn't it? You see, she had this burning ambition to be an international show-jumper. Both Saul and I used to be a bit worried on her behalf, thinking about the precariousness of the life, and the danger too I suppose. But now I've got the feeling she's lost the drive and impetus for competition work. In fact when I saw her last there was no talk of a career of any sort, she was simply wanting to be with her man.'

Michael was listening carefully, nodding from time to time, making no comment.

'And now that she seems to have given up the idea of show-jumping, perversely I feel disappointed on her behalf.' Tara shook her head and gave a slow wistful smile. 'Stupid, isn't it?'

'No, it strikes me as quite natural. What does Saul think about it?'

Tara felt a cold stillness inside herself. 'I don't know Michael,' she said regretfully. 'I truly couldn't say.'

She realized that the confession was in some way a betrayal of Saul, because she had let an outsider know that her husband was shutting her out of his most private feelings about their only child. She guessed, however, that Michael was a man who could be trusted to treat the revelation with respect and understanding – and to keep it to himself.

Again she felt a surge of warmth and gratefulness to her flame-haired companion. It was so good, at long last, to talk frankly and freely about her confusion and hurt with regard to Alessandra.

'You know,' she said thoughtfully, spreading her

fingers to catch the spray of the fountain, 'when I was younger I thought that as you got older you'd learn how to share your feelings with the people closest to you, that you'd get the knack of being able to say even the most delicate and risky things without upsetting anyone. I believed that sharing your thoughts would just get easier and easier. And instead . . .' she broke off, unable to go any further.

Michael stood up and pulled her gently to her feet. 'Where's your car?' he asked.

'At home in Oxfordshire. Roland drove me up to town.'

'It's too late to get back on the train,' he said. 'Come and stay at my hotel.'

'Michael! I'm not a bed hopper.'

'I didn't ask you to be. Although if you gave me the slightest hint . . .'

'I won't!'

He gave her a huge hug and pressed a big firm kiss on her cheek. 'At least I'll know you're under the same roof and that you're safe. And that's fine.'

They walked on together, arms linked around each other's waists in warmly affectionate companionship.

In the morning, having slept sweetly and separately, they met up in the dining room for breakfast.

'If anyone were to see us here, having a *tête à tête* over the bacon and eggs,' smiled Michael, 'they'd never believe how honourably we've behaved.'

'As pure as the driven snow,' agreed Tara wryly. As she shook out her very pure and snowy linen napkin, she glanced around the room with interest. A couple in the corner caught her eye. Although the woman's face was partly turned away, Tara recognized her immediately as a lovably notorious member of the British Royal Family. And the man whose eyes were gazing into hers, were most definitely not those of her royal husband.

Buttering a warmed roll, Tara smiled to herself, pretty certain that the illicit couple's night together had been nothing like as chaste as hers and Michael's.

'Can we meet again?' Michael asked. 'Strictly good friends.'

Tara considered for a moment. 'Why not?' she said softly.

She noticed a discreetly suited man bending over the lovers in the corner. There were some murmurings. The woman gave a smothered guffaw. Tara caught her delighted, only half muffled exclamation. 'The fire escape!' she spluttered. 'Gosh how exciting.'

Michael glanced at Tara and winked. 'I don't think that'll be necessary for us.'

'No, we'll live *really* dangerously and go out by the front door,' she chuckled.

The four or five press photographers waiting outside the hotel for a juicy royal scandal picture, were becoming restless. In the main they ignored the departure of Tara and Michael. But there was one young man who recognized them both and was intrigued. This wouldn't make any front pages, but there was always cash to be had for fillers. Raising his camera he started clicking.

CHAPTER 21

Georgiana examined her face in the mirror. It was really quite remarkable how techniques in cosmetic surgery had improved in the past few years. Only three days after going under the knife, there was hardly any discoloration or bruising to be seen on her chin or neck. Just lovely firm smooth skin.

She laid the mirror down on the white cotton bedcover and leaned back against the pile of soft squashy pillows. She felt immensely pleased with herself as though she had performed this latest miracle with her own hand.

In fact, she reflected, life in general had been going along rather nicely in the past few weeks, ever since her chance glimpse of Tara, which had triggered the conception of a fascinating and absorbing project, now gestating most satisfactorily.

Georgiana had decided to take the option of staying on at the clinic for a longer period than was medically recommended. She could have gone home the day before, but it was so pleasantly soothing to be looked after in the clinic. And besides, Daneman was all tied up with a therapy convention at some learned institute or other this week, which meant he had to stay late for evening sessions, so that she would have been on her own in the house, with no one to admire the results of her suffering.

Moreover, she felt freer in the anonymous atmosphere of the clinic to do certain things which she judged she might have baulked at in her own home, where the quiet presence of her husband – whether he were actually present or not – acted as a partial brake on her more questionably devious schemes. Daneman loved her, she knew that. But she sometimes thought that he was just a little in awe of the range of her daring and imagination.

He would, perhaps, not be pleased to hear that her inventiveness in finding ways to delve into Tara's personal secrets had gone as far as hiring an unremarkable company-style car in which to keep track of her former husband's one-time mistress, and her comings and goings to consult with her gynaecologist. At least that was the initial plan.

Finding it rather fun driving around in her little purple Vauxhall, Georgiana had then amused herself further by purchasing a fetching dark brown wig in a short waved style the entire opposite of her own long straight one. Things had progressed from there to the selection of a number of entertaining new clothes which projected the perfect image of a smart middle management executive rather than a beautiful lady of leisure which was her own cherished signature.

Driving out for the first time in her full disguise (put on in stealthy secret after Daneman had left for his consulting rooms) she had felt a delicious thrill of excitement, as though she had assumed an entirely new personality.

When Tara turned up for her next gynaecological appointment, Georgiana had been in place in her Vauxhall, in prime position to observe Tara spring lightly up the steps and disappear into the spacious hallway leading to the doctor's suite of rooms.

She had waited patiently for half an hour, and then when Tara re-emerged and got back into her car she had discreetly followed the green Jaguar as it moved down the street.

Tara had driven north, eventually parking her car on Islington High Street and then walking along a little way before turning into a Turkish restaurant. Georgiana had allowed a few minutes to pass and then had followed in Tara's footsteps, casually glancing in shop windows, but unfortunately the restaurant had deep red curtains hung on a brass pole screening the customers inside and so she was unable to gain any information on Tara's possible lunch companions and had eventually been obliged to retreat back to the Vauxhall.

Tara spent a full two hours in the restaurant. When she left she had got into her car and driven off in a northerly direction.

Georgiana, concluding that Tara was simply returning to her Oxfordshire house (which used to be *her*, Georgiana's house) had decided not to pursue her. Instead she had waited a little and watched the other diners leave the restaurant. There was no one she recognized, although she was rather struck by a tall young man with a mane of unruly red curls.

On the next occasion Tara had simply driven to

Roland Grant's offices in Piccadilly after leaving her doctor's and Georgiana had decided to abandon her vigil and do some shopping instead.

There was not much to go on yet. In fact Georgiana had to admit to herself that she was not entirely sure what it was she wanted to find out, she just knew that this game of pursuit and observation was utterly fascinating and curiously fulfilling. She was also pretty certain now that Tara must be pregnant. If she had some dreadful disease she would certainly not look so healthy and springy. And surely the only reason for regular visits to a gynaecologist must be pregnancy. Hormone treatment, such as oestrogen patches or implants, did not require a steady number of regular visits. Georgiana should know, she had had all the menopausal treatment necessary to keep her young, stop her bones from going brittle and prevent those parts most cherished by a husband from shrivelling up like a dried prune.

Coming out of her thoughts into the here and now, she stretched, deciding she was rather tired of lounging about in bed. She would get up, make herself very lovely, and take lunch in the dining room.

Sipping a dry pre-lunch sherry in the lounge she chatted with one or two other patients. Her eye was drawn to a glossy society magazine open on the heavy brass and glass coffee table in front of her. As her companions drifted into the dining room and she was left briefly on her own, she picked it up and scrutinized the picture which had caught her eye. It was one of several in a page feature, titled, 'Out and about in London'.

Georgiana stared, little thrills darting about in her nerves. It was a picture of Tara in the company of a young man. She was smiling up into his face and he was looking down at her as though he would like to gobble her up. The accompanying caption simply said, 'Conductors Tara Silk and Michael Olshak leave London's Dorchester Hotel on the morning after Olshak's triumphant concert at the Barbican'.

Georgiana felt a stab of pure excitement, thinking that without a doubt people only left hotels together in the morning when they had spent the night together. She also realized that the young man she had seen leaving the restaurant was clearly the same as the one in the picture she now held in her hands.

Well, well, well! Saul's wife Tara was lunching with a glamorous young conductor, and spending nights with him at the Dorchester. She was doing this even though she was pregnant.

And where was Saul in all this? Georgiana's head began to spin with conjecture.

A gentle voice disturbed her ponderings. 'Mrs Daneman, your lunch is served.'

Georgiana looked up at the polite, white-coated young woman speaking to her. 'Ah, yes,' she said vaguely.

'Are you all right Mrs Daneman?'

'Oh yes. Perfectly.'

'You're looking very well, I must say.' The young woman's appreciation was obvious and obviously genuine.

Georgiana smiled at her in gracious acknowledgement. She placed the magazine under her arm, rose to her feet with the grace of a prima ballerina and moved forward into the dining room.

Sometimes, she thought, things all fall into place. Simply too good to be true.

Tara poured Saul a whisky, dropped two cubes of ice into it and took the chinking glass into the drawing room where she found him sat listening to the newly released compact disc he had recorded some months earlier.

The music was Handel. The piece *The Messiah*.

'*Oh who may abide the day of His coming*?' sang the choir.

'*And who shall stand when He appeareth*?' Tara joined in, singing along. She put the whisky glass in Saul's hands, leaning down to him and dropping a kiss on his forehead.

He looked up, his grey eyes assessing her with that sharp and penetrating glance that still made her pulse quicken.

'I used to play your 1970s recording of this piece quite a lot when you first brought me to live here,' she said.

His lips curved into a smile. 'And?'

'And I used to chuckle over the bit about "who shall stand when He appeareth", because that's what I felt I ought to do each time you walked into the room.'

'So deluded,' he commented drily. 'I hadn't realized I was nurturing such a dangerous little viper in my bosom. If I had of course . . .'

They looked into each other's eyes. There was a tiny pause.

He put the glass down on the floor beside him, flung out his arm and with one swift movement pulled Tara onto his knee. She landed in a heap and he spread her legs apart so that she was sitting astride him.

'Aah,' she gasped as he crushed her hard against him and began to strafe her lips with his. Her heart roared in her chest and hot longing sang through her nerves.

She hadn't anticipated this; she had never included the obstacle of explosive desire as one of the hurdles she might have to surmount when approaching the issue of telling Saul her significant news.

She began to kiss him back, her urgency raw and relentless. It was weeks since they had made love. She felt his hand moving up her thigh, heard the subdued metallic tearing sound as he undid his zip.

She drew back. 'No. Saul. Darling. Wait!'

His body froze into stillness, and as she looked into his eyes she was sure she could see the dark pupils contract.

'What is it?' he asked, instantly on the alert, instantly in control again.

'I . . .' Her voice seemed to become swallowed up in her throat.

'Yes?'

The stiffness in her spine suddenly crumpled. 'Oh Saul,' she whispered, 'I'm sorry.'

'Go on.' His face was suddenly cold and guarded. She had the sense that he was filled with suspicion.

'I should have told you before. I shouldn't have let this happen.' She looked down at herself, seeing her skirt wrinkled up to her hips, the lacy tops of her stockings exposed, the shadowy hazing of dark hair, the deep hollows of the intimate insides of her thighs.

She saw herself as he must have seen her just a few moments ago, playing the seductive coquettish wife. And all the time she had been hugging to herself this secret that he knew nothing about.

She pulled away from him slightly. She had the horrible impression that she had behaved like a teasing tart, leading her man on only to say no to him at the final moment. She kept wanting to repeat, sorry, sorry, sorry.

'Tara,' he said evenly, 'will you please tell me right away what is making you look at me as though I were some kind of demon?' On receiving no instant response, he sighed, picked up his glass and took a sip of whisky. 'What have I done?'

Tara made a move as though to wriggle from his lap, but he held her tight with a restraining hand. 'Tell me!' he demanded.

'It's not you,' she said, 'it's me.'

'Explain!' His hold on her arm was now a fierce grip.

She swallowed. 'It's something very important. I was wrong not to tell you straight away.'

'Tell me,' he insisted with icy calm.

'I'm pregnant Saul.' She heard her voice echoing round the big empty room. 'I'm going to have another baby.'

His glance moved away from her, and then moved back. 'But that's *good* news Tara. Splendid news.'

'You think so?'

'Yes.' He grasped her hand, pressing it so hard he was hurting her. 'So why didn't you tell me before? Why did you think I wouldn't be delighted?'

She bowed her head, truly not knowing the honest answer to this eminently reasonable question. 'Sometimes Saul,' she said eventually, with courageous openness, 'I don't think I have very much idea at all what you will feel or think or say.'

'I find that hard to believe.' His voice was cold and detached, but when she looked into his face she thought she saw flickers of vulnerability. Her words had hurt him.

He zipped himself up and ran a smoothing hand over the front of his shirt. 'How long have you known?'

'Not long,' she lied swiftly, not wanting to wound him further. 'I needed to be sure.'

His eyes searched hers, and she could tell that he was filled with speculation. 'I was under the impression that there were to be no more children for us,' he said eventually and there was a faint challenge in his tone.

'Apparently damaged tissue can repair itself over time,' Tara told him, going on to explain to him just what the doctor had said to her.

'Did you know there was a possibility of conceiving a child before you became pregnant?' he asked. He was like a coolly formidable prosecuting barrister with a trembling witness.

'No. Why?'

'Oh, just idle curiosity.' He turned his face to one side, his cowled lids half covering his eyes.

'Like hell it's idle curiosity!' She shook his arm. 'Saul, tell me what you're getting at.' The sharp teeth of guilt nibbled at her insides.

'I suppose,' he said slowly, 'that for a man, there's a difference in making love to a woman who is fertile, than to one who isn't.'

Her mouth dropped open. 'What?'

He gave a wry smile. 'Now I've shocked you.'

'You certainly have. What on earth do you mean? You're talking as though I were some kind of brood mare, an incubation unit.' Tara felt suddenly furious. Her eyes blazed at him. 'And I'm not a woman you make love with, I'm your wife!'

He shook his head, loving and indulgent. 'You were always such a little tigress before when you were pregnant,' he said softly.

'Huh!' she snorted, jumping off his knee and pulling her skirt down.

Saul took another slow sip of his drink. 'Listen to me Tara,' he said quietly. 'It's a question of responsibilities. If a man is making love to a woman, even if that woman is his wife whom he knows and loves very dearly and very well, he still has a duty to her.'

She frowned, perplexed.

'He might need to protect her from an unwanted pregnancy, for example. How can he do that if he doesn't know there is a chance it might happen?' He looked up, shooting her a glance that made her shiver. 'And she has a duty to him too, because their bodies are something they share more deeply and fully than any other part of their existence.'

She swallowed. She was not entirely sure she followed his argument. But she thought he was trying to say something very important and fundamental about trust.

Again guilt struck.

She had a sudden picture of herself with Michael Olshak, her head resting against his shoulder, her arm encircling his waist whilst his encircled hers. Her heart slowed.

But all of that had been truly innocent. Her behaviour and relationship with Michael were utterly blameless, implying no betrayal or treachery, no loss of love for Saul. Being with Michael was something she couldn't *tell* Saul about. But it was harmless. Surely?

'However,' said Saul cutting into her thoughts, 'You didn't know that you had become fertile again. So you must forgive my little outburst of moralizing.'

She stared at him, her mouth drying as though she were the quivering mouse fixed with the gaze of the cat. She turned from him. *Get a grip on yourself! Be sensible!* She told herself it was far too early yet for her hormones to be taking a hold on her reason.

'Forgiven,' she said, and made a huge effort to make her voice as light as a nicely risen soufflé.

Saul gave her a long look, and then he smiled. 'So,' he said slowly, 'another child.'

'Yes. It's strange. In fact it seems like some kind of miracle.'

'Indeed it is.' He turned his glass in his long fingers. 'I hope I'm not too old,' he said.

'Old!' she looked at him shocked. She never thought of him as old. He had more energy, more drive, more sheer life in him than a whole clutch of some of the men she knew who were twenty years younger.

'When this child is Alessandra's age, I shall most probably be dead,' he reminded her drily.

'Saul, don't!'

'It's simply stating the possibilities, facing reality.'

He shot her a deep glance. 'Tara, is this baby a replacement for Alessandra?'

'No!' she exclaimed hotly, before going on to think about it and then becoming chilled when she considered the possible truth embedded in his words. They seemed to emphasize how bereft she had been feeling, as though Alessandra were truly lost to her.

'No,' she repeated firmly. 'Not consciously, at any rate. No child could replace Alessandra. And anyway it didn't happen like that Saul. This baby wasn't calculated. It just came into being, like some kind of gift.'

She saw a kind of calm, resigned scepticism in his face. She had a sharp horror of things spiralling down between them, a gap widening. For one terrible moment she even thought about Saul and other women. *If a man is making love to a woman . . .*

Saul with another woman. She simply couldn't bear it.

She knelt down and wrapped her arms around his knees. She rubbed her hands along his thighs. 'The doctor said it was quite safe – as long as we weren't too vigorous.'

He dropped a light kiss on her nose. 'All in good time,' he said enigmatically.

'Darling,' she murmured, laying her head on his lap, her feelings in confusion, her body full of longing. 'Please.'

The phone pealed into the soft breathing stillness. Saul made no move.

He and Tara listened transfixed as Alessandra's voice sounded on the tape. 'Mummy, Daddy – it's me. I want to come home.'

CHAPTER 22

Raphael paced to and fro in his mother's studio. Outside the late afternoon was heavy-lidded and sultry, like the face of a flamenco dancer. Clouds were beginning to gather, herded together and steered by an insistent wind coming in from the Atlantic far in the south west. A livid olive green light lay on the vineyard and tinted the roof of the winery to a dull metallic gold.

In this atmosphere of heavy thunderous expectancy Raphael was waiting for his family whom he had summoned earlier. His mother and sister and nephew. The three who had conspired to make his beloved Alessandra's life a misery, whilst all the time he, the only one who had the power to curb them, had stubbornly refused to see the full depth of that misery, until it was almost too late. He didn't think he had felt so wretched with shame and guilt in his life.

He paused in front of one of his mother's current canvases, now nearing completion. For years he had tried to bring himself to look at his mother's paintings square on; to face them in all their savage

290

turmoil and waywardness and rage. But in the main he had failed, and in recent months he had made certain to avoid them.

Almost wincing he allowed his eyes now to roam over the slashing swathes of black and magenta and green, the random blood-red blobs, the distorted purple ovoids that looked like a devil's smile. It seemed to him like a picture of furious frustration, an ever raging battle that would never be resolved.

He guessed that some psychiatrists might judge this to be the work of a person of unsound mind; someone with a personality disturbance or even perhaps some variety of psychotic disorder. But they would be wrong. He was quite confident that his mother was frighteningly sane and perfectly well aware of what she was doing, which in a nutshell was trying to make someone else's life hell, and in doing so forcing them into giving up any claims of sharing, her, the queen bee's, territory.

His mother's rages and frustration, for so long ignored and repressed, had suddenly thrust themselves into the forefront of Raphael's thoughts, ever since the horrible evening a few days ago when she had truly gone too far.

Alessandra had crumpled in a way which had horrified him. And for a moment he had felt a breathless fear that he might lose her.

His heartbeat stumbled now just thinking about it, the impossibility of living without her. But after the brief terror subsided and he had paused to consider calmly, he had come to the conclusion that, on balance, their steadily growing love for each other would still manage to triumph over all the rancour and bitterness and mischief.

It was most probably the wine that had been to blame, he thought with an ironic smile. The wine had loosened his mother's tongue so that it had spun out of control, flicking from her mouth like the tongue of a serpent, whippy and deadly.

All that day Alessandra had been raw and on edge. In the morning, finding her in the bathroom with a box of tricks like a chemistry experiment, he had suddenly lost his temper. He had gone so far as to shout at her, not wanting to engage in yet another of their seemingly endless discussions on the subject of babies.

And this time they had truly quarrelled and at the end of it she had shied away from him like an abused thorougbred race horse. He could tell that she was deeply agitated, by the way she frequently fingered her plait when he went to find her later in order to apologize, going so far as to pull it against her mouth on one or two occasions like a child seeking the comfort of a well sucked security blanket.

On that fateful evening, when Isabella and Catriona had come down to dine they had both been silently simmering with their own private grievances and concerns. Raphael had not at first taken much notice of their repressed storminess, being used to their fluctuating moods. His concerns were all for Alessandra. He had, of course, realized at once that Catriona was well 'tanked up' on vodka, before she so much as made a start on the sherries, a variety of which María always kept well stocked up on the silver drinks tray.

Isabella, in contrast, had initially been most regally sober. She had spent a difficult hour with Emilio before retiring to her room to dress for dinner and was still recovering from the shock of having had to listen to him yelling at her in contemptuous anger, something which had never occurred before.

Arrayed in emerald green silk, with diamonds and emeralds around her neck and swaying from her ears with an evil glinting, she had erupted into the drawing room in no mood to be trifled with.

Alessandra, insecure and unnerved from the earlier row with Raphael, who was the one raft she could cling to in this shifting sea of hostility, had sought refuge at the piano and was still there, continuing to play even after Isabella had made her entrance.

Raphael had noticed that his wife had been spending the lion's share of her time at the piano in recent weeks. And when she was not playing he knew that she had been absorbed in reading through Isabella's untouched, leather bound volume of the complete sonatas of Beethoven. He had been pleased for her to return to an area of interest and skill he knew she was still greatly attached to. Yet concerned also.

Isabella was not pleased. It was not so much hearing her prized piano being played by a stranger's, a foreigner's hands, that irritated her. In secret she had a steadily growing appreciation of Alessandra's talents as a pianist and on occasions, when they had friends to dine, she had actually requested Alessandra to play, showing her off as a kind of cultural trophy. But on that particular evening it was merely the fact that Alessandra was still *there* that triggered Isabella's fury. In spite of all her efforts to dislodge this young beautiful fair-skinned intruder, she was still there in her house.

Hers! Isabella Carlotta Luisa Saventos, who had been the queen of her domain for a quarter of a century and was by no means ready to be relegated to the role of dowager.

Isabella still clung to her hopes of banishing the young usurper and regaining her full powers as she saw them. The fact that Raphael had married the girl was only a partial deterrent. They had been married in secret. A civil ceremony only. No one from either of the families had attended. During the weeks and months following the marriage, whilst jabbing and lunging at her canvases in the studio, Isabella had gradually managed to persuade herself that the couple were not truly married at all.

Alessandra had now come to the end of the movement she was playing. She looked across to Isabella and, noting the dangerous glints in her jewels and her eyes, slowly closed the heavy book of sonatas and got up from the piano stool.

'I have that sonata on a record,' said Isabella importantly. 'The player is Alfred Brendel who I very much admire.'

'Yes, so do I,' agreed Alessandra. She smoothed her simple sleeveless navy shift dress over her slender figure with graceful elegant hands.

Isabella followed the movement of her hands, her glance noting the perfectly curved breasts and the enviably taut flat stomach. As she caught sight of the big Saventos ruby on Alessandra's wedding finger a flame of feeling leapt inside her and she took in a deep breath. 'The splendid thing about Alfred Brendel's playing is that he plays *all* of the notes,' she announced with a certain pointed satisfaction. She spoke with the confidence of one who is a knowledgeable music critic, omitting to mention that she was enabled to do this by having heard a famous critic make exactly the same remark on the radio a day or two before.

'My father recorded several of the Beethoven sonatas when he was a young man,' Alessandra said. 'We've got them on the old 78 rpm shellac discs.'

'Really,' said Isabella.

'*He* plays all the notes too,' said Alessandra, crossing to the sherry tray, pouring herself a glass and then placing it untouched on the mantelpiece.

Catriona, sitting on the sofa flicking through a pile of magazines, gave a little yawn. She hated it when her mother launched into cultural talk; anything to do with painting, or music or literature. She judged her mother did it all for effect, that she was not truly interested in 'art' at all. Her mother was one of those people who would spend a fortune going off to Paris to see some dire contemporary opera. She would sit through three hours of ear-piercing atonal squeaks and shrieks and at the end would experience some spurious feeling of artistic fulfilment – or so she claimed.

Catriona was pretty sure her mother simply liked being seen all dressed up in some very smart places. Catriona could understand that. It was what she herself liked to do, although she preferred a fabulously exclusive rock concert with tickets only obtainable if you knew someone who knew someone, and a star of the status of Mick Jagger topping the bill.

Catriona took a deep sip of her tongue-tinglingly dry sherry and lit a long menthol cigarette. For some days now she had been hoping to be invited to just such a concert; a diamond-dripping charity event in New York.

It had all come about entirely unexpectedly, in the best tradition of the most exciting things in life. Whilst visiting an antique jewellery shop in Barcelona during her and her mother's last trip there, she had met a very attractive American dealer who had asked her out to dine with him on two separate occasions. He had obviously been interested in her recent buying and selling of some unusual Austrian masonic jewellery dating from the last half of the eighteenth century. And they had whiled away a few very pleasant hours discussing the fascinating ins and outs of the antique jewellery business.

He had been extremely attentive, listening carefully to everything she had to say. After a time she had sensed that his interest went beyond hard-headed business matters. Even in the highly cynical and suspicious Catriona's eyes he had seemed quite heavily attracted to her. And for a single woman of her age who had had two previous disastrous love affairs with highly unsuitable men, he had seemed like unexpected manna from heaven. Just when she found herself getting to that state of feeling over the hill, just when things at home were becoming impossible – Raphael finally married, her mother like a box of explosives, Emilio sullen and intractable – here was an answer to her prayers. A rich, sexy entrepreneur who would take her away from it all. Maybe even marry her. The road to freedom gleamed suddenly golden ahead of her.

But her antique dealer hadn't phoned this afternoon when he said he would. His line in New York was constantly busy. She feared the old familiar rejection.

'Maybe they should have a little competition,' Catriona suggested, looking at her mother through calculating eyes screwed up against the smoke from her cigarette. 'Brendel and Xavier – see who plays the most notes.' She shot a malicious glance at Alessandra who was looking most hatefully gorgeous, and oh so slim. 'What do you think?'

Alessandra shrugged, refusing to be drawn.

'But I don't suppose,' Catriona went on in a languidly bored voice, 'that your father would be interested in vulgar games like that.'

Alessandra turned to face her. 'Competitions of virtuosity are nothing new. Did you know that Mozart once had a competition on the keyboard with a musician called Clementi? The emperor Joseph set it up and offered a cash reward.'

'Is that so? Who won?'

'Who do you think?' Alessandra glanced down at her sister-in-law, warning her to stop needling. 'Actually,' she said with a little smile, 'a competition between my father and Brendel could be quite intriguing. And fun too, they're close friends you see.'

'Really.' Catriona got up, poured her mother an enormous goblet of sherry, then topped up her own glass and returned to the magazines.

Isabella sat down beside her daughter and asked Raphael one or two perfunctory questions about the

297

progress of the grape harvesting. He gave thoughtful answers to her queries, surprised at her sudden interest in the work aspects of the business. Usually she was only concerned to see the yearly balance sheet and the profits made, or to sample the best wines in the current crop.

'Oh see this!' declared Catriona, squashing her cigarette to death in the ash tray and tapping her fingers on the magazine which rested on her knee.

'What?' snapped Isabella.

But Catriona was not interested in her mother, she was looking at Alessandra. 'Here,' she said, offering the magazine for her inspection. 'Something to interest you. The picture at the top of the page.'

Alessandra took the magazine and stared at it for a moment in silence.

'What is it?' asked Isabella impatiently, hating to be left out of things. She took a gulp of sherry.

'A picture of Alessandra's mother.' Catriona leaned back and smiled. 'How nice it must be,' she commented slyly, 'to have parents who are famous enough to be in the gossip columns.'

'Oh!' exclaimed Isabella. 'Let me look at it.'

'You'll need your glasses mother.'

'Nonsense,' Isabella protested annoyed. 'I can see pictures without my glasses!'

'Yes but you can't read small print. And the caption's quite entertaining.' Catriona lit another cigarette. She had heard the swallowing sounds coming from Alessandra's throat and knew that she had succeeded in getting the younger woman rattled at long last. For a time this wife of Raphael's had seemed so self-contained and assured Catriona had wondered if she would ever penetrate her immaculate defences.

Isabella peered at the picture. 'Is this your mother?' she asked Alessandra as though doubtful.

'Yes.'

'She looks very young,' said Isabella, making it sound as if this were something to disapprove of.

'Yes,' said Alessandra.

'But this man with her – this isn't your father,' Isabella commented, holding the picture at a distance and trying to get a sharper focus.

'No.'

Alessandra looked pleadingly across at Raphael. He was busy arranging the sherry bottles, and she knew that he was trying to ignore the rancour between the members of his family and that he had not quite reached the point of realizing there was real trouble ahead.

'I think I do need my glasses,' said Isabella.

'Where are they?' asked Catriona with a sigh.

'Oh, I don't know. The stupid things, I hardly ever need them. You read the caption to me Catriona.'

Catriona took the magazine out of her mother's hands, making a show of sighing. She cleared her throat. 'Conductors Tara Silk and Michael Olshak . . .' she began.

As she read the awful damning words in her bland bored tones, Alessandra crossed swiftly to stand beside Raphael. She grasped at his hand, taking it in hers and squeezing hard. Instantly he was alert to her need. He put his arm around her shoulders and murmured into her ear. 'You mustn't worry *amor*. You must not be upset.'

'Well!' exclaimed Isabella, her eyes flashing with a complex medley of emotions as her daughter completed her reading task and dropped the magazine onto the sofa.

'I said you'd need your glasses,' Catriona said, drawing deeply on her cigarette and taking a huge drink of sherry. A strange little smile lit her face.

She was prevented from the invention of further means to drive home the dart she had so fortuitously chanced on and accurately thrown, with the abrupt arrival of Emilio who flung himself into the room, his glowering bad temper temporarily diverting attention from the company's contemplation of the apparently shocking misconduct of Alessandra's mother.

'Ottavio was out loose in the yard,' he proclaimed, accusingly staring at Alessandra. 'His door hadn't been fastened properly.'

'Oh heavens!' moaned Alessandra, dropping her forehead into her hand. 'The catch has been coming loose for a day or two. Ferdinand said he would look at it.'

'Ferdinand!' scoffed Emilio, pouring himself a generous sherry and spilling little runny dribbles all over the tray. 'He'll do it today, tomorrow, sometime, never. He's a lazy oaf.'

'Rubbish,' snapped Alessandra. 'Ferdinand is a very hard worker. He was probably busy with a million other things today!' She glared at Emilio. *Unlike you*, she was saying silently.

'Ottavio is a prize-winning horse. He is irreplaceable,' announced Emilio with a heavy self-righteousness which Alessandra though ludicrous.

'Is he safe now?'

'Yes, thanks to me,' said Emilio.

'You will please sit down and shut up,' Raphael snapped, rounding on him fiercely. 'Your record with Ottavio is not a shining one Emilio.'

'He could have been hit by a car, running around loose like that at the top of the lane,' Emilio said, throwing himself into a carved antique chair and making its legs quiver.

'Yes. And that car would most likely have been yours,' Raphael told him furiously. 'Who else drives a car in our lane like a madman? And such a ridiculous car too,' he added in a low ferocious growl.

Isabella jerked into alertness and sat up very straight. Whilst furious to see her grandson, her own flesh and blood, chided in this way in the presence of the female enemy, she was nevertheless inclined to caution. Raphael did not often exert his superiority, but when he did she knew that it was wise to tread warily. She felt suddenly rather overwhelmed and tired. She drained her glass and held it out to Raphael for a refill.

Catriona drew on her cigarette. 'How are things coming along with Ottavio?' she asked Alessandra in vague not especially interested tones. She tapped a grossly elongated funnel of ash into the tray whilst appraising her long immaculately manicured coral nails with leisurely approval.

'Very well,' said Alessandra. She was still grappling with the shock that had come from seeing the photograph of her mother thrust at her in such a brutal way. But outwardly she had made a remarkable recovery and gave every appearance of being her normal self again.

'How did he do at that show you took him to a while back?' Catriona wondered.

'We pulled out after the first class. He banged his hocks on one of the poles and I was afraid he might go lame if he did any more jumping straight afterwards,' said Alessandra, adding, 'Surely Emilio told you that.'

Catriona shrugged. 'Possibly. What bad luck.'

Alessandra did not add that she had been almost relieved to withdraw and devote herself to Ottavio's well being and comfort rather than career yet again round a set of gigantic fences. She had somehow felt no heart for the feverish rivalry seething in the atmosphere at the show. She had found herself asking what the hell it mattered if one rider got round clear a split second faster than another one. She had been astounded at herself.

Raphael, now officially her sponsor, had simply laughed and told her she was getting old and wise before her time. He had helped her bandage Ottavio's leg, driven the lorry home and then taken her to bed and made gentle but firm love to her.

'Hah!' exclaimed Emilio. 'What have you ever done with that horse that I couldn't do? Nothing!'

'Given him back his confidence,' Alessandra said coldly. 'You'll find he's a far better jumper now than he was when you last rode him.'

'Hah! You talk nonsense. Since you came here and stole away my horses you've done nothing with them. You just ride around in the field over a few fences and take them out walking in the countryside like an English person with their dogs.'

'Stop it!' warned Raphael, his eyes flaring.

302

But Emilio was in full cry now, his pent up rage pouring out in a torrent. 'What big events have you been to?' he demanded, glaring with hatred at Alessandra. 'What prizes have you won eh? Tell me that! None! You do *nothing* of any use here at all!'

There was a communal gasp of shock as Raphael grasped the front of Emilio's shirt, hauled him from his chair and slapped his face so hard that the blow rang out like the crack of a shotgun.

'How dare you?' Raphael shouted at him. 'How dare you speak to Alessandra in that way? What do you do with your time that gives you the arrogance to take *her* to task?' As Emilio stared at him speechless, Raphael grasped his shoulders and shook him, determined to force him into some kind of response. 'Tell me that. Tell me!'

'I am a member of the family,' said Emilio eventually, at first uncertain and then with growing conviction and a heavy tone of sanctimoniousness.

'And that gives you the right to be an idle and ill-mannered idiot does it?' Raphael growled. 'You're more of an oaf than Ferdinand will ever be.'

Emilio fingered the livid mark on his cheekbone, feeling wounded and aggrieved. He stole a glance of appeal at his grandmother. But Isabella, whilst outraged at the way Raphael had lashed out at Emilio and taken him to task, seemed disinclined to make any direct intervention. When she glanced towards Raphael, her eyes were filled with a certain fearful respect.

'I ought to send you to your room in disgrace without any dinner,' Raphael told Emilio grimly. 'If I'd done that once or twice when you were a boy

303

maybe you'd have grown up into a man by now.' His glance moved in stern disapproval over the three members of his family. 'The women in this house have ruined you,' he concluded eventually.

'No!' Isabella decided it was time to assert herself, even though her head was beginning to feel dizzy, her thoughts unfocused. 'You go too far Raphael. I am your mother. I will not be spoken to in that way.'

'I'm afraid it's only what you deserve,' Raphael said, but his voice was more controlled now, more reserved and wistful.

'It is most certainly not what I deserve. I deserve respect in my own house. From all of you.'

'Dear, dear,' drawled Catriona, sitting back and enjoying watching others stir the brew she had carefully prepared. 'How we Saventos people all fight like cats and dogs. Poor Alessandra must think she's landed in a bear garden.'

Isabella's eyes were full of fire. 'You speak to her of *our* family in that way. We from the Saventos dynasty!' Her bracelets flashed and jangled ferociously as she flung out an arm, pointing her finger at Alessandra. 'Think of *her* family. She is a bastard love-child, from parents who were adulterers. And her mother . . .'

'You bitch!' Alessandra said softly. 'You mean minded, wicked prejudiced bitch. You say another word about my mother and . . .'

'And you'll leave?' interrupted Isabella. 'You'll go back to England where you came from, and where you belong? That would be most satisfactory.'

'Mother, stop this!' roared Raphael.

'No, I won't stop!' Isabella yelled back. 'What does she do all day this girl of yours? She plays with

304

the horses and she plays my piano. She makes a show of helping you in the winery! Huh! What use is that? You should have married a good healthy Spanish girl. And then you could have controlled her properly. And she would have given you babies,' she concluded with vicious satisfaction.

There was dead silence as Isabella delivered this final and terrible *coup de grâce*. Even Catriona was taken aback.

Alessandra went very pale. She seemed dumb and frozen.

Raphael crossed to her side but she gave no sign of registering his presence. He put his arm around her. '*Amor!*' he murmured. He could feel her shivering.

'It's not too late,' Isabella said to her, sensing uncharacteristic vulnerability. 'You have not been married in church. In truth, you are not truly married as far as I'm concerned.'

Alessandra's eyes had opened very wide. And then she had disengaged herself from Raphael's arm and walked slowly from the room.

Looking back now, on this sultry dark evening with Alessandra temporarily gone from him, Raphael saw quite clearly all that he had unwittingly allowed to go wrong in the past year. And all that must, without question, be put right without delay.

As he heard the sound of his mother's and sister's footsteps making their way to the door he steeled himself.

CHAPTER 23

Alessandra flew into Gatwick airport as a brilliant September dawn was lighting the Surrey fields. Looking down as the aircraft came in to land she could see the complex system of the motorways beneath; gleaming black cables snaking through the green of the countryside with twinkling insect cars crawling all over them.

Her parents were both there to meet her. Her delight to see them was for a moment overpowering. The hugs and kisses between the three of them were warm and unrestrained, with no hint of unease or awkwardness as they walked linked arm in arm through the lower concourse.

They had chosen her mother's Jaguar for this outing, but it was her father who was driving. He always preferred to be at the wheel, to be in charge, thought Alessandra, relaxing into the comfort of the back seat of the car and looking at the back of his head with a wry and fond smile.

Tara, sitting with Saul in the front, kept turning round and smiling, she was so pleased to see her daughter again.

Alessandra felt a surge of love and pride. She thought her mother looked frail and very lovely. Her dark hair had grown a little since she last saw her. It fell on her shoulders in soft dark waves, framing her face which, although lightly made up, was unusually pale. Alessandra thought about the photograph of her mother with Michael Olshak. And then tried not to think of it.

'Well,' said Saul drily, 'we weren't able to see you actually step down from the plane. Did you kneel and kiss the tarmac?'

Alessandra, despite being exhausted with emotional turmoil and a terrible longing for Raphael, found herself entertained. 'Like the Pope?'

'Mmm.'

'Not quite. Although there was a wonderful feeling of coming home.'

'Good,' he said. 'That's exactly how we feel about your coming back also.'

Alessandra leaned back against the soft leather seat and gave a small sigh of relief. She realized that with her parents there would be no brittleness or hints of recriminations about her long absence and her coolness, and now this sudden and dramatic re-entry into their lives. There would be no danger of their herding her into a confrontational corner where she would be forced to make swift revelations of all that had happened to make her flee Spain so suddenly, and then give them a clear account of her plans for the future.

She felt their understanding and sensitivity reaching down deep and strong and solid beneath her. When she recalled how carelessly, almost cruelly, she had pushed them from her thoughts in the past year she felt great regret. But she knew they would not harbour resentment. And she resolved to try and put things right so that the three of them could be in harmony once again.

At the Xaviers' Oxfordshire home Mrs Lockton was cooking a traditional English breakfast of bacon, mushrooms, tomatoes and fried eggs. A pot of fragrant coffee was percolating.

Alessandra leaned over to inspect the contents of the frying pan and gave Mrs Lockton a hug. 'Hi.'

'Hello.' Mrs Lockton turned and smiled. 'Welcome back to England,' she said simply.

Here's another person from my childhood who isn't going to insinuate or pry, thought Alessandra. The contrast with the secrecy and manipulation in the Saventos ménage was so stark she could hardly reconcile the two.

Allegro appeared, his tail stiff like a periscope, not relaxing until Alessandra picked him up and tickled his chin, making his throat vibrate with eager purrs.

During breakfast, whilst Alessandra got to grips with Mrs Lockton's superb cooking and made up for having eaten virtually nothing the day before, her parents chatted lightly about music and orchestras and performances as was their usual habit.

Tara told them of her experiences the previous week when she had been asked to conduct the North East Symphonia at short notice. 'Those chaps up in the north east are real male chauvinists of the old school,' she laughed. 'When we started off, the blokes in the violin section were all playing a semi-tone flat, just to see if I'd notice. You know, me, being a mere woman! As if I'd no eyes or ears. And certainly no brain. I'm telling you, classical music is one of the last bastions of male dominance and prejudice.'

'The bastards,' said Saul ironically. 'Thinking they could get the better of you. Wait till I have a chance to get my hands on them.'

'Oh, and there's more,' she grinned. 'After that the lead horn player had the nerve to ask me what note he should be playing in his first entry in the Mahler Four. We weren't even doing that piece!'

'So you wouldn't have the score to look at,' said an interested Alessandra, spearing a mushroom.

'No. I'd only got the score of Mahler One which was what we were going to play.'

'So what happened?'

'I miraculously remembered what the note he was asking about was. You should have seen his face, when I told him. They all shut up and behaved after that.'

'So – the final score was decidedly in your favour,' smiled Saul.

Tara chuckled. 'I have to admit to feeling just a tiny bit smug.'

Alessandra looked at the food on her mother's plate, which looked as though it would hardly qualify as a sparrow's breakfast. 'Aren't you hungry?' she asked.

There was a tiny beating pause. 'No.' Tara pushed the bacon and tomatoes away. 'I think I'll just stick with the toast this morning.'

Alessandra put down her fork and looked hard at her mother. 'Are you all right Mummy? You're terribly white and your face looks thinner. Have you lost weight?'

Tara gave a hurried smile. She looked faintly haunted.

'She's been working too hard,' said Saul. 'I'm trying to think of a way of putting my foot down so she'll take notice of my advice and slow down a bit.'

Alessandra felt wretchedly guilty, wondering if her mother's paleness and thinness was a result of worrying about her, Alessandra, miles away in Spain and shockingly uncommunicative. She remembered the endless sharp retorts she had made to her mother on the phone and gave a small internal shudder.

Saul got up and refilled the coffee cups.

Tara picked up her cup. Her nose seemed to wrinkle in distaste as she inhaled the strong fragrant steam coming off the hot liquid. She made a little sound in her throat. 'I won't be a minute,' she said, standing up abruptly and almost running from the room.

Alessandra stared after her, and then looked towards her father, her eyes filled with alarm and questions. 'What's wrong?'

'Nothing,' he said shortly. 'There's nothing wrong. She's just a trifle under the weather.'

Alessandra reached for a slice of toast and began to butter it with long careful strokes, needing to have her fingers steadily occupied whilst her mind raced. This isn't about me she thought, her intuition guiding her. This is something quite different.

She dug a spoon into Mrs Lockton's home-made damson jam and placed a blob of it on her toast. She found her head filled with memories of the hateful photograph of her mother with Michael Olshak. And following that the scorn and disdain in Isabella Saventos's venomous black eyes.

She took a quick further glance at her father, but he was stirring his coffee in a slow anti-clockwise rhythm, his expression thoughtful and abstracted. In other words his normal expression.

'Has she seen a doctor?' Alessandra asked, unable to contain this sudden, completely unexpected anxiety about her mother. She felt as though she had only just re-discovered Tara, and now she might be really ill.

Saul looked up. 'Yes,' he said mildly. 'There's nothing to worry about.'

Alessandra was now absolutely convinced that there was. The internal spotlight in her head switched from herself as a key to her mother's troubles and landed fair and square on Michael Olshak instead.

She returned to her toast.

'What will Raphael be doing at this moment?' asked Saul, smoothly changing the subject.

Alessandra gave a little start. She glanced at her watch. 'He'll be out in the vineyard checking on the progress of the harvesting.' *I ought to be there for him*. She mourned silently.

She felt that she had deserted Raphael, even though he had said he perfectly understood her feelings, her need to have a little time with her own family. He had made all the arrangements, then driven her to the airport. He had held her so tenderly before she boarded the plane that she had almost decided against taking the flight.

Oh Raphael!

'So,' said Saul. 'He attends to all the practicalities personally? The real hands-on winemaker, mmm?'

'Oh yes,' exclaimed Alessandra, her eyes shining. 'He lives and breathes wine and grapes.' Her heart twisted with love and pride as she thought of Raphael's dedication to his work. In the past few weeks, when they had been out picking at the crack of dawn because the daytime heat had been so fierce, he had been out there with the pickers every single day. She could see his face now, lined with fatigue, yet still filled with the strength and dogged steadfastness that kept him relentlessly going.

And then she thought of his constant silent battles with his family which occasionally erupted into open warfare when he had to attempt the role of peacemaker. And on top of all that he had had to deal with a wife who had a weepy obsession with bathrooms and pregnancy testing kits.

'Good,' said Saul, rising from the table.

Alessandra emerged from her reflections, looking at him questioningly. She frowned. 'I'm sorry?'

He gave a dry short laugh. 'I was simply expressing satisfaction. It's perfectly obvious to me that your dash back to England doesn't appear to be an indication of a permanent rift.'

'Is that what you thought?'

'It was a possibility that crossed my mind.'

She gave a huge sigh. 'Oh, it's all so complicated.'

'Is it?' His grey eyes were cool and shrewd.

'Maybe not.' She picked up her coffee spoon and turned it in her fingers reflectively, making it catch the morning sunshine and throw a luminous patch of brightness on the wall. 'I just need a bit of time out,' she concluded vaguely.

'But not from Raphael?'

Tears filled her eyes. She blinked them away and shook her head. 'No, not from him.'

'I repeat – good! Well then, now that you've put my mind at rest I'm going to go and get on with a little work. I've a meeting with Roland at eleven. Maybe after that you'd like to come up to town and have lunch with me?'

'The Ritz or the Savoy Grill?' she said mischievously.

'Wherever you like,' he shrugged. 'Although I'm led to believe that all the smartest people lunch in dark basement wine bars these days. Especially the young ones.'

'What about Mummy?' she asked.

'I think her diary's pretty full today,' he commented drily, then smiling as Tara came back into the room and sat down once more at the table.

'Sorry about that,' Tara said briskly.

Alessandra was not sure whether her mother was referring to her abrupt flight from the breakfast table, or her full diary. She stared at her with renewed anxiety.

Saul dropped a light kiss on the heads of both his loved ones and departed unobtrusively.

'Mummy, I'm worried about you,' Alessandra said sternly.

'No need,' said Tara brightly. 'I'm fine. In the pink as they say.'

'You're working too hard,' Alessandra insisted. 'If Daddy says you are it must be really bad. He's the definitive workaholic.'

'Yes. But you have to remember that he doesn't apply the same exacting standards to everyone else in the world as he does to himself.'

'That sounds a bit barbed.'

'No, just a statement of reality. Daddy gives himself license to work all hours God sends and that's simply fine. But he holds the view that normal mortals have to take things a bit easier!'

'Yes,' said Alessandra slowly, 'I suppose that's right.'

Tara gave a little private smile. She took toast from the rack and started on the same spreading exercise that Alessandra had just completed.

Fingers of unease clutched Alessandra's stomach. She couldn't recall her mother ever before having said anything even faintly critical about her father. 'So what musical furrows are you ploughing today Mummy?' she asked with a smile which felt falsely bright.

Tara took a bite of her toast. 'None,' she said after a short pause.

'Oh! Daddy said your diary was full.'

Tara smiled. 'Not with work. I have to get my hair trimmed and do a little shopping,' she said vaguely.

'Fine. Then after that you can come and have lunch with me and Daddy. I'll tell you both my tale of Spanish drama.'

Tara prepared to have another bite of her toast and then put the bread back on her plate and pushed it away, with a little grimace.

'You really should eat something,' Alessandra said sternly. 'Keep up your strength for more work!'

'Yes. Don't worry, I'll be fine by lunch-time.'

'Great.' said Alessandra.

'But I can't meet you and Daddy for lunch. I'm really sorry darling,' said Tara, glancing swiftly at Alessandra and smiling with anxious apology. 'If I'd known you were coming I'd have made sure to be free.'

'I know, I know. I did rather spring out of the blue. It's me that should apologize,' said Alessandra stiffly, now convinced something was desperately wrong between her parents.

She was also horribly suspicious that Tara's unavailability to dine with her husband and daughter must be a sure sign that she was only too available to dine with Michael Olshak – please God not her lover.

Olshak you bastard! Alessandra said to herself. She had always been so certain of her parents' love for each other. In fact in her adolesence she had sometimes felt shut out from the warm circle of their mutual love. And now, could it really be that things were falling apart for them?

'Let's take a walk in the garden,' said Tara crisply, pouring and draining a glass of cold milk in a rather determined way. 'Come on, we could both do with some fresh air. There may not be many more mornings as sunny as this!'

They wandered across the dew-soaked lawn and Alessandra smelled the damp warm earthiness of an English garden – a blend of scents which brought her childhood memories flooding back.

'Tell me if you're unhappy,' said Tara abruptly without preamble. 'I need to know. And then I can help.'

Alessandra put her arm around her mother's shoulders. She had forgotten how small and delicate Tara was. Her bones felt almost twig-like.

'I love Raphael so much it's like an ache inside me,' she said softly.

'There's been no quarrel between you?'

'Well – yes and no.'

Tara sighed. 'Explain please.'

'There was a horrendous family row yesterday evening. His mother and sister and Emilio were all at each other's throats, but mainly at mine. Raphael's family just seem to hate me. They still see me as some kind of foreign invader. But I think a lot of their hostility's to do with money. There's this horrific will . . .'

They walked along, heads bowed, Alessandra talking and explaining, Tara listening attentively.

Alessandra wished she could be totally frank. But when she got to the part of her story that involved Tara and Olshak she simply left it out and then drew things to a sudden conclusion. It struck her that the story might have come across as rather disjointed.

'It would be so much better if you could simply have your own place,' said Tara thoughtfully, putting her finger right on the spot. 'Living with in-laws must be hell. Even if they were all angels.'

'Oh that would be bliss,' Alessandra exclaimed. 'A place just of our own.'

'Couldn't Raphael organize it? Surely he could.'

'It's not that simple. You don't understand Mummy. Things are really difficult for him. The Spanish are just so . . . different to us.' Alessandra's

316

protest was vehement and sharp, having sensed an implied criticism of Raphael.

Tara smiled. 'Oh, how you defend him,' she said, glancing at Alessandra fondly.

'Yes,' said Alessandra. 'Just like you always do with Daddy.' Or always used to she added to herself.

'And what else?' asked Tara.

'Else?'

'What else is making you unhappy?'

'I'm not unhappy?'

'You must be. Otherwise you wouldn't be here.'

'Goodness Mummy! I'd forgotten how blunt you can be.'

'Put it down to female intuition and maternal concern. You don't have to tell me if you don't want to.'

Alessandra sighed. 'I want to have a baby. I want to have Raphael's baby so much it's become like an obsession.'

'Is that what he said – an obsession?'

'Yes. He's so touchy about it. Sometimes, he's been quite angry. Not like himself at all.'

'But of course he's been angry.'

'I don't see why.'

Tara laughed. 'You're thinking of nothing except what you consider your "inability" to conceive. You're thinking that not being able to produce an instant baby is all your responsibility. All your fault.'

'Yes.'

'Men have worries too. Worries about infertility are very threatening to the masculine ego. They're all bound up with maleness and virility, just as ours are bound up with femaleness.'

Alessandra stared at her. She felt as though a small weight had rolled off her. 'Why didn't I think of that? You're brilliant Mummy!'

'Put it down to my advanced age. And besides,' she added softly, 'as I'm sure Raphael too will have said, it's far too early to start being obsessive.'

Alessandra suddenly wanted to go back to the house and call Raphael immediately. She wanted to tell him she was fine again. That she was coming back to him on the very next flight.

She smiled to herself, understanding that there was no mad panic. Raphael, although miles away, was there for her in spirit. He knew that she loved him. He would always be there, a living breathing part of her, just as she would be there for him. Somehow they would make everything come right: their marriage, his family, their baby . . .

And perhaps, just at this moment, her parents truly needed her. Perhaps this was a time of real trouble for them.

Turning to Tara, Alessandra touched her cheek onto hers in a gesture of impulsive affectionate closeness.

A light wind came across the lawn. It stirred the long strands of Alessandra's loose hair. And then it went on to play a little game with Tara's loose floating dress, flattening it against her body.

Alessandra stared at the faintly egg shaped outline of Tara's stomach. And suddenly the puzzling anxiety about her mother's medical condition fell into place with a great heavy thud.

CHAPTER 24

'I will not be spoken to like this. Here in my own house, in my own studio.' This was just one of several protests which Isabella had felt bound to make to her son as he battered her ears with words she had never imagined she would hear from his lips.

Of course, even from the days of his early childhood she had known that Raphael had a strong, determined personality. And from the onset of his early manhood it had become a source of pride to her that her son was growing into a high-minded, resourceful Spaniard. He was a man of impeccable moral qualities also, scrupulously honest in his business dealings and unerringly fair to his staff. He was not a demonstrative man, but he had treated his sister and nephew with consideration and kindness. And he had always, *always* treated her, his mother, with love and respect.

But now, he seemed to be quite changed. To hear him shouting like this, at her – at all of them – was truly shocking. He was criticizing them, chiding them, threatening even. In order to crush the creeping unease of fear that was stealing over her, Isabella felt the need to voice her objections ever louder.

'You *will* listen to me, Mother,' Raphael snapped. 'You will all listen to me.'

Catriona, leaning up against a stack of her mother's old canvases, rolled her head back, staring out of the window and giving a huge sigh. She had the demeanour of a truculent adolescent who had been brought to task by the school principal and was determined to demonstrate her refusal to be intimidated.

Emilio, similarly truculent, but blustering rather than languid, suddenly decided against making any further angry retorts. Looking into Raphael's hard set face he judged it might be wise to do as he said.

'Very well,' said Isabella with dignity into the growing silence. 'Now we are all listening to you.'

'I am sad to say,' Raphael told her, 'that you will all continue to listen to me, not because you value what I have to tell you, but because you are all self-centered people who know it will not be in your interest to cross me too far.'

'No, no,' said Isabella thinking she should try to placate. 'Of course we value what you have to say . . .'

'Do you? Have any of you thought of me or my feelings in the past year?' he asked hotly. 'I doubt it. You simply followed your own instincts and emotions in order to express your reactions to my marriage and my wife.'

He paused, his thoughts flying to Alessandra. All the love and pain she had brought him.

'I shall spell it out to you,' Raphael said. He turned to Isabella, his dark eyes boring into her. 'You Mother,' he said slowly, 'are jealous and intolerant. You can't bear to have Alessandra, a younger

320

woman living in the house, usurping what you see as your position of seniority in the household.'

'It is not what I "see". It is what I am. I *am* in the senior position,' Isabella said indignantly.

'Yes, that can't be disputed. And Alessandra has never behaved to you in a way which suggested she didn't acknowledge that.'

'Hah! She spoke to me as she liked.' Isabella was deliberate in her use of the past tense.

'She defends herself when you attack her,' Raphael countered. 'That is entirely justifiable. And very courageous of her.'

Emilio snorted.

'And you Emilio,' Raphael said, rounding on him angrily, 'you are a selfish, wilful boy who can't bear to be faced with your inadequacies, your foolish behaviour and your appalling idleness.'

'You gave her my prize horse,' Emilio exploded, enraged. 'How do you think that made me feel?'

'Oh, how tired I am of those words. How many times have I heard them? It is time you learned a new song Emilio. Well I will tell you why I gave her Ottavio. I gave him to her because she knew how to treat him so as to get the best out of him. I gave him to her because you weren't interested in the animal at all. You were only interested in getting dressed up in your red show-jumping jacket and showing off. Ottavio meant nothing to you. Some people would show more consideration to a furry toy than you showed to that horse.'

Emilio went very red. His adam's apple bobbed up and down in his throat.

'And I gave him to her because she's a better rider,' Raphael finished.

'Poor Emilio. To be compared to a mere female in riding skill. That's an unnecessarily cruel cut isn't it?' said Catriona, in her laziest most laconic tones.

'You be quiet,' snapped Raphael. 'You've caused a good deal of trouble with your calculated remarks. I'm coming to you soon.'

Raphael wondered if his astute sister had realized that he was playing a rather similar game to the one she so often indulged in herself. Deliberately drawing out people's secret feelings. Teasing them, goading them. Getting them to show their hands.

He turned back to Emilio. 'When are you going to take some responsibility for your own life?' he demanded.

Emilio scowled at the floor.

'When are you going to grow up and stop relying on gifts and handouts?'

'I *am* grown up,' Emilio exclaimed, trembling with indignation.

'No. You're still a child, playing with toys. Very expensive toys that your grandmother buys you.'

Emilio screwed up his face in a tight grimace. He found himself driven into a very difficult corner.

Raphael swung back to Isabella. 'Have you encouraged him to take any lessons or training in this sport of motor racing he claims he wants to join?'

'You don't have lessons,' Emilio protested scornfully. 'You must just drive.'

'You need experience. You need sponsorship. You need a whole back-up team in top class motor sport. Have you thought of that?'

'Yes!'

'And?'

Emilio breathed heavily, pushing out his lips out

like a toddler on the brink of a tantrum. He glared at Isabella. 'She won't pay for anything like that. She is stopping me from doing what I want.'

'You've asked her for the money to employ a back-up team?'

'Yes.'

He looked at Isabella who flinched under his hostile gaze.

'I wouldn't give him any more,' she said, her voice low and shaky. 'Enough is enough.'

'You wouldn't listen to what I explained to you; how I could win all the money back for you, and much more. You stupid old woman!' Emilio yelled at her. 'You understand nothing at all about cars and racing.'

Isabella blinked. Tears sprang up in her eyes.

'Apologize!' thundered Raphael. 'Now.' He took a step towards his nephew.

'I'm sorry,' muttered Emilio very swiftly, flicking a split second glance in the direction of his grandmother.

Catriona sighed. 'What's all this leading up to Raphael? I think you've made the point that you're angry with us. Perhaps we could just have our punishment and then go and get on with our lives.'

'Not just angry,' said Raphael very softly. 'I am sick of you all. Sick!'

'I know the feeling,' Catriona agreed, spreading her fingers and staring at her nails.

Raphael ignored her. 'You all presumed to sit in judgement on my wife. She tried her best to be pleasant to you, to be unassuming, to be tactful. But all you gave her in return was rudeness and spite and cunning. She received more respect and consideration from María and Ferdinand than from any of you. A worker sweeping the streets in Barcelona would be dishonored to act in the way you have. I am ashamed of you all. You disgrace the family name of Saventos.'

Catriona said something crude under her breath, but Isabella and Emilio were suddenly subdued. The family name meant a lot to both of them.

'And in hurting my wife,' Raphael continued, 'you have hurt me. Didn't you think of that? What have I done to deserve such contempt? Do you all hate me?'

Isabella gasped in dismay. 'We all love you Raphael. We love you very much, and that is why we have been . . . worried that . . . maybe this marriage was not the best thing for you.' She looked deeply uncomfortable as she spoke, and when she had finished took to tinkering with her bracelets with shaking fingers.

'Well you are speaking honestly at least and I thank you for that Mother. But why do you think this marriage isn't the best thing for me? Tell me. Come along, I want to know.'

His mother looked up. She wished she had never spoken those last few words. Because now she had no choice but to try to think of some further ones without making Raphael terribly angry all over again.

'Is it because Alessandra isn't a Spanish girl. Is that it?' he suggested.

'Well, no,' said Isabella, wanting to make peace. 'But sometimes it's easier to marry someone of your own nationality.'

'Very well. So basically, it's not a question of her being English – a foreigner. What then? Alessandra is beautiful, talented, hard-working, cultured. She is the best possible woman I could have wished for myself. She has given me her love and her loyalty and made me extremely happy. So what could you possibly hold against her?'

There was a painful silence.

'You wouldn't like to bring up her parentage again would you Mother? That seemed to trouble you before, the fact that Alessandra was born out of wedlock – a bastard love-child, as you put it. And also the fact that her mother might be an adulteress.' He tilted his head, staring mercilessly at Isabella, whose cheeks flamed with a dull rust. She bowed her head.

'A picture in a magazine means very little if one doesn't know the full context,' Raphael went on. 'A photograph of Alessandra's mother in the company of a music colleague probably means nothing significant at all. But even if it did indicate some illicit relationship, that is nothing to do with Alessandra. She stands on her own. She has her own worth. And on our wedding night she was a virgin.'

Eyes glanced furtively, lips were pressed.

'You approve of that kind of thing? Adultery?' Isabella demanded, rallying.

'I was an adulterer myself for many years,' Raphael pointed out calmly. 'You didn't seem to have any difficulty accepting that.'

Isabella made a dismissive sound in her throat. 'It is different for men!'

'Is it? Morally? I think it is just the same. So let's not have any more hypocrisy on that score.' He turned his head very slowly and looked at Catriona. 'You should have something to say on that particular issue. You've had a number of adulterous relationships haven't you? To my knowledge at least two of your lovers have been married.'

Isabella's eyes opened wide and she gave a low groan.

'You low down bastard,' said Catriona, with quiet deadly dislike. 'Why don't you go screw yourself – in the absence of your wife being around to screw!'

Isabella rounded on her daughter, her eyes shooting darts of venom. 'Is this true? You have had married lovers?'

'Yes, yes,' said Catriona wearily. 'Do you think I've been living like a nun all these years? Of course I've had married lovers. When you get to my age the only juicy male meat available is married. And I've never been keen on the idea of fumbling boys.'

Isabella and Emilio suddenly connected with a shared glance. Both of them wore the exact same expression of shock and sanctimonious outrage. Grandmother and grandson shared many of the old fashioned values based on male privilege.

Catriona looked up at Raphael with a certain reluctant respect. 'I rather think you've done for my chances of staying around here for much longer,' she said, taking out a cigarette despite her mother's fierce injunctions earlier, and lighting it with unsteady fingers.

'Yes. And maybe I've done you a good turn,' he said with a faint smile.

He looked around at his family, knowing that he had temporarily checked and overpowered them. Now was the time to speak out about the future.

'I wouldn't like you to think that I regard my own recent conduct as perfect,' he said. 'I've made the error of trying to serve too many masters. Too many masters of conscience. I have tried, mistakenly as it turns out, to consider the feelings and sensitivities of

326

all of you in this matter of my marriage. In doing that I'm afraid that I've been sadly lacking in my duty to my wife. I knew she was strong and so I expected her to survive – even in the bear's pit that you dug for her and tossed her into. I was wrong. And I regret that from the bottom of my heart. I intend to tell her all of this myself in person very soon, with a promise to her that everything will now change.'

He stopped. The silence was complete, charged with the electricity of feeling and suspense.

'I am also aware that the main reason for your hostility to my wife is nothing to do with her at all – or any of the rather pathetic reasons you have put forward. Your hostility is based on one simple thing. Money. Money and the fear of not getting as much of it as you would all like.'

'The Saventos will,' said Isabella majestically, raising her head like a woman of true nobility.

'Yes, that archaic anachronistic document that binds us all together in mistrust and envy,' Raphael agreed.

'The will must stand,' declared Isabella. 'It is our heritage. Something very private just to us.'

'You think I haven't told Alessandra about the will?' Raphael exclaimed in disbelief. 'Alessandra my wife!'

Isabella flinched in dismay. 'So, she will be determined to have a son and push all our noses out of joint,' she countered coldly. 'But I see no signs of it yet.'

'You will,' he said. 'And Señora Alessandra Saventos,' he added with great emphasis, 'doesn't want a child just to make sure she gets even richer than she already is, or to spitefully deprive other people. She simply wants a child because that is what women who are happy with their husbands and their lives want.'

The silence that followed this impassioned statement seemed interminable.

'So what is going to happen? What will you do?' asked Isabella in a quavering voice.

'Firstly I shall have an architect draw up plans for a new family house to be built on the south side of the estate. In fact I have already issued instructions to that effect.'

'For you and . . . her?' Isabella asked.

'Yes. We shall have a new home and make a new start.' He looked at his mother, understanding her thoughts, noting how her eyes had illuminated at the prospect of new rooms to design and furnish. 'Unless you would like to make a new start Mother. In which case Alessandra will take over here.'

Isabella was at a loss, caught in a dilemma of choice both disagreeable and enticing. Raphael did not feel sorry for her.

'Catriona?' he enquired. 'Have you a comment?'

'I know you too well, Raphael,' she said, with a dry humorless laugh. 'You couldn't be cruel or wicked to save your life. Which means that you aren't going to throw me out or try to cut off my money supply.'

'Yes. You're right. So?'

'So, I'll have to start thinking fast. I've no intention of staying on here as some kind of passive satellite, revolving round your sun, waiting to catch the crumbs that fall from your table.'

Raphael watched her carefully. Maybe, at last, she was showing signs of being sprung from her façade of boredom and inertia.

'I might,' she said with a crooked smile, 'even have to get off my arse and get a proper job, as I'm sure you, and probably Alessandra, have been wishing I would for some time.'

Raphael stared regretfully at her. He still had some love left for his only sister. She was, after all, a rather sad and lonely figure.

'Or a rich husband,' said Catriona, her eyes suddenly dulled and bitter. She squashed her cigarette into the blood red section of one of her mother's paint palettes. 'That would surprise you wouldn't it? You'd all be so pleased to get rid of me.' She suddenly walked swiftly to the door, as though she were a thief spotting the opportunity to make a quick escape. About to exit she turned back. 'But not nearly so pleased as I would be.'

Emilio and Isabella stared up at Raphael as though awaiting a judge's sentence.

'I'm flying to England this evening,' Raphael said quietly. His two listeners were astounded. They had not realized the fight was all over.

'You can't do that!' Isabella cried.

'Why not?'

'It's harvest time. You never go away at harvest time.'

'Well I'm making an exception for once. Going to England to be with my wife is the most important thing for me at the moment.'

'But what will we do?' asked Isabella in agitation. 'Who will see to the picking of the grapes and . . . everything . . .' She stopped, completely at a loss.

'Emilio can take over.'

'What?' Emilio gave a violent involuntary jerk as

though he were about to have a fit. 'I can't take over from you. I don't . . . know enough.'

'It's time you did. Because from now on you either work in the vineyard, learn the business and pull your full weight, or you enrol for a proper training in some other profession. Because if you don't you might find yourself rather poor. You too might have to look for a rich partner. There are plenty of old wealthy widows around who would be only too happy to take on a young stud,' Raphael continued, suddenly tired of the heaviness in the atmosphere and desperate for a little joking and lightness.

But Emilio's face was crumpled in horror and woe. He was a portrait of tragedy.

'You don't have to decide now,' Raphael said more kindly. 'Just stand in for me for a day or two.'

Emilio stared at him in mute appeal.

Maybe he does have an inkling of what real work is, Raphael thought, willing it to be so. 'Ferdinand will help you. He'll tell you what to do.'

Emilio's look of incredulousness almost made him burst into laughter. He glanced at his watch. 'I need to set off to the airport now,' he said briskly.

'Have you finished with us?' Isabella asked, subjecting him to a tragic stare.

'For now. But not for ever, Mother,' he said gently. 'I do still love you all.'

'We shall try to do better,' Isabella murmured.

'Good. I'm sure you will. Perhaps as a start you'd like to investigate the arrangements that need to be made for my marriage to be blessed in the cathedral in Barcelona. And it would be very helpful if you could draw up a guest list for the reception afterwards. Alessandra and I would like all this to take place very soon after we get back from England.'

And on that positive note, he left them, leaving Emilio and Isabella staring at each other open-mouthed.

CHAPTER 25

Alessandra met her father in the waiting area of Roland Grant's central London office. Given that Roland's musical enterprises were world-wide and rumoured to be worth mega millions, his premises were modest in size and simple in decoration.

Whilst she waited for her father's meeting with Grant to finish, she looked around the walls where famous faces stared down from stylish publicity posters. Here was a roll call of all the most talented, famous and successful in the world of performing music: instrumentalists, singers, dancers and conductors. Their faces would be easily recognisable to the general public, even to those not especially interested in classical music.

Alessandra looked with interest at the latest publicity picture of Saul, a blow-up from the cover of his recently released disc of Handel's *Messiah*. The sharp-focus photograph, done in black and white, and taken with the lighting slanting up from below gave a heavily sculpted appearance to his face emphasising the carved bone structure under the skin. He looked hawk-like, austere, frighteningly knowledgeable and sternly thrilling.

It struck Alessandra that all of those qualities had some part to play in the make up of her father's personality. But surely, she thought, the man himself, the father that she knew, had never been as cold and harsh as this arresting image. And yet, presumably it was precisely this quality of remoteness, laced with a faint hint of the sadistic, that touched a chord in a million fantasies. And made people buy his discs.

Or was it simply a reflection of the tastes of the publicity agents, she wondered with a wry twist of humour. Did the creative re-inventing of charismatic figures like her father, serve mainly to keep them amused? Would people buy Handel's music conducted by Saul Xavier even if the disc were wrapped in nothing more than a brown paper bag printed with the composer's and the conductor's names?

Smiling to herself, she moved across to the opposite wall which was dominated by a large poster of Michael Olshak. Alessandra had tried to ignore it, and if Saul's interview had not overrun she could well have succeeded.

But waiting around had left her mind free to rumble away down the bumpy roads of her relationship with the Saventos family and the amazing discovery about her mother's current state, and so it was necessary to have a diversion. Even this particular one.

She stared in fascination at the picture, at the face which conveyed traits so totally different from those of her father. This was a sunny portrait, the background tones cream and amber in order to bring out the startling beauty of the man's bronzey auburn colouring. Here was a man with a wide, frank smile, a great floppy lion-like tangle of hair and a decided twinkle in his eye. Easy-going, amusing, warm. He was in no way handsome but he was loaded with sackfuls of charm.

'Not my type,' she murmured to herself. But she had to admit that it would not be too difficult to fall under the spell of a man like that if he turned the spotlight of his big blue eyes full on you.

Saul came out of Roland's office. 'Darling!' he called out to Alessandra, who swung round guiltily as though caught in a naughty, deceitful act. 'Sorry to keep you waiting.'

He took her arm. 'You know how it is with Roland. He simply never knows when to shut up.'

Roland, following Saul from the office, laughed in agreement. 'If I'd learned how to shut up I'd be a retired civil servant by now, living quietly in the suburbs eeking out my modest pension. How are you Alessandra?'

'Well thank you Roland.'

'Good, excellent.' He took her hand and held it for a moment in his. 'And just you remember that I'm always in need of good pianists on my books. It's a while since I heard you play but I haven't forgotten how good you were.'

Alessandra smiled, gratified and amused. 'Thanks Roland. I won't forget. But I don't think I'll ever be a concert performer. Give me a horse to ride around on and I can cope with six foot fences and an audience of thousands. But the Albert Hall and a Bechstein. They'd scare me to death. No, definitely not!'

Saul chuckled. He guided her down the steps to the street outside. 'The Ritz?' he enquired with faint mockery.

'No. I liked the suggestion of a dark wine bar.'

'Good. Me too.'

Alessandra wanted to blurt out to him, 'Daddy I've found out Mummy's pregnant. And I was so jealous when I realized, I could hardly speak. How could she do this when she's over forty and she's got a child already? It's not right somehow. And it's not *fair*. Oh, it's simply too unfair to even think about!'

She restrained herself. Just as she had restrained herself in the moments following the sickening discovery of Tara's pregnancy a few hours before whilst they were out strolling in the garden.

'Mummy!' she had exclaimed, stopping dead in her tracks, her shoes squeaking in the grass of the dewy lawn.

'Oh. So you've guessed?' Tara said with a dry, wry grin.

'I only had to use my eyes to *see*! Oh Mummy!'

'Oh dear! As bad as that?'

'Yes. Oh I don't mean that. No.' Alessandra looked at her mother. 'Are you pleased?'

Tara sighed. 'I'm not entirely sure. I think I'm still in a state of shock.'

Alessandra was silent, bewildered and uncertain. And then horribly, crushingly envious.

Tara said, 'I'm really sorry that you're having to absorb this piece of news on top of everything else you're trying to deal with. Especially after what we were talking about earlier on.'

Alessandra sighed.

'Listen darling, it's much too soon for you to worry about not getting started with a baby,' Tara said gently. 'You've been under awful stress coping with that terrible family of Raphael's. That sort of thing can play havoc with your hormones.'

'Don't Mummy,' Alessandra said sharply. 'Don't try to be light-hearted and make out it's all OK. Don't tell me I've no need to worry. Because I am worrying, in fact sometimes I'm almost frantic with worry. And I can't do a thing about it. It's like trying to tell your finger not to bleed when you cut yourself. Not possible.'

Tara put an arm up around her daughter's shoulder and squeezed.

'When you got started with me,' Alessandra asked bluntly, 'how many times had you made love with Daddy?'

Oh goodness! thought Tara. 'Once.'

'Yes,' Alessandra responded crisply, her heart giving a thump against her ribs. 'Well, thanks for not covering up with a lie. But that information doesn't exactly comfort me. And it certainly underlines my point!'

'I suppose so,' Tara admitted regretfully.

'How far on are you?' asked Alessandra, thinking that this must be one of the most absurd conversations she had ever taken part in.

'Sixteen weeks, most probably. It could be a little more advanced than that, they're not entirely sure.'

'But you've gone so thin in your face and – well, everywhere except *there*!' Alessandra looked once more at her mother's stomach, a wry mocking reproof in her eye.

'I was always like that before. When I was first carrying you my bones were sticking out like little

336

sticks.'

'I hope you're going to be all right,' Alessandra had said warmly in a sudden burst of anxiety on her mother's behalf. 'I hope it all goes right.'

She had genuinely meant that. But when Tara had then begun to relax and talk more easily Alessandra had found her mind humming with all kinds of questions. She had thought, does Daddy know? She had thought, does Michael Olshak know? And then she had thought things she had felt deeply ashamed to think.

'Down these steps,' said Saul, holding Alessandra's arm and guiding her in the right direction.

'Oh cool!' said Alessandra staring around the dim, candle-lit bar with its terracotta brick work and its polished dark oak tables and benches.

'Do you refer to temperature or ambience?' Saul enquired, pulling out a chair for her and settling her down.

'The latter. Everywhere in England is cool temperature-wise.' She looked up at the menu, chalked in flowing script on little boards around the bar.

Saul, knowing the menu by heart, as this was one of Roland's many haunts, raised his hand to summon service from behind the bar and looked at his daughter.

'Has Mummy told you her news?' he asked lightly.

'No. But I put the proverbial two and two together.'

'I'm going to have the smoked salmon followed by the bean and bacon cassoulet,' he decided. 'And what were your reactions?'

'Oh, you know,' said Alessandra matching his *sang froid*, 'the usual. Shock, outrage, blinding jealousy and a terrible worry about whether she'll come through it all right. And I'll have the same please.'

Saul placed their food order. 'Do you want wine?' he asked her with a faint smile. 'I don't see anything from the Saventos vineyard on the list.'

'I'll have mineral water.' Alessandra found she was somehow not in the mood for wine. With Raphael so far away and her emotions stirred into an unexpected new turmoil by the unfolding of events at home she was aware of a hollow uneasiness in her stomach.

'I'll have the same,' said Saul. 'Drinking at lunch-time's a killer if you want to get any work done later.'

Alessandra toyed with her ruby ring. 'How do you feel about it Daddy? Having another baby.'

His cool grey eyes gazed into hers, steady and inscrutable. 'I feel old,' he said eventually.

'No!'

'Yes. Think of me when this child is your age.' He tilted his head. 'Mmm?'

'Think of Segovia,' she said. 'Think of Picasso.'

'You choose very flattering examples of other elderly fathers with whom to compare me,' he commented with a faint smile.

'Age just isn't an issue with you Daddy,' she protested, spreading her hands out in a gesture to emphasize the point.

He rested his wrists on the table and laced his long slender fingers together. 'What do you think is an issue with me?'

'Music,' she said unhesitatingly. 'And Mummy. And me too, most likely.'

'In that order?' he enquired drily.

'Probably.'

'Ah, I see.' He paused. 'Is this hard for you?' he asked abruptly, his voice low and intense. 'To think of us having another child. To think of having a brother or a sister at this stage in your own life?'

Alessandra stared at him for a few moments. 'You mean do I feel about to be attacked by a severe bout of sibling rivalry?'

He smiled, raised his eyebrows.

'Daddy, that never even crossed my mind!' she told him with a certain warm indignation. 'I have my own life now. With Raphael. Do you understand what I'm saying?'

'I believe you're saying that you think of yourself as a wife now to Raphael, no longer a child to Saul and Tara. And I'm very glad to hear it.'

'Do you think Mummy feels the same?'

'I think so.'

'But I think it's been much harder for her to let go,' said Alessandra, recalling all the anxious phone conversations with her mother.

Saul rolled a piece of bread between his fingers. 'Do you?' he said with cool reflectiveness. 'It's strange isn't it how our perceptions of ourselves don't always match with the perceptions of others.'

'Oh Daddy!'

'Don't waste any pity on me,' he said with a smile of self-mockery. 'So now, Señora Saventos, we'll change the subject and talk about you,' he decreed, raising his hands gracefully from the table in order to allow a plate of smoked salmon to be placed in front of him. 'And Spain.'

'Spain,' she said with a smile. 'I'll drink to that.'

'Are you already wishing you were back there?'

'A little.'

'And you will be soon?'

'Oh yes.'

'Good.' He tapped his fingers on the table. 'And what about the family from hell?'

Alessandra grinned ruefully. 'You're putting words into my mouth that I've never allowed to get there by themselves!'

'I take it the in-laws are the flies in your particular ointment.'

'Yes.' She sighed. 'But I'm just going to have to deal with them.' Her heart sank when she thought of facing them all again. The glaring faces distorted with ugly hate. The anger, the hostility, the needling and the relentless unspoken disdain.

Watching her expression, Saul wondered how much she had suffered at that family's hands. How much more she was prepared to suffer. He had a fierce paternal longing to protect her from any further hurt. And he knew he must keep it in check, because she had a husband whose job it was to do that now instead. But was he willing to do it. Was he *able* to do it?

Alessandra put down her fork. A large fat tear had squeezed itself from her eye, rolling steadily downwards, and now she brushed it into the skin of her cheek with her fingers. 'It all got out of control,' she said shakily. 'There was this awful shouting and anger. Wild and primitive. Spanish is a marvellous language to abuse people with.'

She made it sound like a medieval battle! Saul felt a hot flame of rage. What the hell was Raphael doing, letting all this 'abuse' happen? And where the hell was he? Why wasn't he here for Alessandra when she needed him?

He then recalled that he had not been there for Tara during the lion's share of all the past few months when she needed *him*. He wondered about the price there might be to pay for that.

'What is to be done?' Saul asked.

She grasped at the thick rope of her plait, fingering it in agitation. 'I need to go back to Raphael,' she exclaimed in sudden panic. 'I shouldn't have come away. It was cowardly. I was only thinking of myself.'

'I should think it was just about time that you did,' Saul cut in.

'No,' she said shaking her head fiercely. 'I ran away from him. Even though he knew what I was going to do, even though he drove me to the airport, it still feels like I ran away from him.' She stared at her father, her eyes wide with feelng. 'I have to go back.'

'Go back to face the music?' he suggested.

'Go back to be with him whilst we both do.'

Saul nodded. 'Won't you just stay on for this evening? I truly think Mummy needs you too. And me,' he added in an almost inaudible murmur.

Alessandra saw that his eyes were alight with a strange intense emotion. 'Where is Mummy this lunchtime?' she asked quietly.

'I don't know,' he said, and she caught a tone of bleakness in his voice. 'We don't check each other's diaries.'

There was a tiny silence between them and then Saul's mobile phone, sitting quietly on the table, gave a peal. Saul snatched it up, swearing quietly about his carelessness in not having switched it off. 'Yes.'

Alessandra watched in fascination as his face registered a number of fleeting emotions: wariness, realization, irritation and finally resignation. 'Thank you. There's no need for concern. It's all in hand,' he said finally, snapping the aerial back into its housing.

Alessandra began to gather up her things. 'I have the feeling you're going to have to leave,' she said drily.

'I'm sorry. Another appointment . . .'

'It's OK Daddy.'

They went up the steps into the street. She saw that he was looking grim and strained.

'What will you do?' he asked her.

'Now this minute, do you mean?' Making herself smile so as to reassure him. 'I'll probably take a walk and do some hard thinking.'

'Yes,' he said. 'A sound plan.'

'Don't worry Daddy,' she said reaching up to kiss his cheek. 'I won't fly away as suddenly as I flew in.'

'You must do what is best for you and Raphael,' he said. 'If you truly love him that's the only option you can take.' He stared down into her face and then he turned abruptly away from her.

She watched him walk down the street, a tall straight figure, gaunt and somehow very alone. A small beating wing of fear fluttered in her chest when she reflected on the frailty of human relationships, even an alliance she had always before regarded as unshakeable and eternal. The marriage of her parents.

CHAPTER 26

Taking afternoon tea at the Ritz was a charming and luxurious ritual. Whilst Georgiana waited for Saul to join her, she passed a few pleasurable moments gazing in wonder at fragile white china plates bearing wafer thin sandwiches as frail as leaves newly burst from the bud, and slices of plain bread and butter that reminded her of the frosting of ice on a cold window pane.

She crossed her long slender legs and arranged her skirt so that it just tipped over her knee cap. She fluffed out her newly shampooed hair with careful fingers.

She judged that she was fully prepared. She had all the necessary material to hand; the props required for the drama she had so painstakingly scripted and produced in the past few weeks, and in which she was now about to play a starring role.

The locations of her drama had not all been as stylish and opulent as the current one. The private detective she had hired to monitor Tara's meetings with Michael Olshak had plied his trade from headquarters situated above a very doubtful looking pub in a seedy back street in Tower Hamlets.

His one room (cupboard size) could only be reached by a rickety staircase leading from the pub's tap room, a depressing nicotine-stained saloon, which reeked of beer, acrid smoke and stale sweat. Georgiana had tip-toed across the vinyl flooring flinching with distaste as the soles of her Dior court shoes lisped and squeaked with every beer-spattered step.

Her efforts and long suffering had not been in vain however, for her sleuth, Dicky Dawson, whose name she had selected at random from the advertisements in the local press, had turned out to be as sharp and on the ball as his premises were down at heel and past their sell-by date.

Dawson had reassured her that there would be no difficulty in putting her requests into practice. 'Absolutely no problem,' he had reassured her. 'This is the bread and butter of our work madam!'

She had explained to him that she needed specific dates and times and locations. She had shown him pictures of Tara and Olshak. She had expressed the need for great discretion. 'These are not anonymous nobodies, ordinary people in the streets,' she had told him with grave severity. 'These are famous people. Musicians, artists.'

She recalled that at that point he had grinned and murmured, 'Piece of cake.'

To tell the truth she had been almost sorry not to have encountered more expressions of surprise and worried reservations.

She had offered him money, a bundle of used notes in a brown envelope, as she had seen commissioners of these kinds of services do in films. 'Here is something in advance. Cash up front,' she had said to him enjoying her knowledge of the appropriate jargon.

He had smiled again, and for a moment she had wondered if she had done the wrong thing, like breaching some rule of etiquette in a strange household. But he had taken the money quite readily, stashed it in a drawer in his desk and then written out a receipt for her.

And a few days later he had been able to offer her a good deal of most intriguing and useful information, backed up with some irrefutable photographic evidence. The operation had all been extremely satisfactory.

She looked up and saw Saul come through the doors at the far end of the room. Her nerves jumped with feeling at the sight of his lean athletic figure and his stern forbidding face. She felt excitement and a brand of anticipation laced with faint alarm which made it especially thrilling.

She swivelled her body towards him as he came near and tilted her face up. But he did not kiss her. He touched her lightly on the shoulder and sat down opposite her. 'You're looking very well,' he said.

'I am well,' she agreed smiling. She leaned forward and began to pour tea for him, showing off her narrow wrists and beautiful white hands.

'Yes. You know how to take care of yourself,' Saul said evenly.

Georgiana glanced at him. She was so used to flattery that she had been initially pleased with his words. Now she wondered if he might have been critisizing.

He allowed his lips to twitch with a faint smile and she was instantly reassured.

'How is Daneman?' Saul asked politely.

'Oh, he is well too.' She handed Saul the cup which he accepted politely and then placed on the table in front of him as though it were an unwanted gift.

Georgiana took a dainty sip of her own tea and took a sandwich from the plate. She glanced again at Saul and decided against encouraging him to take one too. He was looking very grave and she reminded herself that he had always hated to be cajoled into things.

'I'm glad you're well,' Saul commented. 'And are you also happy Georgiana?'

She gave a little start. She had forgotten how direct he could be. 'Happy? Yes, of course I am.'

'Then why have you suddenly decided that you want to see me?' The grey eyes were like shiny steel orbs.

'It's a shame for us never to see each other. People who have shared the past sometimes like to share a little of the present,' she told him lightly.

'Is that so? Where did you get that pearl from my dear? From a glossy magazine or from Daneman?'

Georgiana opened her blue eyes very wide indeed, a gesture which always drew the mantle of her femininity closely around her. She saw that he was in a combative mood and for a tiny moment her courage flagged. She took another sandwich and reminded herself of her mission.

'Aren't you going to ask me about Tara?' Saul enquired. 'Oh and you'll want to know about Alessandra too. She's married now you know. To a Spanish winegrower. A most exceptional man.' He smiled, an expression of soft intimidation which would have had many without the thickness of Georgiana's skin running for cover.

'I was going to ask you about Tara,' Georgiana admitted.

'Yes I rather thought so. She's pregnant.' His eyes fastened on Georgiana's face like a leech on a blood vein. Swiftly he drank in the information her face gave him in the unguarded fraction of time following his words. 'But I have the feeling you know that already.'

Georgiana wiped the side of her lips with a dainty finger, wondering how she should return this trickily sliced volley he had driven into her court. 'Actually I did guess something of the sort. Her gynaecologist has rooms in the same street as one of my doctors.'

'Ah.'

'She should be very careful,' said Georgiana, full of female wisdom and holding up a warning finger. 'At her age.'

'I shall take very good care of her, don't worry at all on that account.'

Jealousy rose suddenly in Georgiana's throat like the regurgitation of an over-rich meal. The long buried fury about Tara's stealing away her husband and pocketing all his love and concern resurrected itself, and with it came a renewed desire to punish them both.

'You should be careful for yourself as well Saul,' she said, and her tone had tipped over from the light and playful to something darker and more portentous.

'Oh yes.'

Georgiana picked up the magazine she had laid on

the table in front of her earlier and passed it to Saul for his scrutiny.

He gave a cursory glance to the photograph of Tara with Olshak outside the Dorchester. He made a low chuckle in his throat. 'I've told Tara that if she's going to be photographed with Olshak she should stand on a stool or make sure that he kneels down so he doesn't dominate the shot.'

'You've seen it before then?' She could not quite hide her disappointment.

'I should think everyone's seen it. It's a marvellous stick with which to beat my little wife if she steps out of line.' He raised his eyebrows in a sardonically suggestive manner, hinting at all sorts of interesting sexy games with Tara. And also a tenderly loving playfulness which sparked off Georgiana's jealousy all over again.

'You shouldn't make a joke of it Saul!' she reproved.

When he simply leaned back in his chair, smiling at her and showing no evidence of sharing her concern or taking her seriously, she was suddenly incensed. She had wondered if she would really manage to go through with what she had planned at this interview, but it was at that moment she decided to throw caution to the winds. It was now or never – time to take the plunge into dangerous waters.

'Did you know that the conductor Michael Olshak was in Manchester at the same time as Tara early this summer?' she enquired with an air of innocence, arching her eyebrows. 'Whilst you were in Japan?'

Saul's pause, the tiny downward shift of his gaze, were almost imperceptible, but Georgiana picked up on them. This was something he didn't know. She felt triumph.

'Georgiana,' Saul told her, his eyes cold and impassive, 'one day your over active imagination will get you into real trouble.' He unfurled himself from his chair. He smiled down at her, a smile which did not transmit any warmth. 'I came here because you gave me the impression you needed to speak to me on some serious matter about which you needed my advice. I came rather reluctantly but in a spirit of kindness. I most certainly didn't come here to listen to insinuations and petty gossip about my wife,' he finished with steely emphasis. His departure was clearly imminent.

'No!' cried Georgiana, jumping up and clutching at his arm to restrain him. He stopped, turned. She fumbled in her bag, pulled out a sheaf of photographs and thrust them into his hand. 'It's not just petty gossip.'

Saul took a perfunctory glance at the pictures and then dropped them onto the table as though they were diseased. They lay there shiny and glinting: pictures of Tara and Olshak walking in London streets, their arms around each other. Pictures of Olshak bending to kiss Tara's dark hair. Pictures of Tara looking up at him, her eyes alight.

'This has got to stop,' he told Georgiana in low tight-lipped fury.

'Yes!' she agreed eagerly. 'And you must put a stop to it, Saul.'

'For goodness' sake Georgiana, I'm talking about you and your mischievous meddling.' His eyes blazed like firearms. 'Don't you dare do anything like this again! Ever! And call off your bloodhound now!'

Georgiana started back from him, flinching as though he might physically attack her.

'You meddled like this before and caused mayhem. I thought you were cured,' he said savagely.

She gasped with shock. She was sure no one had ever spoken to her so brutally, not even Saul.

'And don't ever call me at home again!' he told her, his eyes spiced with danger. 'Who did you expect to speak to when you telephoned this lunch time? Tara? Were you going to suggest a meeting with her as well? Thank goodness it was Mrs Lockton you got instead. She called me straight away afterwards. Do you think we're all fools? That we can't recognize the pathetic little games played by a woman who has more time and money than sense?'

Georgiana swallowed painfully. Everything was going horribly wrong. But there was just one arrow left in her quiver. She breathed in hard, stubbornly determined to say her piece. 'You should ask Tara when this baby is due,' she told him. 'You should remember that you've been away a great deal in recent months,' she concluded on a shuddering breath of release, relishing a moment of pure triumph.

Surely now he would understand what she was warning him against. Surely now he would react.

But his defences were impregnable. He gave no sign of any feeling whatsoever, except a lip curling disdain for his former wife. 'You hint darkly Georgiana,' he said, 'but Tara and I live our lives in the open light of day. We have no secrets from each other. Not even that sort,' he concluded glancing in scorn at the photographs.

'I was just trying to warn you,' said Georgiana desperate to salvage something from the growing mess.

'No, you were just amusing yourself. I've nothing against your having a little fun Georgiana, but not at Tara's and my expense. Don't you realize,' he added, almost detonating with suppressed anger, 'that you're simply going down a road on which you've travelled before?'

The china blue eyes stared at him in incomprehension.

'A road with a cruel tragedy at the end of it,' he said meaningfully.

'Tragedy?' She was all innocence. A truly genuine seeming innocence. 'Do you mean the accident?'

'Yes. Among other things.'

'But that was not my fault Saul,' she said helplessly. 'You were driving together in the car and had an accident. Tara was hurt . . .'

Saul gave a rasping sigh of exasperation. 'Georgiana,' he said, trying hard to control the mounting dislike in his voice, 'I've heard and said all I'm prepared to. And now I'm going to leave you. Go home to your husband Daneman and leave me alone. Please don't ever call me again to arrange any more little meetings. Not even on my mobile number. Do you understand?'

'Yes.'

'Good.'

'Good-bye,' she whispered hesitantly, but he had already vanished from view.

* * *

Alessandra took the tube to Regent's Park and walked down the path leading to the boating lake. She recalled her parents taking her there when she was a small child. Her mother would bring crusts of bread in a bag and Alessandra would try to tempt the haughty swans to come and eat.

Today in early autumn the park looked serene and mellow, the water of the lake shifting in undulating sparkles under a veiled creamy gold sun. It was a softly tranquil image in total contrast to her own internal landscape which seethed with brittle uncertainties and an underlying throb of dark apprehension.

She walked along, kicking up a few early fallen leaves, whilst in her head she picked the bones of her recent discussions with her parents.

Most of all she picked at a certain short phrase which had lodged in her memory, the way in which her father had asked a certain question. 'Has Mummy told you her news?' he had asked. *Her* news, he had said, not *our* news. Was his choice of that word horribly significant?

Alessandra's mind leapt onwards, grasshopper-like, landing on the inevitable loathsome suspicion that this pregnancy of her mother's might have more to do with Michael than with her father.

No, surely not. But just supposing. And if her father had any idea, what effect would that have on him – and on her parents' marriage?

Alessandra considered the grim black comedy of a scenario where Tara produced a baby with flaming ginger curls. Surely then it would be obvious without a doubt that Olshak had fathered this child Tara was carrying. The whole world would know!

Which all went to show, thought Alessandra grimly, that her mother had no business getting herself pregnant at this stage in her life.

She squeezed her eyes tight shut and then opened them again. 'Raphael,' she breathed to the grass and the water and the sky. 'I need you. I need you just now. So very much.'

A lone black swan came gliding to the bank of the lake, its fluid head moving from side to side as though listening to her impassioned plea.

She smiled at it, although there was no sympathy of communication in its remote glittery eye. The bird was solely interested in the possibility of food. She spread her hands. 'Nothing,' she told it. She wrapped her arms around herself. 'Empty. I'm sorry. All empty.'

Saul telephoned Daneman at his consulting rooms.

'Xavier,' he announced tersely. 'Listen carefully. Georgiana is up to her tricks again.'

'Ah,' said Daneman. Saul Xavier always elicited a faint stiffening in the spine. A need to be on guard.

'She's been having Tara followed. Some seedy private detective I imagine. She's got photographs with dates and times recorded on the back. The whole tawdry works.'

The dry clipped sarcasm of the tones was almost more alarming than bellowing rage or soft menace. Daneman gave a sigh. 'Oh dear.'

'This isn't the first time she's used hired hands. She seems to have a real taste for it. She went through a phase of hiring high class escorts in the dying stages of our marriage. Glamorous sophisticated call girls. She had them delivered to me like little gifts, thinking they would 'service my needs' in the absence of her being willing to oblige.'

'I know,' said Daneman. 'I was her therapist at the time.'

'Ah yes of course. There are no secrets from one's therapist.'

Probably not, agreed Daneman silently.

'You have to put a stop to it,' Xavier snapped.

'I'll try. I'll speak to her,' Daneman said placatingly.

'You won't try, you'll do it,' said Xavier.

'I'll try,' repeated Daneman calmly. Whilst mild in demeanour Daneman was not easily intimidated even though Saul Xavier was more of a threat than anyone else he could think of. And not because he was Georgiana's former husband. Simply because he was him.

'Do it with something from your psychologist's bag of tricks,' Saul directed him. 'Hypnosis or whatever wizardry you like. Just do it quickly.'

'Yes,' Daneman said reflectively. As he drew tiny squiggles on his note pad, in brief contemplation of the job to be done, he heard the connection click off abruptly and a soft rushing sound pour into his ears.

Tara returned home late in the afternoon. She accepted Mrs Lockton's offer of hot tea and took a mug up to her bedroom. Climbing onto the bed as though she were already heavy and unbalanced with a kicking internal baby, she stretched out with relief and closed her eyes, feeling as though she had done a gruelling day's work.

She had gone first of all to the hospital. There had been a fault with the ultrasound equipment and she had had to wait for an hour before the staff were able to carry out the abdominal scan which had been arranged for her some time previously.

She had then gone on to Harley Street for a further appointment with her gynaecologist. It seemed that everything was going along fine. Her doctor had already been in contact with the hospital and ascertained that the scan had shown up a normal healthy foetus. She was also able to tell Tara that the results of the amniocentesis carried out the week before were heartening, indicating no sign of any developmental or genetic abnormalities considered a risk factor for babies of older pregnant mothers.

But despite the good news, after all the waiting about and probing and discussion, she had felt utterly worn out and curiously low-spirited. It had been a real effort to concentrate as she drove home.

All the time she was thinking of Alessandra, grieving for her daughter's unhappiness. Tara's feelings about this bolt-out-of-the-blue pregnancy were still confused. But whereas before her main worries had centred around Saul's true feelings regarding another child, now she felt a sickening guilt at the thought of this gift which had been so lightly bestowed on her. Whilst she had been agonizing about coming to terms with a miracle, Alessandra had been desperately striving to achieve what had simply been tossed to her, Tara, without giving it so much as a thought.

If only I could make my daughter's dream come true, she thought. She needs a little Saventos growing happily inside her just as I need this little Xavier growing inside me.

* * *

The three of them sat around the table, a simple supper of cold meats, salads and cheese in front of them.

Tara looked pale, and not nearly as self-possessed as Alessandra always thought of her. She was wearing very soft, very washed old denims and a huge white shirt. Her hair was not quite dry from having been washed just before she came down. She looked like a girl.

Saul passed the plates of food around and volunteered snippets of information about his meeting with Roland Grant earlier.

Alessandra thought that it was a good thing her father had such smooth social skills. Otherwise the three of them might have been condemned to the unthinkable humiliation of having to stave off dangerous silences like strangers unexpectedly thrown together, whilst at the same time keeping up the pretence of being a blissfully happy family.

She found herself surreptitiously watching her parents, like a newly appointed detective sent on an interview with a brief to look for clues.

'Roland's still trying to persuade me to let Miles King do my biography,' said Saul, slicing a baguette into marvellously uniform chunks.

Alessandra, now driven to focus intensely on the reactions of her parents to each other, glanced at her mother and saw her eyes give a little flicker of movement.

'Haven't I told you about this before?' Saul asked. 'Surely!'

'No,' Tara said shortly, tearing a chunk of bread in half.

'I'm sorry!' said Saul, raising his eyebrows.

'But Roland did.'

'Ah, I see.'

'He thought it was very odd I didn't know,' Tara said with a mysterious little smile. 'He thinks we have no secrets from each other.'

Alessandra found herself holding her breath as a tiny glance shot between her parents like a current of electricity. She was suddenly reminded of the call that had come in on Saul's mobile in the wine bar, of his brusque compact responses. Oh no! Not him as well.

'Miles King's a brilliant writer,' Alessandra volunteered.

'So Roland tells me,' Saul smiled. 'He wants to spend a month tailing me in my work and play before he starts writing.'

Tara gave a chuckle. 'That should be fascinating.'

'For him or me?' enquired Saul.

'Both I should think. Are you going to go ahead?'

'I don't know.' He paused, his body very still, his grey eyes staring into some unseen distance. 'Raking over the past. The whole thing could be very painful. Not just a breeze as the saying goes.'

This time the look that passed between him and Tara was really high voltage.

It occurred to Alessandra that the unsheathed clashing of swords in the Saventos household had something to be said for it in preference to this tense, restrained parrying.

Mumuring an excuse she slipped unobtrusively from the room and ran upstairs to her bedroom and put through a call to the Saventos house.

Her heart began to beat and throb as the connection was established and the warning purrs sounded.

She had made three previous attempts to contact Raphael earlier in the evening. Each time, when the purrs had been responded to, she could have sworn she heard breathing. She had given her name and asked for Raphael. There had been silence and then a click as the contact was instantly broken. Isabella, she had thought. The bitch.

Frustration and anxiety had begun to mount. She had felt as though all contact with Raphael had been broken. A wave of dizzy nausea had swamped her.

Her fingers trembling she punched out the long sequence of numbers, then waited, her heart a heavy weight in her chest.

But now all she got was the answerphone. A bland message in Catriona's flat rejecting voice.

She sat on the edge of the bed and closed her eyes. A frightening and savage sense of having squandered something that had been most infinitely precious engulfed her in a dark tide.

Night seeped into the Xaviers' Oxfordshire house, reaching out into all the farthest corners and cracks and filling them with mysteries.

Alessandra lay in bed listening to the sounds which announced the final passing of this long day. The house creaked softly into silence as the heating pipes cooled and contracted. Outside an owl crooned its unique and mournful appeal.

She heard the soft footfalls of her parents on the stairs. First her mother, and then about an hour later her father.

She imagined them lying in their big bed, turned away from each other. Close and yet far apart.

She tried to soothe herself into sleepiness. She imagined herself on the plane returning to Spain the next day. In the ferment of worries her imagination became inflamed. She saw herself returning to her lover like the runaway Jane Eyre, she saw the Saventos winery and the house burnt to a ruin like Mr Rochester's Thornfield Hall.

She jerked into full consciousness. In her ears was the clacking engine of a London taxi. Then a door slamming, then silence and after that an intensification of the clacking, gradually growing distant and diminishing.

A tiny scrunching sounded on the gravel beneath her window.

Hairs stood up at the back of her neck as a shower of stones grazed the latticed panes.

She sprang out of bed and flung open the window, Juliet on her balcony.

The figure below was wrapped in shadow. It was tall and broad-shouldered, dark and very significant.

'I am Raphael Godeval Saventos,' it said flinging its arms wide in a commanding show of strength. 'I have come for my wife. Open the door immediately.'

Alessandra stuffed her hand in her mouth to muffle the sounds of laughter and incandescent joy. 'Hush! I'm coming down.'

CHAPTER 27

Supper at the Danemans' house was an elaborate and dainty affair. Daneman and Georgiana ate red mullet with a salad of roquette and crushed hazelnuts dressed in fresh orange juice and virgin olive oil. To follow they had passion fruit sorbet with a raspberry coulis. Georgiana had carefully selected the items for this feast in the Harrods food department. The effort involved had taken her mind off the horrible rebuff Saul had given her earlier. And when she got home there had been further occupation in arranging it all so as to be a feast for the eyes as well as the taste buds.

Daneman greeted her exertions with extravagant praise. He selected a bottle of her favourite Sancerre to drink with the fish and a fine Montbazillac to complement the sorbet.

He found himself feeling very tender towards her, thinking of her tonight as a young girl who has been rather silly, realizes the error of her ways and now needs comforting.

Because she was subdued and unusually quiet, and because he knew the reason – at the same time knowing she did not know he knew – he made sure to keep the conversation rolling nicely along. He asked her about her day and without prolonging his wait for an answer went on to tell her some amusing anecdotes he had heard from his secretarial assistant, Celia, who was always in the forefront of knowledge regarding all the latest celebrity scandals.

Georgiana listened politely. Occasionally she smiled. Daneman knew that his gentle attentiveness was soothing her.

Passing her chair on the way to open the Montbazillac, he bent towards her and placed a soft kiss on her neck. 'You look simply lovely tonight,' he murmured in her ear, eliciting a faint smile.

Her pale fragile beauty still moved him. She was like a precious ornament, as vulnerable as an egg shell if not treated with the proper care.

He uncorked the wine, reflecting that Georgiana's matchingly pale fragile psyche also gave him pleasure. Having spent years in picking up the pieces of distressed people's lives, and being battered with the intense emotions of a stream of demanding patients, it was delightfully restful to come home to the uncomplaining, pliable and basically shallow Georgiana. He saw no point at this stage of her life in confronting her with the harshness of the real world. After all she was able to live quite happily in the one she had constructed for herself. The egotistical world of a child.

Daneman was well aware that in a different setting, with a lack of the money to fund her extravagances, and with no partner to shield her from reality, Georgiana might well reveal a vicious streak and maybe land herself in bad trouble. He also recognized that her irresistible fascination for schemes and cunning was still potentially dangerous. But basically he judged that she was still a child, an innocent abroad, who needed his protection.

He recalled being attracted to her the first time she lay on his therapist's couch. He had wanted to possess her and also to care for her. He knew she was now utterly dependent on his good will and his guidance and his love. Deftly and unobtrusively he controlled her life as he saw fit. In dire circumstances he had even resorted to deliberate artifice on her mind, but that was not an indication of a lack of love.

He crumbled half of a ten milligram tablet from a medicine bottle into her wine. In around thirty minutes she would be relaxed and filled with contented well-being. But the reasoning part of her brain would still be alert.

When the wine was all finished, he said to her, 'Darling, you're looking so tired.'

She nodded. She liked to be spoken to in such caring tones.

He took her hand and led her upstairs. As gently as a lady's maid he undressed her and helped her into bed.

He knelt down beside her and lifted her hand to lie in his. He began to stroke it with a steady rhythm.

'Aah,' she murmured.

He went on stroking, moving his hand to her waist and then over her hips. 'Let me take you down the long curving staircase with the beautiful garden at the bottom,' he said softly.

'Ah yes,' she smiled. 'I like that.'

He began to talk to her, guiding her mind down the long long steps into the sunny garden fragrant with flowers.

'Feel your mind float,' he said dreamily. 'Feel all your worries drift away like lazy fishes.'

Soon she became limp and heavy. He pulled a needle from the back of his lapel and raised her hand again. 'You will feel no pain Georgiana. Just a tingle of warmth and a sense of love and trust.' He drove the needle in at the knuckle, cleanly against the bone. She sighed and smiled.

'There. You can trust me. You're safe with me. This is Daneman, your husband.' He stroked her cheek.

She made a low sound of contentment.

'Georgiana! Listen to me. This time you *will* feel pain. But you will be able to bear it.' He drove the needle in again. Her smooth features contorted and she gasped.

'Good. Now, Georgiana, listen very carefully. Tara is having another baby,' he said with slow emphasis, placing his hands on her face as it convulsed with dismay. 'Yes that is painful for you, but you can bear it,' he reminded her. 'You know that you would not like to have a baby. You would grow very fat and there would be marks and lines on your skin.'

Georgiana murmured in agreement.

'The last time Tara had a baby you were very unhappy,' he told her in a soft droning voice. 'You were so unhappy that you stole Tara's little child from her and took her away with you.'

Georgiana's body gave a convulsive jerk.

'The part of your mind that feels all the pain and the shame has forgotten what you did,' Daneman told her. 'But now you are going to remember. You went into the garden when no one was looking and stole Alessandra away. It was a very dangerous thing to do. And very wrong.'

Daneman relived the ugly moments of that dreadful morning. He had been summoned by a demented Xavier and compelled to accompany him on a journey to find the thieving Georgiana.

Daneman recalled discovering her in the kitchen of the Cornwall cottage that used to be her childhood holiday home. Little Alessandra, just one year old, had been a captive in the bedroom upstairs. The child's anguished shrieking had echoed through the house. And Georgiana had stood in the kitchen like a zombie, idly fingering the bread knife and drawing blood.

Meanwhile in London, Tara had lain in a hospital bed, the nerves in her spinal column fractionally but fatefully injured from a terrible crash in Saul's Porsche. He had been driving like a madman, desperate to gain news of his daughter. And at the same time as Tara lost her virtuoso capacity to play her violin so she also lost the baby she was carrying; her second child, the trigger for Georgiana's act of madness.

'Georgiana, it hurts you for Tara to have a baby,' said Daneman with soft emphasis. 'It makes you very angry to think of her having a baby with Saul. It makes you so angry that you want to do something to hurt back. Isn't that right?'

'Yes.'

He stroked her hand. 'That is something I can understand, Georgiana. I'm not angry with you for the bad feelings you have. You know I love you don't you?'

'Yes.'

He was still stroking her hand. 'I want you to keep listening hard – and you will feel pain again. When you kidnapped little Alessandra you didn't mean to kill the baby Tara was carrying, but that is what happened. It was because of what you did that Tara's baby died. And now you have tried to hurt Tara again. If she lost this baby Saul might think that you were to blame for another baby's death. Do you understand what I'm saying?'

'Yes,' she whispered, her face crumpling pathetically, so that suddenly it was possible to imagine her as an old woman.

'You must not be responsible for another death Georgiana, must you?'

'No.' Her eyes were shiny with tears.

'You must leave Saul and Tara alone. You have another life now. A better life. You have a husband who loves you and cares for you more than Saul did. Don't you?'

'Yes.'

'Are you feeling the pain Georgiana? The pain of what you did which hurt other people?'

'Yes.'

'Soon I'm going to wake you up. You will remember what we have talked about. You will think about it and remember what you promised me. You will feel pain. But it will not be too hard to bear, because you will remember that I understand why you did the things you did and that I don't blame you. You're not a wicked person Georgiana. And I forgive you for what you did.'

365

'Yes.'

'And you must leave Saul and Tara alone.' He paused. 'Tell me what you must do?'

She repeated his words in slow flat tones.

He took both her hands in his. 'Now we're going to walk through the garden together. And then we're going to climb up the steps. Up and up, until you're awake. And when you wake you'll feel quite peaceful and rested. And I shall be there.'

Slowly he brought her back into the here and now of the living, conscious world.

She opened her startling blue eyes and smiled at him, holding out her arms.

He wondered how fully her mind had assimilated his suggestions, how many times he would need to repeat the mesmeric process in order to fully stamp in the message.

With his cheek against Georgiana's he gave a dry smile, running through a projected phone call to Xavier telling him that a mission had been accomplished and advising him of the wisdom of Tara's finding other amusements than being pregnant.

CHAPTER 28

'I have to tell you that you must never never leave me again,' said Raphael when she woke.

Alessandra reached out hungrily to him, still a little drugged with the sweet dreaming sleep in which she had relived the passion of the lovemaking which had followed their ecstatic reunion.

Before he began his story of the Saventos family conference, before he told her of his plans for a new future, before he told her that never again would he allow things to happen which he so bitterly regretted having allowed before, he had taken her to bed and told her he loved her with his lips and hands and his body.

'I want you again,' she breathed, pulling his naked solid body against her. 'I want to feel you, smell you, breathe you . . .'

'You will wear me out,' he chided shaking his head. 'You must think I have the stamina of a bull.'

'I know you have,' she whispered seductively, parting her lips with irresistible invitation and rolling herself beneath him.

He knew that she liked to feel him covering her,

that she relished the weight of him pressing on her, restraining her, closing out all other images except their loving. And he loved her for that particular aspect of her femaleness.

She sighed, spreading her legs wide and arching her back so as to take him deep inside her.

She began to moan in low ecstasy. He clamped his hand over her mouth. 'Be quiet my *amor*! Your parents will think I am making an indecent assault on you.'

'You are,' she whispered in awed gratefulness, as the waves of ecstasy began to roll in, sucking insistently at every vein in her body.

At breakfast Alessandra had to resist the feeling of showing Raphael off like a glittering trophy she had won.

But it was almost impossible. Somehow, in the very English atmosphere of her home, Raphael was even more romantic-looking and exotically attractive than ever before. Exotic not only in looks but in his whole demeanour.

Even in the presence of her parents he kept gazing at her with a long intense stare, as though drinking her in and slowly relishing her. Once or twice he put up his hand to touch her face, murmuring, 'My Alessandra.'

Tara, refreshed from a night's sleep and delighted at the turn of events, or rather the turning up of Raphael, was glad to find herself able to play hostess in her usual lively way, and even more glad to have the privilege of witnessing her daughter's obvious new found happiness.

368

Whilst she talked and re-filled coffee cups and poured fruit juice, she was highly alert to Raphael's long glances at Alessandra. His stares seemed to her like those of a man seeing a vision. And the looks that passed between the two of them spoke of such unity and tenderness that a pang shot through her. A powerful pang both for their joy and for something she wondered if she and Saul had lost.

Saul had come to the breakfast table earlier on and then quickly gone, promising to be back within a few hours for a celebratory family lunch. 'I'll believe it when I see him,' Tara said to herself wistfully.

At least this morning she didn't feel the need to writhe with guilt because of her pregnancy. She judged that at this particular moment Alessandra's cup was running over simply to have her beloved Raphael with her once more.

And it was infectious all this happiness streaming from the two of them. Tara felt she could almost grasp it: a golden beam of radiance touching all around it with new warmth and hope.

Outside the window came the roar of a small red van. Raphael looked up. 'The Royal Mail!' he exclaimed. 'How impressive. How English.'

'British,' Tara corrected him. 'We're a united kingdom you know. England, N. Ireland, Scotland, Wales.'

'With red vans everywhere?' Raphael enquired, his eyes twinkling.

'Oh yes. And when you live in as far flung a place as this, they even deliver to your front door.'

'You must tell me some more of your very quaint English, I'm sorry British, customs,' Raphael invited her.

Alessandra grinned. 'I'll go collect the post. You two continue to improve on Anglo-Spanish relations.'

Glancing through the window occasionally, Tara noticed her smiling and chatting to the delivery man, taking the letters and packets he held out. She looked so different from the Alessandra who had flown in from Spain, white and strained. She looked so happy, so secure.

At Raphael's request Tara took him outside to show him the garden.

It was an hour or so before they came back into the house. Tara went into the kitchen to discuss the lunch preparations with Mrs Lockton. They decided on a meal of roast duck served with sage and onion stuffing and apple sauce.

'Good traditional English cooking,' commented Mrs Lockton approvingly. 'I'm going to enjoy myself!' She jotted down a list of ingredients she would need and set off to the nearby village shops in her bright red 1960s Mini.

Tara searched among Saul's wine collection, amusing herself with selecting wines she thought would please both her own husband and Alessandra's. Slotting some bottles of white into the refrigerator to cool, she found her mood more buoyant and calmly contented than it had been for months.

She heard footsteps coming swiftly down the stairs and then Raphael was standing in the doorway. 'Where is Alessandra?' he asked and urgency crackled around him.

Tara looked up. 'I thought she would be upstairs.'

'No.'

'She's probably in the drawing room, browsing through the music on the piano. She likes to do that when she's been away for a time.'

'No, I looked in as I passed.'

Tara straightened up from her crouched position. 'Raphael, is something wrong?'

'I fear so,' he said. 'Very badly wrong.'

Tara felt a lurch of nausea. She heard the roar of Saul's Porsche in the drive, saw him jump from the car. As he came to find them she saw that his face was calm and expectant, much as hers had been a few moments ago. She watched his expression change as he sensed the tension in the atmosphere. 'What?' he demanded sharply.

'I think Alessandra has gone,' said Raphael.

'Gone! What do you mean?' Saul's eyes were sharp with speculation.

Raphael sighed. 'I found a letter open on the dressing table. It must have come just this morning. I think she read it – and then left.'

'Go on,' said Tara, her tone low and urgent.

'It's a letter from my former mistress.'

'For Alessandra?' Tara's voice was hoarse with shock.

'Yes. It's a letter telling Alessandra that she and I are still seeing each other, that we're still lovers.'

'And are you?' asked Saul coolly.

'No. I haven't seen her for well over a year.'

'Oh hell,' said Tara. 'She'll be so unhappy. Oh poor darling. But where will she have gone?'

'She will have gone back to Spain,' said Raphael.

Saul and Tara stared at him in disbelief.

'I can see you think I'm mad to say that. But I'm sure of it,' Raphael insisted quietly.

'Oh hell,' said Tara again, her voice faint at the thought of Alessandra's unhappiness, her terrible aloneness. 'Sweet heaven!' she burst out suddenly, her eyes blazing at Raphael, 'do something!'

'Yes,' said Raphael. 'I will. I shall find her. I shall make things right for her. Please, you must believe me. But first there is something important I want to say.'

'Go ahead.' Saul put his arm around Tara, pulling her to him, giving her the comfort of his firm stroking hands.

'I have been much at fault this year,' Raphael told them, his voice heavy with regret. 'I have allowed the glue of secrecy and deviousness and lies that has always held my family together to remain undisturbed. When I should have been tearing the old fabric of our secretive relationships apart and demanding openness and sincerity, I simply allowed things to continue as they have been for years. Ever since I can remember. It was our way of existing together. And until Alessandra came into our family, it seemed to work, because we were all very good at playing our games of pretence. But Alessandra dared to be open you see, she was brave. And gradually I learned from her how to be splendidly brave too.' He paused for a few moments. Quickly and without embellishment he explained to them the difficulties of the Saventos will and the bare bones of his recent showdown with his family. 'And now,' he concluded grimly, 'everything is going to change.'

Tara felt Saul's fingers tighten against her ribs. 'Go and find her Raphael,' he said quietly.

'Yes,' said Raphael. 'I will.' He turned back to them just before he left. 'I think what I said just now applies to many relationships, don't you?' His dark eyes seemed to reproach them as he walked out of the house and climbed into the taxi that had arrived and now swept away in a flying storm of gravel.

Tara and Saul stood in the doorway, their arms tightly around each other.

'She will be all right,' Saul said reassuringly. 'I know what you're thinking and how afraid you are. But this is not like the time she was kidnapped. Alessandra will come to no harm. I'm sure of it.' He spoke the truth, at the same time praying it would be so.

'Yes,' Tara said slowly. 'I can accept that. She's strong, and she's not a fool. She will look after herself. And he is a good man,' she added.

'She's like me when things go wrong,' said Saul. 'She has to be alone so as to think things through.'

Tara nodded, biting her lips until blood came.

'And shall *we* be all right?' Saul asked after a pause.

She looked up at him. 'Oh Saul!'

'Raphael was right wasn't he? About openness, about trust?'

'Yes.' Her voice was just a breathing sigh. She wanted to go on, to explain things to him, but there seemed to be no power of breath left in her lungs.

'Georgiana summoned me to a tea-party,' Saul said drily. 'She had things to tell me, things to show me. The sleuth she'd employed had produced some very nice photographs for her to brandish in my face.'

The blood in the great vessels around Tara's heart stilled. 'Me and Michael Olshak?'

'Yes.'

'Oh Saul!' She forced herself to meet his eyes. And to her astonishment there was no anger there, no suspicion, simply a great tenderness. And absolute trust. She made a low cry of distress in her throat.

'I didn't look at the pictures all that carefully. I understood all I wanted to just in a glance.'

'What did you understand?'

'Just how precious you are to me. Oh Tara, when I saw the way you were looking at Olshak, so full of life and warmth I realized how much I still love you, how desperately I want you.'

'I was so lonely,' she protested. 'I was wanting you so much, missing you. You went away, shut me off.'

'Yes. I know.'

'Michael and I were never lovers!' she cried out. 'We are friends, loving friends. He's a sweet man, and I do feel a kind of love for him. But there is only you Saul. You are the only love of my life.'

'Yes,' he said softly. 'I know.'

She sank against him as he bent to kiss her.

'We couldn't face up to losing Alessandra could we?' she whispered to him. 'Giving our precious child to another man?'

'I think that hits the nail on the head,' agreed Saul.

'And then I had to have the monopoly on parental anxiety. You weren't allowed to hurt anything like me.' Tara gave a small rueful grimace.

He nodded. 'I felt so distanced from you. As though I couldn't get near you. That was hell Tara.'

'And so you put a real distance between us? Mountains and seas and thousands of miles.'

'Yes.' His eyes beamed down into hers. 'And now,'

he said meaningfully, lifting her into his arms, 'It's time to put things right and become close again.'

He ran up the stairs carrying her as though she were no more than kitten weight.

Even through the drone of anxiety for Alessandra Tara felt giddy with joy and relief.

He laid her on the bed and placed his hand on her stomach. 'I shall be very very gentle,' he said. 'I think I'm starting to love this new child already – provided it doesn't pop out with a mop of carroty curls.'

As he caressed her a warm joy began to flood through her, filling her body and her mind until it could be contained no longer and burst out of her in soft laughter. 'Oh you dreadful mocking man, my wonderful Saul.'

They lay together in each other's arms for a while. Through Tara's new happiness the anxiety about Alessandra refused to be ignored.

'Saul,' she murmured into his shoulder. 'What would Raphael's former mistress think she had to gain from writing such a wicked and pointless letter? Why did she do it?'

'Perhaps,' said Saul slowly, '*she* didn't.'

CHAPTER 29

Raphael arrived in Barcelona in the early evening. The sun was still intense and the airport smelled of diesel fumes and burning tarmac.

He picked up his car, drove like a madman and arrived at the winery just after dark. There were few lights on in the house and at first he thought it was empty.

As he went through the inner courtyard his mother came hurrying from her studio, her face anxious and fearful.

'Where is she?' Raphael asked, trying to keep the fury from his voice.

'Who?'

'Alessandra of course.'

'I don't know.' She looked mystified. Her eyes pleaded with him not to be angry with her, and he realized she was telling him the truth. 'The horse has gone,' she said. 'Ottavio.'

'What?' He put his hands over his face and gave a silent groan. Of course, he should have known she would come back for Ottavio.

'Emilio has been out to look for him,' Isabella said.

'How long has he been missing?'

Isabella hesitated. 'We're not sure. We have done all we could. Emilio has been looking and looking for him. I am sure he will be found safe.'

'Dear God, I'm thinking about my wife, not a horse!'

'Yes, yes, of course.' Isabella looked truly frightened now, as though she were faced with a mad bull. 'But what is this about Alessandra?'

'Don't you know?' he snarled. 'Surely you can guess?'

Emilio burst in. It struck Raphael with grim irony that his lazy nephew was actually managing to move fast without the aid of four wheels and a six litre engine. He too looked frightened. 'I can't find him anywhere,' he said, staring at Raphael in dreadful apprehension.

'I'm not about to turn you both out of the house on account of a lost horse,' he snapped. 'There are more important issues at stake.'

Whilst Isabella and Emilio stared at him in apprehensive fascination he took the letter out of his pocket. The letter purporting to be from Luisa Victoria de Mena, his former lover. He knew now that it was a fake, a counterfeit. Given time to reflect, that much at least had become obvious. He thrust the letter into his mother's face, his anger incandescent.

Isabella took it and examined it. She stared up at him in dumb appeal and then she looked again at the letter. 'Oh God be merciful to us,' she breathed.

'Well?' Raphael demanded, conscious of his lips pulling away from his teeth so that they were bared like those of a wild animal.

'I never dreamed that . . . anything like this would happen!' Isabella cried.

'No?' hissed Raphael, looming over her so that she cringed away from him in terror. 'Then what did you mean to happen?'

Isabella stepped back. 'Please! Don't shout like this at me Raphael. I feel I don't know you as my son.' Her words were a trembling supplication. 'And listen I have spoken to the priests at the cathedral in Barcelona as you asked to arrange a blessing of your marriage, I have made a list of guests . . .'

Raphael looked into her face and felt a surge of compassion. She seemed so vulnerable and tired and bewildered. Seeds of new ideas began to form in his mind as he came to doubt the validity of his first suspicions. As he stared at her, frowning in thought, Emilio stepped forward, placing himself between Raphael and the anxious Isabella.

'You mustn't blame her,' he said in a low voice. 'It's not fair to shout at her . . .'

Isabella jerked into new life. 'No Emilio. No! Be quiet!'

Emilio ignored the warning hand she had placed on his arm and finished what he had been planning to say. 'It was not Grandmother who wrote this letter. Please Raphael, believe me. Please, don't be angry with her.'

Raphael swung round to him. 'Tell me then,' he commanded, grabbing at the offending letter with his fingers. 'Tell me who did this.' As he looked from the dumb Isabella to the silent Emilio realization came to him without the aid of any response. 'This is Catriona's work,' he said slowly. 'Of course, why didn't I think of that?'

He felt ashamed to have suspected his mother of such a vicious and spiteful act. His mind had been full of her angry and hateful words to Alessandra on that dreadful evening when she had forced her daughter-in-law to flee from the house in distress and rush back to her parents. He had thought also of Isabella's terrible jealousy of his new wife, and then finally of her artistic skills, her potential ability to mimic another woman's handwriting so that it could fool even him.

Catriona had never entered into his mental equation. Because she had been self-effacing and insidious she had lulled him into a state of simply ignoring her. He recalled now that Catriona had plenty of reason to be sickeningly envious of a young woman as beautiful, energetic and talented as Alessandra. A young woman who had suddenly intruded into the household she, Catriona, the eldest daughter, had grown up in. He also recalled that his sister used to have considerable talents as a cartoonist when she was younger. She could mimic other artists' work like an impersonator could mimic gestures and voices.

'Poor Catriona was upset,' said Isabella, desperately striving to defend her daughter and placate her son. 'Emilio will tell you.'

Emilio screwed up his face into a grimace of distaste. 'She was drunk,' he said baldly. 'She was waiting for the telephone. Some American man was going to call her. I know this because I was wanting to make a call and she yelled at me to leave the line free so this man could get through to her.'

'Oh my poor sad girl,' said Isabella mournfully.

'Hmm!' snorted Emilio. 'She waited and waited and she was drinking vodka the whole time. One glass after another. If I had drunk as much as that, I should have been on the floor. And then Grandmother shouted at her and they had a terrible argument.'

Raphael sighed. He could imagine.

'She went up to her room and came down with a letter. She was waving it about at us, telling us it was something she had written earlier as a joke, but that now she was going to mail it. We didn't have any idea what it was, I swear to you.'

Isabella nodded. 'It's true. If I had known I would have tried to stop her. Truly Raphael, I would.'

'Very well, I believe you.' Raphael laid his hand briefly on his mother's shoulder.

'Anyway,' said Emilio, recovering some of his old swagger, 'when she arrived back the call she had been wanting came through for her. And suddenly she was all smiles. She went upstairs, packed her things and called a taxi. And we haven't seen her since.'

Raphael looked at his mother. 'Oh, how terrible for you. I'm so sorry.' Raphael wrapped his arms around Isabella and held her to him for a moment.

'No, not terrible,' said Isabella wearily. 'I think she will be happier away from here. I think we all will. And I just hope she has the sense to stay away.' She dabbed at her eyes and then thrust the handkerchief away. 'Now!' she decreed, 'the important task is to find Alessandra. Raphael! You and Emilio must be a team. Go! Find her.' She raised her head, her eyes flashing with tears and purpose, once more the latter-day matriarch.

* * *

Raphael and Emilio planned a route and drove out into the countryside. But in the dark it was a thankless task looking for a lone horse and rider. By first light they were exhausted, although they continued to search.

Raphael eventually decided that he would have to alert the police. He drove Emilio back to the winery and told him to go to his room and get some sleep.

A sense of deep loneliness invaded him. He felt as though he had been washed up on a desert island and that in front of his eyes there was nothing but a vast impersonal sea and a shimmering sky that made his eyes ache.

Staring down the drive from the terrace with a cup of strong black coffee on the table before him, he saw Alessandra in his mind's eye: her knowing eyes, her lovely face, now so dear to him. The idea of the day stretching ahead without her was intolerable. It would be so long and empty and lonely. Even with people buzzing around him he would be desperately alone.

Weariness seized him and sleep crept up, swallowing him into itself like the folded arms of a black-cloaked spectre.

When he woke the sun was like fire, throbbing down. He put a hand over his eyes shading them. His body too was like fire and he was thirsty.

At the bottom of the lane a small cloud of dust rose. It was like looking at the desert he thought, everything so dry and parched in this burning sultry autumn.

The cloud of dust grew bigger. Through it a shape began to define itself. A moving shape, a head

381

suspended in cloud. He stared, not sure he was fully conscious, his mind still trailing the tattered cloak of sleep. The head moved, rocking rhythmically up and down. An equine head, ghostly pale through the fog of dust.

He stood up, his heart quickening. He recognised the animal. And now he saw the figure astride him. A young woman, lithe and graceful, her body moving in perfect harmony with that of her horse. The sight of her made a rolling wave break inside his body.

He leapt up and with a great cry began to run down the long lane towards her. 'My *amor*!' he cried, flinging his face up to the sun. 'My Alessandra.'

'I'm sorry, I'm sorry,' she wept as he pulled her from Ottavio's back and folded her against him.

'*You* are sorry!' He shook his head in disbelief.

'I should have known to trust you. I should have let you explain. You see I'd been so worried about my parents and then . . .'

'Ssh. You must always be so correct, apologizing when all we must do is make love to each other.' Holding Ottavio's reins in one hand he pulled her face up to his with his other. He kissed her. A long deep kiss.

'It wasn't your mistress who wrote that dreadful letter was it?' she said.

'Former mistress,' he corrected. 'No, of course not.'

'No. And . . .' she paused, her voice low with a quickening beat of urgency, 'it wasn't Isabella either?' Her words were muffled against his chest, so soft he could hardly hear them.

'No.' Very briefly he sketched out the story of Catriona's latest exploits.

'Oh thank goodness!' exclaimed Alessandra astonishing him.

'How so?' He stroked her hair tenderly.

'How could I learn to love Isabella if she'd done that?'

'Learn to love her?'

'Yes.' She made a wry face. 'I've had so much time on my own to think about things. I thought a lot about your mother, and I began to understand that I haven't tried hard enough to understand her point of view, how she must have felt when I came along – and then stayed for ever. Catriona can make her own life, but your mother isn't young now. And she still loves and needs you so much.'

'Good grief, have you gone crazy my precious one? Has your flight into the wilderness with Ottavio turned you into a saint?'

'Absolutely no chance of that.' She looked at him. 'Were you mad with worry about me?' she asked anxiously.

'No. Well not entirely. I know you're pretty tough. Even so, please don't think of flying away from me ever again.' His eyes slimmed to dangerous black slashes. 'I did tell you once before!'

'I won't. I couldn't.'

They began to walk up to the house, two people very close, breathing as one.

'Raphael,' she said quietly, 'I think I'm pregnant.'

There was a slight falter in the rhythm of his steps and then he walked on. 'Yes?' he said calmly, inviting further information.

'I haven't been busy with my little chemistry experiments. You can't do that when you're walking through the fields on a horse and spending the night in an old disused stable . . .'

'What?' he cut in, his eyes flaring. 'Is that what you did? You are a crazy woman after all. What am I going to do with such a reckless, wilful wife?'

'Beat her into submission with your adoration, I hope.' She looked up at him, her heart melting with love. 'I'm sure that I'm pregnant. I just know. I haven't had any bleeding now for three weeks and there's a strange new feeling inside me, a whole different way of seeing and tasting and smelling things. I don't need my chemistry set. I simply know.'

'Well, well,' he said.

'I think you're just a little pleased!' she smiled, recalling his previous displeasure when the subject had come up.

'Oh, just a little!'

Coming out of the winery Emilio spotted them. He stopped dead in his tracks and then broke into a run. 'Thank heaven,' he breathed as he came close to them.

'Emilio, I truly believe you're pleased to see me,' Alessandra said mischievously.

'I am.' agreed Emilio, glancing at Raphael and adding, 'He would have killed me if you hadn't returned in one piece.' He looked in wonder at her crumpled clothes and her riding boots thick with dust. Who in their right mind would go walkabout in the fields in this heat like some tramp? She must be mad. He remembered a saying, 'Mad dogs and Englishmen . . .' 'I'll go tell Grandmother,' he said, thinking it was time someone did something practical.

Turning away Alessandra heard him growl, 'Women!'

She took Raphael's arm, grinning in amusement. 'He's not very politically correct is he? I'll have to start working on him now we're at least on speaking terms again.'

'You just be gentle with him,' warned Raphael, highly entertained. 'He's done very well in the vineyard since I left him holding the reins. I have hope for him yet. And plenty of work for you too my precious. So don't think you'll be getting away with a life of leisure and luxury.'

'Who'd want one?' Alessandra thought of working alongside Raphael in the winery, of rubbing along with Emilio and forming some kind of bond with Isabella. She thought of her and Raphael's child growing inside her and all their future together. She wondered if it was possible to endure such perfect happiness.

Isabella came hurrying from the house, her jewellery clinking, her hair gleaming like a raven's wing in the sun. She enclosed her daughter-in-law in a stiff embrace. 'We are so pleased you are back Alessandra,' she said, as though she had spent some time carefully rehearsing the words. 'But you must never run away again.' she said severely. 'You must always be here. For Raphael.'

Alessandra and he exchanged glances. She felt a spark of joyful laughter bubble up. She gave Isabella a tiny squeeze.

It was a start.

EPILOGUE

Alessandra relaxed into the plump white pillows, her body at peace after all the labouring and effort of the past twelve hours. Her mind was filled with images, past and present.

It was six months now since she and Raphael had stood together in the ancient cathedral in Barcelona whilst the priest blessed their marriage in the presence of his mother and her parents and a huge assembled company of guests.

Only Catriona had been absent. She was living in New York now, the fiancée of the antique dealer who had so fortuitously plucked her from the Saventos household. The family received brief post cards from her occasionally. She had scribbled on one that her fiancé had some really fast track lawyers who would kick the Saventos will into the twenty-first century with a vengeance. Raphael had smiled. Alessandra knew that he thought he was progressing very nicely with his Spanish lawyers, doing things his way. They needed no help from Catriona. She had her new life.

At the elegant reception Isabella had arranged afterwards Alessandra had been overjoyed to see her parents so well and happy – and so clearly in loving harmony again. Tara, six months pregnant, but with only a moderate egg-shaped bump giving her away, had been glowing with life. Saul had held her closely to him, his eyes had followed her everywhere.

In the spring the new house on the south side of the vineyard had been completed. Isabella, claiming that it was only just and proper for the older woman in the family to occupy the smaller premises, had moved in there and set about entertaining herself with elaborate schemes of furnishing and decorating. Raphael and Alessandra had been left in blissful peace in the old family house.

Emilio had elected to live in a small self-contained flat adjoining his grandmother's house. He was working hard in the winery and now had a new girl friend, a curvy black-eyed Catalan girl who was busy getting him under her thumb and was much approved of by Isabella.

Alessandra felt the touch of lips on her and opened her eyes. The black gaze which was fastened on her was full of fervour, full of ardour. '*Amor*,' he murmured.

She put her arms around his neck. 'My Raphael,' she sighed. 'Are you happy?' she whispered.

'Happy? I hardly know what to say.' His voice was hoarse and trembling with passion. His cheeks were moist with tears. 'How do you feel my wonderful Alessandra?'

'Ecstatic! As though I rule the whole world!'

'I telephoned to England to tell your parents.'

'And?'

'They were ecstatic too. They are flying out to see you straight away. With baby Richard, who is apparently already waving his arms in time to Beethoven symphonies and is the image of your father.' His eyes gleamed. 'As you can guess my mother is whipping María and her staff into a great frenzy of cooking and cleaning and bed making.'

'Ah, your mother.' Alessandra leaned across to the two sleeping babies in the two matching cradles beside her bed. 'And what did she say?'

Raphael made a wry face. 'She too was delighted. I told her that the little girl has fair hair and dark eyes and is just like you, and that the boy has dark hair and dark eyes just like me. And that they are both perfect.'

'What could she say to all that?' Alessandra smiled. She put her finger on his lips. 'Let me guess, I can hear her now. She's saying, "That Alessandra. Twins! That girl must always have everything – and more." She's right!'

THE EXCITING NEW NAME
IN WOMEN'S FICTION!

PLEASE HELP ME TO HELP YOU!

Dear *Scarlet* Reader,

Don't forget we are now holding another Prize Draw, which means that **you could win 6 months worth of free *Scarlets*!** Just return your completed questionnaire to us **before 31 January 1998** and you will automatically be entered in the draw that takes place on that day. If you are lucky enough to be one of the first two names out of the hat we will send you four new *Scarlet* romances, every month for six months.

So don't delay – return your form straight away!*

Looking forward to hearing from you,

Sally Cooper

Editor-in-Chief, *Scarlet*

*Prize draw offer available only in the UK, USA or Canada. Draw is not open to employees of Robinson Publishing, or of their agents, families or households. Winners will be informed by post, and details of winners can be obtained after 31 January 1998, by sending a stamped addressed envelope to address given at end of questionnaire.

Note: further offers which might be of interest may be sent to you by other, carefully selected, companies. If you do not want to receive them, please write to Robinson Publishing Ltd, 7 Kensington Church Court, London W8 4SP, UK.

QUESTIONNAIRE

Please tick the appropriate boxes to indicate your answers

1 Where did you get this Scarlet title?
Bought in supermarket ☐
Bought at my local bookstore ☐ Bought at chain bookstore ☐
Bought at book exchange or used bookstore ☐
Borrowed from a friend ☐
Other (please indicate) _____

2 Did you enjoy reading it?
A lot ☐   A little ☐   Not at all ☐

3 What did you particularly like about this book?
Believable characters ☐   Easy to read ☐
Good value for money ☐   Enjoyable locations ☐
Interesting story ☐   Modern setting ☐
Other _____

4 What did you particularly dislike about this book?
_____

5 Would you buy another Scarlet book?
Yes ☐   No ☐

6 What other kinds of book do you enjoy reading?
Horror ☐   Puzzle books ☐   Historical fiction ☐
General fiction ☐   Crime/Detective ☐   Cookery ☐
Other (please indicate) _____

7 Which magazines do you enjoy reading?
1. _____
2. _____
3. _____

And now a little about you –
8 How old are you?
Under 25 ☐   25–34 ☐   35–44 ☐
45–54 ☐   55–64 ☐   over 65 ☐

cont.

9 What is your marital status?
   Single ☐   Married/living with partner   ☐
   Widowed ☐   Separated/divorced ☐

10 What is your current occupation?
   Employed full-time ☐   Employed part-time   ☐
   Student ☐   Housewife full-time ☐
   Unemployed ☐   Retired ☐

11 Do you have children? If so, how many and how old are they?
   _____
   _____

12 What is your annual household income?
   under $15,000   ☐   or   £10,000   ☐
   $15–25,000   ☐   or   £10–20,000   ☐
   $25–35,000   ☐   or   £20–30,000   ☐
   $35–50,000   ☐   or   £30–40,000   ☐
   over $50,000   ☐   or   £40,000   ☐

Miss/Mrs/Ms _____
Address _____
   _____
   _____

Thank you for completing this questionnaire. Now tear it out – put
it in an envelope and send it, before 31 January 1998, to:

Sally Cooper; Editor-in-Chief

USA/Can. address	*UK address/No stamp required*
SCARLET c/o London Bridge	SCARLET
85 River Rock Drive	FREEPOST LON 3335
Suite 202	LONDON W8 4BR
Buffalo	*Please use block capitals for*
NY 14207	*address*
USA	

LOCHI/11/97

Scarlet titles coming next month:

HARTE'S GOLD   Jane Toombs
No-nonsense rancher Carole Harte can't believe that she, of all people, would fall for a film star. But that's exactly what she's done! Trouble is, she's never heard of 'the star', Jerrold Telford, and fears he's out to con her grandmother!

THE SECOND WIFE   Angela Arney
When Felicity decides to marry Tony she thinks the decision is theirs alone, and that love will conquer all. What she's forgotten is that other people have a stake in their future too, and then Felicity realizes just how difficult it is to be _the second wife_ . . .

WILDE AFFAIR   Margaret Callaghan
Rich, powerful, ruthless – the Jared Wildes of this world don't make commitments. Oh yes, Stevie has come across men like Jared before. Her daughter Rosa's father for one!

A BITTER INHERITANCE   Clare Benedict
'A scheming little gold digger. Her husband not cold in his grave and she's involved with another man!' That's how Sam Redmond thinks of Gina. How can she change his mind, when he clearly can't forget or forgive how badly she treated _him_ in the past?